DIAMOND FORTRESS

BOOK 2 IN THE MASTERMIND DUET

MORGAN ELIZABETH

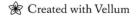

Cover Designed by Madison Lee with Love Lee Designs.

Find her on socials @madicantstopreading

❋ Created with Vellum

To all the little girls who thought the princess should get a shot at slaying the dragon.

A NOTE FROM MORGAN

Hey Reader!

Thank you so much for choosing to read Diamond Fortress! I hated leaving you on that cliff hanger in Ivory Tower, but I PROMISE it was worth it!

If you have not read Ivory Tower, stop here! Do not collect $200! Go back and read it first then meet me back here.

Already read it? You can keep going!

Diamond Fortress contains mentions of cheating, verbal, physical, and financial abuse, assault, violence, gambling and addiction, and murder. Please always put yourself first when reading—it's meant to be our happy place.

I love you all with my whole being.

-Morgan Elizabeth.

PLAYLIST

Ivy - Taylor swift
   Everywhere, Everything - Noah Kahan
   god sent me as karma - emlyn
   Killer Queen - Queen
   Weight of the World - Valencia
   Snooze - SZA
   Dangerous Woman - Ariana Grande
   The Great War -Taylor Swift
   I See Red - Everybody Love an Outlaw
   Only Love Can Hurt Like This - Paloma Faith
   You Should See Me in a Crown - Billie Eilish
   Make Out With Me - Maren Morris
   This is Why We Can't Have Nice Things - Taylor Swift

ONE

-Lilah-

The world shatters around me as people cheer.

A hand pats me on the back.

A man grabs my cheeks, turning my face to press a kiss to one.

Another says, "Welcome to the family."

A third wraps cold, thin fingers around my own, twining them like we're familiar.

They aren't Dante's fingers, which are always warm and thick, callused as if he doesn't work in the back room of a strip club.

I should look over at who is next to me, who is grabbing my hands.

But my eyes are locked across the way on the man I love.

The man whose dark eyes are round—not in shock, but in warning.

His expressive eyes normally have a shield, hiding away the deepest secrets, but not today. Not right now.

Finally, after weeks of trying to get him to talk, to explain, to open up, weeks of promises, of *not now*s, of *later*s—everything is there.

Love pouring through them.

The fiery need to protect.

The overwhelming urge to hide me away.

The desire to give me everything I want.

All the things he's told me over the weeks come together to form a plan.

I can see everything now—except for how the *fuck* this is all going to work out.

But there in his eyes, I see it.

Trust me?

And with that, I nod, turn my head, and smile at the man who is holding my hand.

Paulie Carluccio.

My new fucking fiancé.

TWO

-Lilah-

I sit in my room cross-legged, staring at the door.

Waiting.

Waiting for him.

Or maybe I'm waiting for this all to be a horrific nightmare. To wake up and look around and see we're still in the cabin in Lake George.

Maybe we decided to stay, change our names, and become new people after all.

Marco walked me back to my room an hour ago, holding my eyes as he spoke, giving me clear instructions.

"Go in, lock the door. He'll be here. You wait, Delilah. Understand?"

I don't have an option anymore. I've been thrown in the fire, no longer in my safe tower. No longer able to back down, to run off, to pretend I'm someone else.

But this is what I wanted, right?

To be involved in the plans. To be a part of the sacrifice.

I mull on that as I wait, mull on how stupid I was to want this.

Why couldn't I have had a desire for *easy*?

But then, the doorknob moves, and I panic.

If it's Paulie, am I expected to open the door?

To let him in?

He is my fiancé, after all.

My *fiancé*.

Oh, god.

What a fucking mess.

Thankfully, I watch as the lock moves, turning with a key. Not even Marco has the key to that lock.

"It's me," a voice says before the door even opens, and my body melts, the panic gone.

But then it's back.

It's back because *where the fuck do we stand?*

Who am I now?

Who is he?

Who are *we*?

But I want answers and he's the only one who can give them to me, so I undo the chain, moving back to sit on the center of my bed and staring at the door as it creaks open. Dante stands there, still in his suit, as if he finished whatever he was doing with his family, his men, his . . . girlfriend and came right here.

A small concession.

"You look gorgeous in that, *fiorella*," he says of the lacy nightgown I found in the closet, the closet of brand-new clothes he picked out for me.

I run my tongue over my teeth, annoyed because I wanted him to come in and beg forgiveness and *explain*.

Now that the panic is abating, the frustration is storming in, dark and angry and volatile.

That is, until I see his hand.

On his ring finger is the thick gold band I slipped on in a courtroom chapel in New York before we arrived at Lake George.

The ring he put on the chain with his St. Christopher before we arrived home.

My fingers go to my own necklace where the medal lies on top of a ring of my own.

The one he slipped on my finger.

In his hand with the gold band is a gun.

In the other is a brown paper bag with a familiar logo.

He tracks where my eyes are and smiles. Placing the bag on the vanity, he pulls out the drawer where Marco stored my gun, laying his there as well.

A weapon marital bed of sorts.

Lovely.

This is my life now.

"You must be hungry," he says, stepping forward as he grabs the paper bag again. "You didn't eat at all."

Like I'm a child.

Like I'm someone he should be protecting.

Like nothing happened a few hours ago.

"I brought you this." He lifts the bag. "Your favorite." From the logo, I know it's chicken nuggets and French fries, and suddenly, it hits me.

A single kind gesture takes all of the bravado I was trying to hold tight to.

The fear.

The betrayal.

The horror.

All of it hits at once, and the wall I put between reality and myself to keep my mental state safe collapses.

"What the *fuck just happened, Dante?*"

I make an attempt not to scream.

Dante drops the brown bag back down and moves quickly to where I'm sitting on the edge of the pretty bed he bought for me, clearly on the verge of a full-blown panic attack.

He kneels in front of me, looking up and holding my face in his hands. He's holding me tighter than necessary, like he sees the cracks in my facade, the ones only he can ever detect, and is doing whatever he can to hold me together.

It's not working.

"He knew," is all he says.

"Who knew *what*, Dante!? Because all I know is that I'm now somehow *engaged to your fucking nephew* and everyone in that *fucking room* knows I'm a *fucking* Russo! You put a target between my eyes, Dante!"

"I saved you." His words are so calm compared to how frantic mine sound. "Lilah, it was the only thing I could do. Paulie was calling me this morning because he found out. He knows who you are now."

"Everyone knows who I am!" His jaw is tight.

"He called me this morning because Carmine told him you are a Russo. He found out and wanted to use you."

"Use me?"

"I promise you, none of his options would benefit you or your own grand plan." Dante's eyes have gone wide, panicked. "I didn't know what to do, Delilah. I needed to buy time. I sold him a story. Told him I was vetting you all along, making sure your intentions were pure. That I was making sure you wouldn't betray us. That my plan all along was to set him up with you."

"How do I know that's not what you *were* doing this whole time?"

"Don't play that. You know how to know." He stares at me, and I guess I do. I know exactly what he's talking about. It's the single thing keeping my feet nailed to the floor as I float through this panic and confusion.

"So, what, was marrying me a test?"

"That was me being fucking selfish and making sure you were mine forever."

"So you marry me in secret, binding me to you so you can just offer me up to your nephew two days later? Am I your property now, free to do whatever you want? Can you trade me like a collectible card?" I want to scream, rage, but my words come through gritted teeth.

Dante smiles the smile that brings me back to the car, to that trip, to Lake George, where everything changed.

※

The Friday before:

We stop in front of a municipal building twenty minutes outside New York City.

"Dante, what are we doing here?" I ask, looking around. This isn't a . . . vacation.

"Getting married," he says, turning the key to stop the car, and I think it also somehow is wired to my body because every muscle freezes.

"What?" I ask in disbelief when he doesn't say anything more, just sits there, meeting my astonished look with a hand on the door.

"We're getting married, *fiorella.*"

My lips suddenly feel so freaking dry.

"What?"

"Come on. We have to go. I called in a favor for them to let us in after hours, but a favor only does so much. Can't work a miracle with this kind of shit."

"You called in a favor."

"Three, actually." He opens the door and steps out, walking around the car and opening mine. Cold air comes in and wakes me up a bit.

"You want to marry me?" I ask, still buckled in, still confused. He smiles that handsome fucking smile and squats outside my door. Leaning over, he unbuckles my belt before putting his hand on my cheek and moving so we're face-to-face.

"Is that even a question, Delilah?"

After everything that's happened over the past few months?

I guess not.

Maybe?

I change my question.

"You want to marry me in a random municipality building outside the city?"

"Not especially, but it's far enough away from Hudson City that the whispers shouldn't travel for a while. Our little secret."

"You want to marry me in *secret*?"

The loving nature of his gaze evaporates, irritation taking its place.

"Are you fucking kidding me? When the time is right, I'm marrying you in a ceremony with 500 fuckin' people in attendance. Announcements in the paper, huge fuckin' reception." His look is . . . determined.

He *wants* that.

A small part of me warms.

"I don't think I even know 500 people," I say in a whisper.

"We'll invite people off the street. That's not the point. The point is, when the time is right, when it's safe? I'm marrying you in front of God and our family and friends and all the bastards who will be mourning you being off the market." I fight a smile and lose. He, of course, sees the small tilt of my lips and gives me one of his own.

"You really want that?"

I've always wanted that. A small girly part of my belly wants the lavish flowers and the big dress and the huge church. Lola will probably elope. Hell, a municipal building would probably be ideal for her—she could renew her business license at the same time.

But me?

I want that.

"More than fuckin' anything, Delilah," he says, eyes burning.

"So why not wait?" He sighs, sitting back on his heels and running his scarred hand over his face.

"Because I need this, Lilah. If I get called in right now, you're a person of interest. My assistant? A hole-in-fuckin'-one for the DA, the feds. You marry me, you walk out, and they can't make you testify against your husband. Spousal privilege." My heart sinks and the hint of a smile falls from my lips.

"So you want to marry me because it's convenient? To save your ass?" He moves again, grabbing my face firmer this time.

"Fuck no. Lilah, I need to marry you because I *need* to know you're mine. That if you wake up one day and it's too much, you'll have to work to get rid of me. I'll have time to change your mind." A small smile is on his lips and it's contagious—I feel it growing on mine.

"Why would I want to get rid of you?" His thumb runs along my bottom lip.

"Because I drive you insane," he says, that smile growing. "Because in our line of work, secrets pile up and eat at you. Calling this pre-marriage insurance."

"Our line of work?" I ask with a raised eyebrow.

"Our. You want in, yeah? You wanna rule? You'll be in deep with me. And when you're a gorgeous queen ruling your kingdom, I want to have time in case you decide you find some other prince more to your liking."

It's a joke but I see it now: the honesty.

He really feels that.

He really needs this.

He's so fucking vulnerable right now.

And so I nod.

And I let him help me out of the car.

And I let him walk me into the building.

And I become Mrs. Carmine Dante Romano Carluccio.

And I smile the whole way through.

"Delilah, I wouldn't trade you for the fucking world. I wouldn't trade you if someone had a gun to my head. I am *not trading you.*"

"Then what is this?"

"You were right."

"About what? I'm right about a lot of things." He shakes his head, fighting a smile, but it's gone almost immediately.

"Carmine told Paulie who you are. I think he's tired of watching us argue and wants to see bloodshed. I'm not sure if he knows who you are to me or what, but for right now, I think he just sees you as a vehicle. Paulie called me threatening you. Said he was either giving you to the highest bidder or taking you out. No Russos means the family is vulnerable."

I chew on my lips.

"I froze, Lilah. I needed to buy time. We need to win Paulie's and Carmine's men over. We need to get shit stable with your family. *They* are gonna need time. If war starts, we need to be strategic. I needed to buy time."

"So you sold me for time?"

"I didn't fucking *sell you,* Delilah. Honestly, what was I supposed to do? In a room with Carmine, my whole fucking life falling apart because I realize you were right about what a fucked-up person he is. No idea what my mom saw, if she was just so wrapped up she missed it or what. But my father was smiling watching Paulie and me fight like the sick fuck you told me he is. Then he says, *he freed up the pathway to the head of the Russos for my brother, that he fucked that up by letting your mom say no.* You were right. He knew who you were all along. Made plans for a goddamn baby, the sick fuck."

My stomach churns, and I lick my lips.

"Why not offer to marry me?"

"I couldn't look too eager, Lilah. The way these two work, I seem eager, they start sniffing. They start nipping at you, see what I'm so excited about. This wasn't my plan, but now you get what you wanted, baby. You get to be neck deep in this."

"How the hell do I help with this?" He smiles that devilish smile I love so damned much.

"You're a siren. You're going to use that to tear Paulie down."

A shiver runs down my spine with the words.

A sick form of excitement.

"While I'm married to him? Dante—"

"We have nine months. A summer wedding. Teresa insisted."

Teresa. Paulie's mother.

"Nine months for what?"

"To help Paulie dig himself a hole."

"How do I do that, Dante?"

"You don't even have to try, really. Look at what you've done to all my men. Roddy, Marco, Tino. They all love you. You just walk around, smile your smile, and they fall at your feet. We need them to love you. You need to make them swear fealty to you, so when you try and take down Paulie, they're not loyal to him, but to *you*. We're clearing the path."

I don't know what to say.

It makes sense, in a way.

He stands, smiling and walking over to the bag he left on my vanity.

"Come on. Let me feed my wife and then fuck her. After that, we'll work on the plan."

And really, who am I to argue with an offer like that?

THREE

"You're going to have to go to events with him," Dante says much later, hands running through my hair.

It's been three hours since he walked in and told me everything.

That Carmine knew who I was.

That he needed to revise his plan on the fly.

And most importantly, what the damn plan was.

The new plan—one both Dante and I have crafted, rather than Dante working alone—is simple.

I have nine months to pull the men to my side. The key to a safe, simple take over is to make sure that the men in the family are no longer loyal to Paulie or Carmine, but to me.

Or, at the very least *more* loyal to me than they are to them.

My focus will be the Capos. Paulie has a handful of men he recruited and a few who were loyal to Tony that I'll need to win, and Carmine has his men who have been in the family longer than I've been on this earth.

Dante will do what he can without kicking up too much dust or suspicion, but it's my job to learn who each man is, learn where his loyalties lie, and figure out how to pull them over to me.

And most importantly, do it without causing too much suspicion from Carmine.

It feels good, knowing the plan. Even better knowing that I have a balanced part in our mission.

And now, my husband has both fed and fucked me as promised and I'm slightly less irritated.

That is, until he says that.

"Paulie?" I feel more than see him nod in the dimly lit room and I groan. "Don't have to make it look like a love match, but you gotta at least try and look happy."

"I hate him, Dante." I move, climbing over him and resting my chin into my hands on his chest.

"You need to play the siren, baby." His hands move my hair over my shoulder. "You gotta win the men over."

I stare at him, waiting for him to continue, to explain.

"Paulie is in the ears of the men he recruited, making it so if anyone but him hits the top, they'll cause trouble. There are a few that are loyal to Carmine, a few that were Tony's. I've got my men, but I can't just start talking to their recruits without raising suspicion. It helps that it seems like I gave the family to Paulie, but it would still look off."

"So, I . . ."

"You're beautiful and you're smart. You know what to say to make them turn against him. Or turn to you. Look at what you've done to my men. I even look at you funny, Marco, Roddy? They're planning how to whack me." I smile at that but then remember something.

"Dante. Today . . . Marco—"

"I know. We'll have a talk with him some time soon at the club. No ears. I don't even want to think about that added mess until then. But . . . I'd be hard-pressed to believe Marco's anything but a good man."

"He said he doesn't work for you. Said he works with you, but not for you."

"News to me," he grumbles, irritated, and I try not to smile.

"He made it seem . . . He made it seem like he worked for . . . me. Like he was here for me."

"No idea, Lilah. He's always been protective of you, even before I knew who you were, what you were to me. Didn't have to assign him to watch you, not really. He wanted to do it. If he's working for the Russo's . . ." A sigh falls from my husband's lips. "It would track. The timing of when he came to the family . . . let's just say it would all make sense." I stare at him, and I think he's just as lost about what to expect as I am, so I let it be.

Long minutes pass before I speak again. "When does it start?"

"When does what start?"

"The show? This whole . . . plan?"

"As soon as possible. You did fucking amazing tonight, not letting it show on your face." I glare at him, and he stares back, pushing a loose lock of hair behind my ear.

"I wish you had told me what to expect," I say.

"I didn't want you nervous. I didn't want you thinking about it all night."

"I'm mad at you, Dante."

"Mad at me?" he says with a smile. I slap his chest.

"Yes, mad at you. I don't like this. Fucking engaged to stupid ass Paulie as part of your plan? Walking into it without any kind of knowledge?"

"It's not like I'm doing this as punishment, Lilah. It's not like this is a walk in the park for me, knowing the world will think you're his when you're undoubtedly mine." His hands frame my face. "I want to scream about us from the rooftops and I want you by my side, but we need to do this first. We need to make this world safe for us."

"It's still some plan you didn't tell me about before throwing it at me." I take a breath, my body lying on his making a deep breath difficult. "No more, Dante. No more secrets. I know everything from here on out."

He stares at me, reading my face.

I stare back before continuing.

"I'm serious. From now on, I want to know it all. This plan . . . it's no longer just yours. It's *ours*. I get not wanting me to look nervous. I get not wanting me to stress in case it didn't amount to anything. But I still should have known. That wasn't fair to me, to throw it at me like that and hope I reacted well. When he called you that morning, you didn't say a word to me about it. Drove me all the way back from Lake George playing fuckin' question and answer."

His hand wraps in my hair and gives it a playful tug. "I love question and answer with you. It's how we started, after all." I give him a *you know what I mean* look and the smile fades. "You're right," he says. "Next time, you're in on it." I fight the smile. I didn't expect him to concede so easily, so I'll call this a win.

"I'm in on *everything*, Dante. From now on. I'm your wife.

"You are, aren't you?" he asks, grabbing my hand and pressing a kiss to the ring he put on my finger. His words have gone soft, his lips tipping up, and I can tell I lost him there. Any chance of having a real conversation is gone because he's so lost to the idea of *his wife*.

I give him a small smile and shake my head because I kind of love that—how calling myself his wife put that look on his face.

The daydream look, the look of potential. Of happiness. Of *future*.

"I am. And you're my husband. Which means no more secrets."

"No more secrets, Lilah," he says with promise in his voice before he rolls me over and proceeds to remind me just how a husband treats his wife.

FOUR

-*Lilah*-

Heat is pouring through my body as my mind drifts out of the fog of a deep sleep.

I'm warm all over, my breathing heavy.

A moan falls from my lips as something warm grazes my clit, and a low chuckle hits my ears.

My eyes open slowly just as Dante slides two fingers into me. As they focus, I catch his eyes watching as his mouth sucks on my clit. The unexpected pleasure forces me to arch my back off the bed.

"Oh my god," I whisper, my voice still groggy with sleep, and Dante laughs, the vibrations running through me. "Oh my *god.*"

His eyes are still smiling as his fingers crook, my body responding instantly, and I wonder how long this has been going on, how long he's been teasing my body to get me this fucking ready for him already.

I'm on the edge and I've barely even opened my eyes.

He knows, of course.

Dante *always* knows.

His mouth disengages from my clit, and he looks up at me with that smile, the one that makes him look young and carefree, but I can't focus on that.

It's the *words* he says.

It's always the words with him.

The words he says to heat my mind, my soul, my body in ways I didn't realize were even possible.

"You're going to come on my face, *fiorella*. Then as you're coming, I'm going to move and slide into you and fuck you to say good morning." My teeth bite into my lower lip at the thought of a good morning fuck.

"Yes?" he asks, and I nod. "Say it, Lilah."

My pussy reacts to his firm words by clenching around his fingers and *he* reacts by crooking those fingers.

My hips buck, needing more before I answer.

"Yes, Dante. I'll come and then you'll fuck me," I say with a moan as his thumb swipes over my clit.

"That's my good girl," he murmurs, and then his head dips down again, his dark hair mussed from sleep.

Heat furls in my belly as he sucks, as three fingers now start to fuck me mercilessly, swiping at my G-spot with every thrust.

"Dante, god, *fuck*," I moan, my hand moving to his hair and my legs starting to close on him, like I'm trying to keep him there indefinitely, like doing that will help me hit the peak faster.

My man, of course, rarely lets me run this ship, though. His eyes look up my body. His free hand moves to my knee, pushing my leg back open before slapping me on my sensitive inner thigh. I moan loud at the strike and the way his fingers fuck me fiercer, a punishment, and I just know if I could see his mouth, there would be a grin there.

He repeats the action, slapping my inner thigh, the pain spiking quickly before dissipating into sweet, sweet bliss. I clamp down on his fingers, my back arching, moaning his name.

"I'm close, fuck," I murmur to the ceiling, and then because the man knows me better than *I* know me, he slaps me one more time, the same place, the pain higher but the pleasure overpowering it all as I come, screaming his name.

My back is still arched off the bed, my head on the pillow as I come hard when he starts to crawl up my body, his head moving into my neck as one hand guides his cock into me and then he's there, slamming in deep and filling me.

And I'm whole.

He feels it too; I know it when he groans into my neck.

"Fuckin' missed you," he says there, his breath leaving burning trails against my skin, and the way he says it, the way he slams into me as he does, it almost feels like a punishment.

A punishment for making him feel too much.

A punishment for making him wake without me.

A punishment for making it impossible to sneak out like normal.

A punishment for making him give me his mornings.

"Yeah," I whisper, one orgasm fading as another starts to build.

"That's it, Lilah. Come on. I'm not coming in this cunt until you fall again."

"Dante," I moan as he bucks into me, my legs wrapping his hips. He moves, pulling his body back until he's on his knees, staring down as he fucks me. One hand moves down my thigh and pulls it up until it's against his chest, creating an angle that has the head of his cock brushing my G-spot with each thrust.

"Fuck, look at that," he says, watching where he disappears in me. "Fuck, *look* at you."

He's not speaking to me, not really. Just marveling at the perfect fucking way we fit together.

"Honey," I whisper, the pleasure building, a boiling pot about to spill over.

"I know, baby." His eyes move from where we're joined to my face as his hand moves to my hip, holding me there.

"I need more," I whisper. He could tip me over in a moment. All I need is a quick brush of my clit to get me there.

"No," he says with that evil smile of his, tipping his hips and leaning on my thigh on his chest to get in even deeper. I moan loud.

"It's too much."

"You can take it, Delilah," he says.

"It's *too much*," I moan, my body teetering on the edge, already overstimulated from his mouth. The pleasure is too big, the promise of the all-consuming orgasm near terrifying.

"Almost, baby."

"Dante—" I breath, my eyes locking to his and words stopping when I see him.

"Almost," he says, the words low and growly, said through gritted teeth as he continues to fuck me, sweat beading on his forehead as he does.

He's fighting it.

He's so fucking close, but he's fighting it.

"Could do this all day, fuck you." I moan an incoherent string of words and Dante smiles. "Your body? It's mine. You come when I say, not a moment fucking sooner."

He stares at me, challenging me to argue.

And I want to—for a moment, I think about moving my hand, rubbing my clit and making myself come, but I know.

It will be hollow.

The orgasm will curb the intensity, but it won't be the same.

It won't be as good.

It won't be what I need.

"Dante," I plead, my voice soft.

He smiles, knowing he won.

"Alright. Be my good girl and come for me."

And because he tells me to, I do, tipping over the edge, my back arching, my body taking in even more of his hard cock as I moan his name and clamp down on him.

"Fuck yeah," he says through gritted teeth, fucking me through my orgasm, and in a few moments, I come to, just in time to watch his eyes go dark and his jaw go tight. He slams in, staying deep and throbbing in me as he groans his release, but the whole time, he holds my eyes.

⁂

"What was that about?" I ask long minutes later, still a bit dazed both from an orgasm and the early hour. I look over to my bedside table to see it's before five.

"Decided I don't wanna miss mornings anymore."

That makes my heart warm, a smile growing on my lips.

"So you're going to wake me up early every single morning?"

"If I get to see your sleepy-face smile at me like that? Yeah." He pushes hair from my face then rolls away from me and stands. "Come on, I'll help you get dressed before I have to go."

My smile turns to a pout.

"The plan is rolling, Lilah. Couldn't be found here before, but now I definitely can't be caught sneaking out of my nephew's fiancée's room in the morning." I scrunch my nose again and he just bends down to me in the bed and kisses it.

"So when's the first big show?" I ask, rolling to my back and staring at the ceiling.

"We'll have a family meeting sometime this week, I'm sure. Go over expectations."

"A family meeting . . . ," I say, knowing "family" isn't just brothers and uncles and cousins to Dante.

"Yes. Then next Saturday, you'll be attending your engagement party."

I glare now, his hands grabbing mine and tugging until I'm pulled out of bed and finally on two feet. Barefooted, I have to tip my head up to look at him and I fucking love it.

I love this whole thing, little moments when it's just us. When we're normal people in a normal relationship doing normal things.

I love being *normal* with him.

These small moments that we get so freaking few of.

"I'm going to hate this, aren't I?" I murmur, pressing my lips to his collarbone. One arm wraps my waist and the other goes into my hair, tugging a bit until I look up at him.

"What?"

"This game we have to play now. I just want to be yours," I say with a pout.

"You are mine."

"I want to be yours and for every woman in the room to know it. To know they're eye fucking my property." His lips twitch.

"I don't think I've ever been called someone's *property*."

"Get used to it." He smiles again, the big one, the one that makes him look ten years younger. Mine melts when I start thinking about the long fucking road ahead of us. "Being in your presence, so fucking close to you all the damn time and so fucking far . . . I won't be able to look at you, to touch you . . ." I press my lips to the underside of his jaw, not ignorant to the fact that we're still both naked and he needs to get out the door before the house wakes up. "To kiss you."

"Delilah . . . ," he says in a warning tone.

But then, something hits me.

A sick, sour thought that pours cold water on any bit of heat running through me.

I pull back to look in his eyes.

"She'll be there, won't she?"

"What? Who?"

"She'll be there. At this engagement party. Angela. And whatever other bullshit I have to go to. She'll *be there*." He sighs.

"Angela helps take any questions off me. It also makes me look settled and uninteresting."

"So she'll be there and allowed to touch you and I'll be there with fucking Paulie." Dante's face goes hard.

"You do not touch Paulie." *As if I would ever want to.* But still, I raise an eyebrow and point out the hypocrisy.

"Oh, I can't touch my *fiancé*, but she can touch you?"

"It's different." His jaw goes tight with his words.

"No, it's not," I argue.

I step back and stare at him.

"I don't like her." My hands go to my hips. "I don't like her, and I want her gone." His eyes roam my naked body, but still, he sighs.

"Lilah—"

"No. Raise an eyebrow or two, I don't care. At the very least, I want her to stop fucking touching you." My jaw ticks just thinking about the way she put her hand on his chest yesterday, like she belonged there.

Like she was his.

"Lilah. She helps to draw attention away from my interest in you."

"She's a bitch. I don't like her. I'm your wife." I run my tongue over my teeth but can't resist admitting my real source of hatred. My shoulders fall as I speak, and my voice goes softer. "She *touches you*, Dante," I say under my breath. His lips tip up and I know he likes that because he's fucked in the head.

What a pair we make.

"You don't like other women touching me?" he asks, taking a step closer to me but not closing the gap. I raise an eyebrow, my hand going to the thin gold chain on my neck, a necklace that means so much more than just religious protection. His eyes watch it, going warm.

"Do you like other men touching me?"

"Fuck no." His words come quickly, definitively, and I give him a look.

"Exactly."

"I can't just dump her, *fiorella*. But I can tell her no more touching." I'm appeased. But still, I like this. I like seeing how far he'll go with it, like seeing how his eyes warm when he realizes he's not the only jealous, possessive one in this relationship.

"What if that's not enough for me? Even if she's not touching you, she's still yours."

"She's not. You're mine."

It's starting to form in my head, the idea, the demand. But Dante —Dante sees it. He sees how I'm winding myself up, sees how I'm getting possessive and jealous and raging.

And he fucking likes it, the same way I like it when he does it to me.

What a fucked-up, toxic pair we make.

I wouldn't have it any other way.

He reaches out, pulling me back to him, wrapping his hand around my hair like he likes to do. He uses the grip to force my eyes to his where I see that smile on his lips.

"I don't know; maybe I'll keep her around. I like seeing this. You getting all protective."

I blink up at him, fighting a smile of my own at his words, at his challenge.

"Are you for real?"

He smiles, and I just barely manage to keep one off my face.

"Kind of." I move to my tiptoes, trying to get our faces close before lifting an eyebrow and giving him a face.

"Break up with her, Dante," I say in a whisper.

"No," he says. That smile is wide now.

"No?"

"No. She's a good cover."

"*Break up with her,* Dante," I say, the words nearly seductive, a demand. My hands land on his chest, the hair there scratching at my palms, and it has me questioning if what I'm about to do is wise.

"Or what?" He whispers the question, challenging me, on to my game as he slides a hand down my side. I can't fight the shiver of his callused hands running over bare skin.

He can feel it.

He knows.

He also knows that what I'm about to say would be a punishment for me as well.

Worth it.

"Or I won't fuck you again until you get rid of her."

"Excuse me?" he says with a wide smile.

He does like a challenge, after all.

"You heard me. Until you get rid of her, you won't taste my pussy again." There's a purr in my voice, the siren coming out to plan and absolutely loving this game.

She lives for this kind of payback. "You won't fuck me. Won't come inside of me."

"Delilah. I spend every night in your bed." His words aren't angry, but surprised, maybe? Shocked? Confused, definitely.

But he still has that goddamned smile.

"And until she's gone, you'll be spending those nights with me in one of my old-lady muumuus, falling asleep very much unsatisfied." His smile widens and I know then.

I know it's *game fucking on.*

"Baby. You won't last a night."

"You wanna bet?" He stares at me for a long moment, taking in my face, and I think he sees how serious I am about this.

That I won't be fucking him until he cuts that woman off.

The reality is, I know in my heart of hearts that if I were to tell Dante it was a hard no for me, if I stood my ground and said I needed her gone and didn't turn it into some crazy challenge he can't resist, he would stop it with her.

The man is crazy for me after all.

He would do anything I asked just because it was me asking.

But a part of me—a sick, fucked in the head, toxic one—finds the idea kind of exciting.

Who will crack first?

"Fine. Game on, baby," he says, moving back and taking a step to the closet. I grab his wrist before he can leave, stepping forward and wrapping my naked body around his.

"I won't make it easy on you. I'm going to make it so fucking hard for you, honey. Give you some initiative to cut her off and do it fast." My voice is husky and low. The siren is out for blood.

"Lilah . . ." His voice is deep and growly, and he's probably already on the verge of losing our little game.

I step back.

I'm liking the idea of this already. I want to see how long we can last.

This relationship has been based in physical connection since the beginning. What happens if that's gone? What happens if we go to high school rules, if we take the sex out of it?

"Gotta get ready, Dante. You gonna dress me?" He rolls his eyes but smiles still, taking me to my closet and picking a long-sleeve shirt and a pair of jeans out for me.

"By the way, Teresa wants to take you shopping sometime soon. Get something for the engagement party. I'll give you my card."

"I have my own money, Dante," I say as I pull a lacy thong up my legs, even though technically, that is money I earned working for him.

"You'll take my card. Spend whatever you need to make me absolutely miserable, seeing you and knowing I can't touch you until we're alone." I smile, ideas rolling through my mind. "Or, I guess, until you break."

"Me, break?" I say with a smile. "I think not."

"We'll see. Either way, I expect you to put on a fashion show for me when you get back. I want to see everything you pick out." He tugs me close as I snap my bra on, sliding his hands under the lace at the hips of my thong and pressing his lips to mine.

"Oh, honey. You have no idea what kind of misery I'm about to put you through, do you?" I say with a smile against his lips.

"Give me your worst," he says, and minutes later, he's out the door.

FIVE

-Lilah-

There's a knock at my bedroom door an hour later, two hours earlier than when I'm due outside for Roddy to drive me to Jerzy Girls for work. I'm cautious when I open the door, leaving the chain in place, unsure of what or who could be there, but relief fills me when Marco's bulky body comes into sight.

"You ready?" he asks, and my brows furrow.

"I'm not going into the club until noon."

"Yeah, I know. We gotta different stop first," he says.

I stare through the crack in the door at the man Dante has trusted with me from the beginning.

The first person I called a friend when I started this insane mission.

The person who, last night, told me he didn't work for Dante as I assumed. Who told me he works *with* him, but not *for* him.

With the chaos of what happened after, I almost forgot, only mentioning it in passing to Dante, but here he is now, wanting to take me from the compound hours before I leave for work, telling me we have some other stop.

My mind battles, trying to decide what the fuck to do.

It would be stupid to go with him, right?

But what if . . .

"You want answers?" he asks, and of course, he knows I do.

I came here to find answers, but I have more questions than I started with. Dante has answered so many, but with each secret revealed, another seems to pile on at the back.

So the question is, I suppose, can I trust Marco to give me answers?

Or on a larger scale, can I trust Marco at all?

I stare through the slit in the door, contemplating what I should be doing, staring at his stern face that is patiently waiting for my answer.

He's always been that—patient with me. Kind to me.

And then, I think about how he's called me princess since the day I met him.

How he has protected me, talked to me like an equal.

How he told me Dante was good.

And finally, I remember what he said to me last night.

You really think that family would just ignore your existence all these years?

"You work for the Russos?" I ask, the question coming out without my permission, without the assumption even fully forming in my mind. When he moves those ever-present sunglasses to his head, I know he wants me to see his dark eyes and read the sincerity there.

"Yeah, princess. Have since I was 18." His voice is low and kind, but in his very Marco way, he doesn't beat around the bush.

I respect that.

The honesty.

It's rare that people look me in the eyes and tell me the truth—even Dante doesn't always do that.

So with that, I close the door and undo the chain, going with my gut. When I open it again, he's giving me his friendly, easy-going smile.

"So, answers?" I ask, raising my eyebrow. His smile widens, white teeth framed by smooth, dark skin.

"Come on, princess."

And because I trust Marco with my life, I follow him, knowing I'm so totally going to get in trouble for it.

We're in the car when I finally get the nerve to ask the question I already know the answer to.

"Where's Dante?"

"He's not invited," Marco replies, the words firm. Not angry, just concise.

"Not invited?"

"Nope." *Dante is going to lose his fucking mind.*

"Marco," I say slow and low, "Does Dante know we're going here?"

He turns to me and smiles.

"Marco!" I chide, knowing that while Dante might get mad at me for leaving, Marco is most *definitely* going to get it worse.

"You want Dante being Dante when you meet your grandfather for the first time?" His words hit true and I go silent.

It's not that I don't want him there—marrying Dante means we share everything now—the good, the bad, the terrifying. But Marco has a point. Dante *will* be Dante if he comes. It won't be me, daughter of Arturo, long lost heir who is ready to rule, whether they like it or not. It will be me, wife of Dante Carluccio, heir to the Russo's rival family.

So after staring at his profile for a few long seconds, I nod.

But because I'm not a complete idiot, I take out my phone.

"I have to let him know, Marco," I say, swiping until I find his name.

"Lilah—" he starts, slowing at a red light.

"Marco. If I disappear, if he finds out I left with you and I don't show up at the club at noon, he's going to go insane. He's going to worry." Marco's head hits the back of the headrest as he looks at the roof of the car, shaking his head. "Look. I trust you. I believe you and what you've shared with me. He does too, even if it's in a different way. But you know as well as I do that shit is weird and tumultuous right now. We're playing a dangerous fucking game. I can't do that to him, Marco. I won't let him worry like that." He sighs before looking at me.

"Fine. Text him. Tell him you and I are going on a detour then we're headed right to him. Tell him to expect us before noon." I type out my text, cherry picking my words to try and make it better, but still, I just know it's not going to end well.

> Don't freak out. Marco and I are going on a detour before we head to the club. Going to meet the Russos. I need to do this, Dante. I love you.

"It's done," I say, and he makes a left, barely moving ten feet before my phone buzzes with a text from my husband.

"Jesus Christ. That's him, isn't it? Fuck, is your location on?" I look down at my phone to see Dante's response in bold, capital letters.

> WHAT?

It buzzes in my hand once again.

> DELILAH. Where is he taking you?

It rings next, but I don't answer. God, he's going to fucking kill both of us, isn't he?

"Way ahead of you," I say, a small consolation to my partner in crime. "Turned it off before I sent him that text." Mostly because I knew instead of sending me angry texts, he'd just track me down, drag me out kicking and screaming, and possibly beat down his best friend.

Marco's phone rings in the console. I look down at it and see *Boss man* on the screen.

"Jesus Christ," Marco murmurs. "You're lucky you're worth it, you know that?"

I stare at the man, his stern face just a bit softer with his words. He has full lips, lines around his eyes, and his hair is buzzed short, though he's always brushing a big hand over it like he needs to keep it lying flat. He's built in a way that would make most people who don't know him feel small, but to me, he's just . . . Marco.

The bouncer who befriended me.

My husband's best friend and closest confidant.

And apparently, someone who works for my *real* family.

I trust him.

I know deep in my soul nothing will happen to me in his care.

But I need to know.

"Tell me your part in this," I say, ignoring the way my phone is ringing again. I don't look because I know Dante's name will be on the screen.

"What?"

"You said you don't work for the Carluccios, but I know you're a made man in their family. You know an awful lot about my grandfather and have been calling me princess for as long as I can remember. That's not a coincidence, I'm sure. So, what's your part in this?"

He doesn't respond, and when my phone rings again in my hand, I lift it so he can see Dante's name before giving him an ultimatum. "You tell me or I'm sending him a text to tell him where I'm going and turning my location back on." We slow at another red light, and I watch as Marco tips his head to the sky, praying to whoever it is he prays to. "Marco."

Another long moment passes, and he shakes his head at the roof of the car, as if his bartering with the almighty power didn't turn out in his favor, before he sighs and looks at me.

"Fine. I'll explain my involvement. And to be honest, you should text him when we get there anyway. Don't leave it like that, giving the man a fuckin' heart attack. Let him know you're safe, where you are."

And *that* is why I trust Marco to take me to some undisclosed location.

Because in the same breath, he's telling me that I need to let my husband know where I am so he doesn't go into cardiac arrest in my absence.

"You know he's still going to want to kill you when we get back, right?" I ask, smiling. The light turns green and Marco starts driving again.

"Yup."

"He's probably going to punch you."

"Won't be the first time, won't be the last."

I can't help but wonder what the other circumstances were that made Dante punch Marco.

But I don't have time to ask that question because Marco starts to speak.

"I was 20 when I was sent to the Carluccios to become made into the family."

The car is silent as Marco drops that bomb.

It's not the age. Most men get caught up in the life early, from what I've learned, and I am well aware that Marco was made.

It's that he was *sent*.

It's such a tiny word that changes the entire meaning of a sentence.

He doesn't give me time to question that, though.

"Grew up in Hudson City. A street rat, always getting into trouble. I knew from a young age I wasn't going to fit into a normal life, knew I liked the danger too much. When I was 16, I sought out the Russo family, started running errands. Small shit, delivering letters and checking in on people."

The Russo family.

Not the Carluccios.

"I turned 18 and your grandfather had me made. Said I was meant to be a man of the family, that it was my calling."

"You're a Russo," I say in a whisper.

"I'm both and neither, I guess." He laughs but it's not with humor. It's like he just came to an understanding. "I guess, all along I was meant to be yours, Lilah. Your first soldier. You're a Russo and a Carluccio, just like me, and you're who I serve."

"I don't . . . I don't understand, Marco." He sighs, rubbing a hand over his face like he, too, can't quite figure out how to explain himself before making a left turn.

"When I was 20, your mom started getting sick. Think she knew even then she didn't have a lot of time, needed to clear her conscious, make sure you'd be safe. She called up Alfredo, told him a lot shit about a lot of history. Shit with her and Arturo, her and Turner. Shit she heard about Tony and Carmine. Told him all of her theories, some of them unhinged, some worthy of looking into. She told him Carmine knew who you were, how you weren't Turner's. She said you wouldn't be safe, not forever. Carmine would push one of his men to start something with you. She knew his greedy ass wanted that tie to the Russos, and you were an easy way to get that." He licks his lips, turning the car onto an unfamiliar road. "I guess it's a good thing Alfredo believed her. I don't think he ever bought that shit about a drive-by. It was too clean, no suspects. Still, he wouldn't have thought it went that deep, a planned killing to get control of a goddamned infant. Even then, even when you were just little, Lilah, with no ties to anyone, he loved you and wanted the world for you. Wanted you safe."

My heart skips just a bit.

My grandfather loved me.

"He loved me?" I ask, trying to fight the way my voice shakes. "I never . . . He never . . . I thought—" I don't know how to put my thoughts into words

"I'll let him tell you that part, princess," Marco says like he can read my mind, read the confusion there.

"So, princess always had a meaning, huh?" My mind moves to how he's always called me that and I just assumed it was because he thought I was a spoiled princess, daughter of a mayor.

"Queen, now, I guess. But I think I'll always be partial to princess," he says, and there's a smile on his lips when I look over at him. I give him a small shake of my head.

"So, what? You joined the Carluccio family? To keep an eye on Carmine?" He nods.

"Alfredo sent me, told me to get in deep. Win loyalty, keep my ear to the ground, make sure I didn't hear anything about Delilah Turner. Not a whisper. Had a friend in the family, and he put in a good word. I got a meeting, did the work. I was made in three years."

Fast track.

A man unknown to the family, no ties, no nothing shouldn't have taken three years to be made. Shit, Tino took six and he was a childhood friend of Paulie.

"Who's the friend?" I ask, needing to know everything.

"So fuckin' nosey, aren't you?" he says, and I smile.

"Do you expect less?"

"Never. Look how far that nosiness got you." He tips his head at my hand where I'm twisting my wedding band around my right ring finger. I just smile. "It was Jason."

"Jason?" I ask, shocked. If Paulie cared enough about anyone to have a friend, Jason would be his. He's also Paulie's stone-faced second-in-command. "Huh."

"He's a good guy. Just gambled on the wrong Carluccio to take it all."

And Marco gambled on the right one, I suppose.

"So, wait. Why were you sent to the family?"

"Keep tabs. Ear to the ground, keep an eye on anything to do with you. Your mom said they were to blame for Arturo's death, but we weren't going to retaliate without proof. So we needed an in to make sure it didn't happen again. To make sure no one knew about you, make sure there were no whispers. But mostly, Alfredo wanted you safe."

"Great job with Lola," I say and then cringe and instantly cover my mouth. "Shit, that was unnecessary."

"You're not wrong. Had an ear on you, not on your sister. She's all Turner's, no connection to the family besides you. I knew you were out, going to galas and shit for Turner, seemed happy. I didn't expect him to let his shit impact your sister. That man? A piece of shit."

"You're telling me."

"Anyway. I got into the family young, built trust. Kept an eye on shit. Kept my line to Alfredo, but mostly started working with Dante. Things were quiet with you and he had a vision, a vision I liked and could get behind. Tony went away, thought it would be Dante for sure taking the head, thought there was a chance to save this family, but, well, you know how that went."

Paulie got into the running.

And then I got dragged in.

The way everything is slowly linking together keeps blowing me away. My mind moves over 26 years of life, trying to remember little details I missed along the way, little things that I overlooked because I didn't have the whole picture. It stops on the day I walked into Jerzy Girls to make a deal. "You were there. That day I walked into Paulie's office."

"Dante's office." I shake my head because I find it funny how *both* of them are always so quick to correct that. "But yeah. Stayed behind to watch him. Glad I did, watched your dumbass walk in there like you knew what the fuck you were doing, all dolled up like you were going to seduce him."

I turn my head and stare, my mouth open just slightly.

"I was *not* trying to seduce him."

"Princess, you were trying to seduce *someone*. Thank the good Lord every fuckin' day you came on a day Dante was out of the office. I can just see it—you walking in, him going fucking haywire psycho man and then scaring you off."

"Oh, so instead he got to slowly go haywire psycho man?"

"You really trying to tell me if he started his obsessive act as soon as you saw him, you'd be chill with it?" I look away, rolling my lips because he's not wrong. I one thousand percent would have been scared off by his psychoses. He laughs, and then the car is silent for a few more turns as we both mull over the past and the present, the would haves and could haves, before he speaks again.

"He's not shitting you, you know."

"What?"

"Dante. Fell for you before he knew who you were. Two years ago, some blonde came up to him, chatted with him for five fuckin' minutes, and he told me to find you. Swear to God, Lilah, thought he lost his damn mind. *Find me a girl,* he said. *Early twenties, I think. Blonde.*" I smile, loving to hear this side of things and thinking how much Marco *most definitely* thought Dante was going insane when he told him to find an *early twenties blonde* and left it at that.

If I let myself fall into ideals and daydreams, I can convince myself this was always meant to be, always in the cards, Dante and me. Like somehow, we were always meant to find each other. Like it was so important to some version of history, the universe brought us together twice, begging for us to make it happen.

I sit on that thought through the rest of the drive, and it's a few more minutes before we're parked out front of a familiar building.

"Why are you doing this, Marco?" I finally ask what has been bugging me.

He doesn't have to do his, doesn't have to put himself further on the line for me.

But then he looks at me, putting those ever-present sunglasses on top of his head and turning in his seat to stare at me, like he wants to make sure I understand whatever he has to say to me.

"Because you belong at the head of this family and they need to know that." My heart flutters at his words.

"So you're taking me to prove myself to Alfredo?"

"I'm taking you so he can prove himself to you."

"I'm . . . I'm confused," I say, looking at my friend, and then the door of the building where I was turned away last time I came here, then back to Marco. He leans over, grabbing my chin between his thumb and pointer finger. It's not a romantic touch, not even a friendly one. He uses the grip to tip my chin up just a hair and force me to look at him.

Instinctively, like the move reminds me of who I am, my shoulders move back a bit, the siren snapping into place.

"You don't prove yourself to anyone, Lilah. No matter what, you're boss of that family once Alfredo dies." The sentiment is great, but in reality . . .

"But people will argue. No one knows me. People won't just . . . agree to that."

"Fuck 'em," Marco says instantly.

"Fuck 'em?"

"That's your place, Lilah." He moves back, crossing his arms on his chest. "Your father wanted that for you, yeah?" My mind moves back to the carefully scrawled words on a piece of paper that was wrapped around a photo of a man holding a baby, love in his eyes.

A letter my father wrote me before he died.

You will be a queen one day, my Delilah. You will have the power to take this family further, to help our community, to grow and to flourish.

"He left me a letter," I say, my eyes staring off behind Marco's head. "Told me to spit in anyone's face who told me I shouldn't rule." My lips tip up with the memory of the line, and Marco's laugh fills the car.

"Fuck. You're a lot like him, aren't you?" he asks, and I smile.

I've never had that, someone telling me I'm like my father.

And I think I like it a lot.

⚜

Before we walk in the building, I send a text on the cell that hasn't stopped ringing since I sent my last one and trust that he'll heed my wishes.

> I'm good. I'm with Marco. We're going to meet my grandfather. We're at Russo Contracting in Hudson City. I love you more than anything, Dante, but I'll be pissed if you break down the doors. Marco's bringing me to you when we're done. I'm texting you so you don't worry, but I'm also trusting you to listen to me. We're a partnership. No more secrets.

A very long minute passes while Marco and I sit in the car waiting, because I know he's going to respond, before he finally answers.

> No more secrets. I'm fuming, but I'm trusting you on this. I wanted to be there with you when you went.

> I need to do this alone. I need to be Lilah Russo right now. Not Lilah Carluccio.

The pause is long and I know in my own way that my words hurt him.

But he needs the truth.

I also know in his own way, it's a truth he'll understand if he's willing to let himself.

Finally, my phone buzzes in my hand and the tension that I didn't realize was building in my spine eases.

Tell Marco if you're not in the club by noon on the dot, I'm going in guns blazing.

I smile before tapping out my response.

I expect nothing less.

Covered in you, fiorella.

SIX

-Lilah-

We walk into the large, familiar building and I look around.

It's the contracting office I went to months ago, back when this all started. Where I was told I was too innocent, not tough enough for this family.

Sure, the man who told me that thought I was there to bag some kind of mafioso boyfriend, but the sentiment stuck. It hurt all the same.

It's what set me on my mission to prove myself.

I can't quite pinpoint how I feel now, walking back into this building without having *proven* myself yet, not in the way I thought I would when I returned here.

God, it's crazy to think how much has changed in a few months.

Everything has, really.

I tip my head to Marco as I stare up at the big sign reading *Russo Contracting*. "I came here right after Lola was taken." Marco stalls, his hands moving to a lock on the front door, a key in his hand.

The business is closed, doors locked, but it seems Marco has the key.

"You came here?" I shrug, not looking at him as I answer.

"I wasn't sure how to move forward. Everything was confusing. The journals . . . my mom's, when I first found them, they seemed like fairy tales. Stories. But with all of the new information I had, they started to make sense. I wanted revenge for my father and my mother. I . . . wanted family."

"And? What happened when you came here? Alfredo never mentioned—" I shake my head before he can continue.

"I didn't get that far. Walked in and met a woman here. Front desk. Older, dark hair, curvy. Pretty, but . . . rude."

"Fuckin' Roz."

"Yeah. She knew who I was. Said I looked like my father." I blush, remembering the exchange. "Said I wasn't cut out for it. Then some man, her husband, Sal, he came, thought I was . . . I don't know. Some girl looking to hook up with a dangerous man, get a thrill. Told me I was cute but that I wasn't cut out for the life. Acted like he knew me, knew my type."

Finally, Marco undoes the lock, shaking his head. "Fucking asshole. What happened?"

I smile, remembering my words that day.

"I got his name. Told him I wanted to make sure I could see his face when I was in charge in a few months."

Marco's laugh booms as we enter the building, and I feel a small, infinitesimal sense of pride as it does.

"God, I can't wait until that jackass figures out who he was talking to." We walk past the desk and I look to it, remembering the moment and the way it was fuel to my fire.

How it led me to Dante, in a way.

"She's jealous of you," Marco says, leading me back to the sample rooms.

"Who?"

"Roz. Wanted your father. She's always been around, her family not in the family but always sitting on the outskirts. I think she cooked up some fairy tale in her mind that Arturo was hers since they knew each other as kids. But then your mother came along . . .” His voice trails off, and I can't help but smile.

“And then my mother came along.” I look at carpet samples and paint swatches. “So, what, she said all of that to me because she's jealous she didn't get my father?”

Marco sighs and shrugs.

“You didn't hear this from me, Lilah,” he says, tipping his ever-present sunglasses down his nose to look at me as we stop walking in the middle of a fake kitchen. I nod and give him the sign of the cross and he smiles.

“She thinks if the position stays empty, if there's no one to take over when Alfredo passes, that Sal will be Don.”

“Sal, her husband, Sal?”

“One in the same.” I nod, slowly understanding.

“And . . . would he?”

“Who knows what would happen if you don't step in. Maybe. Men aren't crazy loyal to him, but they aren't any more loyal to some other Capo. Who knows how the chips would fall.”

“But it doesn't matter anymore because I'm going to take over,” I say, straightening my shoulders and knowing that's the truth. Even if I've never met these people, even if they all hate me from the start, if I have to crawl from the bottom to win their approval, I will.

I'm meant to rule this family.

And just like I'll win over every last Carluccio until they're loyal to me, I'll win over the Russos too.

SEVEN

-Dante-

Looking around, I wonder if this is how Lilah felt when she threw her own tantrum in this very office.

Not better, but the edge is gone.

The red anger that I felt when she sent me a text to tell me she was going with my second—no, *her second*, I think—to meet with my enemies has dimmed just a bit.

Enough for me to breathe, at least.

Not her enemies, I remind myself. *She's a Russo herself.*

Any loose paper that was on my desk is now littered on the floor, a mix of random mail and important papers I absolutely need to keep.

The pens that were sitting in a fucking stupid fancy pen cup Lilah ordered off of some office supply website are everywhere, a Montblanc fully embedded in the wall.

I might leave it there.

Put a frame around it and a little tag, like it's some kind art installation.

Name it *Lilah Drives Me Fucking Insane.*

But I know as much as I want to search every fucking Russo Contracting building, go to every lot to find Marco's car, walk in guns blazing, she needs this.

She needs this chance to be Delilah Russo, this chance to prove not just to the assholes who told her she was too soft that she's anything but, but to prove to herself that she is a queen.

And I know a part of her needs to know she can trust me to keep it together while she does her half of our plan, while she works to help us win in the end.

So instead of calling again, instead of sending her a text demanding her location or demanding she come right to me, I sit in my desk chair and stew.

And I take deep, calming breaths for the next two hours, knowing that even though Marco might not be who I thought he was, he still loves my wife. He still would put his own life on the line to keep her safe.

EIGHT

-Lilah-

Marco takes me back through an unmarked door, past the display rooms, before stopping in front of yet another door. He knocks three times, then one, then two before there's a noise on the other side and he turns the handle.

In another life, I'd probably bite my lip, chew the skin on the inside of my cheek. I'd let the anxiety show on my face, let the fast pace of my heart make my hands shake.

But now I'm *Delilah Carluccio-Russo.*

I'm a queen.

I'm here to take out anyone who doesn't see things my way.

I'm here to take my rightful place.

So instead, I roll my shoulders back, tip my chin up, and follow Marco into the room.

Inside is a long, old table, initials and letters and designs carved into it, like men have sat around it for centuries, marking it up, only half paying attention to whoever was speaking. Like memories were made and tattooed into the wood.

And when I look down it, past the empty seats, I see him at the very end.

I don't have to ask who he is.

I've never seen a photo of his face but I still know he's my blood.

He has my eyes.

He has the set of my jaw.

His eyebrows are a near exact match of mine, despite the gray flecks in them.

But mostly, he looks identical to the man holding me in that picture, the picture I found what feels like a lifetime ago. A young man holding a tiny baby, his face filled with pure, unadulterated joy.

And here is his clone—older, more worn, tired and gray, his face lined, but still nearly identical.

"Alfredo," I say, tipping my chin to him as Marco pulls out a chair for me a few seats away. I sit, tucking myself in and turning in his direction, my chin still high even though my stomach is in knots.

He stays silent.

I don't let it phase me.

Or at least, I try not to.

My face stays blank except for my eyebrow lifting as if to say, *Yes?* But beneath that, I'm panicking.

What if I'm not what he expected?

What if he called me here to tell me to back off?

What if he's preparing to tell me I'll never be a real Russo?

The thoughts fly at warp speed and for a moment, I wish I had Dante here, my rock who would protect me.

He would know what to do, what to say while I flounder.

But then I see it.

The shine in his eyes.

The man is staring at me intensely and his eyes are glossy with tears before one finally falls.

"Jesus," he says in a croaky whisper. "*Madonn'.*"

I don't say anything.

Instead, I watch eyes I've seen in the mirror my whole life, eyes

I've never seen in another face in person, continue to water before tears start falling from them.

"You look just like him," he says, the words a mere whisper.

"So do you," I say, fighting the croak in my own voice.

"You've seen him?" he asks, his brows coming together. "Your father? You've seen pictures?"

"My mother left me one with a letter from him. I was a newborn, and he was holding me."

Alfredo—my grandfather—stares at me for long moments and there are just more similarities—deeper than features or looks, but personality. He's debating on if he should say what he wants to say next, the questions battling on his face. The average person wouldn't see the warring, but I know it well.

"Do you . . . Would you . . . You think I could get a copy of that? My boy and his girl . . . god." Another tear falls and finally, a part of my facade cracks and I smile, a small, sad thing.

"Yeah. I could get it to you."

He breathes in deep and its like with this exchange, something in him has healed.

Something that's been broken for 26 years.

"God. Look at you. He would have . . . Shit. He'd be fuckin' proud, seeing you. Hear you've been wreaking havoc." I smile, but a swath of panic hits me all the same.

"Heard from whom?" I ask, wondering if maybe the Carluccios haven't been as quiet and unknowing as we assumed or if Sal and Roz ran their mouths.

"Marco," Alfredo says with a smile. "Man's fond of you but says you give everyone you meet a run for their money."

I smile then look back at my friend.

My . . . guard.

He shrugs and I turn back to Alfredo.

"I do my best."

"That's what Arturo would have wanted. He would have babied you like you wouldn't believe, but he would have made it so you were tough. Took no shit." His eyes move to my right hand, where I moved my wedding ring. "Definitely wouldn't have let you marry a goddamn Carluccio on a whim."

The smile drops from my lips and my blood heats a bit in irritation.

"Well, he's not here, so he has no say, right?" Alfredo's face screws up. And I fight the frustration. This is not how I wanted things to go. "Look. I'm here to talk to you, to meet you. To learn about my family. But if you're going to just give me shit for how I'm choosing to live *my life—*" I move, hands pressing into the scarred table to stand.

"Don't. You're right. That wasn't my place."

I sit back down.

"I'm sorry. It's just . . . hard. You're married to the enemy, in a way." My jaw goes tight with his words and I instantly defend my husband.

"Dante isn't the enemy."

"So Marco tells me. I trust Marco's judgement." I raise an eyebrow at him.

"But not mine?" The accusation hangs in the room but he doesn't answer. "If you were so sure I wouldn't have good judgement, why not step in? Why not intervene when you learned about me?"

"It's not that easy."

"Why?" I ask, the words carving through me, the honesty of them revealing something I hadn't wanted to look at too hard.

What does it mean that the family knew of me, knew there was an heir, knew Arturo had a daughter and never tried to make contact? Why did they never try?

I fill in the quiet with a new question, hopefully an easier one. One that hurts a bit less.

"When did you find out about me?"

Part of me wishes that I came on their radar a month ago, six months ago. That would make it hurt less, if it was relatively recent and they were trying to figure out the best plan of action, but I know from Marco it wasn't.

"About five years after you were born, we found out who killed your father. Well, your mother figured it out. She brought to my attention all of her thoughts and worries. You were, what? Four?" Marco nods and Arturo continues. "Took about a year or so to dig up the intel we needed to confirm some things, trying to learn whatever we could about what happened. That's when we found out that it was Carmine who called the hit, and Johnny who carried it out. Tony was involved, but that boy was always just a pawn for his father."

"Just like Paulie," I say, looking at Marco who nods. Because that's the truth—if Paulie rules, it will just be a way of Carmine continuing to manipulate the family and his legacy from the grave. It's why he can't win.

Arturo continues his story.

"Unfortunately, after my son was killed, the family suffered. There was a sense of . . . desolation. Like the family was done. He was the sole heir. What was the point in fighting? But when we realized you were in the world . . ." His words hang in the room, and while talking to him should have me feeling a sense of completion, understanding, I'm even more confused.

They knew I existed since I was a child.

When Arturo passed, the family was lost. When they learned of me, things looked less dark.

But no one came for me.

Instead, I spent 25 years locked in a tower, a protected princess, manipulated to help the villain of my fairy tale grow his power and wealth.

"Why didn't anyone ever come talk to me?" I ask, looking at Alfredo.

This is what I can't understand.

No one came for me.

Not before mom passed, not after. Not when I was suffering the most, not when Lola was in hell.

No one came for us. No one wanted to help.

"We did," he says, and my world turns on its axis.

"I'm sorry?" Alfredo leans forward, the fingers of his hands intertwined and resting on the table.

"From the time you were four to the time you were eight, when your mother got too sick to keep going, I would meet with you once a month." My brow furrows.

"I don't . . . I don't understand."

"It was quiet. Just your mom and me, Tuesday afternoons. When you were in school, she'd take you out."

His words trigger a memory in my mind that was long buried.

Mom taking me out of school once a month in second grade.

We'd drop off Lola and then she'd just not take me to elementary school, instead taking me to breakfast and to the mall for some shopping. A girls' day, she told me. Just us two.

And then . . .

"The park," I say, the word quiet and nearly whispered as the memory emerges, cobwebs pulling back as it comes into the light. Alfredo's eyes go wide.

So insignificant to a six-, seven-, eight-year-old girl playing in a park and having a girls' day, especially considering months later my mother would get sick, those moments overpowering the bulk of my childhood memories.

"The park on Fifth and Broad," he whispers, confirming my memories.

And then my mind moves, flickering through pages of long-buried moments in time and settling on one when I was seven.

I'm standing in a castle, waving at my mom. She's smiling. She looks tired but happy.

She's tired a lot lately.

Mr. R is sitting next to her and he smiles too.

I'm a queen, standing on top of the world.

Mr. R stands up, walking to me and standing below me.

"Rapunzel, Rapunzel, let down your long hair!" he says, and I laugh. I like Rapunzel. She's my favorite princess ever.

But I don't want to *be* her.

"I'm not Rapunzel, Mr. R!" I say with a giggle. His hands go to his hips and he makes a silly, confused face.

"You're not? That pretty blonde hair would have fooled me."

"I'm not a *princess!*" I say it with little-girl frustration, as if to say, *How could you even say that?*

"Oh no?"

"No. Princesses are no fun." He leans against the plastic play structure and smiles.

He's got a nice smile. And he talks to me. Mr. R always talks to me like he doesn't mind if I'm little and only want to talk about kid stuff. Other old people don't like to talk about princesses and fairy tales. All of Daddy's friends always tell me to go play by myself while they have grown-up talk.

Mr. R talks to me, and I like that.

He's nice.

"No fun? They get to wear pretty dresses and sparkly crowns though."

"But queens get to wear sparkly crowns *and* they get to make the rules. And they get to *fight*." His smile grows.

"Yeah?"

"Yeah. I don't want to be a princess. I don't want to be pretty. I want to fight!"

"But you're in a castle. You're in a princess tower."

"Nope! I'm in a . . ." I try and think of the word I read from Lola's vocabulary homework. "A *fortress*."

"A fortress, huh? So, you can fight?"

"Yup. Made of diamonds."

"Well, of course. You can fight in style."

"Diamonds are the strongest rocks in the *world*. I want to be a diamond. Pretty and sparkly and strong."

"Then a diamond you'll be, Delilah."

The memory comes back out of nowhere.

It was buried deep in the recesses of my mind, somewhere safe, warmth surrounding it. But now it's back and I can see it clearly— Mr. R is Alfredo, a younger, less worn version, but that's him, clear as day. All along, the man my mother took me to play with once a month —he was my grandfather.

Mom said he was just an old friend, someone who always just happened to be playing at the park when we went. I remember her telling me if I wanted, I could ignore him, play alone. It wasn't some kind of arranged play date, but I liked him and I liked how he smiled at me and I guess . . . I guess a part of me knew, even then.

He was family.

"Why didn't . . . Why didn't you ever say anything? Tell me who I was? Who you were? Even after . . ."

After mom got sick, I never saw Mr. R again.

"I tried. I swear it, I tried. Your mother . . . was shaken because she also knew what happened all those years ago, knew deep down that you were the reason Arturo was murdered." He sighs. "I wasn't going to push her. She had two young girls and was trying to make things work with a husband who kept getting deeper and deeper in the underworld. I told her I wanted to tell you who you were, who you would be one day. Your destiny and what that meant. But she told me no. She told me it would be your choice one day, and I had to respect that. Said she didn't want you growing up knowing you were already pigeonholed into some life you didn't get to choose. And I respected that because I know it's what your father would have wanted."

It's what your father would have wanted.

Interesting to see the contrast between who I'm learning Arturo was and who Turner is.

Turner made *nothing* my choice, telling me where to be, when to be there, and who to be when I got there. Selling dates with me, using me to his advantage to further his own needs and desires.

Meanwhile, my father wanted things to be *my choice*.

He didn't want me forced into this. Of course, he told me in that letter he left I would be a queen, but thinking back, I recognize he told me he wanted that *if it was what I wanted.*

And really, there's no way he thought that note would be his last line to me, the last and only time he got to tell me about my destiny, of his hopes, dreams, and expectations of me.

"And then she got sick?"

"And then she got sick. She told me she left you things to explain and one day, you'd show up at my door looking to get answers. That I was to be patient, to wait. She was sure of it."

I think of the journals, the insight into her life, the note from my father.

"Every morning, I woke up and prayed it would be that day. The one I got a knock on my door and you'd be standing there, ready to take your seat."

"My seat?" I ask, my heart stuttering.

"You're going to be queen one day," he says then screws up his face in confusion, nerves maybe. "If that's what you want, of course."

So much is running through my mind.

New information is melding with old to create a better, more complete picture. There are still fuzzy spots, questions I have that I think might never be answered because Arturo and my mom took the truth to their graves, but still—the picture is closer than what I had before.

"Do you . . . Do you think they'd let me?" I ask, and for the first time in a long time, my voice is timid. Nervous.

My biggest fear is that he'll say no.

"Delilah, not that it matters because this is your right, but yes. I think the family will be overjoyed to welcome you in. Welcome a piece of your father, a strong, smart woman like yourself."

"Oh," I say, looking to Marco. His eyes are locked on me and I see it clear in his face, his body language. He's ready to leave if I ask him to, but also, a small smile is there on his lips.

A friendly reassurance.

It's then that Alfredo stands, his chair scratching on the floor as he does before he puts his hand out to me.

He doesn't ask for an answer then, whether it's because he knows it already or he wants to give me time. Instead, he says, "Come. Let's meet your family."

My family.

Shit.

That feels really fucking good.

And so, I take his hand and I'm led to another, similar room where men sit around.

Waiting for me.

And as I walk in, the men in the room smile, cheering, giving me a chorus of, *Welcome home*s and *Finally*s, and I know I made the right choice, taking his hand.

In coming here.

Because in a way, I'm home.

NINE

-Lilah-

It's about an hour later when it happens—the moment I'd been waiting for since I left the contracting firm a few months ago.

Or, really, since I read that letter from Arturo, if we're being honest.

I'm chatting with a few Capos, one who knew my father way back when, and they walk in.

Sal and Roz.

Instantly, her eyes lock on mine and her jaw goes tight.

And then she has the gall to roll her eyes like I'm an irritation.

Months ago, when I met her, I was Delilah Turner.

I had no idea who I was, really.

A princess in a tower with no idea of what lay before her.

Roz met a woman she could boss around and, from the look of it, she thought that would be the end of me. She thought her small push would stop me from standing.

"One minute, fellas," I say, then I stand and I hear it.

From behind me, Marco murmurs an, *"Oh, fuck."*

I fight the laugh.

In the last hour, I've fallen back into the new version of me, away from the nervous little girl who feels like she belongs nowhere and toward the queen I turned myself into, starting my first day at Jerzy Girls.

I might have been Delilah Turner when I walked into the Russo office months ago, but now I'm *Delilah Antonia Carluccio-Russo,* and I am a queen.

They can either bow or get the fuck out of my way.

"Hi, I believe we met," I say with a smile. "Roz, right? And Sal? Sal Conte." Roz purses her lips but doesn't reply. Sal gives me a look, brows coming together like he can't place my face.

Of course, walking into this family get-together, he knows who I am in the grand scheme of things, but he can't place where we met, much less where I met his wife.

"I don't . . . think I remember meeting you," Sal says, and to be honest, for a moment, I can't tell if he's stupid or playing games.

"Oh, you don't? I guess I didn't leave an impression. But don't worry. You definitely left one on me. I came into the office a few months ago. You, Sal, told me I didn't have grit. You remember that?" I ask, scrunching my nose up. "And you—" I turn to Roz, who is giving me a face that would kill if it could, I'm sure. "You called me, oh, what was it?" I tap one pointed red nail against my lips, looking at the ceiling, making a show of it. "Oh, yeah. *Some random bastard child.*" The room goes quiet as I say the words just a bit louder, all eyes already on our little trio, and I smile a wide, catty smile.

God, it feels good to be me.

The new me.

I like her a lot.

Sal's hand scrapes down his chin and he finally nods. I can almost see the lightbulb flicker to life inside of his head.

"I remember now. Came in looking to find a made man, right?"

So, he's just really dumb.

Got it.

"No. I actually came looking for my grandfather." I put a hand out. "Delilah Russo-Carluccio," I say, swapping the order of my last names just this once for impact. "Nice to meet you," I say, tipping my head to the side as I smile, personifying the version of a girl with no grit he thought I was.

No one takes my hand.

They both just stare at me.

"Russo?" Sal says, and I give him a wide-eyed nod, like the ditz he clearly thinks I am.

"Yeah. Turns out, you didn't know the full story when you told me I didn't have enough grit. You may have known my father, Arturo?" I smile sweetly and see from the corner of my eye Marco rolling his eyes to the ceiling.

Sal stands there, confused and shocked, his mouth open slightly.

He hasn't met this version of me yet.

I wonder how he'll feel about her.

"But don't worry, we'll have lots of time to get to know each other as I shadow Alfredo more, preparing to take over the family when he passes the torch." My smile at this point has to be nearly comical.

It only grows when Roz speaks next, her own mind hung up on another part of the name I presented.

"*Carluccio?*" she asks in a near screech. "How the fuck are you a Carluccio *and* a Russo? Your mother wasn't a fuckin' Carluccio."

"You knew who she was?" Sal asks, looking over at his wife, but she ignores him, continuing to gape at me with indignation.

"Oh, I married in. Just like you," I say with a lilt in my voice, using the words she used all those months ago. I put a hand innocently to my chest. "Except, I chose better when I did. Got myself a true heir. Can you just imagine how much power our kids would have? A Carluccio Don and a Russo Donna. God. It's almost poetic. So very Romeo and Juliet, but if they didn't die in the end, ya know?"

"You've gotta be fuckin' kidding me," Sal murmurs under his breath, and then it happens.

They must know something about this man that I don't because the room goes silent, anticipating. Marco's body goes just a hair stiller in my periphery, and I watch as Sal's face starts to go a bit red with frustration.

"Oh. Shit. Sorry. I forgot I'd heard that you were hoping to take over when Alfredo was gone. This must be a bummer for you," I say and move my face into a fake pout.

"Oh, fuck," Marco says.

"Who the fuck do you think you are, girl?" Roz asks, as if she has any power at all.

"I'm Delilah. I'm sorry. I thought we already went over this. I'm Lilah Russo, and you're the uptight bitch who was too caught up in trying to sit in a seat that was never going to be hers to help a young girl *trying to find her family.*"

"*Maddon',*" Alfredo says.

"Who the fuck do you think you are?" Sal asks, his face going redder.

"I think that I'm going to be the Donna of this family before you fucking die so your options will be to get the fuck out or back the fuck down." I tip my chin up with my words, crossing my arms on my chest, knowing that this moment is a tipping scale for how the rest of the men in this family will fall into line.

Ruling is my right, but loyalty and respect aren't inherited.

"Like I'll ever listen to some fucking cunt who—" I don't hear the rest of his words.

I block them out, deciding that while I would have preferred to *earn* respect, I'll force it if I have to in this moment.

My hand moves to the waistband of my pants and I hear it again, louder and more exasperated this time.

"*Oh, fuck,*" Marco bemoans.

"*Madonn',*" Alfredo says.

Still, neither stops me as I pull the small gun from the waistband of my jeans, my thumb flipping the safety and pointing it at Sal's chest.

"Feel free to argue with me, but when Alfredo passes, I'm the one who's boots you'll be licking. And I've got a really, really good memory."

"Who the fuck—"

I move the gun, shooting off to the side of his head and hitting a wall.

"Will you fall in line when I'm in charge?" I ask, and I figure this is as good a time as any to show that I'm someone that deserves their respect. That they need to obey. Someone worthy of leading.

I've got a lot of time to make up for, a lifetime where they barely knew I existed, and a lot to learn about this family, but I can't show weakness.

There's no time for second-guessing.

My father's letter runs through my mind as Sal's life flashes before his eyes.

Good.

"I'm waiting, honey," I say, my voice low and soothing, a stark contrast to the literal gun in his face.

Truth be told, I don't know if I'll pull the trigger if he refuses to submit. I don't know if I have it in me to kill a man in cold blood, if that's something I'll ever be able to do.

But I don't have to make that decision right there because finally, he nods, a slow smile crawling on his lips. His hands move up in a placating manner.

"Yeah, Delilah," he says with a smile. "You know, your father would be proud of you."

A little bit of pride runs through me with his words as I put the safety back on and tuck the gun in my jeans.

"Yeah, well, he'd be even more proud of me for this," I say, and then I do it.

I purse my lips before I step forward and I spit in his face.

Because my father once told me that men would tell me I didn't belong in a seat of power and when that happened, he told me to *spit in their face.*

"Sorry. My dad told me to do that," I say, and then I turn my back to him and walk away, not worrying about any kind of reaction but scanning the men's faces as I do.

Wide eyes of shock.

A few small, entertained smiles.

A huge, proud smile on Alfredo's lips.

And finally, Marco shaking his head at me with a smile before tipping his head to the ceiling, praying for patience as always.

TEN

-Lilah-

"Do you think I should call him?" I ask, watching the streets turn familiar again, away from the Russo business and back to the center of the city. Not toward home—toward Jerzy Girls.

My eyes move back to my phone where Dante's last text is still on the screen.

Covered in you.

God, I love that man.

"No need. He knows we're headed back."

"How?" I ask, looking at him.

"Turned my location back on. He's watching us. You should too."

I nod, knowing he's right and doing as he suggested. Before I can even get to the right screen, Marco's phone rings in the center console.

This is not the first time.

I'm actually not sure if he ever *stopped* calling Marco while we were in the Russo compound.

"Why are you ignoring his calls? Let him know we're headed to him now."

"Because I would much rather not waste even a moment getting there. If I don't hand deliver you to your husband as soon as humanly possible, it's only going to hurt more." I cringe a bit, knowing he's probably not wrong.

"Marco, once he—"

"He's gonna be pissed, Lilah. All good, I expect it. Had to do it this way. But he's gonna fuckin' rage at me."

"Why didn't you just *tell him?*"

There's silence before he speaks, like he's trying to explain something without hurting my feelings. He gave me his reason quickly on the way, but I was too wrapped up in the potential of what was happening to ask much more.

But Marco is loyal to Dante.

He loves him.

And still, he didn't want him to come.

"I wanted you to have what you had: meeting Alfredo alone, meeting the men, asserting your crazy brand of dominance—nice touch, spitting in Sal's face, by the way. I've been dying to do that myself." I smile a bit before furrowing my brow again.

"And if Dante came . . ."

"If Dante came, it would've gone a few ways, none that you would have wanted. People would be nervous of Dante, wondering what his motive was."

"Dante doesn't have a—" I interject, trying to defend my husband.

"That man's only motive is to give you the world and keep his family from going too dark. I know that. You know that. The rest of the world? They see Junior Carluccio, the man no one knows much about except that he's a hard ass and his father is a piece of shit who sold his own son out to save his ass."

Fair enough.

"If he were there, there would have been too many questions. You needed to shine, Lilah. You won over an entire family in a single fuckin' morning."

Warmth washes over me with his words because somehow, I know he's not just saying that.

I did.

I won the family over today.

"I'm blood," I say, justifying why it happened so quickly, so easily.

"Doesn't mean shit, Lilah. People see you, they know you're a queen. Know you're the right person to lead the family into the future, not because you're blood, but because you've got . . . it."

"Got it?"

"Something about you, Lilah. Can't explain it but people look at you and know not to fuck with you. Know you've got power, that you've got the ability to tear a man down."

I sit there in the passenger seat of the blacked-out car—an upgrade from my days of sitting in the back and being chauffeured around—and gape at the big man sitting next to me, his eyes on the road.

"I think that's the nicest thing you've ever said to me, Marco," I say after a few silent beats.

"I think that's the nicest thing I've ever said to anyone, Delilah." His words are deadpan, and I can't help but smile.

"Fair enough. So why wouldn't you just tell Dante that? That I should go alone, without him." Marco scoffs.

"Have you ever tried to reason with your husband when he thinks that whatever his decision is is going to be the better one for you?"

I have.

It's not easy.

"Fair enough," I say.

"I wanted you to have today, Lilah. I'm loyal to Dante, loyal to Alfredo. But most of all, I'm loyal to you."

I let that sink in, his words that mean so fucking much to me.

"My very first soldier," I say quietly, tipping my smile in his direction. He doesn't look away from the road when he speaks, but his words fill me with warmth all the same.

"An absolute honor to serve, Lilah."

We park in the familiar lot of the gentleman's club where my whole trajectory really started. I step out of the car, walking ahead of Marco, heels clicking on the asphalt as I head to the front door then clicking on tile as I walk through the club. I tip my chin at the few men I know, waving at the girls, and headed straight for the unmarked door that leads to Dante's office.

But, of course, I don't make it there.

I'm stopped barely twenty feet in, Dante's broad shoulders and fiery face in full *insane man on a rampage* mode.

"Dante," I say instantly, putting my hands up in an attempt at placating him.

"Delilah, get behind me." His words are terse, angry.

"Dante—" I try, wanting to stop this trainwreck.

"Delilah!" His voice booms through the club despite the thumping bass.

"All good, princess. Told you it's coming," Marco says from behind me. I look back and he just smiles.

"Behind. Me. Delilah," Dante says, reaching me and putting a hand on my waist, pushing me aside and then behind him.

I stand there, my hands on my hips, sighing with the knowledge that this will most definitely be my life from here on out.

This is what I signed up for, though, I guess.

Unhinged possessive men with way too fucking much testosterone.

Lord, give me the strength.

"You took her," Dante says, his words finite and damning.

"Dante—" I start, but his head whips back to me, the venom for me too, apparently.

"You're next, Delilah."

"*Excuse* me?" I ask, blinking my eyes indignantly, a hand moving to my chest. He turns to me fully before he starts to speak.

"You disappear for fucking hours, I hear nothing from you, then you try to walk into my club like nothing happened? Yeah, you're fucking next, Delilah." I look around, noting a few of the girls watching with interest but no men other than Roddy, who's got a bored expression.

Seems he *also* knows this will be his life from now on.

"You better rethink the way you're speaking to me if you *ever* want to be sneaking in my bed again, Carmine Dante Romano Carluccio."

And there it is.

The flare of heat in his eyes, the slightest tip of his lips.

He fucking loves this side of me.

I raise my eyebrow at him and he just shakes his head, turning back toward Marco. I'll call that a win.

"You leave with her, give me no fucking heads-up, don't tell me *anything,* and you take her to our fucking *rivals?*"

"Our rivals. Not *hers,* Dante."

"She's a Carluccio."

There must not be anyone he doesn't trust here today because it seems Dante doesn't care who hears what, standing in the back of the club and speaking without much nuance.

"She's also a Russo, man."

"I don't give a shit. She's *mine.*"

Should that give me a flutter both in my heart *and* my pussy?

This, too, I guess, is my life for now on.

"Guys, come on, let's—"

"You sorry?" Dante asks, tipping his chin to Marco, his back stretching as he crosses his arms on his chest, and it's then I know.

I know this will end in blood.

Because Marco, the dumb ass he is, smiles.

And then he shakes his head.

"Not even a little."

And then Dante winds up, stepping forward and pulling his fist back, punching Marco in the jaw.

His stumbles back, and Dante stands there, his jaw tight.

"Jesus Christ, Dante! Was that fucking necessary?" I ask, my hands on my hips but not stepping in. Marco steadies on his feet, his hand going to his face which is already swelling, a smile on his lips as he works his jaw.

Well, at least it's not broken.

"All good, princess. Told you, knew it was coming."

I stare at them both. Dante's jaw is still firm with irritation but a little less so, like the aggression knocked out some of his unhinged rage. Marco smiles like he thinks this whole damn thing is just *hilarious.*

"Fucking men," I mumble then turn on my heel, walking toward Dante's office and shaking my head.

Both men chuckle as I walk off before they follow me.

My life.

"Wow." I look around Dante's office minutes later and note papers all over the place and pens thrown about. One is even lodged into the drywall next to the door. "This looks worse than when I had *my* meltdown in here," I say of the time I destroyed Dante's office when I first found out his real identity.

I look behind me and see Dante still has a bit of his angry face plastered on, but Marco has a small tilt to his lips, despite the quickly swelling jaw. I cringe when I see it, thinking I should have someone grab some ice.

"When I learn that my *wife* is going to go speak with the Don of another family while I sit here, twiddling my fucking thumbs, and that my second is the one who took her, I get a little fucking pissed."

"Marco's my second now," I say with a smile, and I'm pretty sure he growls at me.

Marco laughs.

Seriously, I think the man might just have a death wish.

Or at the very least, *way* too much trust in Dante.

Shaking my head, I move to perch my ass on the edge of Dante's desk, swinging my feet and like magic, the remaining hint of his anger disappears.

It's like when he sees me sitting here, he remembers all the times he's fucked me here—and all the times he's probably *planning* to.

I just smile back at him.

"You were gone for four hours, Delilah. Got a text at seven thirty, then nothing. Then a text from Marco twenty minutes ago saying you were on your way back to me."

Normally, I'd feel bad.

But I was with *Marco*. Dante knows the man loves me almost as much as he does, though in a truly platonic, brotherly way.

Nothing bad was *ever* going to happen to me.

"Aw, honey, were you worried about me?" I ask with pouty lips, fighting a smile. Dante looks a lot less amused.

"Delilah, I swear to God, this is not the right time."

"Alright, you grump." I roll my eyes. "You know nothing bad was going to happen. I was with Marco."

"I know that last night, you told me Marco said he doesn't work for me and implied he works for Alfredo. I know that your family does *not like* the Carluccios, partially because my father had yours killed. I know you went to go meet with the rival family of ours."

I love that—how he says *ours* like the Carluccio family is already mine, like we've never not been a pair.

"You're forgetting, husband of mine, that the Russo family is *my* family."

"You've never met them."

"That's actually . . . not true." I realize now I forgot to tell Dante about the first time I walked into the contracting company. "Before I walked into Jerzy Girls, I went to Russo Contracting. Met some bitch of a woman who, apparently, was just jealous of my mother. She gave me some shit, made me second-guess some things, then one of the Capos came and made it worse."

"Made it worse?" Dante's jaw goes tight again.

"Cool it, Rocky, no need to go punching more made Russo men. He just told me I was too soft for a Russo man, that I'd get eaten alive." Understanding moved over Dante's face.

"He didn't know who you were."

"Nope. But I made sure he won't forget who Delilah Antonia Carluccio-Russo is ever again," I say with a small smile, and in a move so similar to his best friend, Dante looks at the ceiling, his lips moving but no sound coming out.

"You do that a lot, you know. Pray. Both of you, actually," I say, looking at Marco who's holding an ice pack to his jaw that I had Roddy bring in from the bar.

"I'm praying for the patience and energy I need to deal with your volatile ass."

"My volatile ass?! You just punched my second for literally no reason."

"Your second?"

"I've named Marco my first soldier."

"I thought Marco was my man."

"Turns out, Marco was a Russo first, sent to the Carluccios to keep an eye on you dipshits, make sure no one wanted to fuck with me." I look at my husband who *loves* to fuck with me. "He didn't do that part of his job too well."

Dante stares at me, trying to process everything I just told him, his mouth open just a bit. He stares for nearly a minute, mouth opening and closing, trying to decide how to proceed before he shakes his head and waves his hands in front of him.

"You know what? Not touching this one right now. We can handle all of . . ." His hand waves at Marco in an all-consuming gesture. " . . . that later. What did you do to the man who gave you shit?"

I smile.

I smile big and twirl a lock of my hair.

"I spit in his face."

"You . . ." Dante closes his eyes and takes a deep breath. "You spit in his face?"

"My dad told me to." Dante breathes deep before staring at me.

God, I love this.

This is so fucking fun.

Being queen is a goddamn blast.

Giving Dante regular heart attacks is *fun*.

"Lilah, sweetheart, your dad is dead," he says in a slow, panicked way, like he's afraid I might have forgotten or lost my mind.

"In a letter, honey. Arturo told me that any man who questions if I should be the boss of the family, I should spit in their faces."

"I think . . . I think that he probably meant that metaphorically, baby."

"Yeah, well, I took it literally." I shrug and Dante slowly closes his eyes.

And with that, my second bursts into laughter and I do too, watching my husband shake his head at us like we're both the most insane people on this planet.

But we're his people, all the same.

ELEVEN

-Lilah-

The rest of the afternoon includes explaining every moment that occurred while I was in the Russo compound, from when I walked in to learning that I had actually met Alfredo as a child to being welcomed by the men of the family to pulling a gun on Sal. (That one made Dante both angry and proud, which to be honest, is how he normally is with me.)

After my show and tell, I watched as Marco explained his complicated history, how he started with the Russos and how he was recruited to infiltrate the Carluccios. That last part made Dante a little green around the gills, probably from wondering with panic if there were other men in the fold who were there with poor intentions.

I gently remind him when we are alone that once we settle in, we'll have plenty of time to figure out who is loyal to us and who we need to deal with.

The "we" made him smile and with it, I watched the panic ease just a hair.

On Thursday morning, two days after the day I met the Russos, Marco takes me to the club for work. Two days of quiet planning, of keeping to our normal schedule and, unfortunately, not fucking because neither of us have cracked yet.

Instead, our nights have been quiet talks, Dante sneaking into my room as normal but sleep clothes staying on. Nights of gentle kisses, his fingers running thorough my hair, my fingers tracing the soft lines on his face, and talking.

Talking about everything and anything, so reminiscent of those days in the club, when I danced and he asked me questions.

I refuse to admit how much I secretly love it.

I'm at the club for the morning, working with the girls and getting the gossip as per usual, making sure to keep up my relationships with them, before I disappear into the back where I spend the rest of my day hanging out in Dante's office. The key is to spend just long enough for anyone who needs to see me *working* before I can go spend time with the boss man.

But by two, I'm slipping out the back door and getting into the blacked-out Corvette with Dante.

His jaw is tight, his face angry, and even though I'm liking just being us, seeing him like that gives me just a bit of a heart flip, a hint of a throb in my clit.

I hope he doesn't last too much longer, to be honest. And not because I care anymore if stupid Angela Sigano gets to touch my husband.

"I'm still pissed at you for this shit," he says, interrupting my thoughts, eyes focused on the road, and I smile.

"You wouldn't tell me your plan, so I made one of my own."

"A dumb plan," he says, and I shake my head.

"Just because it wasn't *your plan* doesn't make it dumb, Dante."

"Driving to Newark? Dumb. Setting up a sketchy payphone call? Dumb. Getting intel from a man who tried to kidnap your sister and killed your father? Love you, babe, but dumb." I roll my eyes.

"Whatever."

"So what's happening with this call?"

"Johnny has a request and he says he has intel for me. I'm not in the position to turn potential intel down, so I set up the call. Could be nothing, but could also pay off," I say, knowing Dante isn't going to love that, but we're already committed.

He shakes his head at me in a way that is so similar to Marco, it makes me laugh.

And with that, he turns his face to me, smiles, and we're off.

At four pm on the dot, I'm standing outside of a payphone in Newark, shivering.

"Maybe he changed his mind," I say, looking around nervously when the phone doesn't ring on time.

"Or maybe he's in prison and calling at an exact time is hard," Dante says, appeasing my anxieties, even if he thinks this is a shitty idea.

"How *do* you call people in prison?" I ask.

"You'll never find out, Lilah."

"You don't plan on going to the big house anytime soon?" I ask with a smile.

"Lilah—"

And then the phone rings.

I jump, my wide eyes, and turn to Dante.

"*Answer it,*" he says, and with shaking hands, I do as he demands.

I'm glad Dante's here. I'm glad it's him witnessing my cool, calm exterior cracking with nerves and not Marco or some other man who I'd want to see me as strong and self-assured.

Still, I slip on my costume of confident, all-knowing baddie.

"Yes?" I say, my voice smooth.

That mask I used to put on for Turner really does come in handy sometimes.

"It's Johnny," he says, and even though I never had to talk to him, I somehow know it's him.

Shit.

What now?

"Yes?" I say again.

"Surprised you answered. Surprised you took this risk, little girl."

"You call me little girl again and you'll regret it, Vitale." I have no idea how I would *make him* regret it, but my gut says I could find a way.

He laughs like I told some kind of joke.

God, this man is intolerable.

"Should I hang up?" I ask, and it's then that the confident siren snaps into place. The ruthless queen.

His laughter stops and I smile.

"No. We have things to talk about," he says, the words coming out in a panicked rush.

"Then talk. What's the purpose of this call, anyway?" I ask, because the reality is, that when Johnny sent his letter, he requested I contact him in some way but didn't tell me why.

Thursday the third at four, Delilah. Please. I need to speak with you.

Alarm bells rang but more so, my interest was piqued, and after he gave me details I needed about Carmine and Tony, I felt it was only right to give him some of my time.

"God, cut to the chase, why don't you," he says, and it raises my hackles.

"Johnny, I need nothing from you. You are quite literally in state prison paying off what will probably be a life sentence for your measly, shitty, underboss life. Why on earth would I want to spend a *second* more of my precious time talking to scum like you?"

"It's not gonna be a life sentence," he says, his tone gruff, and it seems I've hit a nerve.

"You and I both know that if you don't serve life you'll be *serving life,* Johnny. Whether it's someone from the Carluccio outfit or from the Russos, you've got enemies all around."

"There's always WITSEC," he says.

I laugh.

I actually *laugh.*

The man is out of his mind.

"Johnny, sweetheart. Sweet, delusional Johnny. In what universe would they give a piece of scum *WITSEC?*"

"I know things," he says.

"So do I, Johnny. Lots of people do. Not everyone gets WITSEC just because they *know things.*"

"Look. I just . . . I just need to know if I ever *do* get out, I *get out,* okay?" Ahh and there it is.

He wants the mob's form of immunity, and he wants to convince me to give it to him.

"You want to make a deal?" I ask, my voice near incredulous.

"You work for the Carluccios and now you're in with—"

"I'm marrying into the Carluccios." The line is quiet. "I guess you didn't hear the news over in prison."

"You're . . . marrying in?" My eyes lock to my husband's. Dante's arms are crossed over his chest, his look fierce as he watches me, and I can just *feel* the way he's dying to hear every moment, every syllable of this call.

"Uniting the families and all. I'll head the Russos now *and* the Carluccios—"

"Carmine would never—"

"I don't give a shit what Carmine would or wouldn't do. Now what do you *have* for me?" There's silence again, and I think I might have lost him, but then he speaks.

"Then you need me more than I thought," he says, and his words are smug, like he just won something.

I'm over him.

"Jesus Christ—"

"You'll need to pull the men to your side." His words echo Dante's from the other night and I still.

"I'm sorry?"

"To ensure you'll be safe. Liza? She didn't do that."

"She didn't . . ."

"Never bothered to get to know the men so at the end of the day, they were loyal to Carmine and Carmine alone. We all know how that went for her. The men loyal to Carmine, no one in the family questioned it, just like he knew would happen."

I fight not to show Dante that Johnny's words hold any meaning, fight not to show him this new bit of information that I don't even really understand yet.

Allegedly, Dante's mother was killed in a drive-by because she knew too much. Wrong place, wrong time, dangerous life.

That's what he'd been told. That's how he knows it.

But could it have been more? Something else?

Something *worse?*

"Pretty thing like you, you can convince them to join your side. Pull them in, tell them what they want to hear . . ." He pauses like he's thinking. "You gotta put you first, Lilah, or you'll be eaten alive."

I fight the urge to argue or get mad that just like the rest of the world, he underestimates me.

Sees me as weak and silly and in need of protection.

I want to tell him to fuck off, that no one will be eating me alive, that I can hold my own, thank you very much.

Instead, I lean into it. Instead, I let him think that by sharing whatever information he has, he's doing poor little unprotected me a favor.

Johnny worked with the family for years—my entire life, really. He knows the men and, more importantly, knows their weaknesses.

Whether I want to admit it or not, Johnny probably has information I could use.

"What do you have for me, Johnny?" My voice is bored when I ask it.

"I can tell you how to win over all of Paulie's men, all of Carmine's."

"And Dante's?" I throw that in there to balance the scales, to ensure that no questions will be asked, and Dante raises an eyebrow at me. "How do I win over Dante's men?" I ask, then I wink at my husband who shakes his head.

"Dante's men are ruled by Marco and we both know Marco is really your man."

I fight a tiny smile and watch Dante's eyebrows furrow in confusion.

"Let me guess—Marco's right there with you?" he asks, and instead of arguing, telling him that it's actually Dante who is accompanying me, I cut to the chase. It's none of his business who I'm with, and clearly, the man can't be trusted with fucking anything anyway—he's willing to give me anything to help himself out.

"You've got thirty seconds to give me something interesting, Johnny." I sigh like I'm bored of this exchange.

"Thirty seconds?" he asks, confused and, if I'm not mistaken, indignant.

All men who think they have a modicum of power are indignant when a woman tries to put them in their place.

"Twenty five," I say, starting my countdown.

"Jesus, I—"

"Twenty." The man attempted to kidnap Lola, intentionally hurting her to the point where my sweet, easy-going sister needed stitches.

"Lilah—"

"I have zero patience, Vitale," I say with indifference. "You hurt my sister, killed my father, and now you want immunity. You'd better have something really fuckin' good for me." Out of the corner of my eye, I watch Dante's eyebrow raise and his head tilt in a, *That's my girl,* kind of way.

"Paulie's fucking Dario's wife." I pause.

I pause because Dario is one of Paulie's men.

"Dario actually likes the broad, been trying to knock her up for a year. She's still on birth control, though, so if Paulie knocks her up, it won't get too confusing."

Well.

That would be good information.

Except it could be a death sentence to bring that up without any kind of proof—to insinuate a volatile man's wife was fucking his higher-up?

"Do you have proof?" I ask. It's a long shot but . . .

"How the fuck would I have proof."

"So you're just giving me gossip, then."

"It's not gossip; it's happening."

"Everything is gossip if there's no proof, Johnny. Moving forward with gossip could be a death sentence." Silence. "Anything else?"

"Jason?" *Paulie's second.* "Was recruited by Carmine when he was a kid. He's loyal to both men."

Jason seems like he's going to be the hardest to crack, like if there is one man I need to worry about who will remain loyal to Paulie when the dominos fall, it will be him.

Strange since he was Marco's in.

His words come back to me.

Bet on the wrong Carluccio.

Maybe he just has too much ego to turn away?

"He has a daughter, loves her to death. Paulie's a real shit about giving him time to be with her. Not sure if Jason knows it, but Paulie does it on purpose. Thinks it's funny, watching him struggle with it." I file the information, further sickened by what a fucking asshole I'm "engaged" to.

"Is that it?" I say the words with a sigh, and the silence on the other end tells me he can hear it. I think if he were in front of me, I'd see the start frustration across his face. Irritation that I'm not impressed by what he's handing me.

"I just gave you dirt on two of the Carluccio soldiers most loyal to the man you need to take down."

"No. You told me some gossip and something random as fuck. That's it."

Silence.

"Give me something or I'm hanging up. I'm bored, Johnny. I'm a busy woman. I have shit to do other than stand around in fucking Newark."

"Teresa," he says quickly, like he's afraid if he doesn't, I'll hang up, but also there's an edge of reluctance in his voice.

Whatever he's about to say, he doesn't want to share.

"Teresa?"

"She's feisty." I stay silent. Finally, something that I find interesting. "Tony—he was going to leave her when all that shit went down with your mother. Carmine wanted him to marry Libby, get the connection to you. Fuck, that was the plan all along, why Arturo had to go down." My jaw tightens, and Dante's eyes go dark.

He has no idea what's being said but knows that whatever it is, it's upsetting me, so he hates it by default.

God, I fucking love this man.

"Anyway, she figured out his plan, had some words with him. There was a fuck ton of screaming. Tony threatened to cut her off."

And yet, she's not. She's living in the compound, in control of Tony's money and assets, and living the life.

"Not sure what happened, but then all of a sudden, it was settled. They weren't happily married, and he had his *goumads* like any made man does." I roll my eyes. "But they were good."

"Why are you telling me this?" I ask. "While it's startlingly interesting, the soap opera of the Carluccio family, it doesn't give me anything. You want immunity, you need to give me fucking information, Johnny."

"She has something." Silence. "She has something, something to threaten Tony with."

"What does she have?"

"No idea. But he's locked up and still scared of her." I let that sink in, remembering the pretty woman I met the night Dante announced my engagement to Paulie, remembering her mentioning my mother.

She knew who I was.

"Is that it?" I ask, not giving Johnny insight into my thoughts.

"Is that it?" His voice is incredulous through the crackly line. "I just gave you three pieces of information you didn't already have." I don't answer.

He was Carmine's second-in-command.

He undoubtedly knows more.

I can hear the skeletons rattling from here.

But whatever else Johnny has, he's holding it tight, be it from fear or leverage, I don't know.

"So we're done?" I ask, ready to hang up and move on.

"Paulie." *I knew there was more.*

"What about Paulie?"

"Look. I tell you this . . . and I'm as good as gone." I bite my tongue, trying to bury the excitement.

"As opposed to . . . ?"

"I tell you this, Delilah, and it gets out, I'm not making it to the end of the fuckin' *year*."

"Bummer," I say, staring at my nails.

I need to get them filled sometime soon.

"You're a real cunt, you know that?"

I smile.

I also thank the Lord that Dante isn't listening in to the call.

"At least I'm a free woman, Vitale. At least I'm breathing fresh air."

"For how long?" His question hovers over the phone line. "How long before one of them decides they don't like the idea of a woman in power? Carmine, Paulie? No way they'll be on board with a woman as a boss."

"That's my problem to figure out. Now, do you have more for me, or should I hang up? I'm getting cold."

"He put a hit out on her." He spits out the words quickly, like he needs to do anything he can to keep me on the line.

Bingo.

"Who?"

"Paulie." *Jesus fucking Christ.* "Paulie put out a hit on Teresa."

"Why?"

"He can't stand the bitch. She got power of attorney for Tony, got control of everything: money, investments, real estate. A lot of it went to the state when he was nabbed, but the rest . . . The rest he transferred over to her before they could grab it. No idea why. Paulie thought it would go to him, but here we are."

"So he put a hit out on his mother to inherit it?"

"Seems it."

"But it was never fulfilled? Or is it still out there?"

"Word on the street is that Teresa got wind of it. Spoke to her husband, dangled whatever fuckin' carrot she has, and he reamed Paulie out. Hit was called off."

So, Teresa knows her son tried to have her killed. And she has something on Tony—a man in prison for what appears will be life—and he's still scared of her.

Looks like I need to spend more time with my "future mother-in-law."

"Like grandfather like grandson, though. Callin' hits on beloved women."

What the fuck is that supposed to mean?

Before I can respond, though, we're interrupted.

"This caller has thirty more seconds before the call ends," a robotic woman's voice says through the line.

"Thanks, Johnny," I say, a small smile on my lips. "This was great."

"So, we're good?"

"Oh, we're good. I forgive you for what happened with Lola," I say.

"Lilah, if I get out, I'm good, right?"

"I don't know, Johnny. I'll have to ask my dad, see what he says." There's not even a hint of humor in my voice when I say it, cold venom in the words.

He knows I don't mean Shane Turner.

He knows I mean the father he murdered in cold blood at the command of a sick fucking man.

Dante gives me a smile and shakes his head, but Johnny is yelling.

"Are you fucking kidding m—"

And then the line dies.

Time's up. Good thing I got what I needed.

"Let's go," I say, hanging up the phone. "I'm cold." Dante pulls me into his arms, wrapping his jacket around me and pressing his lips to my hair.

"A fucking queen," he says, and then he walks me toward his car, ready to move on with our plan.

TWELVE

-Lilah-

The family meeting is the next day and I'm dressed for the occasion.

And, possibly, to make my damn husband crack.

It's been seven days since Dante fucked me, and I'd be lying if I said I was *happy* about that.

But I'd also be lying if I said it didn't give me some kind of sick joy to be playing this game.

In my head, it's not even related to stupid fucking Angela, not really. I know if I said jump, Dante'd be looking for a bridge, and if I said, *No more Angela* and didn't turn it into this little game, she'd be gone.

I also understand the purpose of her. We spend a lot of time together and Dante pushed my working and living with him and then he pushed *marrying* me onto Paulie. If he were single, it would be a giant red flag waving, saying that something wasn't right to anyone who could put two and two together.

Angela coming to events as his date gives us some kind of cover to hide behind.

So that's fine.

I just don't want her hands on him.

And I also want to make him suffer while we play this game.

Hence why I'm wearing an outfit where the skirt hits a few inches above my knee, but it's absolutely skintight with a slit on the side ending not far below my hip. The top is a tiny, spaghetti-strapped tank that doesn't quite hit the top of the high-waisted skirt, leaving a sliver of tan skin.

Honestly, I could probably wear it as a dancer or server at Jerzy Girls and make good money in it. I added a loose, oversized, trendy blazer to cover up and make it more *baddie attending a family meeting* appropriate. But in its own way, I feel like it only adds to the sexiness of the outfit—the idea of unwrapping layers, of imagining that blazer as some man's that I'm wearing after a long night . . .

And I know it worked when Marco rolled his eyes and shook his head when I met him in the hall for him to drive me to the building where the meeting is to be held. It's a nondescript building with little to tell you about it from the outside. But last night while we lay in bed, Dante told me it's been in the family for decades and helps to organize and house the *above the board* businesses: HR and the sales side of the disposal company, investments, and holdings.

It's also where *family meetings* happen, in a dim cinderblock basement, conveniently too deep below ground for cellphones or bugs to work.

And when I walk in, my heels clicking on the floors, all eyes move to me.

Ten men—the Capos and the three Carluccios—all stare at me.

I smile when I realize not a *single one of them* doesn't have a hint of that hunger in their eyes. *A win for the outfit.*

But then one last face surprises me.

It has a smile, one of camaraderie, like it's in on a joke I didn't know I told.

Teresa.

I move through the room, my shoulders pulled back, my smile

easy, tipping my chin to some of the men I recognize and smiling at others before I sit next to Paulie's mother. She gives me an approving smile.

"Didn't expect to see you here," I say.

"Stand in for Tony. I'm his power of attorney, after all," she says, and I find it interesting that she's allowed in on these meetings. Dante sees no threat in a woman in power, but Carmine? I just know that man hates giving a vagina any kind of pull in this fucked-up world he rules.

I also know there is no way he was team *give Teresa control over Tony's entire life.*

When I look down the table and see Carmine and Paulie both glaring at her, my thoughts are confirmed.

"We're working on reconsidering that," Paulie says, the words coming like he couldn't hold them back, and Carmine's eyes snap to him.

So very interesting. This meeting seems to be even more fruitful that I thought it would be, and I barely just sat down.

When Dante told me there would be a *family* meeting I'd be expected to attend, I assumed it would be some bullshit where Carmine gives me his *little lady rules* and I smile and nod before normal business goes on.

I figured I could take mental notes on who each man was, who my targets should be, and who would give me the most trouble.

But now . . . I'm getting more than I ever thought.

"You can try, Paulie, but I guarantee your father won't agree to that," she says, a cat-like smile on her lips.

She knows something.

Or she has *something on him.*

And if I'm not mistaken, she's not a fan of her own son.

And with the arrows he's shooting her way and what Johnny shared on our call, it's becoming clear that he isn't too fond of her either.

Very, very interesting.

I wonder if the rumors are true and she knew about the hit.

Before the conversation can continue, Carmine speaks. "Let's get into the meeting, shall we? Delilah, thank you for joining us today."

I can hear it in his words.

Thank you for joining us, this is a special occasion, and don't expect an invite back.

The fuck with that.

"Well, of course. As a member off this family, I expect to be down here, what? Once a month? Every other week? What's the schedule look like?" I sit back in the chair, carefully crossing my legs as I do.

Eyes watch my legs as the move, slightly hidden by the table but not fully.

Men are so fucking simple.

"Meetings are usually exclusive to Capos and the heads of the family. I'm sure you understand," Carmine says with a tight smile, and when I look around the table, I see an equal number of cocky smirks and nervous glances.

Good.

I like when people doubt me.

"Actually, I'll be attending those meetings as well," I say with a broad smile.

"Delilah, that's—"

"Is my purpose in this arranged marriage not so the Carluccios and the Russos can form a bond? Work together moving forward?" My hand moves out, gesturing at Carmine.

"Well, yes, but—"

"As the sole Russo heir, I will be taking the position of Donna. If you want to work with the Russo family, you'll be working with me." I say the words crisp and clear and watch each one hit Carmine.

His tongue runs along his top teeth as he clearly weighs what to say, but eventually, he nods.

"On to business," he says, and I fight the smile that wants to play on my lips.

Until I meet Dante's eyes and see he isn't bothering to fight it, so I let it out as Carmine drones on with business.

When the conversation winds down from general information that doesn't mean much to me, but I still take mental notes on, I speak up.

"I would like to start an event in Eliza's name," I say, looking around. Two of the men at the table are older. Not Dante's men—Carmine's men.

"In Liza's name?" one of them asks, and I smile my siren's smile in his direction.

"I wish I had known her, but I've learned a little about her since I agreed to enter the family. She loved Hudson City and loved doing anything she could to benefit the community, correct? I think it would be a great way to get the family back to its roots."

A test.

"You don't have to worry about where the roots of the family are, sweet thing," one of them says. Silvero Cafro. His heavily graying hair is combed back, the sides short and styled in a way that tells me he hasn't changed barbers in over forty years.

I turn my head to him and raise an eyebrow.

"And why is that?"

"You're marrying in. Paulie will help guide the family into the new generation." My mouth screws up and I raise an eyebrow, refusing to back down.

"And I'll help. My name is on this family now, too. It's clear that there aren't many women who sit at this table, but if I have any say in it, that will change." A scoff comes from Paulie but I ignore it.

He can go fuck himself.

His comeuppance is upon us.

Silvero continues to stare at me, and I wonder if I miscalculated in thinking this man would appreciate and accept a clear speaker, someone who doesn't back down just because some cranky old man likes things the way they are.

But still, I don't change my expression. I continue to stare at him with a look that says, *And?*

A look that challenges him to respond to my words.

And then, finally, he smiles.

A genuine smile, like I passed some kind of test.

"I think I'm gonna like you, *mitica.*"

"*Mitica?*"

"Means legendary. That's what you remind me of. Little thing, but not gonna go down without a fight, are you?" I look around the table at his words, meeting each man's eyes before stopping on Dante's.

He's fighting a smile despite his normal stern mafioso face plastered there.

"Not even a little," I say, locking eyes with my husband as I do. He lets a little of that smile break through at the edges of his lips.

"Well, I think it's a great idea," Vinnie, the other Capo of Carmine's, says. "Liza meant a lot to this family, and her loss should be remembered. A community day. Shit for kids, food, music, games."

"That's a wonderful idea. Delilah and I can work together to plan it," Teresa says, and when I look at her, she's smiling but it's mischievous.

Like she *knows.*

Or maybe like she's proud?

"This is stupid," Paulie says.

"Why is that?" I ask, looking at him with exasperation.

"We're not here to make the community love us. We're here to make *money*, Lilah. That's why women shouldn't be here. All of you are too fuckin' soft about shit."

I want to tell him off.

I want to throw something in his face.

Instead, I give him a smile.

It's not a kind smile, but the type you give a child who is having a temper tantrum.

"Do you think there's a way to do both, Paulie?" I ask the question as though he's a child that I need to reason with by getting on his level. Vinnie scoffs out a laugh and I look over to him, throwing a wink his way. He smiles.

This might be easier than I thought, winning over these men.

"I know it's probably hard for you to understand, what with your head so fucking far up your ass, but getting involved in the community, giving back—it build ties. Connections. It builds trust. So if something *does* go south, we're less likely to be questioned. Or people are less likely to believe it."

"This isn't a PR campaign."

"Why not?" I ask, looking over at Jason who has been watching me skeptically the whole time. "The world is changing. RICO acts and social media. Cameras in everyone's hand ready to make whatever they spot go viral. We need to be focusing on the PR of this family. We need to take how the public sees us seriously."

I have everyone's attention now.

"Right now, the city thinks of you all as thugs. Dangerous men who are stealing from the poor to make themselves rich. They'd *love* to see each and every one of you locked up, to make themselves feel safer by removing the connection between their city and the Carluccio family. You need to rewrite the narrative. Take it back. Become the family they root for because when we succeed, the city succeeds."

Paulie looks exhausted and bored with me.

Dante looks proud.

The men look a mix of intrigued and impressed.

"I grew up as Shane Turner's daughter. Knew no other life than making sure his image was clean. Every gala I went to, I smiled, became the pretty girl next door. I was trained to win the city of Ocean View over, to win the voters. And look at him. A piece of shit, but he's fuckin' beloved in that town. It's why when there are whispers about who he is, they don't stick. No one thinks it could happen, and if they do, they think that it's okay because he's bettering the town they live in while he works his shady shit. He promotes what he's done well—reducing property taxes, bettering the school systems —because he knows how to play the game. The new game, where an opinion is a google away. You guys?" I look around. "Sorry to say, you just don't."

I'm done with my speech and look around, taking in the faces.

Silence takes over the table for a full minute.

I'd be lying if I said it didn't make me nervous.

"She's right, you know," Silvero says. His face says he's not happy about admitting it, though. "Back when Liza was around, when Anthony was in charge, I could walk into Trattoria and everyone smiled at me. Got a table instantly. Now, it's . . . different. I still get my table, still get served, but no one wants to stop and talk." Men around the table nod in agreement.

"The city is scared of us."

"What a bunch of pussies you're all being," Paulie says, throwing his hands in the air. "Who the fuck cares?"

"I do," Vinnie says, and the room settles.

According to Dante, Vinnie is Carmine's second and was in battle with Johnny.

"The old days were good. We helped, but it helped to keep us clean. It took the pressure off us. And the girl's right—everyone has a phone; everyone wants some kind of viral video these days."

"A community event could start rebuilding trust in the community," I say, looking around. "It's a step into the future. A world where made men aren't having fingers pointed at them, the newspapers gleefully covering their demise," I say, staring at Carmine.

He doesn't blink.

"We could hold it in River Park on third," Silvero says, ending the staring contest when Carmine looks his way.

A slight look of shock covers his face, like he's stunned that one of *his* men is on the side of the stupid little girl.

It's only going to get worse, old man.

"What do you think, Carmine? For Liza?" I ask, and even though I don't move my eyes from him, I can see from my periphery that Dante's brow furrows.

Confused.

He didn't hear the accusation Johnny made.

And I didn't see fit to share without some kind of evidence.

That kind of information would kill him.

Finally, with a long minute between us, Carmine's jaw gets tight before he nods. The look is filled with venom though, like he's trying to tell me that I won't get away with whatever I'm planning.

But that he's also annoyed he can't figure out *what* I'm planning.

"For Liza," he says.

"So, it's on. Teresa and I will plan it," I say, a smile on my lips as I continue to stare at the Don I can't wait to tear down.

And then, I do the unexpected.

Not unexpected for me, but for the rest of the family in the room, I'm sure.

I look at my wrist where a small, dainty watch is and I smile, putting my hands to the table and standing.

"It's been real, boys, but I have plans. See you all later."

The faces at the table look shocked, minus Marco and Dante who both look a mix of exasperated and humored.

And I know why.

No one stands before the Don.

No one leaves before Carmine does. It's a respect thing, and by ignoring it, I'm delivering a fatal blow.

Good, I think as my heels click on concrete, and then Marco's chair scrapes and his heavy footsteps follow me.

We get into the car, not even bothering to say goodbye to anyone, and when the door shuts on us, Marco turns to me.

"You did good," he says with a wide smile.

"Did I?" I ask, half proud, half nervous. "I'm worried I went too far for the first time most of them met me."

"No, it was perfect. Carmine's men don't like Paulie as it is and they remember what it was like when Carmine's father, Anthony, was in power: easy, safer, community focused. They also all loved Liza from what I know."

"So, I didn't totally blow it all up?"

"You pissed off Paulie and definitely pissed off Carmine, even though he won't show it, but fuck it. They'll be gone soon enough."

"Hell yeah, they will," I say.

He smiles before starting the car and backing up, taking me to Jerzy Girls because I can't head home right yet—I told everyone I have some important plans.

While he drives, I reach into my bag and grab the notebook I brought with me and start scribbling down everything I learned at today's meeting. I take note of where the weak spots might lie and who I think will be the hardest to turn.

THIRTEEN

-Lilah-

The door creaks as Dante slips into my room that night, earlier than usual.

Not that I'm complaining.

He does his normal routine of locking the door, stepping to the vanity, laying his gun inside, and placing the brown paper bag with some kind of meal to feed me on top before moving to me.

"Hey," I say, standing from where I was sitting on the bed scrolling mindlessly and padding over to him. My arms go up to his neck as I move to my tippy toes to kiss him, his own arm wrapping my lower back and pulling me closer.

The kiss is gentle and sweet, but the heat of untamed lust still burns beneath.

"Missed you," he whispers when he breaks the kiss, pressing his forehead to mine, and as always, I get flutters in my belly with the words.

"You're early tonight."

"The men are going out tonight, part one of Paulie's bachelor party or something, I think." His hand moves up, tangling in the hair at the back of my neck, and he presses his lips to mine again, this time a bit longer, a bit hotter.

"We haven't even had an engagement party," I say with a laugh when it breaks, my words a bit breathless.

"He'll take any excuse to go out and party, get drunk and do something fucking stupid," Dante says, his voice exhausted.

"Hmm," I hum, then I step back and tip my head to the brown bag. "What's in the bag?" I ask because I never really know what he's going to bring me.

"Nuggets, fries," he says with a smile.

"Mmmm," I say, moving around him and grabbing the bag excitedly.

"Your reward," he says with a smile as I bounce on my bed with the bag.

"My reward?"

"Your reward for being so fucking amazing today." I smile, basking in the sunshine of his compliment.

"You think I did okay? I was nervous I went too far."

"Nope. You left and I could see the steam rolling off my father the whole rest of the meeting." I smile. "You got Vinnie for sure."

"Did I?" I ask with a smile.

"To be fair, the man is nearly seventy and is won over by a pretty smile almost every time, so there's that. It's why he wasn't Carmine's second. But you won him over with the event idea. That was a good one, by the way."

"Thank you," I say, munching on a fry. "I thought of it on the way over. I mean, I wanted to start doing that kind of stuff anyway, but I figured why not announce it today? If the men were on board, Carmine couldn't argue the idea too much, especially if I did it in your mother's name." He comes up to the bed, sitting next to me and pushing hair behind my ear.

The touch is strange, normally something sweet that makes me feel warm and cozy, but considering I haven't had him in so long, it feels almost electric.

It's barely been a week, but both of us have held strong, trying not to cave, trying to tease the other into losing without breaking our own restraint.

My thread is fraying quickly.

"Genius. I don't think it could have gone better."

"What happened after I left?" I ask as I peel open a container of barbecue sauce, dunking a chicken nugget in.

Dante steals it from my hands, eating it in one bite and smiling at my pout.

"No one had the balls to say anything bad about you, which I thought was interesting," he says, grabbing a new nugget, dunking it, and feeding it to me.

"Why's that?"

"Because that means they either didn't have anything bad to say or anyone who *did* have something bad to say thought they'd be outnumbered." I furrow my brows, still not understanding. "It means that anyone who wanted to talk shit about you thought that if they did, enough men in the room would be on your side that they'd be odd man out."

Interesting.

"It's barely been a week, though." I doubt I've been able to pull men over that quickly.

"You work hard at the club, and you're nice to the men who work there with you. They know your backstory. When you're at the compound, you're not hiding away, scoffing at the family business. You're in the kitchen, eating with them. Learning about them, their families. You're getting to know them and they're getting to know you. It might seem small, but it means a lot to have someone come into the family and immediate try to be a part of it."

I think on that and realize he's not wrong. This week I've spent less time while at work at the club in Dante's office and more time on the floor, talking to the men—both Capos and the lower made men.

I've organized two family meals to be delivered into the shared kitchen this week, writing a note covered in hearts and girly font to tell the men that it was from me and to help themselves.

And each time I see a man, they thank me for it.

They also have been slowly talking to me, learning about me. Asking me questions about Lola and the club, about things I like.

Small talk, sure. But sometimes people underestimate how big small talk can be in your day-to-day interactions.

"It helps that you always look sexy as hell every time they see you, those low-cut tops and tiny skirts." His eyes are heated with his words, breaking me out of my thoughts.

"You like?" I ask with a smile. "I bought all of my new outfits with your money." His hand goes to my bare knee, sliding up as he does, stopping right beneath the line of my little nightgown.

"I would like them a whole lot more if they were just for me." The thumb of his hand moves, swiping against my inner thigh. "And if I could act on it."

"Oh, you can act on it, Mr. Carluccio," I say, moving the food to my bedside table and leaning back on my hands, a smile on my lips. "Just, if you do, you gotta know you'll be losing our little deal."

"But what if you are the one to break first, Mrs. Carluccio?" he says, that thumb strumming delicate flesh, and leans forward to press his lips against mine. "What if you lost the game?"

His breath plays along my lips and I almost say fuck it.

I almost let him win.

It's not even important to me, not really, so what's the point?

But then I remember that if I let him win, I just know I'll be hearing about it until the day I fucking die.

"Not a fucking chance, Dante," I whisper with a smile, pressing my lips to his and then rolling out of his reach.

He sits there, still leaning in, his hand now on the comforter like he's making out with the ghost of me.

"You'll be the death of me, Delilah," he says with a smile before sitting up and adjusting himself.

"But what a death it would be, Dante."

An hour later, I'm fed and still in pajamas, sitting under the covers while watching Dante get undressed for bed. I watch as he reaches behind himself, grabbing the back of the long-sleeve thermal he wore today and tugging it up. I watch the muscles flex, watch as tan skin and that dusting of hair are revealed, and try to ignore the way my body instantly responds.

It's been less than a week since I've had this man, and even though this dumb challenge was my idea, I'm dying a little inside with each minute that passes.

It almost feels like a battle of wills at this point—a game to see which of us is stronger. It's not about the prize, just about power.

And as I watch long, thick fingers work at the button of his pants, I wonder if maybe it *isn't me* who's strongest.

"What?" he asks when he catches me staring.

I lick my lips, unable to answer.

"Delilah . . . ," he starts, looking me over with a hint of worry before that melts with his realization. A smile grows on his lips. "Oh."

"Don't look at me like that, Dante. I'm not losing," I say.

He smiles.

"Yeah, I know." My interest perks up.

"Is that you saying *you'll* lose? For the cause?" My mind starts to move over all of the ways I can have him tonight if he does, all the ways I can enjoy my husband finally.

"Nope."

I glare at him and he laughs.

Fine.

Two can play that game.

I stand from the bed, moving over to my vanity and grabbing my lotion before sitting at the little stool before it. Squeezing some into my hand, I start to slowly spread it onto my skin, starting at my legs and moving up, over my knees, up my thighs.

He's standing there shirtless, his slacks unbuttoned, but his progress stalls as he watches my hands move. *Perfect.*

And then he speaks.

"I'm gonna take a shower," he says, and I give him a weird look. "Keep me company?"

"We were just about to go to bed, Dante," I say. "And I don't want to get my hair wet."

I don't mention how I refuse to get in that shower for fear that I'll break, naked in a small space, hot water beating on our bodies . . .

"Just sit in there with me. You sit on the toilet, get ready for bed, put your lotion on. Keep me company."

I stare at him and his smile, and I know. *I know* this man has some other plan.

But do I care?

Nope.

"Fine," I say, and he smiles wider before moving to the attached bathroom in my room. I listen to the shower start, refusing to follow him until he's under the water, his naked body away from hands and eyes that are quickly becoming their own entity.

"You're safe, Lilah," he says, his voice low from the bathroom. "I'm in the shower." I roll my eyes but also fight a laugh, knowing he knows why I didn't follow him instantly. I head in, eyeing the neat pile of his pants and underwear before sitting on the closed toilet and finishing the process of putting on my lotion.

"I miss you, you know," he says, his voice low.

It's low in a way I know, a way that has that invisible string that connects to my clit tugging.

"Hmm?" I say, not trusting my voice.

"I miss you. Touching you. Tasting you. Being in you." His words fill the room alongside the steam, making it feel like it's everywhere, he's everywhere.

"I—"

"Have you touched yourself, Delilah?" The words are a rumble and I recognize them.

He feels just as unhinged as I do.

And I can almost guarantee his hand is on his cock.

Jesus fucking Christ.

"Dante, I—"

"Answer my question, *fiorella*," he says. A low, barely audible moan falls from his lips.

"No," I whisper, because I haven't.

I'm regretting that now, the need for this man pooling between my legs, a mere week of being without him feeling like torture.

"Me neither," he says, and then another groan comes from the shower.

"Are you . . ." My words trail off as I picture him under the pounding water on the other side of the thin shower curtain, stroking his cock and thinking of me.

"Yes. Now you," he says, his voice low and dark. I don't answer. "Come on, Lilah." The words wind around me, making me heart skip a beat. "It's not cheating if I don't see you. If you don't see me."

I moan despite not having my hands anywhere near my body.

Just the *idea* of it.

"Let me talk you through making yourself come, Lilah. Please. God, that's what I want right now. Let me hear you." His words are a plea now, nearly begging, and I think in some way he knows.

He knows anything he begs of me, I'll do, the same way he does for me.

My hand moves, sliding up my thigh as I lean back, spreading my legs. A finger trails the line at the top of my panties, slipping under the elastic, moving down over tight curls and barely—ever so barely—brushing over my clit.

I moan, the sound quiet but filling the small room all the same.

"Fuck, yes." I hear splashing, and I know—I know his hand sped up with that small noise.

My hand moves farther into my underwear, two fingers circling my clit now as I arch my lower back just a bit, tipping to get more.

"What are you doing, Lilah? Tell me." His voice is a firm demand, and like he's right above me, like it's his hands on my body, I answer.

"I'm circling my clit," I say in a low, quiet whisper.

"Are you wet?" he asks. "Dip down, put one finger in your pussy, and tell me how wet you are. How fuckin' needy that pussy is."

I have no choice but to abide, dipping my hand in and sliding my finger into my entrance.

"Jesus, fuck," I murmur. "I'm so wet. Fuck."

"Fuck yourself with that finger, baby. No clit. One finger," he demands, and I moan again, bucking my hips. "My cock is so hard for you, Lilah. What the fuck are you doing to me?"

"I need more, Dante," I say, but I don't give it to myself.

I wait for his instruction.

I *need* his instruction.

His words.

"Such a good fucking girl, my baby is. Waiting until I let her have more." A deep groan falls from the other side of the curtain. "Spread those thighs for me, baby. Spread them until it hurts, picture me there, holding you open for me, getting you ready for my cock."

I do as he says, spreading and marveling at the slight twinge of pain in my hips, how it intensifies my pleasure. My eyes drift shut and I can see it: Dante standing before me, his hands holding my thighs open, lining the head of his cock up with my entrance.

"Three now, Delilah." I love that too, how his words go fierce, how he uses my full name when he's like this, when the boss takes over. "Fuck yourself with three fingers and ride them. My cock is bigger, but that will have to do. No clit, baby."

Again, I obey, three fingers sliding into my wetness easily. My hips start to buck, moving to meet my fingers that are thrusting into me.

"Fuck, it's so good." I moan. "I miss you. God, I need your fucking cock."

"No. This is good, baby. This is so fucking hot. I miss your cunt but I like this, hearing you get yourself there, listening to that wet cunt take your fingers. Jesus. Are you dripping?"

The water in the shower shuts off and I hear him now, the sound of his wet hand jacking his cock.

"Oh, god," I moan.

"Are you *dripping*, Delilah?" he asks a second time, voice firmer.

"Yes, god, I'm so wet." It's on my hand, the wetness making me so slick, and I know that his cock would slide in so perfectly if he would just . . .

"Take off your panties and toss them over," he says, and I pause.

"What?"

"I said, take off your fucking panties that are wet with you and throw them over to me. I can't have you, but I'll have that."

I moan again with his words as they register and roll through me, bringing heat with them. I do as he asks, closing my legs, sliding my wet panties down, and tossing them over the top of the shower.

"Soaked," he groans. "Go. Finger fuck yourself, baby. Get close."

I slide my legs open once again, filling myself with three fingers and starting to ride them.

It doesn't take long until I'm teetering on the edge.

"Shit, Dante. Oh my god."

"You're so close, baby. Hold on. Not yet."

"*Dante—*"

"Got your wet fuckin' panties wrapped around my cock, jacking myself off to the sound of your wet cunt, of you moaning my fuckin' name. You'll hold the *fuck* on, Delilah."

It's an order.

One that takes my body closer to the edge.

But I don't argue, because he's right.

I will, if that's what he wants—what he needs.

"That's it, baby. Now go," he says what feels like hours later but couldn't have been longer than a minute. "Rub that sweet clit and scream my name as you come for me, but remember that you're only having this right now because I'm telling you you can." I moan as my fingers finally touch my clit, hips bucking at the intense pleasure. "I own your orgasms, baby. They're for me and me alone, and you only come when I say so."

I'm nodding, teetering on the edge, but he can't see me.

"Dante—"

"Now. Go, baby."

And then I scream his name, my body convulsing around my fingers as I do. Somewhere in the recesses of my mind, I hear Dante moan low, hear the groan of his release, and that sparks my own orgasm just a bit more.

It takes long minutes for my breathing to regulate, for me to grab some toilet paper and clean up, but as I stand to wash my hands, something hits the floor by my feet.

"A reminder of what you do to me," Dante says, the water turning back on in the shower.

And on the floor are my panties.

My panties covered in Dante's cum.

When the room is dark, when I'm cuddled in his arms, the blanket pulled up around us, I finally whisper my truth.

"I kind of like it, you know," I say. His lips move to the spot beneath my ear, pressing there sweetly.

"Like what, *fiorella?*"

"This. You and me." He laughs a deep laugh that's laced with sleepiness.

"I'd hope so. You're pretty stuck with me." I roll in his arms, laughing gently, slapping a hand on his bare chest, the hair there tickling my palm.

"No, you dummy." I think and then revise. "Well, yeah, but that's a given." My lips move to his collarbone, pressing there, and his hand moves down my side to my hip then trails down the back of my leg to my knee, hitching it up over his hip.

It's not sexual, just a way to get even closer to me.

He's like that always, trying to get his body as close as humanly possible to mine, like if he doesn't, he's afraid I might disappear forever.

"Then what?" he whispers, the hand from my hip moving back up, skimming Dante's oversized tee shirt I'm wearing, moving to brush hair from my face before stopping to cup my jaw. His face moves in, and he presses his lips to mine gently, altering my brain chemistry for a moment before I can answer.

"This. Us. Just . . . being. I love sex with you, but I like this, too." I'm shy, trying to figure out how to say what I want to say.

How do I explain that this forced celibacy, this challenge of sorts has made me feel closer to him than ever. Made us talk more, find new ways to be together, and has nurtured and strengthened the bond between us.

I don't, of course.

I don't have to explain.

"I know, baby. Me too," he says, and then I fall asleep with the knowledge that somehow, when it matters, we're always on the same page.

FOURTEEN

The Carluccio Family:

Jason: Paulie's number two. According to Johnny, has a daughter. Paulie gives him shit for it. Angle?

Dario: Paulie's man. Seems loyal. Paulie is fucking his wife.

Gian: Paulie's man. Wouldn't stop looking at my tits. Easy.

Roddy: Dante's man. Already loves me. :)

Marco: My man.

Vinnie: Carmine's man. Old school. I don't think he likes Paulie. Stir the pot?

Silvero: Likes me already. Misses the old days.

Tino: Technically Paulie's man, but I think I won him already. Fucking Sammi. Talk to her about him.

Paulie: Piece of shit. Too arrogant for his own good.

Carmine: Manipulative. Has a plan no one knows about.

Dante: Mine.

And with that list, I know where I need to start.

Teresa.

FIFTEEN

-Lilah-

The Monday after the family meeting and exactly one week after the announcement of Paulie's and my engagement, I let Dante know I will not be at work the normal time, instead working toward my goal of creating a friendship with my seemingly potential mother-in-law.

Teresa.

The woman is an interesting conundrum, appearing to play the part of the perfect mob wife and also acting as the all-knowing, potentially devious super sleuth.

I need to know more.

I remember the words she said to me that first night we met.

I knew your mom. She was a good friend to me in my time of need.

It couldn't have been when Tony went away—those trials took place when she was her sickest.

And what would Mom—a politician's wife and the lover of the heir to Teresa's rival family—possibly have in common with Teresa Carluccio?

And then there was that family meeting, where she said she was the power of attorney for Tony. Where she fought with her son.

Where she looked at him with such distaste, it made me question her motherly love for the man.

And finally, there was Johnny's insight.

Paulie put a hit out on Teresa.

For money?

For power?

Does she know?

I have no idea, and when I asked him, neither did Dante. I need to know more, to figure out what the puzzle of Teresa looks like and decide if she's friend or foe.

But I know I won't find my answers at the club working.

So instead of heading into work today, I find myself walking across the property to a small cottage on the outskirts ad knocking on the door I know to be that of Teresa Carluccio.

She opens the door with zero hesitation, telling me she either expected me or saw my approach on some kind of security camera, but either way, she greets me with a friendly smile.

"Good morning, Delilah. What a lovely surprise," she says, moving to the side and using her arm to sweep across the small but stylish expanse of her entryway. "Please, come in, come in!"

I do as she asks, moving into the room which is decorated mostly in stark whites and chromes, everything new and top of the line. A plush white rug sits under an expensive-looking all glass coffee table, a comfy but elegant light-colored suede couch sitting before it.

"What brings you to my little corner of the compound? Can I get you some coffee?" she asks, walking toward a kitchen area, and I follow, my heels clicking on the hardwood as I do.

"Maybe later, thank you. I was actually hoping to do a little shopping today and wanted to know if you wanted to come along? I need to get a dress for the engagement party, and we can get lunch after. Maybe start planning for the community event, if that works for you. I booked the pavilion in the park for three weeks from now, so the turnaround is a little tight, but I'd love to start working on getting the community back on our side as soon as possible."

Teresa stops and turns to me with a smile on her lips.

"Just like your mother, you know," she says with a small shake of her head, that smile staying in place. I pause, unsure of what to say. "She got an idea, wouldn't drop it until she saw it happen." She turns again, headed away from the kitchen and toward a closet. "We met before you were born, families running in the same circles and all." She smiles over her shoulder at me. "You know how that goes."

"Yes, I do. I didn't know you were such good friends with my mom."

Teresa grabs a gorgeous dark-leather jacket, slipping it on her arms and smiling my way with a smile I recognize.

A woman with a secret plan.

"She helped me when I was at my absolute lowest point," she says, grabbing her purse and stepping out of her home. "Come on, Delilah. I think we have a lot to talk about."

An hour later, I'm following Teresa around the mall, watching as she elegantly moves from rack to rack, tossing things aside, inspecting others, tossing items into a pile over her arm. Jason, who drove us here, is standing in the corner of the department store, scrolling on his phone and pretending not to watch us.

"You know. The men are going to love you," she says, clacking hangers. "I mean, most of them already do, but the rest . . . they'll come around. That was always my biggest worry when Tony was around. If the men would like me, if they'd whisper in his ear I wasn't good enough." She laughs, clacking another hanger. "Not that Tony didn't already think that about me. He had half a dozen *goumads*, you know."

My eyes are wide but I don't say anything, leaving the conversation open for her to keep speaking.

To reveal more.

"Thankfully, I convinced them all to like me well enough," she says, looking over to Jason, who is leaning against a wall ten or so feet away, a bored look on his face, before looking back at me with a small smile. "And when he was gone, I knew I needed to pull the next rest to my side. Tony's men might as well have been mine at that point, but Paulie's men. Carmine's. The more of them who liked me, the safer I was."

Her words are so casual, like it's just a part of life.

Like it's not an exact mirror of my own plan.

"Safer?" I ask, though I don't need to. I understand how important having the men of this family on your side can be.

"Oh, no one told you?" she asks as she looks at me with a raised eyebrow. Then she puts her hand around my elbow, pulling me close like we're old friends or a close mother-in-law/daughter pair, before speaking in my ear in a low voice. "Paulie tried to put a hit out on me."

My ears go a bit static with her words.

Johnny shared this information on the payphone, but I've been unable to find anything that confirms it. Not a receipt or a whisper. Even Dante and Marco hadn't heard anything. It must have been such a closely held secret.

"I'm sorry. I think I heard wrong—" She shakes her head with a smile, stopping my words before they leave my mouth.

"Nope, you heard correctly. My dipshit of a son tried to put a hit out on me. Lucky for me, knowing his father was a piece of shit and his grandfather is a conniving piece of *trash*, I saw something like that coming. It's in his blood, that poison. Too much of Carmine's, not enough of Liza's."

I don't respond.

I'm not sure *how* to.

She's talking so casually about her son—a man she *brought into this world*—putting a hit out on her life. Of him trying to have her *killed*.

And then she looks at me, eyes dipping to where my necklace is, the St. Christopher medal hidden beneath the neckline of my shirt, burning my skin, then down at my hand at the engagement ring Dante gave me.

The engagement ring the world thinks is a symbol of my devotion to her son.

Does she know different?

She smiles then moves to another rack.

"See, Tony went away for life. And when he did, I got power of attorney." There's a small smile there, like she's proud of that fact, like a wife getting power of attorney when her husband goes away is an accomplishment instead of an obvious choice. "Of course, the feds probably would have locked him up for longer, put him in federal instead of a cushy state pen if they knew everything. So I told my sweet, devoted husband that if he signed everything over to me, I'd keep my mouth shut."

I look around the store, scanning for eyes, for ears.

There's just Jason, staring at his phone, looking bored, too far to hear our conversation.

"No one's around, trust me. Tracked every last employee when we walked in. You should, too. A good skill to have, knowing where everyone is in any room you walk into. Jason's distracted, but even if he were listening, none of this is a family secret. Not really." She flits to a rack of earrings, spinning the display like she actually cares what the options are. "Anyway, I said to Tony, I said, you give me power of attorney instead of our dipshit son or that conniving father of yours, and I'll keep it to myself."

She finally turns and smiles at me.

"I'd tell you that's a lesson to learn, that you should hold your cards close and gather whatever you can, but you're like your mother. You already have been, haven't you?" She stares at me, not necessarily waiting for a response but reading my face all the same. When she sees an answer I'm not sure I gave, she smiles and nods. "Good girl. Staying quiet."

She walks off, moving toward a table with black slacks. "Anyway. That pissed off Paulie. The kid thought he'd get all of Tony's assets, the money, the cars. Tony sold the compound to Dante before the feds got wind of all of his assets and put a freeze on them, put the cash offshore, signed a bunch of shit off in my name." A feline smile creeps over her lips. "Paulie thought if I were out of the way, it would all be his. But he's stupid and can't see past the excitement. Can't see the game. Throws a fit when things don't go his way." She shakes her head, her curtain of dark hair moving with it, and sighs. "He was always that way. A terrible temper and hated to lose. Fuck, once we had the Gambini kids over, they were playing Monopoly while their mother . . . God, I can never remember her name. Anyway, they were playing and it looked like he was losing, so he took the board and chucked it at the little boy's head."

Another shake of her head and a sigh, the perfect portrait of a disappointed Italian-American mother. "He could have gotten far, you know. He's a smart kid. But he never wanted to put in the work." As I follow her toward a display of summery dresses, I interrupt her slowly.

"I'm sorry, Teresa, but . . . I'm very lost."

"You won't be. Eventually. This family is one big mess of secrets that will all reveal themselves to you eventually. But first things first, you gotta win them over. You know that, though." She moves farther into the racks and I watch from the corner of my eye as Jason moves as well. Despite looking entirely out of the happenings of two women shopping, he's got an eye on us.

"He's going to be the hardest nut to crack," she says, shifting her eyes to our bodyguard and lowering her voice. "He's a sweet kid, a little high strung, but loyal to the bone."

It feels like everything this woman says is a giant riddle I need to decode. I don't understand a single bit of it.

Actually, that's not fair. I understand the *what*, I just don't understand the *why*.

"He's got a daughter, you know."

I did know that. According to what I've been able to find out from Dante, Marco, and even Johnny, Jason is a single dad with a daughter he absolutely adores.

"Tensions are high between them. Some of it's normal preteen girl shit, part of it is he's never around for her. She's got some kind of father-daughter dance in a few weeks. Jason asked Paulie to give him the time off, but of course the ass won't confirm or deny if he'll be on that night."

I try not to seem too eager to learn this new information as I file it away and try to figure out how to use it to my advantage.

"On?" I ask. "Does Paulie have some kind of . . . job?"

"On for the family. Paulie thinks he's hot shit, makes his men take shifts 'on' just in case. Makes no fuckin' sense, but he loves the power. So he puts them on call like fuckin' police officers or doctors, makes sure they can't make any plans during that time *just in case.*" There's a scoff and a shake of her head. "Can you believe that he'll actually make shit up, call whoever is on, and have them do some dumb ass errand for him just to make sure they haven't made any sort of plan? Last week, he called Tino and had him bring over a fuckin' pizza."

How the fuck does this woman know that?

"That's . . . That's crazy," I say, choosing my words carefully because, again, Paulie is her *son,* after all, and I don't know this woman well enough to understand if she's the type that is okay with me bad mouthing her son so long as she did it first.

"You're tellin' me. Problem is, like I said, Paulie loves that power. Fuckin' asshole makes sure he always puts men 'on' when he knows they have somethin' going on."

"So, he schedules them for . . . a . . ." I try to figure out how to phrase it. "An unnecessary workday, but he does it when they have something going on?"

"Gian missed his brother's wedding three months ago."

"Wow," I say in a whisper. She stops her perusing and stares at me, taking me in like it's the first time she's done it.

"You know, heard about this whole thing—" She moves her hand around in my direction. "Thought it might be crazy. Thought that Dante might actually be giving that dumbass the family, that we were all fuckin' doomed. Then you walk in and my mind was . . . changed." A smile grows on her lips. Not one of joy, but of . . . satisfaction.

"I don't—"

"Like I said, you'll need to pull them to your side," she says, her voice low, grabbing a dress on a hanger and not even bothering to look at the size or the price. "If you want to make your plan work, you need them on your side." She repeats what she started earlier and again, my gut drops. Teresa continues to pull me along through the store, keeping Jason at a distance and adding clothes to the piles in her hands, handing some off to me.

"I don't know what you're talking about," I say, accepting another little black dress from the woman before she nods at me, walking away from me quickly as I follow, trying to keep up.

"Marissa!" Teresa says, waving at a woman standing near the dressing rooms of the expensive department store. She tips her head in my direction before jerking it in a *this way* move as she tosses her pile of clothes to a chair, moving to the stranger. Her hands are on her arms when she leans forwards, pressing a kiss to each cheek.

"Can we get the big room and share?" Teresa asks the woman after a minute of useless small talk.

"Of course! Anything for my favorite customer!" the woman says before grabbing a key ring and jingling it in our direction, indicating we should follow her.

"Teresa, I—" I start, trying to tell the woman kindly that I have zero desire to undress in front of her.

"Jason's too close," she murmurs through gritted teeth, grabbing my hand and squeezing.

I go quiet, understanding.

Whatever she's about to tell me is not for *mixed company.*

As soon as the doors close behind us, Teresa waits thirty seconds, listening to Marissa's heels clicking, the sound getting farther and farther before she finally speaks.

She doesn't start small.

"I'm on your side," she says. "Your plan? I want in. I can help, Lilah."

My gut churns, thoughts flying in my head.

This isn't where I thought this shopping trip would go.

I thought I'd be the one working on growing her trust, on pulling her to my side, getting intel.

But instead, it seems she wants to prove herself to me.

"Why?" I ask. "No offense, Teresa, I don't know much about you other than you've been loyal to the family who killed my father for quite some time."

There's a smile on her lips, a sad one, before she speaks. "God, your mother would be so fucking proud of you, Delilah Antonia."

She stares at me and I hold her gaze, waiting for more. Then she sits in the chair in the corner and gone from her face is the mystery. Gone is the cloak and dagger.

Instead, there's honesty there.

There's heartbreak.

There's a long life of secrets and betrayal.

"Your mom was the same age as I. We grew up in the same circles, so I knew her most of my life. We were best friends." My eyes go wide with that news.

Teresa Carluccio was best friends with my mom?

I was actually there the night she met Arturo, watched her go to that rooftop and not come down. I knew it was the beginning of the end for them." She looks to the side and shakes her head. "She lived with her head in the clouds. She wanted to find her soulmate. Wanted to fall in love and grow old with him, to have babies and watch them grow." There's a shimmer in her eyes as she continues. "Wanted grandbabies." Teresa smiles. "When we were young, we said we'd have baby girls and we'd name them after each other. That they'd be best friends forever."

Teresa shakes her head gently with a smile.

"Anyway. You know what happened with all that. No need to dig up the past. But when Arturo . . . When he was murdered, it broke your mom. A part of her died that day, Delilah." I roll my lips in, fighting emotion.

I knew that, of course.

But hearing it, seeing in Teresa's eyes how bad it was . . .

It breaks a part of me too.

My mind moves to Dante and how I don't think I'd recover if something happened to him.

"We got together one night, after everything. I had just found out the plan had been to get rid of me, to take on Libby and you, to get that tie to the Russos." She shakes her head. "God, I was so fucking mad. Your mom had moved from grief to anger too." A sad laugh comes from her lips. "We started planning. Got so drunk I couldn't look at wine for a month, cried a lot, and we started planning. Got whatever information we already had, figured out what else we needed . . ."

Silence hangs in the dressing room.

"What plan?" I ask, confused.

"You know, people think the men in this life hold all the power. But men get distracted by a nice pair of tits. A woman? She wants revenge? It's all she can fucking breathe until it's hers." Her words resonate so deeply, turning my blood to fire.

Because that's the life I've been living, isn't it? Living to get revenge on the people who hurt my family. Who killed my father, used my mother, hurt my sister.

"Your mom helped me put Tony in prison for life."

And then for the millionth time, my idea of the past falls apart before Teresa helps me reassemble it, leaving me with a clearer image of what happened all those years ago.

SIXTEEN

An entry from Libby's journals, written ten years after Arturo's death.

We've done it.

Finally.

It's not all the family deserves, but we've gotten at least some part of our own retribution for what happened to my love, for what that man put his own wife through.

I know my time is coming soon, and I'll be back with him again.

I know that the future is murky, that Delilah isn't old enough to know everything, that the world still isn't safe for her.

But I can rest easy knowing we did this small part.

And that my friend was able to get everything she deserves.

-Libby

SEVENTEEN

-Lilah-

The dress is black—tight and low up top before flaring to a sweet, knee-skimming circle skirt.

Black because this is not a celebratory experience for me.

The shoes are deep emerald green. The soles are red.

The whole ensemble was bought on Dante's card, of course.

The nails, just like my lips, are red, and sometimes I wonder if I'll ever go back to any other color.

Not anytime soon—I like the subtle reminder that I'm a siren.

That I'm here to destroy anyone who isn't worthy of serving under my rule.

When Marco knocks on my door, I open the third drawer of my vanity, grab the small gun that is there, putting the safety on and slipping it into the tiny garter holster I had Marco buy for me.

I'm done letting everyone else protect me, done being a helpless victim.

An hour later, I just finished having an absolutely mind-numbing conversation with a man who, to be quite honest, had bigger balls than anyone I've ever met.

I mean, to incessantly stare at the tits of a woman who you know is the sole heir to one powerful family and the fiancée to another . . . you have to have some balls.

But I smiled through it, playing the game I was trained to excel at.

"You don't have to smile at everyone, *fiorella*," I hear behind me. I don't even look at him, crossing my arms on my chest.

"Don't you have a date, Dante? Or should I call you *zio?*" He's silent, and when I finally break and give in, he's looking around.

Checking for ears.

"My bride will not be calling me fucking *zio*," he says under his breath. I roll my eyes and his lips tip.

I should have known something filthy is coming. "You wanna call me Daddy, though . . ."

"Dante Romano Carluccio!" I whisper under a hushed breath.

But still, a wave of heat runs through me.

He sees it, of course.

"Huh. You don't hate that. Good to know."

"Oh, dear god," I say, but still, I cross my legs.

It's been so damn long since I've had him.

"But really, Lilah, you don't have to smile at every man who talks to you."

"What?"

"That man. He was talking to you. I can read you better than I can read anyone. You hated it. But you kept your pretty smile on your lips despite the man staring at your tits the whole time."

"Now, now, don't get possessive," I say with a smile, still not looking at him.

"I'm always possessive when it comes to you. Stop giving people a smile when they don't deserve it."

"That's how the game is played, Dante. Women smile."

"Not you." My brows furrow in confusion, and I look around the room. "You don't give the gift of your smile to anyone who doesn't deserve it, Delilah."

My mind goes to days when I would be at a gala and Shane would whisper through gritted teeth in my ear, *Smile, Delilah. Smile when you are being spoken to. Make it actually look like you enjoy being here.*

"In the real world, Dante, when a woman isn't smiling, she gets told that she should do it more."

"This *is* the real world. This is *your* real world. Anyone says that to you, you kick them in the fuckin' shin for even deigning to tell you what to do."

Finally, I let my eyes drift over to him where he's standing next to me. He's leaning against the wall, ankles and arms crossed like he doesn't give a shit about anything going on.

But his jaw is tight, irritated.

"You mean that," I say, my words low.

"You don't let anyone tell you what to do anymore, Delilah. Ever." My eyes scan the room before I murmur my next words low.

"Not even you?"

"There's only one time when I'm allowed to tell you what to do."

"It's been a while since you did."

He doesn't smile but even in his profile, I can see the smile in his eyes.

"Whose fault is that?"

My eyes scan the room, finding the culprit. *His date.*

"Not mine," I say.

"How much longer is this going to go on?" he asks me. "Sleeping with you is nice, watching you make yourself come was fucking spectacular, but I know you need me just as much as I need you, baby," he says.

He's not wrong.

Two weeks.

It's been nearly two weeks of sleeping next to Dante in little nighties, of kissing and touching but not much more, except that one night a week ago.

And as much as I hate to admit it, because he's not wrong, I do need him in that way, it's been nice.

A change.

We never had this, always so desperate for each other's bodies. We never had time to just be together without that. To talk, to touch, to kiss.

"I like it too, *fiorella*," he whispers, always knowing what I'm saying, always able to read between the lines.

And then he walks off before I can respond, waving to some random person in the room, or maybe no one at all, as always, leaving me wanting more.

Less than twenty minutes later, though, I'm standing with Marco when I look around the room and see it.

Angela, standing in front of Dante, a hand to his chest, clearly waiting for him to kiss her.

He doesn't even look at her, simply moving back a step and leaving her hanging, forced to make it look like it wasn't the rejection it was. It's a consolation, him denying her and stepping back, but still.

She's still there.

She's still *his*.

And while I understand the need for her presence, I'm done with her putting her *grubby little hands* on what's mine.

I take a step in that direction and feel Marco try to put a hand on my wrist.

It slips from his grasp as I keep walking.

"Delilah—" he tries, but he can't really stop me—it would cause a scene, after all.

I would cause a scene.

So I keep walking, pasting a huge, friendly smile to my face as I stop in front of them.

"Excuse me, so sorry, Angie, but I just got a super important call and I need to inform Dante of something." Her eyes move to mine, daggers bouncing off my armor.

I didn't even bother to make my voice sound kind or apologetic.

I fucking hate this woman.

"You don't even have a phone in your hands," Angela says, looking me over.

"Okay, and?" I ask, raising an eyebrow.

"How did you get a call?" The look is catty, like she wants to hit me, and honestly?

I wish she fucking would.

I'm dying for an excuse to tug on those shitty extensions.

"Junior, you've got to be kidding me," she says, and a part of me blossoms at the fact she calls him that, a moniker he absolutely despises. "We're at an *event*." I smile, mouth closed, lips pursed, nose scrunched.

"To be fair, the event is to celebrate me. Engaged, remember?" I say, lifting my hand even though my thumb spins the thin gold band on my right ring finger.

Dante doesn't miss it, of course, his own hand moving to the chain around his neck where his ring lies beneath his own medal.

But instead of smiling at Dante, I look at her hand that's wrapped around my husband's arm, the ring finger empty. My eyes linger there, then I look at her her face, a catty smile on my lips.

At least it's obvious she knows what I mean, knows I have something she doesn't.

Something she'll never have.

She sucks her teeth in a very unladylike way before opening her mouth to say something more.

But her *date* cuts her off.

"Angela. Leave me and Delilah."

"Dante—"

"Angela."

I don't even *try* to hide the smile. Not even a little. Her jaw tightens before she puts her hand on his chest, moving to her toes to press a kiss to his cheek before giving me a bitchy finger wave and walking off.

I want to pull her hair out.

I can't pull her hair out.

Yet.

I turn, walking toward a quiet corner, knowing Dante will follow me. When we're far enough from the crowd, I turn back to him before scanning the room, looking for any eyes watching us.

Always looking for eyes.

"Tell her she can't touch you," I demand, turning to Dante once I see the coast is clear and crossing my arms on my chest. He puts his hand on my arm, directing me into a coat closet I didn't see before.

"What?" he says once he turns the light on and closes us inside.

"Tell her that she cannot touch you," I say through gritted teeth as he moves me farther into the dark closet, a dim bulb overhead barely letting me see his expression.

"Lilah—"

"I'm not kidding, Dante. I'm done. I'm going to lose my mind. Every time I see her hands on you, my hands twitch to slap her. If you need to keep her around so bad for the image, fine. I get it. But I don't want her touching you. Definitely not fucking kissing you." He steps closer, an arm sliding around my lower back.

"Are you jealous, baby?" he says. I wrap my arms around his neck and tip my head up to look at him.

"Very much so." That makes him smile.

"I kind of like this side of you, all jealous and possessive."

"Speed up this grand scheme of yours and I'll be jealous and possessive all the time, when any woman looks at you." He rubs his nose against mine.

"You gonna let me fuck my wife tonight?" His head moves down, and he rubs his nose along my neck, kissing the spot he loves beneath my ear.

"Are you gonna cut her off?"

"I don't know. This is kind of fun." His words are growled into my neck, the vibrations moving straight to my needy clit.

"You don't cut her off, you're not getting your wife tonight."

"Punishment for both of us," he says, voice low as his tongue moves out, licking my skin. I try and take in a breath, ignoring how shaky it is.

Dante, of course, does not ignore that.

"I need it, Dante," I say.

There's a knock on the door before he can answer.

The door cracks and I'm hidden behind my husband's large body before I hear Marco's voice, Dante going slack with relief.

"You two better not be fucking in here," my second says, his booming voice filling the small closet.

"Lilah won't let me fuck her," Dante complains like a petulant child.

"That's because he's still letting his little *goumad* touch him," I say, stepping away.

"She's not my *goumad*, Lilah."

"Oh, yeah, I forgot, I'm the *goumad* technically."

"Jesus Christ, Lilah—" He sees the small tilt of my lips, sees the game, the teasing, and shakes his head.

"You two done in here?"

"I mean . . . ," Dante starts.

"You gotta be done in here. Dinner's in five," Marco says, changing his request to a demand.

"Got it. I'll leave. You let Lilah know when three minutes have passed," Dante says, stepping forward, but I grab his arm and move him back.

"No. Marco, you let *Dante* know when three minutes have passed. I'll be heading out now," I say, ducking under the big man's arm.

"Marco—" I turn to face my husband, looking over Marco's arm as I do.

"Remember, Dante. Marco's one of my men now," I say with a smile and then walk out the closet, Marco clicking the door behind me.

But as I walk away, I hear that deep, bone-warming laugh softly following me in the distance.

EIGHTEEN

-Dante-

Dinner starts and I'm seated next to Lilah by some stroke of luck, with Angela across from me and Paulie across from Lilah.

It's lucky because I think if Angela were next to my wife, she might just slap her, and if Angela were next to me, I don't even want to know what Lilah would do.

I can just imagine her kicking a pointy heel into the other woman's shin and giving her a sweet smile of fake apology.

It's been an eye-opening experience, seeing how my sweet wife is just as possessive about me as I am about her. The past week of this game, of her demanding I drop Angela, was just that—a game. Who would break first? Who could resist the other?

But it was also so much more.

It was a chance to learn my wife in a different way. The first night I was alone with Delilah, I couldn't keep my hands off her and that never changed. Having this forced celibacy has almost been a cleanse. It was much more similar to how things were during those days at the club, when I would sit in the shadows and pester her with questions, dying to learn more about her—anything about her.

The nights have been spent like teenagers, kissing and giggling and talking, but not much more, despite how much I know we both would have enjoyed it.

How much we both wanted it.

But, while those nights have been nice, I'm done with this.

I need my wife.

And now that she's seated next to me, I know I can plot my defeat of this woman.

The game starts during the dinner course, some kind of ravioli in a cream sauce that I know before she even picks up her fork, Lilah will just push around to make it look like she ate.

I also know I'll be bringing her food tonight, making sure she's fed and happy, always.

"So, Delilah, what do you do over at Jerzy Girls?" Teresa asks, looking genuinely intrigued. "You work as Dante's assistant, yes?"

I've always been fond of Teresa, despite her bringing Paulie into the world and choosing to hook herself to Tony. I like even more how my wife seems to have created a friendship with the woman who once knew her mother.

Lilah needs that, a woman in her life. Bonus, she's a woman in her life who knows *this* life.

"You know, a bit of this, a bit of that. I help make sure the girls have anything they need, get payroll in line—that kind of thing." As I listen to them talk, I finish my meal and place my fork down before moving both of my hands to my lap and sitting back in my chair. Then I slowly creep one hand over, over, over until it lands on the fabric on her sweet knee-length dress.

It's beautiful, of course, but when I saw her in it, the first thing I thought of was flipping the floaty skirt up and bending her over in a corner while I fucked her from behind.

Since that isn't in the cards just yet, I move my fingers, pulling the fabric up until my hand is on her warm skin.

From the very corner of my eye, I see the tiniest tip of her tongue leave her mouth, wetting her lips.

But other than that, she's as unfazed as ever.

My hand stays there for a minute, a long minute as I feel the heat of her sin, before her hand—the one not holding her fork—moves under the table, covering mine. And then, as always, she surprises me.

I don't know how, since it seems Lilah *only knows* how to surprise me.

But I definitely wasn't expecting her to gently take my hand and slide it up her thigh until my pinky finger gently grazes her pussy.

Her bare pussy.

The woman has no fucking panties on.

All my brain can think of is her warning to me two long weeks ago.

I'm not going to make it easy on you.

"Well, you know, Delilah worked as a stripper before she came to us," Angela says, sitting across from me, and my eyes cut to her.

I truly hate the woman.

Having my hand on Lilah's warm thigh helps the urge to say something mean and aggressive to Angela, something that could ruin her as my cover. Except for when the pointy fucking nails Lilah always has dig into the skin of my hand.

In response, I move my pinky to soothe her, to quell her anger, grazing where she's already getting wet for me.

It's been too fucking long.

She needs me just as badly as I need her.

Watching her make herself come in her room last week was nice —a new experience, a taunting one, knowing I couldn't help or take over, but my own orgasm barely cut the edge off my need for her.

And each day since, that need has doubled like some kind of

radioactive ingredient, taking over my body until fucking her is all I can think about.

"And that's relevant, how?" Teresa asks. She's sitting across the table, next to her son, and leans forward to get a better look at Angela. I can nearly see the unique brand of Italian-American mother rage pouring off her in waves.

Angela, though, is dumb as a box of rocks.

"I'm just saying, is all." She shrugs. "Maybe her intentions are, you know, money."

Lilah snorts.

She snorts and then, unable to hold it back, actually laughs out loud for nearly a minute, a minute where I have to fight the urge to either join in on laughing or grab her face and pull it to me because I fucking love that sound and this woman to my core. Finally, she wipes a tear from her eyes, waving at her face with a huge smile on her lips.

"God, Angie. That's good!" Angela grits her teeth. She despises when anyone shortens her name, and since she clearly hates Lilah, it probably pisses her off even more. "I guess it takes one to know one, right?"

I watch Teresa's eyes go wide, her lips rolling between her teeth as she fights a laugh.

"I don't—" Angela starts, her cheeks turning pink.

"You know I'm a *Russo*, right? I don't need the money, sweetheart." Lilah's voice does from friendly giggling to catty queen and I think my dick gets a little hard at the tone.

That can't be normal, right?

She pauses for a moment, and I don't look her way, but I just know her eyes are travelling over Angela, and I just *know* she's going in for a killing blow. "Nice dress, though." Again, I don't look at my wife, playing it cool, but I just know there's a catty look on her face.

It also makes me a little hard.

Definitely something wrong with me.

And when I watch Angela's face turn a deeper shade of red, I know that the woman-only burn hit hard.

"I guess your Dad doesn't give you the kind of allowance you need to prepare for these kind of events," she says, and Angela actually gapes at her.

I can't resist it.

My hand moves again. It slides between her legs and tugs just a bit until she spreads her legs gently, giving me room to play.

"So, Lilah, I was just telling Silvero about the event we're planning for next month in Liza's honor. He's got the contacts for Trattoria Seven and a few other local places that might want to contribute."

"That's wonderful," Lilah says. "Ideally, I'd love to foot the majority of the bill if we can. Dante and I made it a line item in the family budget so we can make sure that we keep contributing to it, more events and more community involvement."

"Why would you throw an event for *Hudson City?*" Angela asks with a disgusted voice. She's mentioned more than once to me how much she hates this *trashy* town, as if it isn't the city I was born and raised in. "It's not even worth it."

I open my mouth to speak, but Lilah beats me there.

"Some of us understand the value of being a part of a community. Of building up trust in the people where you live and work. We all benefit when our city flourishes." There's a pause as Lilah winds up for another hard hit. "But don't worry. You can leave the important stuff to the grown-ups."

Angela's face goes full-on red with embarrassment and frustration, and her jaw goes tight in a very unattractive way.

My wife deserves to be rewarded.

With that thought, I move my hand up her thigh again, a single finger dipping barely into her then dragging the wet up and circling her clit. My own heart races at the move, at touching her like this after two weeks of nothing, at feeling how fucking wet she is from the slightest graze of my fingers on her flesh.

But Lilah's breathing doesn't change.

Her face doesn't change.

In fact, she turns her head to Teresa.

"Anyway. That dress you picked when we were out shopping was stunning—why didn't you wear it tonight?"

Casual conversation.

As if I don't have my hand on her pussy beneath the table.

I look away from my sister-in-law, away from Lilah as I lick my lips and circle her clit once more, pressing harder this time, and her legs spread just a bit more.

Asking for more.

I want her begging though.

My finger moves, slowly sliding into her and feeling her tight cunt clamp down already.

If we were alone, a low moan would leave her lips.

If we were alone, I'd watch her lower lip drop, her eyes drift shut the way they always do when I first enter her.

But I can't see that.

And I know that my queen has her face of ice on, not allowing anything to pass through. Instead, both elbows go to the table and she leans her chin into her hands, eager to listen to whatever Teresa tells her.

"Oh, you know, I thought that might be better for the bridal shower in a few weeks." Lilah's legs open wider, her hips tilting almost unnoticeably before she speaks once more, and I slide a second finger in.

"That makes sense. When is that, again?"

I don't hear the answer because Lilah's cunt is clamping down on me as I move out, pressing her clit once again, then slide in.

But even though I know my girl is on the edge, when she answers, not a single quaver is in her voice.

"That's going to be such a wonderful time. I might invite some of the girls from the club."

"*Strippers?*" Paulie asks, finally speaking up. My eyes move to him and he has a look of disgust, like he can't believe someone would invite dancers at a gentlemen's club to anything.

"Dancers. But yes. I was a dancer once, remember?" Lilah says, and this time, I do look over at her.

She's raising an eyebrow in her *Do you really wanna place this game?* way, and I sink my fingers in, grinding the heel of my hand on her clit as she starts to quiver around my fingers.

Her only tell is a tiny flush on her cheeks which could be interpreted as embarrassment or irritation.

Not lust.

Surely not the edge of orgasm.

"Well, you're not anymore, so don't invite them."

Wrong answer, nephew of mine, I think, knowing how close Lilah has grown to the women of Jerzy Girls.

"You never seem to have much of an issue with them, Paulie," she says, tipping her head to the side like she's confused. "I mean, you've been fucking Fancy for at least a month, right?"

My nephew's face goes fire red and, to my shock, his *mother* scoffs out a laugh.

"I don't—"

"It's fine. That's not part of the deal anyway, right, *fiancé?*" she asks with that same cutthroat, sugar-sweet tone in her voice.

I *fucking adore this woman.*

And even more, I love how when I grind down on her clit harder, her hips buck almost infinitesimally because she's so fucking close, but not a moment of it shows on her face.

And right then, when I know she's on the cusp of shattering on my hand, I pull out.

I move my hand from under the table to my glass, rubbing the edge with my wet finger casually before dipping it into the brown liquor and then into my mouth.

I don't look at my wife, but I know her eyes are burning on me.

The fire furls in my gut, the need for her almost painful.

"You just started war, Dante," she whispers under her breath, not looking at me as conversation continues around us, shifting in her chair like she's uncomfortable.

Good.

Me too.

"Give me your worst, baby," I say back in the same whisper, but then I wonder if I might have made a critical error.

Because I can see without even looking right at her that my wife smiles big before taking a large sip of wine.

I mimic her movement, taking a sip of my own whiskey, and I can't help but think that I'm going to need it for whatever this woman has in store for me.

NINETEEN

-Lilah-

When I finally get the chance to leave the party, I slip out and Marco walks me back to my room. I grab my burner phone as soon as I lock the door and text my husband.

> ETA?

He replies near immediately.

> About an hour. Gotta clear the house.

> Be quick.

And then I wait.

I wait about thirty minutes to set my plan in motion and when I do, I make sure the chain is latched as well as the deadbolt. When I roll to my side, to the bedside table I stocked as soon as I knew this game was on, I have a smile on my face.

I'm dressed in the skimpiest, laciest of the nightgowns I bought with Dante's card, and now I am holding a bright-pink vibrator in my hand.

Let the games begin.

-Dante-

My phone buzzes in my pocket and I know it's her.

My girl.

My wife.

God, I fuckin' love that.

Never thought I'd be the type of man to settle down, get married, but here we are.

As I'm watching the caterers close up the rest of the tables, I'm wondering if maybe she's texting to tell me she's tired, going to bed early before I can crawl into her bed with her. It's nearly one after a long as fuck day.

I'm also wondering if when I get to her room, if I crawl between her legs and start eating her sweet pussy, will she let me finish her off?

Before I walked Angela to the door, I brushed off her touch on my arm, telling the heiress that I don't want PDA anymore. And considering I'm never alone with the woman, I think the message got through loud and clear, especially when she gave me a forced, stiff smile before letting Tino help her into her car.

I don't blame Lilah for hating her, if only because Angela gets to be seen in public with me. I get it. Watching her walk into a room on *fuckin' Paulie's arm* killed me. Knowing everyone in that room didn't know she's mine made fire rage in my veins, but it's all part of the plan.

It won't take long—I've watched the men already shift in a room to cover their future queen rather than who they think is their future boss, Lilah's little siren working overtime.

But we need a reason not to raise alarm when we're together so often. Angela is an excuse for people not to question who Lilah is to me.

Everything, the voice in my head reminds me. *She's everything.*

I pull the phone out as it buzzes a third time with another text from her.

> How long will you take to get here?

> I need you.

> My hand is on my pussy and it feels so good, Dante.

> Fuck, I'm so wet.

Jesus fucking Christ.

I read over the texts again, and then a third time, trying to understand and decode them.

To decide if it's really happening or if my needy, sex-deprived brain is just hallucinating things.

Is this woman *sexting* me? While I'm still halfway across the house, closing shit up?

Before I can reply, another text comes through.

> Did I tell you I bought a vibrator? It's so big, baby.

> Almost as good as you.

Oh, fuck no.

The only things that go into that sweet pussy are attached to me.

"Marco!" I shout, already headed toward the door. "Finish up here, I've got business to attend to." I don't even care when I hear his deep laugh following me as I start to run.

And then I'm headed to Lilah's wing of this stupid monstrosity of a house. No one else stays there, except for Marco whose room is at the entrance of the hallway. He's always on guard, ensuring my girl stays safe when I can't keep my eye on her.

I'm already pulling the key out of my pocket when I approach her door.

I don't bother to knock.

I just unlock the knob then use the other key for the deadbolt, turning the door and pushing it in to open it.

As soon as I do, I hear her. I hear a wet noise, the wet of her fucking pussy, and a low hum.

And I hear her moan, low and deep.

But I don't see it. I don't see her, legs spread wide as she plays with herself.

Because she left the fucking chain on the door.

"Delilah!" I say through gritted teeth, my voice firm and frustrated.

"Dante," she moans.

"Delilah, undo the fucking chain."

"Are you going to stop seeing her?" Her words are breathy, and when I look through the crack of the door, I can see a sliver of her: her hand moving quickly, the side of one leg, her hair spread around her like the fucking goddess she is. Another moan falls from her.

"What?"

"Oh, fuck," she moans, like she can't stop, can't get thoughts out through the pleasure. "Are you . . . Are you going to stop seeing her?"

Despite my anger, I can't help but smile.

This *fucking woman.*

"If you don't open this goddamn door, I'm breaking the chain."

Her breathing is getting heavier.

She's getting closer.

I'm not sure if it's the vibrator or the rush of knowing she's getting to me that's turning her on.

Knowing Lilah, it's probably both.

"Oh, god," she moans, and through the crack, I see her head moving side to side.

Thrashing.

"Do not fucking come, Delilah. Let me in."

"I . . . I can't . . . Oh shit, fuck, *fuck*."

That's it.

"Stay there. Don't move, Lilah."

"What?" Her words are breathy and confused and I smile.

Then I take a step back and kick my shoe right where the chain would be attached to the wall, ripping it from the doorframe.

Explaining that when I need one of the men to fix it will be a tomorrow problem because now the door is swinging open and Lilah is lying on her bed, a lacy nightgown up to her waist, pumping a pink fucking vibrator inside her wet pussy.

Her eyes are dilated with pleasure, despite the look of shock on her face.

"What the fuck, Dante!?"

She keeps fucking working it, though, keeps moving it in, her hips twitching. The other hand, that I can almost guarantee was alternating between playing with her tits and rubbing her clit, is stalled just inches above it.

I lock the door without fully turning my back to her before taking my gun from where it's tucked into the waistband of my pants, placing it in her drawer, and taking three long strides to her.

To where she's *still* working that fucking buzzing vibrator inside of her.

I grab it, and as it slides out, she moans.

I smile.

"What's this?"

"Dante—"

"What is it, Lilah?"

"It's a vibrator. Now give it back so I can finish off and go to sleep." She's pouting and it's fucking adorable.

But I don't need *adorable* Lilah right now.

"The only thing finishing you off is my cock, Delilah."

"Not until you agree."

I smile, knowing I can win no matter what.

Two weeks without her is way too fucking long, and I know she feels the same. I take the tip of the vibrator and move it through her wet, making her back arch off the bed.

"You sure about that?" I say, my voice low.

"Tell me you're done with her," she moans.

"It's not that easy, *fiorella*."

The reality is, it could be that easy.

Is life a little bit easier and are there fewer questions when I have Angela on my arm at events? Of course.

But would I risk it all, deal with the questions, handle Angela's inevitable fuckin' tantrum if Lilah told me it was important to her? If she didn't make this all a little game where we see who could hold out the longest?

Absolutely.

I'd take a bullet for Delilah Antonia Carluccio-Russo.

God, I fuckin' love that name.

"I hate her, Dante," she whimpers. I take the pink vibrator, dipping it inside just a bit then dragging it up, circling her clit, and repeating the circuit. Pleasure to ease the pain I've caused.

"I know, baby."

"I hate when she touches you," she says, and this time, it's not said through a moan. I look up and her eyes are on mine.

Now this—this she means.

I pull the vibrator away from her, turning it off and setting it to the side, and then I move to cover her body with mine.

I love this—her nearly naked, me fully dressed. It's always my favorite way to have her and the way I find myself taking her most because as soon as I'm in her presence, I *need* her.

Always.

"Then she doesn't touch me anymore," I whisper. Lilah's eyes go wide.

"What?" My hand moves, brushing hair back.

"You don't want her to touch me? She doesn't touch me. Easy

as that. What my wife wants, she gets." A small smile tips up her lips.

"Really?"

"Lilah. You think if you stood there and told me you genuinely were against something, *especially* if it's because you're possessive of me, I'd say no?" I press my lips to the spot below her ear. "Fuck, you think if you ask me for *anything*, I'll be able to deny you?"

"Well, technically, I'm lying down," she says, and I move my head from her neck to look at her and then to the ceiling, praying for patience.

"Yeah, you're lying down with a wet pussy I haven't tasted in almost two weeks. You *really* think I could tell you no?" She smiles.

"Maybe I should reevaluate other things I want."

"I'd give you the entire world, Delilah." Her eyes are too much—too sweet, too kind, too much love and adoration there that I'm forced to return to kisses, running my lips down her neck. "But what I won't give you is a fucking orgasm with a pink vibrating dildo." She barks out a laugh as I reach for the offending object and throw it in the corner. "At least not for the first time."

Her laughter fills the room, a room that will be filled with her moans in just minutes, and as always, it's a reminder as to why we're doing this. Why we're going through this trouble and strife and cloak and dagger bullshit. Because this free, happy laugh—I want to hear it always.

"Okay, now that that's gone," I say. "Let's fix the next issue." My head moves down to her hand, where her thin gold wedding band is just a bit too big on her right ring finger, and I pull the entire digit into my mouth and tug the ring off with my teeth. Her chest rises as her breathing goes wonky.

I grab her left hand and slip it on with my mouth. When I pull back, I smile at the ring on its rightful finger and spin and settle it on top of the huge engagement ring.

The only good part about this plan was I was able to buy Lilah the most outrageous, gorgeous ring, knowing she could actually wear it daily on the correct finger. The world thinks it's from Paulie, but she and I know the truth.

"Better. Now, if you're going to touch your pussy, you use this fucking hand and you make sure my fucking ring is there." I move off her until I'm standing. "Now show me." Her big eyes go wide.

"What?"

"Show me what you were doing before, but do it with your pretty hands, and do it wearing my ring." She licks her lips.

I expect her to argue.

To say no.

But as always, my Lilah surprises me and takes one finger—her ring finger, the temptress—and runs it from her wet center, dragging it up until she circles her clit.

A small moan falls from her lips.

My fingers move to the buttons of my shirt, undoing them with haste.

"That's it, baby. You can play with that pretty pussy for your man, but you don't forget who owns it." Another moan because my girl likes when I talk to her. "How does it feel, baby? Having your fingers rub your clit, knowing you're going to get my cock soon?"

"Oh, god, fuck, Dante. I need you so bad." Gone is the teasing from her voice as her hips buck up, trying to get something only I can give her.

"I know, baby. It's been too fucking long." I shrug off my shirt, but my eyes are fixated on her hand, on her red nails and her glittering rings and the fact that she is mine.

All fucking mine.

I move my hands to my hips, undoing my belt and the button on my slacks before pushing them down and stepping out of them. I move to the edge of the bed, climb on, and settle between her spread legs.

"Jesus, look at that. Look at you lying there, waiting for me."

"Dante, I *need* you," she whispers, that finger with her wedding band rubbing incessantly.

I haven't missed how that's the only finger she's been using, following my directions so fucking well.

"I know, baby. I'll take care of you," I say, my left hand moving up her body, between her breasts, until I reach the delicate gold chain. I reach behind her hair, grabbing onto the St. Christopher medal and moving it until it's settled on her warm skin. She leaves the chain on every day, manipulating the necklace until the medal sits on the back of her neck.

A quiet symbol that she's mine, a symbol only I understand.

My hand trails back down, brushing her hand aside and taking its place with small circles on her clit.

"You gonna give me ultimatums again?" I ask with a smile, my thumb rubbing her swollen clit.

She licks her lips, her eyes going hooded as they meet mine.

"Probably," she says, a small smile on her lips. I smile wide and shake my head, leaning down to press my lips to hers.

"That's my girl," I whisper before I line my cock up with her opening and slam in.

Lilah's back arches off the bed, her low, needy moans floating in the air around us until it feels like she's everywhere.

I stay there, deep in her, my forehead to hers, both of us panting.

"You ever gonna keep this cunt from me again?"

"No," she whispers, her hips moving to try and get me deeper. I smile, slowly pulling out and pressing back in. Another low moan fills the room.

I think I would give it all up to hear that sound every moment of every day.

"Whose is it?" I ask when I'm deep in her again, one of her legs wrapping my back.

"It's yours, Dante." Her words are breathy.

"That's fuckin' right," I murmur then tip my head down to look where I'm disappearing in her, ready to fuck her until we both come. But as always, she has her own plans. Lilah's hand moves, a single red-tipped nail going to my chin and tipping it up until I'm looking at her once more.

"Are you going to let her touch you ever again?" I slow my thrusts but don't stop.

"What?"

"Are you ever going to let her—or any other woman—" She fights a moan as I slide in again. "Touch you?"

I smile.

It's a smile filled with pride because this woman always shocks me at every turn. This woman will never let me get away with anything, always keeping the scales even, and I fucking love it.

How anyone could ever look at her and see a meek, breakable thing is beyond me. How anyone could see her and not think she could hold her own, not think that if you betray her, she'll cut your head off is unthinkable.

She is made of unbreakable diamonds, her only weakness being herself.

The only thing that can tear Delilah down is the doubt that quietly hides in her.

And I'll work to remove every last bit of that doubt for the rest of my damned life.

So I tell her what she wants to hear, and I tell her the truth.

"Only you, *fiorella*."

Because from here on out, Angela Sigano will no longer touch me.

No one will touch me but my wife.

My siren told me her demands and I'll do anything to make her happy.

I move the hand on her hip in, my thumb hitting her clit, and instantly, her back arches off the bed as she moans, clamping down on me.

But her eyes stay locked to mine.

Always.

"Now be a good fucking girl and come for your man," I say,

moving to sit on my heels and pulling her by the hips until she sits up and is in my lap, seated on my thighs. The moan that falls from her lips tells me that she's close as it is, which is fine by me—we have a lot of making up to do anyway. This round can be quick.

"I wanna make it last," she says with a lie, my little siren always ready to play. I nip at her bottom lip, lifting her by the hips and slamming her back down onto my cock, filling her deep.

"Make it last next time, baby. Need you to come on me right now."

"No," she moans, and god, this women will be the death of me.

Completely and totally.

"Delilah, come right fucking now," I say, lifting and slamming her once again, and this time, when she's full, she grinds her clit, rubbing against my pelvic bone. She moans loud as she does, her eyes fighting to drift shut.

There she is.

"No, it's been so long, Dante." Another moan. "I want it to last."

I wonder in that moment if she'll ever do as I ask.

If she'll ever stop fighting me on every single move I make.

I really hope not.

Because then I can't fight back.

"Fine, then I'll make you," I say through gritted teeth, trying to hold back my own orgasm as she clamps down again, my balls tightening and my cock throbbing near painfully.

I haven't even jacked off except for that one time in her shower since she cut me off, the need just building and building, waiting for one of us to just give the fuck in.

I lift her one last time, one arm wrapped around her waist, the other around her shoulder so when I slam her down, I force myself even deeper then move, grinding her against my pelvis and listening as her breathing increases, a small squeal coming from her throat, but she holds tight, refusing.

"Jesus fucking Christ, Delilah, come on my fucking cock," I say, pressing my hips up, grinding her down, and moving a hand out to slap her ass.

A punishment for holding out on me, for making me wait for her to fall before I can follow her.

It's the slap that does it, that has her screaming my name into my neck, clamping down on my cock, her little body shaking on mine as I fill her.

Finally.

TWENTY

-Dante-

Walking down the hall of the compound toward the wing the men spend the most time in, I'm hoping to find my dipshit nephew, hopefully without Dario.

I know he's not at fuckin' work, so there's a good shot he's here.

And when I walk toward the games room, his voice carries over all the other noise and down the hall.

And when I enter the room, I see that Paulie isn't alone, a few men loitering with him, but Dario is not one of them.

Gotta love when shit works in your favor.

"Can I get a minute, Paulie?" I ask, trying to give a least the idea that I care about maintaining his image in front of his men.

"No," he says, not even bothering to look at me.

Such a little shit.

"Let me rephrase: I need a minute with you. We can do it here or somewhere more private."

"Don't care what it is, you can say it in front of my men," he says, and I want to shake him. I want to tell him what a fucking moron he is, that the fact that he cares so fucking little is going to be his downfall.

Instead, I toss the photo onto the green felt, leaning a hip into the table and crossing my arms on my chest.

"What the fuck, Dante?" he asks, not even looking at the photo.

But I don't miss Tino and Gian both leaning in, taking a look, and then leaning back with wide eyes.

"Is that you?" I ask, knowing damn well it is.

I didn't want to have to see this fuckin' image, but when it landed in my possession, I knew it could be of use.

This morning, Marco told me he'd gotten some mail from Russo, that he didn't look at it, but the old man told him it was important to *the cause.*

Of course, I was intrigued, but my expectations weren't high. It could be something as simple as a receipt, something that was once Arturo's, something that was given to them by Libby Turner before her death.

But still, when I went to my room and found a small yellow envelope on my pillow, I wasn't eager to open it.

It was nondescript, the kind with a silver fastener holding the flap down, the kind that might hold important documents or photos or files.

It's also the kind that never bodes well, in my experience.

And on it, my name was written in clean, crisp black letters.

DANTE

Not Marco's handwriting, and also not what I would peg Russo's handwriting to look like.

I undid the metal prongs, carefully opening it and peeking inside to see a stack of black and white photos.

Surveillance photos.

Confirmation. Someone sneaking you surveillance photos is *never* a good sign.

Gently, I spilled the contents onto my bed, for some reason afraid to touch the images.

But in reality, I should have been afraid to *look* at them.

Because in gritty, long lens photography were photos of Paulie fucking a woman. They clearly weren't commissioned by Paulie, not something that either of them knew was happening, and for a moment, I'm left even more confused than before I had them.

Until I flip one over and see that same thick black penmanship on the back.

Dario's wife is written in the same dark letters.

My mind moves back to what Johnny told Lilah, about Paulie fucking his Capo's wife, about her secretly popping birth control despite the fact that Dario wants to build their family.

I think about how my wife told Johnny she couldn't use that information without proof.

Proof that, apparently, I was given.

Proof that Paulie and two of his men are now staring at.

"Is that you?" I repeat, enunciating like he doesn't understand.

"Where the fuck did you get this?" he asks, looking to me like I'm the one who took the fucking pictures.

Like I'm at fault here.

"It was fuckin' *given* to me by a little birdie. The fact that you're not denying this shit says a fucking lot."

"Why would I deny what's right here?" he asks, and I want to fucking knock him out.

The fact that he shows zero shame, zero remorse for breaking the omertà, for fucking the wife of one of his men?

Just another reason not to let him have power.

"Paulie, is that Kelsey?" Tino asks, his voice low and astonished.

"Who the fuck cares?"

"Uh, Dario's gonna care," Gian says. Gian's a good one, brought on six or seven years ago. He's single, but when he does date a woman, he treats her well, doesn't have any *goumads*.

He values relationships and is always kind and respectful to any of the men's wives or girlfriends.

The look on his face tells me that seeing this just lost Paulie a shit ton of respect.

"Dario spends too much time worrying about his fuckin' wife and not enough time worrying about the family," Paulie says. "Maybe if he finds out his wife is a whore, he'll shift his priorities."

"Jesus, man," Tino says, eyes wide.

"Wives and children *are* the family, Paulie. We don't fuck with that shit. We don't fuck made men's wives."

He turns to me and I see the ice there, in his eyes. The look tells me he does not give a shit about family or community. About growth or respect.

He cares about power and what having it can get him.

"Maybe you should mind your own business," he says, his voice cool.

I shake my head, making it seem like I'm disappointed in him.

Like I care.

I look to Tino and Gian, both clearly shaken by Paulie's lack of empathy, before stepping back.

"You're going down a shit path, Paulie."

"Worry about yourself, Dante."

"When it starts to impact the men, we all gotta worry about it. That shit bleeds, Paulie." And then I walk out, but the whole way I feel the men's eyes on me and the looming doubt in the would-be Don.

Perfect.

TWENTY-ONE

-Lilah-

Two weeks after the engagement party, Teresa and I throw the community event in Dante's mother's name. I'm up early, the men meeting me at the large park in the middle of town where I instantly start bossing them around. Within minutes of us all arriving, I have them opening tables and chairs, hanging decorations, and running to stores to pick up food, drinks, and any other bits and bobs we forgot along the way.

By noon, it seems like the entire city of Hudson is in the center of town, celebrating a woman I never got the chance to meet.

The first handful of attendees looked hesitant, eyes wide as a handful of known mafiosos stood around, urging them to sit and eat, taking little kids to face painting stations, and handing out goodie bags.

But then more people started to come, the air moving from tense and nervous to welcome and excited. Now laughter can be heard on the thankfully warm late winter day. Families are sitting around and enjoying the event, members of the family mingling and reacquainting themselves with the community they once abandoned.

"You did good, you know," Silvero says, leaning against the picnic table I'm standing next to as I overlook the party. I look at him and smile.

Over the last three weeks, since the family meeting, I've been able to talk with nearly all the men, giving them pretty smiles and learning a bit about them, but Silvero—he's been standoffish.

He always says hello, he's always polite, but he leaves it at that.

Being Carmine's second, I knew he'd be tough, but it's hard to get past tough when he doesn't even bother to say more than hi to you.

So this is a surprise.

"You think?" I ask.

"Yeah. Kids are all having a blast; town is here. Fuck, I think this is the first time in fifteen, twenty years we've done one of these."

"Here's to making it a yearly thing, yeah?" I ask with a smile, expecting one in return from the older man, but I don't get it. Instead, when I look at him, with his combed back hair and arms crossed on his chest, he's staring at me intently, trying to read me.

"She loved this kind of shit, you know? That's why she convinced her father to let her marry into the family. She loved this city and how the family nurtured it. The Romanos, the family Eliza was born into —they actually wanted to build ties with the Russos, you know."

I smile at the new information, the irony not lost on me. Silvero smiles back.

"I didn't know that," I say.

"Would have been a different world, Liza marrying Alfredo. Instead, she hung her star on Carmine, and Alfredo Russo got sweet Antonia."

Antonia.

My middle name.

And, apparently, my grandmother's name.

I wonder just when I'll stop getting hints of my past, of my family history, from other people. My heart warms a little at the thought of being connected to a woman I didn't get to meet, but Silvero keeps talking.

"Carmine's father, Anthony—he loved this shit. Giving back to Hudson City, making sure no one who deserved better was struggling. Loved helping good people who were on hard times. Used to say there was no need for us to be swimming in wealthy if the people next door couldn't put food on the table. Not saying everything the man did was good, but he had good intentions, at the end of the day. A real Robin Hood, ya know?"

"I've heard. I'd love to be able to bring that back to the family. I think . . ." I look around, trying to decide how much to reveal before looking back at Silvero.

He seems like the kind of man who appreciates someone being honest, giving their opinion even if it doesn't align perfectly with his own. He seems like that's a trait he would respect in someone.

He started this conversation. Here's hoping he's open to hearing more, and that *more* might help to pull him to my side.

"I think the Carluccios went too far in the wrong direction," I say, looking around and fighting the urge to look at him, to gauge his reaction. I try to look like I'm confident in what I'm saying, not nervous. "The family got distracted. It's easy, you know? To get caught up in the greed and the money and the . . . adrenaline." I keep my eyes away from him as I watch Dante chase a little boy, a raucous game of tag being played in the grass. "My father—well, the man who raised me, I think he fell into that. The adrenaline. Got caught up in it and forgot everything." I look back to Silvero, finally, to see he's still staring at me with an interested look. Not mad, just . . . intrigued. Open to listening to me.

"I'd like to think I have that in common with Liza: being attached to someone who accidentally went too far and forgot that it's not just them in the world."

I'm careful not to put blame on anyone, not to imply it's a weakness or a wrongdoing on Turner's or Carmine's part, but an easy accident anyone could make. A long beat goes by, and I pray I didn't go too far, implying that Carmine is anything but perfect and exceptional.

"No offense, Lilah," he starts, and my gut drops. "Don't think Turner was ever good. I think he knew what he was doing all along, knew how to hide it well enough to trick your mother. But that man was always powered by greed." He turns his head, looking around, trying to find . . . someone.

When his brow furrows with frustration, or maybe disappointment, I think it's a someone who isn't here. I also scan the get-together, trying to take note of who is here and who isn't . . .

And then I know.

Carmine.

Carmine isn't in attendance, despite it being held in his deceased wife's name.

I have to wonder what that says about him to his men. To the men who knew Liza, who knew how important community was to her. To men like Silvero, who remember when this kind of event was the norm. Men who might miss those days.

What does it mean to see their "leader" shows no interest?

"It happens. A man wants power so bad, he changes who he shows the world to win them over. Seems good until he wins that trust. Then he does what he wants with it," Silvero says.

Funny.

He might be talking about Carmine or Paulie or even Tony, but he also could be talking about . . . me.

The deceit has never weighed on me much before, not until this man, who clearly longs for the way the world used to work, calls me out, intentionally or not.

"All we can do as a collective is move forward, hope that we have the best interests of both the family and those around us in mind," I say, trying to give him what I can—reassurance, a molecule of understanding.

Common ground.

"Do you?" he asks, looking at me.

His face has changed from contemplative to stern.

"Do I what?"

"Have the best interest of the family in mind?"

I look at him and I don't feel the panic I probably should.

Instead, I feel at ease because I know now that I can answer honestly.

"I believe so. I think . . . I think there's room for the family to grow and to still benefit the community. It doesn't have to be all or nothing —greed and deceit or giving everything away. There has to be a middle ground where everyone wins. I think . . ." I look around. "I think if the family shifts priorities, we can do both. No one has to suffer. And we can make it safe. No more worrying about crack downs, about getting into hot water. Be quieter, but also louder in the community. There's . . ."

I'm really about to go here, aren't I?

I turn to Silvero fully.

"The community is scared of you guys. They see thugs, there to fuck things up in order to make a buck. The whispers . . . they aren't good. But we could change that. I mean, look at this." My hand moves over the field where families are all gathered. "This is what Anthony had in mind. It's what Liza loved. We all just . . . got distracted."

"You don't have to take responsibility for that. It's not a we, Lilah." His words are soft, almost like he's embarrassed. I put a hand on his arm.

"It's a we, Silvero. I'm part of this family now. Whether Paulie or Carmine or Dante or whoever wants me involved, I'm here. I'm not going anywhere."

I mean that.

Because despite coming here with a very specific plan, starting this mission with the desire to tear down this family, things have gotten twisted.

Feelings have gotten complicated.

Some of the men in this family—they aren't bad. They're just being run by bad people. I feel a strange connection to them all. The desire to push them in the right direction, to ensure we all benefit in the end.

The silence between us grows and then slowly, so slowly, Silvero's lips tip up.

"I think you're going to fit in just fine here, Delilah. Don't let those *stugots* put out your fire, yeah?" he says with a smile then tousles my hair like I'm a little kid. Still, I smile.

"Never. Now, can you do me a favor?" I ask.

"Anything," he says, and the way he says it, it's like he already knows I'm in power. Like he truly means *anything*—he'd go wack some guy down the street for looking at me funny or run whatever errand I decide I need done.

I tip my head to where there's a large grill set up.

"Go help Tino with the grill. I haven't seen him take a single item off that thing that isn't charred to shit."

With that, Silvero tips his head back and laughs before walking off.

And as I cross his name off my mental list, I see Teresa in the distance and watch her give me a covert thumbs-up.

Seems the queen herself agrees I'm doing okay at this.

TWENTY-TWO

-Lilah-

A bridal shower is the absolute *last* place I want to be today.

Much less a bridal shower where I have to pretend I'm excited to be marrying *Paulie Carluccio* and that I'm not already fucking his uncle nightly.

But just when I thought things couldn't possibly be more irritating, I see her.

"Why is she here?" I say through gritted teeth.

"Who?" Sammi asks. She was invited by Teresa, who knows about her involvement with Tino and her friendship with me from work.

"*Her,*" I say, tipping my chin as Angela *fucking* Sigano walks into the quaint but luxurious teahouse where Teresa planned my bridal shower.

"Is that . . . ?"

"That's Dante's *girlfriend,*" I say through gritted teeth. "And she hates me. She's the world's biggest bitch." She air kisses a few other guests as she walks into the room, looking around like this is a party for her instead of a for woman she can't stand.

Not that I care, but I don't miss that she didn't bring even an envelope as a gift.

Poor manners.

But when her eyes scan the room and land on me at the end of the table, the entire thing set up so that I look like a princess, happily ready to be wed, she lifts a lip in a sneer.

The woman sneers at me at my own party.

"Ope, well, pretty clear how she feels about you," Sammi says with a laugh. "Wouldn't have anything to do with how much time you spend in Big Boss's office, now would it?" My eyes go wide as I look at my friend. She instantly starts laughing. "Girl, I knew it. Don't worry, my lips are sealed. Fuck, I've been in messier situations with lower stakes." Her smile goes friendly, sisterly, almost, as she slows her laughter.

"I see how that man looks at you. Can deduce there is some method to this madness." Her hand moves to indicate the room.

I sigh.

I like Sammi. I like having a friend who doesn't care about all . . . this.

But still . . .

"Don't say anything. I'm neither confirming nor denying, but just . . . hush."

"Babe, you think I've worked for this family for this long without knowing when to keep my lips sealed? Shit. But when the coast is clear, I fully expect a deep dive on how that man is when he's not glaring at everyone in a ten-foot radius."

And then it's my turn to laugh, drawing attention to our little huddle, but I don't care.

Because I finally have girlfriends to gossip with, with zero strings attached.

The afternoon goes as well as one can expect—stupid games are played, gifts are opened, food is eaten, and now I'm staring at the clock, knowing I only have about thirty minutes left of this sham to endure.

I can handle thirty minutes.

Or so I think, until I'm moving toward the refreshments table and I hear it.

"Well, you know she wouldn't even be here if her mother wasn't a whore, out fucking that politician and then going behind his back with a Russo."

It's almost like a record scratches.

"What did you say?" I ask, turning around to face the speaker.

None other than Angela *fucking* Sigano.

The room goes quiet. The women she was gossiping with wisely take a step back—they must see the fucking venom flowing in my veins, dying to be spit at someone.

If I didn't already hate this woman for being able to be seen with *my husband* out in public while I can't, I really fucking hate her now for talking shit about my mother.

Would she be so confident in her bullshit if she knew my entire life has become dedicated to wreaking revenge for my family? If she knew that I fully plan on tearing down anyone who gets in my way?

But she just stands there, not moving, staring at me like she can't comprehend the words I just spoke.

Angela clearly has not a single fucking light on in that empty, empty head of hers.

"What?" Her eyes go wide, big blue ones that I'm sure let her get away with a lot of shit.

Not with me.

I've been looking for a single solitary reason to go at this woman, and she handed it to me on a silver fucking platter.

It's my party and I'll beat your ass if I want to.

Or however that song goes.

"I said, what did you say?" I enunciate the words like she's a child who needs me to speak slowly as I take a step closer to her.

"I don't understand."

"I get that there's literally nothing but a fucking hamster on a wheel in that thick skull of yours, but don't play games with me. What the fuck did you just say?"

"Lilah, maybe—" someone starts. I'm not sure who. I'm solely focused on Angela, who still can't seem to understand that I have the full intention of inflicting harm on her for what she said.

"What did you say about my mother?"

A smile forms on her lips.

"Oh, that?" I smile, too, because I just *know* she's about to make a huge fucking mistake. "I said your mother is a whore. And that if she wasn't a *whore*, you wouldn't even be here."

My smile widens.

"And you stand by that?" I ask.

"What?" Again, she's confused because, well, of course she is.

"You stand by what you said? You believe it wholeheartedly? That my mother, who died of *cancer* when I was ten, is a whore?" Her smile returns along with a catty look.

"Yup," she says, popping the p.

"That's it," I say, stretching my head to the left and the right.

"What?" Angela asks with a nervous laugh, looking around at everyone like I'm a fucking lunatic.

Oh, I am. I am completely un-fucking-hinged.

And I am *so incredibly done* with this woman.

So, I reach out and I grab her hair, tugging until she falls toward me and I can get an arm around her neck.

"What the fuck!" she shouts as we fall to the ground. As we go down, I nick my head on the side of a table, the pain searing, but I don't care.

I'm seeing red.

"You psycho! What the *fuck!*" She's shouting as I move, wrestling her to the ground until I'm sitting on her chest, my pretty white dress pushed up to my hips, my ass in a thong bared to the entire, classy party.

I give zero fucks.

"Take it back," I say, my hand still fisted in her hair.

"No! It's the truth! Your mom was a whore!" Her voice is whining, I've got her pinned to the ground, and still, she has a shitty fucking attitude.

So I punch her.

I punch her right in the cheek, hard.

And *fuck,* it feels good.

"Jesus Christ." I hear murmurs from somewhere behind me and even though I'm not looking, I know its Marco. I know he's probably shaking his head and looking at the ceiling, praying to God and wondering what he did to deserve Lilah duty.

I also know I have approximately thirty more seconds before he comes and pulls me off her.

Need to make it worth it, I suppose.

With that in mind, I keep going, slapping her, tugging her hair. I snap the strap of her dress, every moment of her putting her *fucking grubby little hands* on my husband rushing to mind.

"Take it back!" I shout like we're kids on a playground.

"Fine! I take it back! Just stop!" She's crying now, hands covering her face, makeup dripping.

Good.

I don't stop, though, my hand tugging harder at her hair.

But I'm forced to when big hands are under my armpits and I'm being lifted.

"No! No! I'm not done!" I shout because I'm lost in the zone and it feels so good to finally put my hands on this woman.

"Yeah, you are, princess. Got her good. Now, let's get you home."

"No fucking way! I'm calling the cops! I'm getting her ass locked up!" Angela shouts, sitting up on the floor. She looks around the room like she's waiting for someone to help her up, but no one moves.

With her words, though, it's confirmed that this woman truly is a moron.

"Down, Marco," I say.

"Nope."

"Promise I won't hit her again," I say, watching with pleasure as it takes two women to help Angela stand. She looks like shit, blood dripping out of her nose, black mascara running down her face, the strap of her dress ripped. I don't think I broke her nose, but a truly sick part of me thinks that would have been fucking *awesome*.

Roddy stands in the corner, grabbing my purse, well aware that I'm going to break whatever deal I make with Marco and will need to be escorted out quickly.

"Promise?"

"Yes, Marco." I put sugary syrup in my voice to try and convince him and it seems to work when he sighs and places me down on the floor. My heels click on the tile, and I push down my white dress that had ridden up to my waist.

And then I smile.

Three steps takes me a foot away from Angela, whose eyes are wide and angry.

"You're going to fucking *prison*. Do you know who I am?" I smile. Angela Sigano is absolutely no one: a daughter of a man who is a Don of the least powerful family in the state. A Don mostly because he forced it into existence with enough money, not because of blood or legacy. "Dante's going to fucking lose it when he hears this! You're *done!*" she says, spit flying from her mouth, and that one actually makes me laugh as I wipe my hand down my face, swiping at her spittle.

"Oh, honey. You know? I actually feel bad for you." I smile sweet and she keeps glaring. I just *know* the type of child she was—the *roll on the floor in a department store screaming until she got her way* type. "You hold no fucking sway, but you want to so badly, don't you?" Her face twists with anger. I put my hand on my chest, leaning in a bit. "Me? I'm a queen. I'm a goddamn Russo. I'm a fucking

Carluccio." A single red-tipped nail points at her. "You? You're nothing."

"You'll be nothing in *jail*." I laugh at her words and her face gets angrier. Uglier.

"Do you *really* think that's gonna happen? Do you think anyone in this room will be on your side?" Teresa actually snorts a laugh at that and fuck, I really freaking like her. "And Dante? Guarantee *that's* done."

"Fuck you," she says and then spits on me, on purpose this time. Her last hurrah.

I don't let it even register on my face, not giving her that small hint of a win before I take a step closer.

"Jesus," Marco murmurs, and I try not to smile as I poke my finger into her chest, her face mere inches from mine as I try once again to get my point across.

"You even think about disrespecting my mother again, you won't leave with just a headache and a damaged ego," I say.

And then I slap her again, partly because she needs one last reminder of who she's dealing with, partly because I just really want to.

"Alright, that's it," Marco says before I can get in one last word, his hand going to my elbow.

"What? I was having fun!" I say, stumbling as he pulls me, not slowing for me to get stable footing until Angela is out of ear shot, her shouting trailing behind us.

"You have a fucked-up sense of fun, Delilah Russo," he says, pushing me into the car.

I laugh the whole way home.

TWENTY-THREE

-Lilah-

Except, we don't go home. We don't drive through the iron gates of the Carluccio compound.

We drive right to the center of Hudson City until the buzzing sign that reads *Jersey's Finest Girls* comes into sight. I smile, the move causing a sting of pain at my eyebrow. When I touch it, I find it's tacky and a dot of thick blood is left on my fingers.

"Got yourself on the table when you took her down. Shouldn't need a stitch," Marco says, watching me in the rearview mirror, and even with the sunglasses on, I see the small smile.

He's proud of me, even if he'll never admit it.

Roddy turns around and smiles big at me.

"Not gonna lie, that was pretty fuckin' awesome," he says. "Like WWE but hotter."

"Keep that to yourself, man," Marco says.

"What, just saying it was hot. Lilah tackling some bitch, her dress riding—"

"Yeah, let's *definitely* keep that part to yourself, Roddy. All you need is Dante finding out you got a good view of my ass during a *WWE but hotter* smackdown."

Roddy's face goes a bit white and I can't help but laugh.

"Oh. Shit. Yeah." Marco shakes his head, turning the car off and looking back at me.

"Come on. Let's go show Dante what kind of trouble you got into today," he says as if I regularly get into trouble.

Ehh.

Well, okay. Maybe I do.

We walk into the front door of Jerzy Girls, Marco tipping his chin at Tino, Tino looking me over with a *What the fuck? look,* and Marco shaking his head as if to say, *Trust me, you don't want to know.* Candy walks by, stopping right in front of us.

"Carm?!"

"Hey, Candy."

"What the fuck happened to you, babe!?" Her boobs bounce in her tiny top and I smile.

"Angela Sigano called my mom a whore." I hear Marco sigh and I'm sure he's running a big hand over his face.

Roddy's deep laugh fills the immediate vicinity.

"No fucking way," she murmurs. "Tell me you decked her." I smile and nod, and then she looks over her shoulder. "FANCY! You gotta see this! Carm knocked out Angela fucking Sigano!"

"No way!" Fancy yells then teeters off the stage, jumping down and running my way.

Fancy has *no* top on, but no one blinks an eye.

I love this place and these girls and this family I've created for myself.

"Oh my god! Girl, she got you good!"

"No, I did that myself, hit a table corner as I knocked her to the ground," I say. It's very important to me for everyone and anyone to know that I *did not* let Angela get a single shot in, much less let her make me bleed.

"*No fucking way!*" she shouts, and Marco tugs on my arm.

"Come on, princess. Gotta get you looked at." I roll my eyes at Marco but smile and wave at the girls, who each give me a high five before walking back to work.

"You're a goddamn mess, you know that?" Marco asks, and I just smile as he leads me through the door that leads to Dante's office. "Fuckin' perfect for his crazy ass," he murmurs to himself under his breath. We stop at the door I know all too well, Marco moving to unlock it before he knocks twice.

"What are you doing?"

"I gotta knock. Can't just walk into his office."

"Maybe you can't, but I sure can," I say with a smile, turning the knob.

"Jesus, Lilah—"

I push the door open, seeing a man in the seat in front of Dante, my husband looking hot as ever as he glares at the door, definitely annoyed that someone is interrupting his meeting without his permission.

Until he sees me.

Then the look fades.

I know if he were alone, there'd be a smile that follows that look. Instead, his eyes just warm and I can almost hear the words.

Fiorella. Missed you.

"Tried to stop her," Marco says. "Tried to stop all of it, really. But Lilah . . ."

"Lilah is Lilah." The sweet look turns to concern. "What the fuck happened to your face?"

"Told you. Tried to stop her," Marco says, hands in the air like he had no part in this.

The man sitting for the meeting clears his throat.

"Marco, take Mr. Johnson to a room. I'll have paperwork for him to sign in an hour or so. If he wants, he can go watch the girls while he waits."

"Got it," Marco says, and the man stands, probably used to unconventional business tactics, letting Marco lead him out of the room. "I'll bring in the first-aid kit in a few." Then the door clicks behind him. I look to my husband.

"She called my mother a whore," I say, crossing my arms on my chest. "I'm done with her, Dante." He stands from his desk, taking the three steps to where I'm pouting, then grabs me by the waist, lifts me, and places me on the edge of his desk. His hands go to either side of my face, and he pulls me in and presses a kiss to my lips.

It's like whatever other chaos and questions he has can wait—he needs to kiss me first.

God, I really fucking love this man.

"Who?" he asks then moves his gaze to the cut in my eyebrow. He's got that look like whatever name I say, he's going to go find them and do worse.

I smile wide.

I can only hope.

"Angela Sigano." The words come out almost cheerful, and his eyes snap to mine. "Afterwards, she said I was going to prison and that you'd lose your mind when you found out."

"She said *you* were going to prison after *she* did this to *you?*" The smile gets bigger and I shake my head, ignoring the dull ache there.

"Oh, no. I did this myself," I say, pointing to my face. "I went to tackle her to the ground and clipped my head on the corner of a table." I wonder how many times I'll have to repeat this.

So totally worth it.

"You what?" Dante asks, looking me over, confusion written on his face.

"I hit my head on the table. Marco said it shouldn't need a stitch."

"No, before that."

"I tackled her to the ground." I smile and I kinda feel like a cat who brings in a dead bird. I'm proud; Dante is confused at best.

"*Fiorella* . . . I need an explanation as to why you attacked a Don's daughter at your bridal shower." Marco knocks, and Dante calls out, giving him the okay to come in.

Chances are, Marco thinks we're already fucking in here.

He smiles as he walks in, shaking his head at me and handing off a large first-aid kit to Dante.

"Johnson chose to watch the girls," he says. Dante nods before Marco leaves, the door clicking as he locks it behind himself.

Okay, he *definitely* thinks we're going to fuck in here.

"Angela?" he asks, opening the kit and riffling through it.

I try not to think about why a strip club needs such an intensive first-aid kit the size of a large briefcase, especially not when Dante seems so familiar with all the items in it.

"She called my mom a whore," I say matter-of-factly. He raises an eyebrow at me.

"Okay?"

"So I told her to say it to my face, and she was being a real bitch about it, saying I shouldn't have any power because I was a bastard child, as if *she* has any power. Fuckin' Gio Sigano hasn't had power since the nineties, my god." I roll my eyes and don't miss Dante's smile. He's been giving me my own little course on all the families in the tristate each night after he fucks me into exhaustion. "Anyway, so I tug her hair and she's a real little bitch about it, falls to the ground, and I move to sit on her chest. That's when I hit the table. Then I punched her."

Dante stops halfway through ripping a packet of gauze open.

"You what?"

"I punched her in the face," I say, kicking my feet and smiling.

I like the shock there.

I think I'll have to start doing this kind of thing more, just to see that face.

"You . . . You *punched her in the face?*"

"Don't look so surprised. I've been dying to do it since I saw that press photo forever ago. Every time she touches you, I want to tug her eyelashes out one by one."

"She doesn't touch me anymore, Lilah," he says, and I remember the truce we came to on that, that they would date to maintain the image but no touching.

And then the *way* we came to that agreement rushes to my mind and I give him a different kind of smile. Dante looks at the ceiling, shaking his head.

But there's a smile there all the same. He remembers, too. His hands go to my face, holding me still so he can look at my eyebrow.

"You're lucky you didn't go too deep. Marco's right—you won't need a stitch, but you might get a scar." He turns and grabs a hermetically sealed alcohol wipe, tearing it open.

"We'll match," I say, reaching up and running a thumb over his eyebrow. "How'd you get yours, anyway?"

He smiles then rolls his eyes. "Punched Tony in the face."

"You punched Tony?!"

"That's what brothers do, Delilah."

"Were you mad at him?"

"Nope."

"I'm sorry, what?" I say with a laugh. "How old were you?"

"Twenty."

"So Tony was . . ." I try doing the math in my head. "Thirty five? Isn't that a bit much?" He shrugs.

"Just dumb shit brothers do."

"Dumb shit you do at *thirty five?*"

"You didn't do dumb stuff with Lola?"

"Lola was like a mom to me. So, no, I never punched my sister in the face." He smiles a small smile, grabbing a butterfly bandage from the box.

"And those?" I ask, tipping my chin to his hands. He looks down at the small scars on either side of his fingers and smiles.

"Dumb guy shit." I lift an eyebrow and wince at the pain. "Can't do that for a while, babe." His thumb smooths over my eyebrow.

"Dumb guy shit?"

"Me and the men, especially when I was younger. It's a game. Take a knife, stab the spots between your fingers. See how fast you can go."

"Until you *stab* yourself?"

"It was a challenge. Who had the most balls. Also, it was a way for me to prove myself with men who inevitably would see me as less because I didn't have to prove myself to be in this family."

"That is so fucking stupid." He smiles wide.

"Told you. Dumb guy shit. I have a lot of evidence of dumb guy shit. Lots of men with lots of testosterone trying to rise up the power ladder. Shit happens." I grab the hand not holding the bandage and press my lips to one of the worse-looking ones.

"I want to kiss them all." He smiles at me, using both hands to add the bandage to my eyebrow before grabbing my face.

"When we get home, you can," he says, dipping his head and kissing my neck. "But only if I can do the same." A shiver runs down my spine.

"Can I make up scars?" My voice has gone husky as a smile grows on his lips. I can't see it, but I can feel it on my skin.

"Wherever you point, I'll kiss."

"We have at least an hour . . . ," I say, moving my hands to untuck his shirt from his pants, running my nails up his back.

"Yeah?"

"Yeah," I whisper as he moves, pulling me closer to the edge of the desk until I can feel his already hardening cock pressed between my legs, the short skirt of my pretty white dress leaving little to nothing between us.

And then his phone rings.

One of his phones, I should say. In Dante's line of work—or, *our* line of work—he needs many phones.

But the one in question is buzzing next to me, my least favorite name blaring on the screen.

"Talk about a buzzkill," I murmur, seeing "Angela Sigano" on the screen.

A small part of me smiles because I know that even on his public phone, my name is just "Lilah."

On his private phone, it says "Wife."

On his burner phone, it doesn't say anything, but he has all of my numbers memorized, so it doesn't really matter at the end of the day.

But his "girlfriend" needs her full name, as if using just her first wouldn't give him enough details.

It might be petty, but I really like that.

"I'll ignore it," he says, reaching for the phone.

"No. Answer," I say, and I've got a smile on my lips. A smile Dante knows well as I lean back on his desk into my hands.

"Delilah."

"And put her on speaker."

"Delilah—"

"Put her on speaker, Dante. I won't talk. I just wanna hear this." I smile my sweetest, most innocent smile and bat my lashes. "Consider it a wedding gift." Dante rolls his eyes at me, but he does as I ask because I'm pretty sure he genuinely would find a way to give me the moon if I ask for it. He presses the green button to answer and then the speaker button.

He really, really loves me.

"Angela."

"*She punched me in the face, Dante.*" I smile.

I smile big and I don't even try to hide it.

Dante has a small smile on his lips and shakes his head at me.

"Who?" he asks, and despite the small smile, his voice sounds exasperated. Bored.

Me! I mouth, and his eyes widen in a, *Cut it out, Lilah* kind of way.

"That fucking bitch who's fucking Paulie!"

Uh uh uh. Wrong choice, honey, I think, rolling my lips and biting them as I watch Dante's face get that stern, angry look on it. The same one that he got when that lawyer guy called me a bitch.

Even more, I know the thought that *anyone* thinks I'm fucking anyone but *him* definitely ratchets up his frustration.

Even if it's just stupid Angela.

"*That bitch?*" he asks, and I wonder if she can feel the cold through the line.

I can feel it from where he's standing in front of me. I lift my hand, moving it to his neck and playing with the hair there, twirling it in my fingers and letting my nails scrape his skin. One of the acrylic tips is loose and it's just another reason for me to hate Angela fucking Sigano—she ruined my manicure.

"Delilah. I was at her *stupid fucking bridal shower—*"

"Why?"

"What?" Her voice is an irritating screech, and I wonder how *anyone* could find her attractive.

"Why were you there?" He slows the words down like she's a child and I smile again because my man is funny without even trying.

"I was *invited*, Dante," she says with a snarky attitude. I widen my eyes because I know for a fact that Dante only likes snark from me, and even then, mostly when he knows he can fuck the snark out of me in the near future.

"So send a fuckin' gift and your condolences. All you do is bitch about the woman. Why spend an afternoon with her."

"But everyone was going to be there," she says with a whine. Dante sighs, tired of her.

"Why did you go, Angela?"

"I don't understand the question."

Of course she doesn't. There's probably just a single, lonely brain cell in her head.

"Of course you don't. Fine. Let me tell you why. You went because you wanted to stand in a corner with all the women you think are your friends, making snide fuckin' remarks about Lilah. Women who, sorry to break it to you, when you're not around either a. Talk shit about you, or b. Hit on me. They don't fucking like you. But they like gossip and they like drama, so they tolerate you."

"What the fuck, Dante, I—"

"You do it with fuckin' everyone, so I know you were doing it there. But really, what the fuck do you bring to the table, Angela?" I roll my lips into my mouth, biting them to fight a laugh and ignoring the tug at my eyebrow.

"Excuse me? My fa—"

"Your father is a washed-up boss who is fuckin' broke, trying to sell his daughter to any made man who is willing." Silence is on the line.

My eyes go wide and his meet mine, one hand moving to brush hair behind my shoulders. It's like despite whatever conversation he's having, he's having another, much calmer, loving one with me.

"I can't believe—"

"Don't play dumb. I know most of the time it's not a fuckin' act but I know damn well when it comes to money, you've got sense. Know who has it, who doesn't, and how to fuckin' spend it. You spend mine just fine."

More silence.

I scrunch my nose at him in a, *You've been buying her shit?* way, and he taps my nose.

"I don't understand why you're being so mean, Dante." Her voice has changed, gone from bitchy whining to sad little girl, something I'm sure works on other men.

But I'm sitting on Dante's desk, between his legs, my eyebrow cut because she called me a mean name and it made me mad.

She's never going to win here.

"You hit a made woman," he says, and fuck if that doesn't send a thrill down my spine. *A made woman.* He looks at me with a soft, heated look, like he likes how those words affect me. The mix of his look and his words have me biting my lip, and he see it.

His hand moves, sliding up my thigh, thumb caressing right where my dress that's hiked up ends.

"She's not a fuckin' made woman; she a glorified *goumad.*"

I cringe.

I cringe on her behalf because the look in Dante's eyes?

Pure fire.

Pure anger.

Hatred.

"You hit the fucking Russo heir, Angela."

"She's a fuckin' whore, just like her whore of a mother—"

And ding ding ding, Dante's anger peaks.

I smile.

I also get kind of hot, but that's a whole other issue.

"That's it, Angela. You're done." Silence for long moments, but Dante is patient through them, waiting for her to speak.

"I'm done?" Silence. "What do you mean I'm done, Dante?"

"I mean you're done. This arrangement was convenient and now it's not. You're fighting with the family, causing issues, causing bodily harm to a future boss—"

"That bitch is never going—"

"Argue all you want, Angela. It's over."

"I'm going to tell everyone about this. I'm going to tell everyone how fucking interested you are in your *nephew's fiancée.*" Dante's face goes dark, and I can hear the smile in Angela's voice, like she thinks she won some battle. "Won't that just cause a nice little stir?"

For a moment, my gut drops.

For a moment, I worry that my quick moment of irrational anger won and I fucked up big time.

But then Dante smiles.

He smiles like he was waiting for this.

"Will you?" he asks. "Because I've got some pretty pictures you've been sending my men." My eyes go wide.

"I-I—"

"And I've still got some unpaid debts with your father."

"I don't—"

"I call those debts, your family is done." Silence again. "You're threatening the wrong fucking man, Angela. I don't involve myself with people without ammunition. You want to spew shit, go for it. Just know, it will come back to bite you in the ass and burn your family to the ground."

She waits a beat and then speaks. "So what, we're done just because of some silly—"

"Don't reach out again. You do, your family is done, Angela. Have the shitty life you deserve." Then Dante swipes to end the call before he throws his phone to the side, and I bust out laughing, a strange joy taking over. He shakes his head, grabbing a second bandage from the first-aid kit, placing it on the cut and pressing his lips there.

"You really don't like people calling me names, do you?" I say, wrapping my arms around his neck and tilting my chin up for a kiss. His hands to go my hips, pulling me to the edge of his desk before he bends down to kiss me.

"I don't like any soul on this earth disrespecting my wife." A chill runs down my spine at his words and I press my lips to the corner of his jaw, bristly with five o'clock shadow, to the spot that bulges when he gets annoyed or when someone does something that pisses him off.

Or when he's about to come.

I absolutely love this man's jaw.

"Thank you," I whisper.

"For what?" he asks, his head going into my neck.

"For being mine."

"I'll be yours forever and a day, *fiorella*."

And while he doesn't let me kiss each of his scars this time, he presses kisses to all of my favorite places and I conveniently forget all about Angela Sigano and the disaster of my bridal shower.

TWENTY-FOUR

-Lilah-

The night of my phoney bachelorette party, a full two months into this sham of an engagement, I go in with a plan.

I'm in a teeny white dress with a goofy *bride* crown and recruit all of my favorite girls from the club to go out and bar hop around Jersey City with me.

It's not a sham because I plan to go out and get tipsy and have a good time.

It's a sham because my drivers are Dario and Tino.

Tino, I'm pretty sure, I won over already, if not just because him and Sammi have become a *thing* and I know Sammi does nothing but whisper sweet nothings about me into his ear because she's a good friend.

But Dario has been a bit of a tougher nut to crack.

I need to shake his faith in his Capo and I have just the thing to do it. Because now that Dante confirmed Paulie is in fact fucking his wife, I can move forward with Johnny's tip without fear of it being fake.

The key is to shake his faith without making him question me.

And what's better than a drunk girl with loose lips?

So when I get into the car so that my glorified babysitters can drive me to stop number two, I stumble.

"Woah, Lilah—you good?" Tino asks, careful not to actually touch me as he moves to catch me if needed, but I just giggle a girlish sound and wave a hand at him as I situate myself into the car.

"You're sweet, Tino. All good!"

The s in sweet comes out slurred and I watch his eyes widen just a hair.

God, how the fuck have these men made it this far? They can't even hide a simple reaction.

Then again, that's the point, isn't it? Why would they hide their reaction to the woman they think is just the boss-to-be's fiancée of convenience?

The dumb girl who, just a few months ago, was stripping at the family-owned club?

It takes everything in me not to smile as Tino gets in the front, leans over to Dario in the driver seat, and whispers, "She's hammered."

Dario sighs.

I let a smile come that time.

The trick is, I had one half of drink in that club and then "spilled" it on myself.

So, I *smell* like liquor.

And I'm *acting* like I'm drunk.

And really, men don't ever try to think too hard when you don't make them, so one plus one is equaling two.

As the car moves, I lean from the back seat into the console between the men. "You know, I don't know how you do it, Dario," I say with a heavy sigh, twirling a strand of my hair and leaning over like I've drunk a lot more than I have.

"Do what?" Dario asks, his voice bored, eyes watching the car in front of us. That car has my friends, the girls from the club, and if all goes according to plan, that car will reach our next stop well before I do. He's probably annoyed that he has to drive me and my crew of dancers around from bar to bar to celebrate a marriage that we all know is *absolutely* a fraud.

"Handle it. The whole thing with Paulie. We're not even *married* yet and it's already getting to me. And you've been married for what, two years? Three?"

"Handle what?" he asks, still not paying full attention.

"You know, the whole thing with Kelsey?" I continue to twirl my hair and Candy, the only girl I convinced them to let me take in this car with me, looks over at me, knowing *damn well* that I haven't drunk much more than a sip and also probably knowing about Kelsey.

Somehow, this woman always knows everything.

She's like Gretchen Weiners—her hair is so big because it's full of secrets.

Fuck, she'd make a better Capo than half the men in the family. I think about how maybe I should make her one before I force myself into the game.

"What about Kelsey?" Dario's voice goes slightly lower, his eyes looking at me in the rearview with a different look now—no longer bored, but interested.

Good.

"Well, ya know. She's fucking Paulie. I mean, it's kind of a bummer because like, we aren't even married yet and he's already got a *goumad*, but—oh god!" I say, the car swerving into the shoulder, Dario's hand slamming into the hazard light on the dash as he slows, but not nearly quick enough for the sake of my stomach acid.

"What did you say?" he says, eyes dark in the rearview.

"Yo, Dario, calm the fuck down. Don't kill me," Tino says, putting a hand to the wheel.

"What did you say, Delilah?" The car slows to a stop and I make my eyes wide like I just realized my mistake. Like I didn't *mean* to spill this secret, or that I genuinely though he knew.

"Look, Dario, I thought—" *So, it's obvious that Dario doesn't know his wife is fucking his boss.*

I wasn't totally sure if it was unknown or even frowned upon—Dante said it's against the omertà to fuck another made man's wife, but he couldn't be sure of how the rules for Tony's or Paulie's men work, if their code was different.

"Tell me what you said, Lilah," he says, putting the car into park and turning around in his seat. I sit back, making my eyes wide as saucers, my mouth opening just a tiny bit.

"Dario, you're scaring the girl," Tino says, and even Candy's eyes are wide with shock and not quite fear but . . . awareness. Like she's trying to figure out the next step to keeping herself safe.

My fingers go to the clutch in my lap. I'm pretty sure I won't need the gun Marco encouraged me to slip in there, but then again, you never know what to expect from unhinged men with a modicum of power.

But I'm appeased when Dario takes a deep breath, his jaw going tight before his eyes open again, directed right at me. "Can you just . . . tell me what you mean, Lilah?"

"I just . . . ," I start, playing the part and nervously tucking hair behind my ear. "I shouldn't have said anything. I just thought you knew about them. I didn't think it was a secret." I pull my lip into my mouth, chewing at it.

"About *what?*"

"Paulie and Kelsey. They . . . They're having an affair. Paulie doesn't . . . He doesn't hide it so I figured . . . I don't know how the family works. I just—"

"It doesn't work like that," he says through gritted teeth, tugging out his phone.

"Dario, man, don't—"

"All those nights she said she was out late with her girls, never posting it all over fuckin' Instagram like she does every other fuckin' moment of her life. All those days she came home and went right to bed, said she was *fuckin'* tired."

Ope, sounds like this affair has been going on some time. I widen my eyes and make an "eeek!" face at Candy, who fights a smile. She shakes her head in a, *Girl, you are fuckin' nuts and I want details later* kind of look.

I feel like there is absolutely a conversation that Candy and I really need to have.

But right now, I need to keep my eyes on Dario, whose hand moves on his phone, pressing numbers. I also watch Tino who clearly knew about Kelsey and Paulie but didn't share it with his brother as he wipes a hand down his face in frustration.

He knows exactly what's about to happen.

"It's me," Dario's voice says, an angry edge to it. There's a pause as he waits for an answer. "Your *fuckin'* husband, Kelsey. Dario. Or did you think it was going to be Paulie? You're apparently fucking him like he's your husband." The car fills with squawking, a woman shouting through the line, her tone a mix of angry and defensive.

Strange take but I mean, not my neck on the line.

"So it's true?" Sounds like she ousted herself without my even having to show proof.

God, some people really don't know how to play the game.

I think about how nothing on this earth could get me to admit I'm with Dante before we're ready without full-on torture. Meanwhile, Kelsey folded in seconds.

"*Fuckin' Paulie, Kelsey?!*" The words fill the small car as they boom from Dario, and I can see a muscle in his neck twitching as they do.

I move wide eyes to Candy, hers reflecting mine before I smile a small, smug look, letting it disappear quickly. She gives me a, *You knew this would happen?* look, and I just smile and shrug.

"You have some explaining to do, babe," she whispers under her breath, and I give her a tiny nod before Dario's voice fills the car again.

"I'll be there in ten fuckin' minutes. You better be packing your *fucking* bags." Dario puts the car into drive before he answers again, the phone tucked between his shoulder and his ear. "Who the fuck cares, Kels? Not me. Maybe try *fucking Paulie*. Maybe you can stay with him."

There's a pause before Dario throws his phone down, bouncing it on the console and landing it in the back seat where I can see he didn't even bother to hang up. Kelsey's tinny voice still comes through the speaker like a little mouse squeaking—no words actually audible, just noise. Then he moves, the car jerking as he drives off the shoulder and back onto the highway.

"Man, we're on Lilah duty," Tino says, looking around the car in a panic. From what I've come to understand, Tino was recruited by Paulie, but his trust lies with Dante and Dante was the one to assign my detail tonight.

Funny that I didn't tell Dante my plan and he still played it so I could win.

"Paulie has been fucking my wife for a year. Someone else can cart his fiancée he treats like shit around. I'm going to make sure Kelsey doesn't take anything that's not fucking hers." I bite my lips to fight a laugh as I watch Tino sigh and pull out his phone. "No offense, Lilah," Dario says a bit softer, anger still in his voice though.

"None taken, Dario. I'm sorry you found out like this."

And my night gets just a little bit better when I hear Tino speak into his phone.

"Marco? Yeah, Tino. We gotta problem."

TWENTY-FIVE

-Lilah-

Thirty minutes later, a blacked-out Corvette pulls up outside Dario's house and I fight the smile that is dying to come to my lips as it does.

Mission accomplished.

God, I love when a plan works out. There is screaming and crashing coming from the house even though the doors and windows are closed, and I just know that can't be good for their marriage. Or Dario's loyalty to Paulie.

A tall man with broad shoulders and familiar shoes steps out of the car as the door opens, and I don't even need him to step into the streetlight to feel the cool darkness pouring from him. Power and confidence and danger.

He's in Don mode.

My panties get just a bit wet thinking about it.

Marco opens the passenger door, slamming it loud, and when his eyes meet mine, he shakes his head.

That seems to be Marco's go-to move when he doesn't know what to do with me.

They walk up to us and Dante and Tino do that dumb man hand-shake thing while Marco simply tips his chin up, eyes on the house.

"You stay here," Dante says to Tino then points at the big house with no neighbors. "Make sure he doesn't kill her. Also make sure Paulie doesn't get dragged in just yet. We'll have a family meeting on Monday." Tino nods. "You got his phone?" he asks, and I smile.

"I got it!" I say with a proud wave of the phone I grabbed from the back seat. Slowly, Dante turns to me and then just shakes his head as I smile.

"Got it, Boss man." I think that wording is interesting, one of Paulie's men calling Dante *Boss man*. Seems I won't have to do any additional work on Tino. "You really think he'd do that? Paulie? Fuck a made man's wife?"

Dante sighs and runs his hand through his hair.

When he pulled up with Marco, the belly flutter was because for the first time, he looked like a boss. He looked like the rightful heir in all black, coming to clean up a mess one of his men made, his second walking right behind him. The air of it, the appeal of it has heat pooling in my belly.

My man.

The king to my queen.

Fuck, I can't wait to rule with him.

And now, he's playing into the dutifully disappointed uncle.

"Paulie is . . . Paulie. He thinks for himself. Carmine thinks it will change, that when he's in charge, he'll . . . settle."

He doesn't even add a *but*, not leaving room for interpretation that he disagrees. Instead, he methodically puts any disapproval or disbelief directly on Camine's decision-making.

My panties get just a bit wetter as I watch him in action.

I've been doing my work on the men, gaining their trust or destroying their trust in Paulie, but Dante has been doing his job, continuing to look like the solid, reliable option for the family.

"So I guess this ends our party, " I say, looking to Candy with a very fake sad face.

"Ah, shit, I'm sorry, Lilah," Tino says, running his hand in his hair. "I feel bad. I know you were excited for tonight."

"It's okay, Tino. I feel bad for all of this," I say, cringing, waving my hand at the house where glass just shattered—a vase or a glass or something. Dante tips his chin to Jason, who showed up without my noticing, and Jason walks to the house, presumable to make sure no one is near death.

"It was bound to happen. No way you could have known."

"Don't worry, we'll take over Lilah duty," Dante says, and my eyes go wide.

"What?"

"You finish your bachelorette. Marco and I will escort you around. Your girls are already at the next stop, yeah?" My phone has been blowing up with "Where are you?" texts for an hour.

I nod.

"All good. We'll handle it," he says. And then in five minutes, we're all in the car, Dante and Marco driving us to our next stop.

And suddenly, the night looks a whole lot brighter.

TWENTY-SIX

-Lilah-

By eleven, I'm drunk and not the fake drunk I was when Tino and Dario were driving me around.

Full on hammered and, if I'm being honest, I can't remember the last time I drank this much.

My entire adult life was about being prepared if a journalist or some kind of press stumbled upon me—drunk at a club wouldn't have looked great.

But here I am, drunk in a club with a bunch of dancers and mafiosos, and, most of all—I feel safe.

Because I know *nothing* could ever happen to me. Not when Marco and Dante are on "Lilah Patrol," as they called it.

I fucking love this tiny glimpse into what the future could be when this all turns out the way I want.

Living carefree and going out, Dante keeping watch to make sure I have fun and don't get into trouble then taking me home to do whatever he can dream up.

I'm dancing with Candy and Fancy, and we're grinding on each other on the dance floor with a remarkable *lack* of men coming over to join in. I just *know* that is my husband's doing.

Whether it's just vibes alone or if he and Marco talked to every single man in this place and told them to stay away, I'm not sure. But it does, in a way, add to the fun, knowing that there's no harm in the vicinity. Knowing I can shake my ass with my friends without having to worry about some rando who smells like AXE and BO coming to join in is freeing.

But the best part of all is knowing Dante is there, watching.

Sometimes I can't see him, just know he's there. Others, I turn and he's leaning against a wall, watching me, a tumbler in his hand as if he's drinking, but I know damn well it's all for show.

That's what's happening right now, Dante standing twenty feet away as I grind into Candy, Marco standing next to him, arms crossed on his chest, glasses on.

I bet Marco feels at home here, a loud club, girls dancing, keeping the men in line.

But Dante . . . Dante is watching me and me alone. I know with him around, no harm will come to me.

But the way his eyes are burning on mine . . . It has me thinking I might like a little harm. Between that and the way the liquor is coursing in my veins, I think I might just want some trouble.

With him.

I reach into my bra, pulling out my phone as I grind my ass into Candy and even from here, I see his eyebrow lift.

> I need you.

That's all I send.

My clit is already pulsing just thinking about the possibilities.

I watch him open his phone, watch him read my text, watch his eyes shift to mine instantly . . .

And I smile.

Later.

That's his response.

Later.

That just won't do. My tongue grazes my lips as I type, continuing to dance, hoping the letters come out sensible.

Now or I find another way.

His jaw goes tight and I hear Candy cackle behind me.

She *so* totally knows what's going on between Dante and me, even if I haven't told her.

Like I said, Candy knows *everything*.

I so need to chat with her.

Maybe she could be the Marco to my Dante.

A part of me wants to let my mind trail into an alternate universe where I have my own team of made *women* ruling the town of Hudson City, but then I watch Dante type something on his phone. I'm confused when my phone doesn't buzz, when he doesn't look at me for a response.

Instead, his eyes look over to Marco, who pulls out his phone then tips his chin in confirmation of whatever my husband said.

Dante's eyes finally meet mine again before he nods and turns, walking away.

That's my cue.

"I'll be back!" I shout to Candy, who laughs hysterically at my words.

"Get it, girl!" She keeps dancing and it's fascinating to watch the men come over as soon as I leave, like I have some kind of *don't dance here* force field.

But I don't have long to think on that because my tipsy mind is trying to focus on Dante's back, on his wide shoulders and slim waist as he walks ahead of me, not even slowing to check if I'm behind him.

That man knows damn well I am. I'd follow him to the ends of the earth if need be.

The ends of the earth end up being one of the fancy VIP sections that is occupied by a group, all drinking expensive bottle service, and I know that they paid a pretty penny to be up here. Regardless, Dante leans into the bouncer watching the section, slips him something, and the man nods then looks over Dante's shoulder to me and nods again.

Dante keeps walking.

I follow not far behind, walking right past the bouncer.

No one questions it.

And no one questions when he walks into the private bathroom in the VIP section or when I follow him inside.

The room gets quiet as the door closes behind me, Dante locking it and instantly pinning me to the wall.

"What are you doing to me?" he asks, his breath on my neck.

"You're the one that dragged me into a club bathroom."

"You have me so fucked up, Lilah. Can't spent three hours out with you without needing my cock in your pussy. *Fuck,*" he groans as he pushes into me, his hard cock pressing into my belly.

"Oh god," I whimper. His hands move down my side then up, lifting the skirt I wore as he does before a thumb hooks into my panties and he moves back down. "Oh *god.*"

"I'll be whatever the fuck you want, Lilah, but when you come, it's my fuckin' name you say."

Who knew a god complex could be so hot?

Then he's moving down, kneeling on the floor, and I forget about everything except the man in front of me.

He looks up at me with a cocky smile, heat in his eyes as he helps me step out of my panties before he speaks. "You know what to do, baby," he says. "Let me serve my queen."

A new rush of heat fills my veins and it has absolutely nothing to do with the liquor in my system and everything to do with remembering a moment not long ago where he said similar words and blew my damn mind.

Of course, I acquiesce, lifting my leg and placing it on his shoulder, spreading myself for his eyes.

"Jesus Christ, every time I forget just how pretty you are." A thick finger runs through me. "And so fucking wet for me." That finger circles my clit and I moan, forgetting where we are.

"Shit," I murmur, quieter.

"No need. You better scream my fucking name, Delilah." His fingers holding me dig into my thigh nearly painfully and I moan. "I own the club. This bathroom is soundproof."

"You wha—" I start, looking down to question him, but then he's using two thumbs to spread me farther and his tongue is licking me from entrance to clit, stopping there to suck on it, and my head is falling back as I moan, knocking into the door. "Oh god."

He chuckles against me, the vibrations moving through my body as a thick finger slides into my pussy. "Jesus Christ," I moan, bucking my hips and praying that in my drunken state I don't fall over.

But I know that if I do, Dante will catch me.

He always does.

"It's too good. Fuck, Dante, I'm gonna come," I say frantically, barely any time later, but my body is so oversensitized with drink and lust and *Dante*. My hands are in his hair, my mind battling with if I want to pull him back or press him closer. He groans against me, his finger moving harder, like he wants me to get there, needs me to get there.

But I want more.

And I remember that in my own way, I am in control.

So unlike the last time we were like this, I tug at his hair, pulling his face back, only for him to give me a confused look.

"I want to come on your cock, Dante," I say, my eyes hooded and my voice full of need and want but also, determination.

"Fuck," he says, the side of his mouth tipping up in a smirk and that head shaking just a bit and leaning in.

"Dant—" I start to whine, but he presses a quick kiss to my clit, sending a bolt of heat through me before his hand comes to my ankle, moving it from his shoulder to the floor. He stands, his body close to mine.

One hand goes to the door next to my head while the other moves, the sound of a belt and zipper filling the tiled bathroom, the echo of it sending shivers down my spine.

"Up," he says, his hands going to my hips and lifting me, pressing me to the wall as I continue to kiss his neck.

"I need you," I whisper into the skin below his ear, the words throaty as he uses a hand to drag the head of his cock through me, tapping at my clit and making me moan again.

"I've got you, baby," he says, then he slams in, both of us moaning as he fills me completely.

There's something about this man being inside of me that makes me feel whole. Like this is how I was always supposed to be, like the tiny piece that's been missing my entire life is back.

When he's deep in me, he grinds against me, rubbing my clit with his pelvis, and I clamp down with need.

"Holy shit," I murmur, the feeling he was already building in my belly getting hot.

I'm already so fucking close.

He pulls back and moves into me again, the groan he lets out urging me to tighten and wrap my legs around his hips. I'm desperate to get closer to him and get him deeper in me somehow.

"That's, it baby," he moans, his face in my neck.

"Dante," I whisper, having a hard time getting air into my lungs. "It's too good, fuck."

"Love that. Love you moaning my name like that. Fuck." He says the words through gritted teeth, his hips slamming into mine as he fucks me relentlessly, the heat building and cresting. "That's it, Lilah. Squeeze my cock."

"You're gonna make me come," I moan, my lips going to his neck and sucking there.

I hope I leave a mark, I think drunkenly. *Something that will make people question, something that I'll still see when his necklace*

*holding his ring is tucked into his shirt and that tattoo is beneath
clothes.*

Marking him as mine.

"Come for me, Lilah," he says, grinding once more against my
clit, and this time, I can't resist.

I come, my head falling back but not hitting the door, his hand
there before it can even cause pain. I love that, how he always antici-
pates me, knows what I'll need to stay safe without my even saying a
word.

I moan as I quake against him, against the door, my legs tightening, but through it all, he holds my eyes, looking at me like what he's
witnessing is the most glorious thing in the world.

I love that, too. How he always looks at me like I'm some miracle,
like he can't believe he gets to see me in real life.

Like he can't believe I'm his.

And then he pulls out again, fucking me more brutally now that
he knows I got mine, chasing his own orgasm, and I can't help but
urge him on.

I whisper in his ear the same filth that I love when he says it to
me. How fucking good he feels, how hard he is, how much I need his
cock at any moment of the day. And as I do, I start to build again, the
feeling in my belly curling in on itself.

"Jesus, you're gonna come again, aren't you?" I moan in his neck
in confirmation and he *growls* my name. I can't decide if it's in lust or
appreciation or what, but either way, the sound has me building
higher, bucking just a bit.

"Yeah, like that," he says then moves, looking down, watching
himself disappear into me, pinned against a wall in the bathroom of a
club. "Fuck, just look at that. Look at you take me like you were made
for it. Never seen anything so fuckin' beautiful, Delilah."

"Dante," I moan.

"Now. Come for me right fucking now while I fill this cunt with
my cum. *Fuck*, Lilah, it's gonna be dripping out of you the rest of the
fucking night, isn't it?" he says, and that's it. I scream, convulsing

around him as he groans, and I feel him pulsing deep inside of me, coming.

And he's right.

For the next two hours, I can feel him in me until he finally, *finally* takes me home and climbs into my bed with me.

The perfect bachelorette party.

TWENTY-SEVEN

-Dante-

Lilah is fully gone by the time we're finally driving home. Marco and Tino took the other girls home, and it's just me and Lilah in the Corvette, headed back to the Carluccio compound.

It takes everything in me not to drive to Lake George, to drag her to our little hideaway and fuck her until we both can't see straight. I'd spend hours and days in bed with her, doing nothing more than devouring her.

Soon, I remind myself. *The plan is moving along. Don't fuck it up now.*

Lilah did a great job with Dario, who was admittedly one of my bigger concerns of Paulie's detail. She already won Tino over when she was working at the club as a dancer, whether she knows it or not.

But watching her do her thing, slowly pull the men to her side, use her siren's smile to win them over so when she's ruling, they'll bow to her . . . well, it's part of the reason I had to fuck her in the bathroom of my club.

And good thing I did because there is no way she's going to be up for anything by the time I get her into bed.

"Dante," she says, her voice tired, her head against the glass of the passenger seat door.

"Yeah, *fiorella*."

"Ugh. God. I love that, you know?"

"Hmm?"

"*Fiorella*," she says it in a comically deep voice, trying to mimic me, I assume. "Love that. Love it, Dante."

"And I love *you*, Lilah." She hums a noncommittal sound and I think I lost her, that she's on her way to passing out. But then she speaks and as always, she surprises me.

"What's an Eiffel Tower?" I nearly swerve off the road, increasingly thankful that Marco isn't in the car with us because there is no universe where I want *another man* in the vicinity when Lilah is talking about shit like that.

"I'm sorry, what?"

"An Eiffel Tower."

I play dumb.

"It's a monument in Paris," I say, putting on my blinker and merging onto the highway.

"I'm not *dumb*, Dante," she says, her words slurring.

"Know that, baby."

"So what is it?"

"Why are you asking that?"

"Fancy was talking about it. Said she wouldn't mind being Eiffel Towered by you and Marco." I cough. "Everyone laughed and agreed but like . . . what is that?"

"Maybe this is a conversation for another day." Her eyes open now and she looks at me, failing to focus on me.

"Is it sexual?" I smile.

"Yeah, baby. It's sexual."

"Like a threesome." *Jesus Christ.*

"Yes."

"How does it . . . How does it work?" she asks, and there it is.

Just the tiniest hint of curiosity laced with intrigue and maybe even little bit of heat.

Jesus fucking Christ.

I clear my throat before glancing over at her. The back of her head is against the head rest, her face turned toward me, eyelids heavy.

"You really want to know?" I ask, and she nods so I sigh and like every other moment since Lilah has walked into my life, I do as she asked, explaining what an *Eiffel Tower* is to my sweet, nearly virginal wife. "So, one guy is . . . behind. And the girls is bent over—"

"Ooh, I like that," she says, and her eyes go warm the way they do when she's turned on, but a drunken version of that. I can't help but laugh and move a hand to her thigh, squeezing before moving back to the shifter.

"Yeah, I know. So, then the second guy stands in front of her and she gives him a blow job." Her nose crinkles and her brow furrows.

"But . . . that's not very French." I snort because how can you not. I turn off the highway.

"Yeah, it's more of a . . . shape thing. If the guys, say, give each other a high five—" Her eyes are closed and she's nodding her head.

"Ah, yeah, I can see it now. It looks like the Eiffel Tower." She makes a face like she's thinking hard about it before her eyes open lazily again. "It is weird that that's kind of hot? Like, it kind of made me wet thinking about it."

I might love drunk Lilah most of all.

"Not weird but know right the fuck now that's never happening. You're not even *looking* at another man for the rest of your very long life, Delilah Carluccio."

"Okay, now *that* made me wet," she says, her eyes closing and a small smile playing on her lips.

This fucking woman.

"But, I meant like . . . if I could clone you, that would be hot." I adjust myself as my mind shifts from anger to heat, but she keeps talking. "You know, you fucking me from behind but me sucking you off at the same time? Your hand in my hair but also on my hips?" She hums a small sound of pleasure and intrigue and fuck if my cock doesn't take note. "Too bad there's not two of you, ya know?"

"Baby, you want me to figure out how to clone myself so I can fuck you every which way, I'm on it." Her eyes drift shut as a smile is on her lips.

"Yeah. You would, wouldn't you? I think you'd do anything for me, Dante," she says, and then her breathing slows and I'm pretty sure she passes out.

But it's good to know she understands just how far I'd go for her.

TWENTY-EIGHT

-Lilah-

My next opportunity to win over the men comes when I overhear an argument as I'm walking through the Carluccio compound.

Truth be told, I cannot wait to get out of this place. Despite Dante owning the giant freaking mansion, I've already informed him that not a single part of me intends to stay in this home long-term.

It's too *big*.

I absolutely hate it.

I grew up in a big house—not as big as this, but still too large and obnoxious—and I hated it. I had friends with small homes, and when I was there, they were always filled with warmth.

Family.

That's what I want with whatever family I end up with.

But right now, as I'm forced to walk the entire length of the house just to get to the kitchen, I'm almost thankful.

"No, it's not okay. I need you tonight," I hear Paulie say.

Interesting.

"Paulie, I gotta go to the hospital. Visiting hours are until eight and then I'll be out. I'll be free to do whatever you need."

"Go tomorrow."

"Man, she's nine. She won't understand—"

"Should I find another second?" Paulie says, and even though I can't see into the room, the chill nearly creeps through the open door and into the hall. "Know Dario would be more than happy . . ." His voice trails off and once again, I'm reminded how much I hate this fucking man.

"Come on, Paulie. Don't fuckin' be like this."

"I need you there. You're not, you're telling me you're not committed. That's it. Decision is yours, Jason."

There's silence.

And then the door slams and the sound of shoes on marble starts to come my way. I move quietly then begin walking in the direction of the noise, staring at my phone and startling when I nearly run into Jason.

Perfect.

God, maybe I was made to be a super sleuth.

His face is set with anger and frustration when he grabs my arms, steadying me before he tries to keep moving, not even a word shared.

"Oh, gosh, I'm so sorry! I wasn't even paying attention," I say quickly, putting a hand to his bicep.

"No worries, Delilah," he says, using my full name the way very few people in this house do these days.

When I first moved here, nearly every man in the family except for Marco, Roddy, and Tino called me Delilah. Now it's just Jason.

That wall of professionalism is still there and strong.

And when he keeps walking in the direction I came from, I try not to curse at the lack of interest, at the missed opportunity.

He's alone.

He's already mad at Paulie.

I just need a way to break through, to contrast what a fucking douche Paulie is. A way for his brain to associate me with good and Paulie with trash.

So I run after him, trying to thick quick as I do.

"Hey, Jason!" I say, my heels clicking on the hardwood. "Wait up!"

Just like I feared would be the case, of all the men I need to flip, Jason has been the hardest to even begin to soften. I don't think he hates me per se, but I'm pretty sure he's dead set on being Paulie's second when he's Don.

He's definitely the most loyal.

So loyal, I definitely wouldn't mind having him on my side when I'm in power alongside Dante. Jason slows his strides but doesn't stop, which, honestly? I'm still calling a win.

"How's Bethanny?" I ask when I catch up to him, my mind coming in clutch as it pulls the name from the depths of my mental files.

He stops walking and turns to me.

"Bethanny?" His brow is furrowed in confusion, but he doesn't look annoyed.

"You're daughter, right? I heard from some of the men she's been in the hospital for a bit. Pneumonia?" I watch my words play through his mind like he heard me but can't quite understand why I'm bringing this up randomly. Or even, why I'm talking to him, since it's not like we're friends or anything.

"I had pneumonia in kindergarten. Stayed in the children's hospital for almost a month. It was stressful," I say in explanation. Finally, his face softens just a fraction.

Bingo.

"Yeah, I uh . . ." He runs his hand over his hair. "She's good."

"You going there to see her tonight? I looked it up, said visiting hours are until nine?" I ask, knowing full fucking well he's been told he can't.

"Eight," he corrects, rubbing a hand on the back of his neck, sighing. "No, I, uh . . . I got . . . family stuff. I'll see her tomorrow."

"Your daughter's important, Jason. Have you told Paulie it's a family thing? I can't imagine not letting a father see a sick kid." I give him wide eyes like I'm not aware what a tool my *fiancé* is, and he lets out another sigh.

I actually feel bad—this is clearly weighing heavily on him.

"Yeah. It's uh, I guess it's important. He needs me."

Needs to make a fucking douchey power play, I think.

"Oh, what a bummer. I'm sure she'd love to see her dad." I scrunch up my nose and try to make it look like I'm thinking, even though I've already made my decision on what to do. "I'd love to help. I got her a little something—a doll and a coloring book and some girly stuff. I'd love to bring it to her this afternoon. Say you sent me in your stead?" I shrug my shoulder as if to say it's the least I can do.

A look of relief flows through his eyes.

"You really don't have to—"

"I want to. I know how hard Paulie has you all working. It's the least I can do. Family is incredibly important to me." I smile my sweet politician's daughter smile, on a campaign run of my own, and hope it hasn't gotten too rusty.

"You sure?" he asks after a few moments. "God, that honestly would be a huge help."

"Absolutely. Just tell Lisa I'll be stopping in, make sure she knows to expect me," I say of his ex-wife, and he nods.

"You just saved my ass, Lilah," he says, putting a hand on my shoulder and squeezing in a friendly way.

"Of course, Jason. I know it's not official yet, but we're family in a way. And once it is official, I'll be pushing to make sure we focus on supporting all of the men *and* their families." He nods.

"Know a lot of men would appreciate that. It's been . . . tough."

And there I see it.

I won him.

Another man down, I think as I nod and smile, turning to go figure out how to completely spoil a sick little girl.

TWENTY-NINE

-Dante-

Two weeks later, I tell Marco to have my wife pack a bag and prepare for an overnight stay.

"Are we going on vacation again?!" she says as she hops into my car with a little red overnight bag. I smile at her and shake my head.

Half because she's so fuckin' cute and half because before we left, she was sending me photos of lingerie laid out on her bed, asking me which to bring.

I told her I wanted a fashion show.

"Soon. I owe you a honeymoon," I say, my mind moving over the many ideas I've had over the last few months of what would make a good honeymoon for my wife and me.

"You owe me a *wedding,* Dante Carluccio."

"And a wedding you'll get, Delilah Carluccio-Russo."

We came to an agreement that she could hyphenate her name, so long as my surname came first.

I wanted that, to call her Delilah Carluccio.

She's mine. I know she's dying to be a Russo, to finally have that tie to the family she never really knew, but I needed the world to know she was mine.

So the way Lilah always seems to do, she gave me that.

And the way her eyes get soft every time I say it, the way my chest tightens a bit, I would fight her all over again for that.

"We're headed to Ocean View, actually. Thought you'd want to go."

"Ocean View?" she says with a smile, her voice lifting a bit with excitement.

This was the kind of meeting I technically could have done over the phone or with a video call, but give me the option of spending the day out of Hudson City with my wife on my arm *and* having her look at me with those warm, excited eyes?

Yeah, it was going to have to be in person.

"Yes. Gotta check in on the site there. I thought you might want to go see your sister. Gotta meet my sister-in-law and all." Her eyes go wide and her smile goes wider.

"Really?" Her voice has gone up a full octave with excitement and it's even more confirmation that this was the right move.

"Well, the way you're looking at me right now, even if I wasn't planning that I am now," I say, starting the car and moving toward the parkway.

THIRTY

"It . . . smells better than I would have thought here," Lilah says, her high heels clicking on the cement floors of the Carluccio Disposal transfer station in Ocean View.

"You don't want to know how much it costs to keep it that way," I say, and she smiles.

"I'm nosy. I so totally want to know." She looks around the empty space before leaning a bit into me. "So where are the bodies buried?"

I had made the mistake of taking a sip of my to-go coffee we grabbed at a Wawa on the way in before she spoke and sputter, spewing brown liquid to the floor. She slaps my back as I cough, her laugh floating around us.

"Jesus! Are you okay?" A few more coughs and my airway is cleared, but my heart still feels like it's a beat behind.

"We try to keep the, uh, family business and our business separate, Lilah. Jesus." I lower my voice, looking around and grateful there was no one nearby to witness my near death.

"I was joking, you know," she says, eyes wide with my answer.

Ahh, I just showed my hand, I suppose.

"Me too." *Cover, Carluccio. Play it cool. Don't scare off the pretty woman who didn't grow up in this life.*

"You so weren't," she says with a smile, as always taking shit so much better than I could ever imagine, and before I can answer, I see Sergio, the manager of the location, walking my way.

"Dante, my friend! I told you to send me a message when you were on your way!" His head moves to Lilah, and he looks her up and down. "Though, if I had a pretty lady driving with me, I'd be distracted too."

"Watch it," I say before I can even curb my words. He lifts his hands up. "She works for the family."

"Got, it, got it." Sergio has worked for the Carluccios for nearly thirty years, starting as a teen washing trucks and moving to my most trusted employee at this site.

"Sergio, this is Lilah, my assistant," I say, hating using that word.

Wife.

Partner.

Queen.

All words I would much rather use.

But for now, assistant will have to do.

"Delilah, this is Sergio, the manager of the Ocean View site." Lilah smiles as we stop in front of the large man, putting out a hand for him to shake. I watch with fascination as she shakes the man's hand firmly, giving him a business-driven look that reminds me just how fucking well she's going to do when she's in charge.

"A pleasure to meet you. Gotta be some kind of woman to deal with his grumpy ass all the time." I roll my eyes, but Lilah's head tips back as she laughs out loud, and it echoes in the concrete building.

I want to bottle it up, the sound filling me like champagne, bubbles and celebration, and pure unadulterated joy.

"Come, I'll take you upstairs to the office. We can talk there," Sergio says, and then we follow him up the winding metal staircase to the offices, her laugh still ricocheting in the empty warehouse.

"We just can't handle the increase, Dante. It's too much," Sergio says almost an hour later. We're sitting at a long table, a stack of papers scattered across the surface as my manager tells me they can't handle the increase in commercial accounts we've recently acquired.

"I don't know what to tell you, Sergio." Those accounts are vital to the business, adding more work but also higher profit margins.

We need higher profit margins to keep the family satisfied as we begin to back out of the shiftier ways of earning money. My plan for a seamless transition with minimal backlash from the men is to counter that loss with increased profits across the board.

"What if . . . ," Lilah says, and I look over to where she's holding the papers Sergio slid to me in front of her. Her head tips up, that sweet brow furrowing before she puts the papers down, turning them Sergio's way and tapping a red-tipped nail on a line. "Right here." She moves her finger. "And here. These are residential routes but they're only running the trucks for three hours. Where are the drivers going after?"

Sergio moves the papers closers and squints at them.

"Those drivers are part-time."

"Can you make them full-time? Or combine the residential half days and add in a day for a commercial route?"

"Those routes are on complete opposite sides of town," he says, shaking his head in the negative.

Lilah stands, walking around the table, her heels clicking, and I fight the desire to stare at her ass as it sways past. Then she bends in front of a map scribbled with different colored lines indicating routes on different days, and my patience is tested even further.

"Here. Combine these two—you can loop right here, assuming the truck wouldn't be at max capacity before you got to Third. And if it is, you could just . . ." A red nail draws an imaginary line to the transfer station and then back. "Then you'd have them take this one." Her nail trails a purple line. "And when you go to get the other side of Seaside Road, you can turn right onto Brighton." She looks up and smiles. "That would clear up a day, I think."

Sergio stares at the map, confused but then slowly, his face clears, and he looks up, smiling at my wife.

"That might just work," he says.

"I know," she counters, her perfectly lined brow lifted. The cut she got while fighting Angela is mostly healed and just as I suspected, it looks like it will scar.

She calls it her badge of honor.

"You know the area?" he asks. She looks over at me and I shrug. If they don't figure it out now, they will eventually

"I grew up here. My sister owns the bakery on the boardwalk," she says. Her demeanor is confident and casual, but I know she's nervous for him to connect the dots.

That she's the dirty mayor's daughter, that she's privileged, that she was some tabloid princess—everything she's trying to forget about her old life. But Sergio is a man and probably can only think of two things: beautiful women and food.

"No shit, Lola's your sister?" She smiles. "Girl's got some good cookies." *Exactly.* Lilah's face morphs with relief before she replies.

"Tell her you know Lilah and she'll throw in an extra next time you're that way." Sergio looks over at me, nodding.

"You said she's your assistant?" he asks, tipping his head to my wife. I nod. "You should keep this one, Dante. She's good for your business."

"Don't I fuckin' know it," I say, wrapping an arm around her shoulder as she walks back around the table, stopping her before she can return to her seat. I want to kiss her, to lift her and spin her, to tell Sergio that she's my wife, but this will have to do. "You couldn't pay me to get rid of my best asset."

And I mean every word.

THIRTY-ONE

-Lilah-

It's after five when we leave the transfer station and make our way to the boardwalk, finding parking easily in the off-season and then heading toward Libby's.

"Lola's shop is probably closed, but Ben's should be open for a bit longer," I say as we walk down the boards of the Ocean View boardwalk, my heels clicking as we go. It's chilly, but just looking out at the water makes me feel at home in some way. "This was my mom's favorite place. This beach, this boardwalk."

Even the sound of my feet on the old wood boards feels good down to my soul. Like a part of me is returning to where it always craves.

Home is funny that way. I spent my entire childhood dying to leave this town where everyone knew me, where everyone protected me, where no one was their true self with me. And when I left, I was happy about it, but a part of me will always need this city. Will always need to come back occasionally, like a touchstone that's forever connected to my mother, to my childhood.

"It's why your sister opened here, right?" he asks, and I nod. He's holding my hand as we walk, and it feels like Lake George.

It feels normal.

Another thing my soul freaking *craves*—normalcy with Dante: a night out without him cosplaying as my babysitter, a day trip without the guise of it being for work.

"Soon, Lilah," he says, gripping my hand a bit, somehow always knowing what I'm thinking without my saying it aloud. "It'll be like this every day soon."

I don't have to ask what he means—I know he means this openness, the freedom of being together.

Soon, we'll have it.

"There they are," I say, pointing to two shops farther down the boardwalk. The perfect opposites—Lola's bakery, Libby's, named after our mother, bright and sunny with the cutest pink awning, next to Ben's tattoo shop, all dark with his thorny logo on the glass. "Let's go into Ben's; the lights are off at Lola's. She's probably over there."

The bell rings above us as we walk into the tattoo shop, me leading the way with Dante's hand on my waist as he follows right behind.

"One sec, I just gotta . . . done!" the dark-haired woman at the desk says before lifting her head and smiling at us. Her black hair is cut blunt to her shoulders with blunt bangs, and her face has at least a dozen piercings in it, but I instantly know who she is.

And apparently, when she sees me, she knows who I am as well.

"No way!" I smile. "No *way!*" She walks around the desk with her arms in the air, squealing with excitement before pulling me in for a hug.

"Is . . . Is this your sister?" Dante asks under his breath with a very confused tone as the woman lets go and then shouts Ben's name down the hall.

"Oh, god, no! But you! You look just like your sister. Well, like your sister if she got a tan and dyed her hair." Her hands go to her hips as she looks me over. "You've got her curves, but you've got more tits." Black eyeliner-lined eyes go wide while staring at said tits. "OH MY GOD, CAN I PIERCE YOU TOO!?"

Dante snorts behind me.

"Hattie, what did I say about yelling at clients?" a deep voice says from behind her, and even from here, I can see the distinct pleats of my sister's red braids following behind him.

"It's not a client—it's family!" she says, stepping aside, and I smile big and put my hands in the air as if to say, *Surprise!*

"Hey ya, sis!"

"Oh, my GOD! Lilah!" my sister yells before rushing to me and hugging me huge, rocking us both side to side like it's been years since she saw me last instead of a few months. "What are you doing here?! When did you get here?! Why didn't you tell me!?" The questions come at rapid speed, and my eyes move to the side, where Dante is watching with a smile on his face.

"Jesus fucking Christ," I hear as Lola lets me go and looks me over like she needs to document every and any physical change that happened since she saw me last. "Let the girl fuckin' breathe, babe."

"Benjamin James, it's my *sister*," she says, turning around and putting her hands on her hips, annoyed with her boyfriend. I watch Hattie sit back with a smile like she knows what's about to happen.

"Then let your fuckin' *sister* breathe, babe. God, you don't see me tackling my fuckin' brother every time I see him."

"That's because the Colemans communicate in head nods and fist bumps. The Turner girls communicate in hugs and squeals."

"She's totally right," I say, nodding at Ben. "That's how we communicate when she's not laid up in a hospital bed dumping world-rocking information on the room."

"Just wait until you knock her ass up, Ben. Give her some girls, your house is just going to be chaotic screaming," Hattie says with a devious smile. Ben gives her a glare that I'm pretty sure any normal person would be afraid of.

But then again, I don't think Hattie is a normal person.

"Who's this guy?" Ben asks with a tip of his head at Dante. I look at him, and my eyes give him the *up to you* look.

He looks back at me with a, *You trust them?* look.

I nod.

He smiles.

"Oh my god, that is so fucking cute," Hattie says under her breath, watching our silent conversation.

Dante steps forward, putting one hand to my lower back in a way that is unmistakably not just a *friendly* move.

"I'm Dante. Lilah's husband," Dante says, putting his hand out for Ben.

It's at that exact moment that the room erupts in absolute unhinged chaos.

THIRTY-TWO

-Dante-

"So that happened quick, yeah?" the big, tattooed man says as he sets up his station. It took nearly forty minutes to calm Lilah's sister enough to go over what all has happened in the last three months. Then another hour to explain everything and another thirty minutes for Lilah to convince her sister that while her mission might sound dangerous, it's really not and we have it under control. That last one was a half lie because no matter how much I try to fool myself that this and Delilah are safe, we all know what we're trying to do has its risks.

"Yeah, well . . . when you know, you know," I say. I don't necessarily feel like I need to explain myself to this man who I've never met and my wife has only met one time before, but I also know that family is important to Lilah.

The big man who is about to put a needle to my skin gives me an incredibly skeptical look.

He's buying none of it.

"Is Lilah in some kind of trouble? Lola worked her ass off to keep her out of all that shit—"

"Lilah does what she wants," I say, cutting him off. Ben snorts and tips his head as if he understands.

Lilah always made it seem like her sister was sweet, down to earth, and, if anything, a bit of a pushover.

But from this small exchange, I can almost guarantee Lola got some of their mother's stubbornness too. I can see a brother in the trenches.

"Her sister is the same way," he says, confirming my thoughts. I smile. I can work with common ground. "Drives me up a fuckin' wall but can't say I hate it all the time." There's a smile that I also recognize but I sure as fuck will not be sharing war stories with this man.

"This good?" he asks finally, showing me the tablet, and I nod.

It's better than good.

It's perfect.

The man took 30 minutes with what I told him and is showing me a damn work of art.

"Great, man."

"Take off your shirt, lie down. Gonna shave you then we can start. This will probably take . . . I don't know. An hour?" He looks at me. "You got an hour?" I blink at him and can't help but smile when I hear the women in the next booth laughing, Lilah's voice carrying over them.

If I didn't, I'd find a way to give Lilah another hour of this—time with her sister being free and easy.

"You've got an hour," I confirm, and he nods at the chair for me to lie on.

Ben and Hattie closed the shop once we showed up, what with Lola's meltdown and immediate tears at the news, and then I said I wanted a piece while we were here. It took about five minutes to convince him that his scheduled 6 o'clock appointment—one I made nearly a month ago—was in fact *my* appointment. Inevitably, Lilah decided she wanted to one-up me, insisting Hattie give her a piercing *and* a tattoo.

Now Ben and I are sitting in silence while he prepares the transfer, shaves a spot on my skin, and sets up his station. The tattoo starts in silence, but ten minutes later, Ben finally breaks it.

"I don't have a sister. I have a brother and he has a fiancée. I've got Hattie. But Lola's got a sister, so that makes her *my* sister."

I fight a smile, liking that for my girl.

A brother.

Not that she won't have an entire *family* of brothers soon enough, but still.

"I have my issues with your wife," he says.

Anyone else, I'd sit up and argue, punch the man in the face.

But this is Lola's man.

And this man holds a needle to my skin.

He also knows who I am and what that means, so I can assume he's not trying to stir up shit by talking about a woman I called my wife to my face.

I'm not stupid, so I stay quiet, let him speak his peace.

"Barely know the girl. But I know Lola. Know Lola spent years sacrificing, giving everything she had to that shit of a father of hers. Know Lola gave their mother a promise and she worked to keep it, to keep Lilah in the dark so she could live free. But I also know my girl *suffered* most of her life for that, and that couldn't have been easy to ignore. So either her sister put on some kind of crazy ass blinders or she didn't want to bother because she was busy living her happy little life."

"I think—"

"Let me finish, man. So I can't say she's my favorite person on the planet. Gonna take me some time to not see all the trauma Lola has every time I look at her. But all the same, she's family. I'm gonna marry Lola. That will make Lilah my sister. You fuck shit up with her, I don't care if you're the goddamn president of the United fuckin' States. I'm gonna fuck you up. You have friends, but so do I."

I wonder what kind of friends Benjamin Coleman has. If he even *has* friends or if it's just a bluff.

Either way, I decide then and there that despite his frustration with my wife, I like the man.

I like him a lot.

There aren't many people who are straight shooters with me, who tell me like it is regardless of any repercussions it might hold.

Marco is one.

Lilah is another.

It seems Ben Coleman is a third.

"We'll get along just fine, you and me, Ben," I say, and he smiles, a wide, gleaming grin. "Not my place to tell you but I will anyway. Not even sure how much Lola knows. Knowing Lilah, it's little to none." Ben stills the needle. "She's good now, trust me," I say, and he continues his work. I sigh before continuing, trying not to move my chest too much as I do.

"Turner . . . It wasn't just Lola he was fucking with. He did it with Lilah too, just in a different way. Lotta shit coming to light right now about her father, about history between Libby and the Russos and the Carluccios and Turner." He pauses again, looking at me. "There's lots to unravel. Not gonna sugar coat it, most of it, you'll never learn about. But some of it . . . Just know that Lilah didn't have it as sunshine and rainbows as she wants Lola to think." Ben's jaw goes tight and I see a million thoughts behind his eyes, but one resonates deep.

Deep because I feel it too. Daily.

He wants to hurt Turner.

"Turner used Lilah, too. Selling dates with her to politicians and sons, trying to help their image. Had every moment of her life tracked. Her best friend was on his payroll. There was no way for her to know what Lola was going through because she was going through her own shit, keeping *that* from her sister. And once she found out about everything that happened . . ." I sigh.

I feel like an ass for revealing Lila's secrets to this man, but he should know if not just so he can stop hating Lilah, but also because if and when Lola finds out, he can help.

The girls' relationship is buried among lies they each told to protect the other. It's going to cut deep when everything comes to light. He'll need to be armed with whatever he can to help his girl when she needs him most.

"Not sure how much she'll tell your girl over there. Lola might have protected her but Lilah protects her sister just as much. She left the hospital, talked to Turner. Went to the Russos, met with some bitch and decided she was gonna get revenge on my family and prove herself to hers at the same time." Ben hits a sensitive part and I cringe, and I watch a hint of a smile hit his lips. "Chill he fuck out, man. I'm not your enemy." His smile grows, a hint of masochism there.

"Not gonna lie, it's kind of fun, making a mafioso twinge."

"Jesus fuckin' Christ." I shake my head, careful not to move my body. "Anyway. She walked into my club—"

That has Ben stopping, sitting up straight, his machine still buzzing in hand.

"Which club?"

I sigh.

"Jerzy Girls."

"For the love of fuck, please tell me the mayor of Ocean View's daughter wasn't taking her clothes off in a fuckin' mafia-owned strip club."

I pause, contemplating how to answer.

"I mean," I start. "Okay, so, the mayor of Ocean View only really has one true daughter and Lola definitely wasn't stripping at Jerzy Girls." His eyes close and he breathes in deep, like he's trying to center himself before he speaks again.

"Yeah, Lola can never find this out. Oh, Jesus. She'll have a fucking heart attack. She'll make Lilah move in with her. Apply for WITSEC. Or maybe have her committed."

"That's why I'm telling you, so you can help if this shit gets out."

He looks at me and nods, a look of . . . appreciation—maybe?—playing on his face.

"Okay so . . . she was working at your club?" The words come through gritted teeth, and he shakes his head to himself before he moves back to the ink on my chest.

"I moved her to waitress quick. Then my assistant." He stops again to glare at me.

"How convenient. You fucked your assistant?"

And that's when *my* death glare comes out.

"Don't you fuckin' even *insinuate* that shit. I knew who she was. She was my assistant so I could spend time with her while keeping her away from my fuckin' nephew. I knew what her plan was from the start, knew it was dangerous, knew I wanted to find a way to help her." He's not buying it.

"Oh, and you just happened to fuck her along the way?"

I take a deep, calming breath before I look at him and he can see it—the pure fury running in my veins.

"That was the last time. Last time I take that shit. You try it again, don't care if we'll be family one day, if one day you'll be marrying my sister-in-law, I'll fuckin' knock your teeth out."

He stares at me for what feels like an eternity and I wonder if I went for it, would he just start swinging with that machine? And if he did, would it end in a bunch of crazy lines all over my body?

But then, he smiles.

"I think I might like you, man," he says.

"Weird fuckin' way of showing it. Not sure how I feel about you." That smile gets wider.

Maybe he's insane.

He's an artist—maybe he's got some kind of Van Gogh complex.

"You were keeping her safe?"

I nod.

"And you're . . . what, keeping her safe still? Workin' some plan?"

I nod again. Time passes and he goes back to working on my piece before finally speaking.

"I think we'll be able to be family just fine." I smile before his words go dark again. "But Lola doesn't get dragged in. Not at all. Yeah?"

I can work with this.

"Yeah, man. Trust me, we're on the same page."

And then he finishes my tattoo.

THIRTY-THREE

-Lilah-

"Are you going to show me?" I ask later in a hotel room, fingers moving around where I can feel plastic cellophane is taped to his chest beneath his tee.

"Are *you* going to show me?" he asks, and I smile.

"You show me yours and I'll show you mine."

"Aren't we a little past that?" he asks with a smile.

"Shut up," I say, smacking him. His hand wraps my wrist, tugging it to his lips and pressing a kiss on the pulse there.

"I'll never be past you showing me yours, Delilah."

"I'd hope not. God, we've been married less than three months and you're already tired of me?" I squeal as his hands move under my armpits, dragging me up his body before burying his face in my neck.

"Never. I could never be tired of you." His hands start to bunch up my long-sleeve shirt. "Now let me figure out what you got."

It's like hide and seek, his hands slowly removing my clothes until he finds the bit of metal Hattie pierced me with on my belly button. He moves me to my back then slides down my body, my shirt bunched under my armpits, until his fingers softly move over the skin there.

"Does it hurt?" he asks, his breath flitting against sensitive skin.

"Only a bit. Mostly when I touch it."

"Why this?" he asks.

"It's hidden. And when I was 16, I really wanted to get it done, but my dad said no."

"You had a scar there," he states matter-of-factly, and I smile.

Of course Dante has made note of every single scar, birthmark, and freckle on my body.

"Yeah, well. I wasn't always the picture-perfect daughter. I rebelled. I wanted my belly button pierced so bad, told my dad I was sleeping at a friend's house, and got it done. Except my father was the mayor so word always got back to him. Not sure why I thought going to the boardwalk in *his town* was smart, but I was young and stupid so . . . Anyway, he found out and made me take it out. He checked every morning until it healed up."

Dante smiles.

"So you've never been able to do as you're told?" His lips press to the warm metal gently, barely a brush.

"I've always *wanted* to do whatever made me happy." I run my hand through his hair that needs a cut. "Thankfully, what makes me happy these days is right in this bed." He moves, crawling up my body, finishing tugging off my shirt before grabbing my right arm. He stares at where the plastic wrap covers my very first tattoo.

"And this?" He's reading the words but I know he wants me to explain.

"Spit in their faces," I say, reading the loopy black text. His face tips to mine, the smile wide on his lips. "It's my shooting arm, just in case they're not in spitting distance."

He shakes his head at me. "You're gonna be quite the Donna, aren't you?"

"I just want to make him proud," I say, a moment of honesty

coming out in the whispered words. His eyes go soft, a hand moving to my cheek.

"Do you really think he's not already unbelievably proud of you? Of all you've done? All you've endured?"

"I haven't really done much, not yet," I say, revealing my deepest thoughts as only Dante seems to be able to make me do.

"*I'm* proud of you," he whispers, straddling me now, a hand to each side of my face. "Do you know how fuckin' proud I am of you, *fiorella?*" My throat closes, my nose itching, tears forming in the backs of my eyes. "No. None of that. Not for you. Not anymore. You don't cry anymore, not unless they're happy tears."

"Dante, you can't—" I start with a laugh.

"No, you don't understand, Delilah. I can, and I will. That's my job now. You don't cry because you're sad anymore. You cry when you marry me again in front of five hundred fucking people. You cry when you tell me you're carrying my kid. You cry when we name a little boy after your dad or a little girl after my mother. You don't cry because of what they took from you. You cry because of what I give you."

My eyes are watering again and honestly, I'm not sure if that fits into his guidelines.

"What if I'm crying because you're just too fuckin' sweet and I don't know who to thank for putting you in my path?" He smiles.

"I'll let that pass," he says with a whisper before pressing his lips to mine again. I roll my eyes at him through the kiss, shaking the tears off before I move, trying to roll so I'm on top of him.

He lets me have that, helping to roll me until I'm straddling his stomach before I say, "Okay, my turn," and start to lift his shirt off. I struggle, tugging and giggling as I do before finally, *finally,* his shirt is off, tossed onto the floor, and I'm looking through plastic wrap at Dante's chest.

"What . . . ," I say, the words drying up on my tongue.

On his chest is the letter D in some kind of bold, Old-English font.

But it's not the letter that has my fingers tracing the plastic, dying to touch his skin to test if it's real.

It's the ivy creeping along the entirety of it that stops my breath.

"Covered in you," he whispers, and my eyes instantly start to water. "I'll let that slide, too," he adds, but I don't have it in me to slap at his chest for making me cry again.

Because a conversation we had what feels like an eternity ago runs through my mind.

"Good thing I'm not allergic to poison ivy then, huh?"

"I guess so. Be careful. You get too close, I might start growing on you, too."

"Baby, I don't think you know what I would give to be covered in you."

I continue to trace the letter and the vines, my fingers shaking a bit as I do. "What are these?" I ask in a whisper, pointing to tiny pink and purple flowers.

"Fiorella," he says in a whisper, moving, rolling until I'm under him once again. "My little flowers." I scrunch my nose, trying not to let the tears burning for the third time tonight come to fruition. "Well, they're actually belladonna," he says, moving hair back from my face as he balances on his hands over me. As much as I want to look at him, see the emotions there, my eyes don't move from the tattoo hidden beneath plastic.

"Why do I know that?" I ask, my mind turning the word over and over, trying to remember what it is.

"They're deadly. They make berries which look like a tasty treat but one or two will kill you." I look at his face finally and see he's smiling. "Just like you."

My fingers keep moving over the plastic, tracing the letter, the vines, the flowers.

"On your chest?" I ask. He has the Carluccio family insignia on the inside of one arm, a tattoo that is such a closely held tradition, there was no record for me to find back in the days when I was researching the family. I remember I once asked him about his only other ink in the shadowed dark of my apartment, tracing the design similarly to how I am now on his chest. I asked him why it was there, such a strange place.

He told me it was close to his heart but not on it.

"If I could tattoo you on my soul, Delilah, I'd do just that. This will have to do for now."

THIRTY-FOUR

-Lilah-

"Hey, Paulie, I have a quick question for you," I say, walking into the games room of the compound later the next week.

There are six men sitting around a table, sprawled on couches, standing and talking. It smells of smoke from cigars that litter the ashtrays. Tino is bent over the pool table, lining up a shot. He winks at me when he sees me walking in, and I wave with a smile.

As I walk farther into the room, each man gives me their own smile and a wave or a small hello or a tip of the chin in greeting.

Each and every one of them.

Each one stops what they're doing to say hi and as I take in their faces, I realize it's not out of duty or politeness.

The smiles are genuine. They're truly happy to see me here.

Except for one, of course.

"What the fuck are you doing here, Delilah?" Paulie asks with a mean glare. He's been drinking from the look of him, and I have to wonder how much. The nearly empty bottle of whiskey on the counter could be old, or it could have been shared with the others, or . . .

But the really interesting part is how the men react to his words. *Confusion.*

Furrowed brows.

The men take notice of the interaction and begin to stand at attention to watch how it unravels.

Tino take his shot and then stands, leaning on his pool stick, taking in what's going on.

Dario crosses his arms on his chest.

And maybe the most surprising, Jason moves just a hair in my direction, a nearly brotherly protective move.

It's then that I know.

I've done it.

I've pulled them all to my side.

They all feel the need to protect me, all of them looking at Paulie with confusion and just a hint of intolerance.

A small thrill runs through me.

Well, I guess it's time to see how deep that loyalty runs.

Time to push the envelope.

"I was wondering if you could look at some of the things for the wedding," I say, lifting a folder. I make my voice sound apologetic and exhausted, like this whole process is taking its toll on me. "Your mom gave me an entire—

"No." I mask my face with a look of confusion, like I can't understand why my *fiancé* wouldn't do me this favor for our *special day.*

And really, he truly is the dick to end all dicks, not even letting me finish my sentence before telling me no.

"I just need—"

"No, Lilah. Get the fuck out of here," he says then moves forward, cutting the distance between us in half.

"Did I . . . Did I interrupt something?" I ask, looking around at the men. "I'm sorry, was this a meeting or something?" I cringe as if I feel bad about just jumping in.

"No, sweetheart, you didn't," Jason says.

Well, that's definitely new, I think to myself, fighting the smile at knowing Jason now treats me as a friend—potentially one to protect.

When Marco told me they were childhood friends, that Jason is the reason Marco was able to easily join this family, I knew he and I could probably be friends if he could get his head out of Paulie's ass. I trust Marco's opinion, and if he said Jason was good people, I just needed to work extra hard to make him *my* people.

And it seems I've succeeded.

Still, I chew on the inside of my lip. From the outside, it would look like I'm nervous, like this interaction is making me question everything. But in reality, I'm fighting the smile that wants to take over.

I have to fight the siren back, fight the urge to become the woman who wants to put Paulie in his place. I work to fight the need to snap back and be catty because that's not the role I need to play with these men.

Not yet, at least.

Right now, I am meek, sweet Lilah. I am the little girl who just wants to bring her family back to its glory. The woman who is *excited* at the prospect of joining the Carluccio family, of marrying Paulie who will one day be Don.

Over my dead fucking body, my mind wants to add.

"It will only take a minute, I promise," I say, stepping closer to him. He stares at me for a long moment, like he's trying to understand my game.

I wonder if he has any idea—if he can tell I've slowly been winning his men over, earning their trust and loyalty so that when I take him down, I'll be safe with men who already respect me. I wonder if he knows all of the tensions I've been quietly stirring.

I'm pretty sure he's absolutely clueless. If he knew, he probably wouldn't be so quick to ignore me, to talk down to me.

He steps back before turning from me, silently dismissing me.

"Paulie, please. It's just a few things like menus and timing for the day of." I hold up the folder of information that Teresa gave me, still planning the wedding as if she genuinely thinks I'll be marrying her son.

We never really did have a come to Jesus moment where I admitted everything, I suppose.

"You know, the ceremony, the rehearsal, th—"

"I don't give a shit, Delilah. Get the fuck out before I make you."

Yes, please do, I think, but instead of saying that, I pout, putting a confused look on my face and stepping closer to him again.

"Hey, man, no need to be a dick. She just has a question," Tino says, putting his stick down onto the felted table and walking our way. Paulie turns to him with anger in his eyes, tipping his chin at the man he recruited.

"What, you're gonna take the side of a fuckin' Russo?" Paulie asks with venom in his voice, betrayal bubbling right beneath it.

"She's gonna be a Carluccio, Paulie," Jason says, his voice low and easy. But with men like Jason, low and easy often means frustrated and on guard.

"If I fuckin' let her," Paulie says, the threat clear in his voice.

"What does that mean?" Dario says. "You're just gonna give up the merging of the Russos?"

I'm surprised he's even in the same room as Paulie. From what Dante told me, the family meeting where he facilitated Paulie and Dario talking about Kelsey's infidelity went about as well as one could expect—Dario hurt and trying to figure out why someone in his family would do that to him, Paulie calling him a little bitch and saying she wasn't even a good lay.

The mark on Paulie's jaw Dario gave him is still there, the lightest yellowing of the bruise the last to fade.

"I appreciate it, guys, but you can keep playing. I just need Paulie —" I start, trying to make it seem like I'm making an effort to keep things copacetic, calm and easy.

"I told you I'm not doing shit, Delilah. Get the fuck out of here," he says, and I see it.

The red around his collar.

He's getting mad.

I've been planning this night for two weeks, waiting for when all of Paulie's men are in one room, calculating the best way for this to happen, and, maybe the most important factor, not telling Dante about this particular step in my plan.

It's the most necessary step, but one Dante will absolutely *rage* over.

"I just don't understand—" I start, following him, my hand moving to his shoulder.

I'm egging him on. Waiting for that hotheaded Italian who moves without thinking to come out. The one everyone has warned me about. The one the made Silvero doubt if he would be the right Carluccio to be in charge when Carmine passes the torch.

And then it happens.

The final step of this particular plan falls into place when Paulie's temper snaps.

When he turns around to face me, pulls his hand back, and back-hands me across the face.

And I let him.

I let him use his full force to hit a woman who did nothing but ask a question in front of all of the men who he thinks are most loyal to him.

I let my body move to the side, let the papers falls to the ground and scatter, showing different wedding information with sweet hearts doodled in the margins, like I'm actually in love and excited for this sham.

I let the pain take over as I fall to my knees, making sure it's written all over my face, holding the place where he struck me.

And even though I was hoping this would happen, even though I *wanted* this, I look up at the man who struck me with watery eyes. The wateriness is from the hit, not emotion, but I know when I widen my eyes and let them water further, the men in the room will catch it.

The men whom I've slowly pulled to my side.

Three men who were sitting and smoking cigars stand quickly in response, the others moving to where I am.

"What the fuck, Paulie!?"

Gian and Tino rush to me, taking an arm each and lifting me from the ground.

Jason is already to Paulie, holding him back, seeming to be worried he might hit me again.

"Why the fuck would you do that?" someone asks, but Paulie keeps staring at me, his chest rising, anger clear on his face. Not a hint of remorse.

Not a hint of concern for his sweet, young bride-to-be.

"You did this to yourself, Lilah. Learn your place." I let my mouth open in shock, not speaking. I keep my eyes wide, move a single delicate hand to my chest. I don't want to cover the place I know is already blooming with red as I lean into Tino, his arm wrapping my shoulder.

I play the part I was born to play.

The princess who needs to be protected at all costs.

I let the men think they need to save me from the dragon in the room, not letting on that he only blew fire after I poked him with a needle.

"You're outta line, Paulie," Dario says, his voice low but firm as he steps between Paulie and me, cutting my line of sight off. It takes everything in me not to lean over to get a better look.

"The fuck are you saying?" Paulie says, trying to shake off Jason, but he holds on tighter.

A flash of pain runs through Paulie's drunken eyes as Jason's hands hold him—he's holding him too tight.

Good.

God, this is going better than I could have ever anticipated.

It takes everything to fight a smile from creeping onto my lips, from letting Paulie see just a hint of how I manipulated this situation.

"You don't hit a woman, Paulie. Definitely not your fuckin'

fiancée. And sure as fuck not *Lilah*," Tino says, and a chorus agrees with him.

"She was just asking you a question, man," Gian agrees. I sniff, moving my face into Tino a bit as if I'm about to have a breakdown, as if I want to hide from the monster who hit me.

"Are you guys *fucking kidding me?* You're giving me shit because I put this fuckin' *puttana* in her place?"

"She's not some piece of ass, Paulie." I'm not sure who says that, but it doesn't even matter anymore.

It's the fact that *someone* said it.

"No shit. She's a convenient wife who will give us the power of the Russos." *There it is.* "She's never even offered me head. A real fuckin' tease."

The air turns sour, men in the room looking around to see if everyone is on the same page and around Dario, I see Paulie's face pierce with pain, Jason's hands tightening intentionally.

So much better than anticipated.

"So what, you're on her fuckin' side? My men on the side of some *whore*? Fuck, a few months ago, she was *stripping!*"

"Nothing wrong with stripping, especially if you're doing it to help out your family," Tino says. He's the most carefree and easy of the crew, and he's also falling for Sammi fast.

"Just because you're fuckin' one of the whore—"

And then the room snaps.

Tino moves, handing me off to Gian as he bolts across the room, decking Paulie in the face, blood instantly pouring from his nose.

"Let's get you out of here," Gian says, quickly ushering me out of the room. And while my face shows fear and concern, a party is happening in my mind.

Another win for Team Carluccio-Russo.

THIRTY-FIVE

-Lilah-

"I'm going to fucking kill him," Dante says later that night, moving the pack of frozen peas he brought me and glancing beneath to the swollen skin.

"I'm fine, honey. Promise. A little sore, but you should have seen it. They were all over him!" I'm nearly bouncing in my seat with excitement, adrenaline still coursing through my veins.

"Delilah, your entire cheek is one giant bruise." I nod excitedly.

"I know. I wanted him to do it." Dante stops and looks at me and my smile widens. The movement hurts a bit, and when he sees the tiny wince, the peas go to my face again.

"Delilah." His voice is equal parts stern and absolutely exasperated, and I put a hand to his cheek, mimicking him in a way, minus an ice pack.

"I promise, this was my plan. I did it, Dante. They aren't loyal to him anymore."

"Explain before I lose my mind." His voice is exhausted but also strained.

It's really taking everything in him not to go find Paulie and kill him. I know this to my soul. I smile, a small, painless tilt of my lips.

"I did it, Dante. I got his men. They aren't his anymore. They're mine."

"I don't . . ." And then he gets it, his mouth dropping just a bit in shock and awe. "Jesus Christ, you're insane. You planned this?"

"I told you I did. Though, to be honest, he's kind of a little bitch, so I didn't think he'd actually hit me that hard." Dante snorts out a laugh and I smile too. "But yeah. It was . . . I guess it was my final test of sorts. To see who they'd be loyal to when push came to shove."

"And they chose you over Paulie?"

"Yeah. They came rushing over to me, helped me up, and then Tino *decked Paulie in the face.* We'll have pretty, matching premarital bruises tomorrow." I smile at the idea. "I knew they were on my side, but before we do anything . . . drastic, I needed to know how far. If it's just because I'm pretty and nice to them or if it goes deeper." Dante sighs, shaking his head.

"But you're Lilah, and you can have the loyalty of just about anyone without even trying." He puts his hands to my face, one holding the peas, the other warm on my uninjured cheek. He looks at me with pride before pressing his lips to my forehead. "You are so fuckin' smart, you know that?"

"Remember that if you ever want to try and get one over on me," I say with a smile. "I already have your men in my pocket."

"Technically, Marco was never my man," Dante says with a sigh.

"Oh, honey." I give him a fake pout. "Are you jealous that Marco loves me more than you?" He looks at me with stark eyes, not a drop of humor in them anymore.

"I want every man under our command to prioritize you, Delilah, so no. If anything ever happens, they're trained to pick you."

"I sure hope not," I say, thinking about how I'll need to make it protocol to pick *both* of us in an emergency.

"Well then, you can go live in your little world of sunshine and rainbows." My gut drops.

"Anything happens to you, I lose my mind, Dante."

"Same, Lilah. Let's make it so that we both make it to the other side of this," he says, moving the peas to the side and pressing his lips ever so gently to my cold cheek.

The move is sweet and kind and beautiful, but the words . . . they churn in me for days.

Because in his own way, Dante just revealed he thinks there is a chance one of us won't make it to the end.

THIRTY-SIX

-Lilah-

The next day, everything falls apart.

Or falls into place, depending on how you look at it.

But in the moment, it feels like a disaster.

I'm walking down a hall when I hear the low, grating voice say my name.

"Delilah."

My mind tells me to keep walking.

To ignore it.

Some kind of sixth sense kicks in and tells me I need to just *go, go, go.*

But the other side—the side that lives for the drama, that sees potential to shake the already cracked foundation in every interaction —it tells me to stop.

And before I can even register it, my heels stop clicking on the luxurious hardwood floors.

"Yes?" I say, not bothering to turn around.

"Come to my office. It's time we spoke," Carmine Carluccio says.

And I know in this moment, I have no option but to agree. Saying no would be way too suspicious. So I nod, turning back to his direction where I don't even see his face, just the side of a shoulder as he turns into a room.

When I walk in, he's already sitting behind a huge dark-wood desk.

It brings back memories of walking into Jerzy Girls that first day, walking up to Paulie while wearing that bright-red dress, except this time, there are no bodyguards in the room and I have absolutely zero plan.

It's just Carmine and me and the all-consuming sense that this is going to be the come to Jesus we've all been waiting for, whether I'm ready for it or not.

"So what's your plan?" he asks, and I furrow my brow, feigning girly, ditzy, blonde confusion.

"I'm sorry, my plan?"

I don't miss how he doesn't tell me to sit, doesn't even make an attempt to make this feel like a cordial conversation.

"A girl like you falls into a family like this, she has a plan."

"I don't know what you're talking about. My plan was always to pay off Turner's debts and learn more about my birth family," I say, giving him a confused smile.

"Ah, yes. Turner. Did you know he and I had quite the friendship years ago?"

Back when you conspired to have my father killed? Back when he knew his platform was stronger with a sweet, whole family and not with his wife leaving him for some mafioso?

"Yes. I did know that."

"I had a feeling. You're pretty, Delilah. But I can tell you're not stupid. You play it, I'll give you that. You play it well and made all of the men fall for you as you bat your lashes and play the game, but you're not some dumb *puttana*." I stare at him and smile, a sickly-sweet thing.

"Why, thank you, sir."

"It wasn't a compliment." I don't know what to say to that, so I let him take the lead. "You know, Dante was never to be the Don."

The shift to speaking about Dante has my stomach churning.

"Yes. Your son Tony was, correct?" I ask. The Carluccio family Don sighs, an exasperated sound.

"Tony was pliable. That's why I liked him. Made him that way, giving him whatever he wanted and taking it away any time he chose not to play things my way."

"Interesting parenting choice."

Carmine smiles, but the look doesn't reach his eyes.

It stays on his lips, becoming incredibly snake-like and terrifying.

"We all make our decisions, don't we? Turner chose to make you into a chameleon, able to shift and fit whatever role you desired." I never thought about it that way, but he's not wrong.

In a way, I used the skills Shane Turner forced upon me—the ability to win the vote, to charm a man with a smile, to use my body as a distraction—and let it benefit me.

"But like your mother, you didn't like the path chosen for you. Wanted something that wasn't yours. Power that wasn't yours."

It takes everything in me to let my old training kick in, to not let my jaw tighten, to not glare.

"Turner didn't so much as choose a path for me as he forced me on one that benefited him."

"Women interpret things in a way that makes sense to them. Still, you decided that being a politician's daughter wasn't enough. Found out about your whore mother, about your dead father and decided that sounded more fun, yes?"

I tip my chin up, refusing to let him know his words hit.

"Made some kind of plan, wormed your way into the Carluccio family business, got a job, started to win the men over."

How the fuck—

"So you come in, make my son fall for you, and then what? Take over both families?"

How does Carmine know so much?

And when did he learn it?

Did he know it all along?

Has anyone confirmed any of this, or is it just whispers? Is it just him putting together pieces, scraps I didn't clean up properly?

Don't let it show, I tell myself. *Don't let it show on your face.*

"I don't think I understand what you mean."

"Let's drop the games, yes? I know you're fucking Dante. Nice necklace, by the way."

His eyes dip between my cleavage where the thin gold chain sits, the medal lying warm against my skin.

The medal that was given to my husband by his mother.

By Carmine's wife.

Don't show anything, Delilah, I tell myself.

"You're fucking Dante and pulling strings with the men to pull them to your side. All the men Dante already won over are yours, all in love with your tits and ass and distracted from the truth."

"The only man who is mine is Marco." That feels safe to say, an obvious answer.

"What about Jason?" he asks, his eyes cool. "He was recruited by me, posted to be Paulie's second, but last I heard, he was protecting you when Paulie was putting you in your place." I ignore his words, letting them bounce off me and refusing to give him the reaction he wants. "Or Tino? Recruited by Paulie and he just hit his Capo for putting his hand on his property. Something he has every right to do."

"I'm no one's property, Carmine."

A mistake.

I should have said Tino hit Paulie because he spoke shit about his woman.

Instead, I leaned into the accusation, not denying that Tino is on my side, that I've won over Jason.

"That's where you're wrong. You're wearing a Carluccio engagement ring, sleeping in a Carluccio home, fucking a Carluccio man.

Any Carluccio man in this home has the right to put you in your place, to use you how they see fit."

The man leans forward and my stomach churns, acid burning up my throat with his words.

Use you how they see fit.

"And I'm a Russo," I argue.

"For now."

"I'll always be a Russo."

"Until the Carluccios take over and there are no more Russos to be."

The room is silent.

Finally.

Carmine's own plan revealed.

I wonder if that puts us on even footing—him assuming he knows my plan and me knowing his.

Him revealing this to me means nothing good for my own safety in this house.

"Years ago, your mother was to marry Tony. I had it all set up. A congressman in my pocket would do the family well. She went and tried to convince her father to let her go with the Russo boy, and when her father said no, she threw a tantrum and went and fucked Turner. That's why I told Liza we'd only have fucking boys, you know. No tantrums, no grand ideas of love and trust and all that bull-shit. Men want power and know how to get it." He rolls his eyes, and I have to wonder what would have happened if she had gotten preg-nant with a girl.

Or if maybe, once upon a time, she *was* pregnant with a little girl.

The blood rushes in my ears as he keeps speaking.

"Things settled, and Tony was paired with Teresa, the giant cunt she is. A consolation prize—a decent family to build ties with, but no congressman. But it went well; Tony gave us an heir, a continuation of the family. And then your fuckin' mother had you."

He slams his fist on the desk in anger, making me jump against my will.

"A disgrace. Cheating on her husband with the Russo boy after turning down the Carluccios because she didn't want to be involved in the life?" He shakes his head and I watch the red that was crawling up his neck start to recede as he takes a few deep breaths, centering himself. "But it gave me an in, an option. It gave me you—the sole heir to the Russo throne.

"You made sure of that," I say, my voice barely an accusing whisper.

"I did," he says with a sick fucking smile.

There it is.

The confession.

"So what was it?" I ask, moving forward, stepping until I'm in front of the back of the luxurious leather chair, leaning my hands on the backrest. I tip my head to the side. "The fact that she didn't want to settle for a Carluccio or that you knew if he was around, there would be no way to get to me? Leverage me?"

He smiles, taking me in.

"You're smarter than I thought."

"I think you probably underestimate women all the time." He stares for long moments.

"You've been spending a lot of time with Teresa."

Interesting.

"She's going to be my mother-in-law. Lots to plan, you know."

"Drop the games, Delilah. We both know you're not going to marry Paulie."

"And why is that?" *How much does he know?*

"Because you're just using it as an excuse to spend time with the men. To lure them to your side. You're working your way in, trying to win over Paulie's men. *My* men."

"Carmine—"

"Did the Russos put you up to it? Was that the plan all along? Was the whole long-lost granddaughter shit all a bit you've been playing up?

"Paulie's too fucking stupid to see it. Can't see past the potential of marrying a fuckin' Russo to see what a shit show this is. Can't see past his own fuckin' ego, trying to be big man. But I see it. You want to take over."

There's no turning back now.

I try and think of what Dante would do in the position, how he would respond.

So I smile a cocky smile.

"So am I succeeding? At winning over the men?" I ask, raising an eyebrow and not confirming nor denying his accusation.

He stands from his desk, the chair scraping back angrily before he's moving around it, stopping five feet from me.

I straighten, the smile still playing on my lips but my pulse rising.

Panic flooding my system.

This can't be good.

The look on his face is like a cat who properly cornered a mouse that's been taunting him for weeks.

"Well, you have a large bruise on your jaw from my grandson, but he has a larger one from one of his men who hit him after he put you in your place."

I lick my lips.

Panic continues to rise, and Carmine comes closer.

He raises a hand, lowering one finger.

"Dante's men were yours as soon as they saw you on that pole like the whore you are."

"I don't—" He takes a step closer and lowers another finger.

"Paulie was fucking Dario's wife, and you conveniently let that little bit slip."

Another step closer, another finger down, and I take one more step back.

"Jason is too focused on his own family to worry about his *true* family, and you giving his little waste of space the time of day won him over."

Another finger down, one remaining as he takes another step closer.

I bump into a buffet table against the wall of the back of the office, nowhere left to go.

Carmine gets closer to me.

The office door is open, and I *pray* someone is close.

I *pray* that if I raise my voice, someone will hear, that my words will echo through the bare hall until it hits the ears of someone who can help me.

Anyone who can help me.

Because the look in this man's eyes . . .

It's what they write about villains.

It's a look that will haunt my nightmares for years to come, should I get out of this in one piece.

"Carmine, please back up," I say, my voice louder than needed when he's barely two feet from me—the space between us not too close, but shrinking quickly.

"Tino is fuckin' that stripper, one of your friends, so he's gone to us, gone from common sense. A woman is twisting his mind just like you all fuckin' do." Another step. "And the rest of the men have been pulled away from me with the promise of a nice pair of tits and playing it safe."

His words come through gritted teeth, fury in them.

But what I find most interesting is the use of *away from me*.

Not from Paulie.

Not from his side.

Not from the family.

From Carmine.

"From you? Not Paulie? I would have thought you'd be more worried that the men wouldn't be loyal to your successor."

"I don't give a shit about that. I care about this family remaining loyal and staying in power. That's where they've all fuckin' gone wrong. *It's me* who is the Don of this family. Not Tony, who was stepping into my shoes well before it was time. Tony, who let a woman plan his demise just because she caught him fuckin' some broad. Not Paulie, who walks around thinking he's already the boss when he can barely tie his fuckin' shoes, much less keep his men loyal and committed. Sure as fuck not Dante, with his grand schemes and ideas of how things should be. It's me." He's fully in my space now, the heat from his body warming mine, and I wonder once again if he would be telling me all of this, confessing this way, if he didn't have some kind of plan.

Some kind of scheme to keep me quiet.

THIRTY-SEVEN

-Lilah-

"Carmine—" I say, loud, panicking now.

But then I feel it.

The heat.

The electricity that always snaps when he's near.

"What's going on here?" Dante says, stepping into the room, and every bone in my body melts.

He's here.

I prayed with everything in me that someone would come, would save me, and here he is: my knight. My savior.

My everything.

Carmine takes a step back, giving me some room to breathe, but when he turns to Dante, it's like I'm not even there anymore.

It's like he's talking about someone who isn't in the same room, making decisions about my life without a care.

"She's gotta go, Dante."

"Go?" Dante says, his face blank, his body loose.

But I see it.

Most wouldn't, of course, Dante is so careful with his emotions.

When I look at Carmine, I know he doesn't.

Doesn't see the pure rage and aggression boil beneath the surface.

Someone deigned to threaten his queen.

"She's planning something to ruin the family, Dante." Carmine looks at me with disgust, remembering I'm here, then back at his son. "She has to *go.*"

"Go where, Carmine? You whack her, and the Russos come after us for revenge. They know about Arturo."

"And how the *fuck* would they know about that? What's there even to know, Dante?"

He steps closer to his son, both questioning and challenging him.

"The man died in a drive-by. Sad story, move on."

"You and I both know that is the furthest from the truth."

No answer from Carmine, and Dante just continues to stare.

It's interesting to watch.

Not the two physically standing off.

But the internal battle of my husband, the war of his father versus his wife. The man he has spent his entire life convincing himself had some sort of redeeming qualities because it's what his mother would have wanted.

God, our stories are so similar in that sense, aren't they? And from experience, I know this moment hurts the most. When the mask drops completely and there is not a single good thing left.

And then he smiles. Carmine smiles at Dante and moves his head from left to right like he's weighing something.

"Well. Fine. You got me," he says with that smile like it's a joke. Like he was caught stealing leftovers from a work fridge instead of committing murder. "That whore insulted the Carluccio name and tied herself to those fuckin' Russos. I'm so fuckin' tired of the men comparing the families, wanting to go back to the old days. To give back and help the city again, blah blah blah. All pussies, so fucking worried about coping charges—"

"Tony went down for that pump and dump scheme, Father."

"He went down because he was being lazy and fuckin' his *goumad* instead of keeping an eye on the business. But really, it worked in my favor. Paulie is much more malleable. So I let it slip that Tony was the one who called the hit on Arturo, got the Bianchi girl all riled up. She was already too friendly with Teresa; the two of them concocted some scheme and down went Tony."

Does Teresa know that Carmine knows what she did?

And should I warn her?

"You set Tony up to fall?" Dante asks.

"No, but I didn't stop it." The sick smile crosses his lips again. "My name was on the papers, too, after all. Step in too far, I rile up interest in me."

He let Tony fall to keep himself safe.

And, apparently, because he thought Paulie would be the easier man to train.

"I know you don't see my vision. Too fuckin' weak, always were. Told your mother that from the start, that she needed to stop fuckin' babying you. But here we are. So I let you and Paulie duke it out, show me who was worthy. Had it all set until this fuckin' cunt came around."

He looks back at me and shakes his head.

"Would have been great, bringing you into the family, getting that tie. But you're fuckin' trouble like that mother of yours. Like that father of yours. *Too* much trouble. When I found out you were working with Dante, told him he could get rid of you and end the family line or give you to Paulie. Knew you weren't working there without some kind of plan, but I thought you could benefit us. He chose well at the time. But you're just a fuckin' rat. A stupid cunt who needs to go." Carmine turns away from his son and steps toward me again.

For a man in his seventies, he's still broad and in shape and could very well cause me the hurt he's threatening.

He could kill me.

"That's where you went wrong," Dante says, stepping between his father and me, voice losing the polite, respectful nature.

A shield.

My knight, serving his queen.

"Wrong?"

"So fuckin' wrong, Carmine," Dante says. Carmine rolls his eyes at his son, a move I see when I peek over Dante's broad shoulders.

"What the fuck are you talking about, Dante? Always with the damn riddles. Be a normal fuckin' man and talk straight." He smiles a sick, evil look that sends a chill down my spine and I take a step back. "That's your mother in you. *Weak.*"

"You should stop now," Dante says, his voice low and menacing, but now I'm seeing it.

Even if Dante doesn't recognize it, I can. There's something in Carmine's words, a secret he's finally willing to reveal.

One that is going to destroy Dante.

I put my hand to his back, trying to tell him we need to go before it happens.

In the same way he wants to protect me, I need to protect him.

But the old man's smile grows, and I can now see fully what a sick fuck he is.

He lets it all out in front of basically a stranger, assuming I'll be gone in a day or so, no loose lips to sink his ship.

A ship that, from what I understand, once loved Eliza Carluccio with a fierceness. And now history is repeating itself as the men of the family are beginning to love another new member the same way.

Me.

"That's why she was killed, you know. Not strong enough for the life. Couldn't take it."

Dante waits for a beat before speaking, his words slow and losing their angry edge.

Tinged in confusion.

"She was killed because she knew too much."

Then Carmine drops a bombshell he's been holding close for some time, I assume.

And he does it with malice in his eyes.

"She was killed because I told her to be outside that deli at noon."

The room turns to ice, and Dante's body stills. The sick grin on his father's face starts to spread.

"Thing is, your mother didn't know when to shut up. Found out about my dealings with that first development downtown. We were working with the city, pushing through the process of evicting people so we could hike prices, and she was giving me shit about it. Telling me it wasn't right, threatening to go to the press, like she had any fuckin' say in the matter. She told me your grandfather would be sick, seeing me, as if I gave a fuck. All the fuckin' kumbaya bullshit of helping out the community, being a staple—it wasn't *profitable*." He shakes his head and sighs.

"She wanted the jewelry and the designer clothes and the big fuckin' house but didn't want to be tied to what *got us those things*. I was over it. Why have a wife when I could have any woman I wanted and not have to deal with her bullshit in my ear? Why fund her life-style when I could live free? Of course, just like this whore, she had pulled all the men to her side. Seems a weakness of us Carluccio men, to get manipulative cunts twisted up in our business. So, I needed to make it seem like an accident, like it was unplanned."

Carmine has moved back as he talked until he's leaning on his desk, arms crossed on his chest, ankles crossed like he has not a care in the world.

Like he either doesn't notice or doesn't care about the ticking time bomb that is Dante.

And that's what my husband is right now. He, too, shifted so I can see his profile as he stares down his father, and the look is bubbling fury. He's struggling to take in all of the information, to process it and respond accordingly.

It kills me to know that the words Carmine is speaking—they make sense to him.

They fit into whatever timeline Dante has as a reference. I watch his face, knowing how much his mother meant to him, knowing how long he spent convincing himself his father was a good man.

And even though he told me he believed me, that he was on my side, that our mission was to take down Carmine *and* Paulie, I think a small part of him still was clinging to the hope his father would surprise us all and turn up decent. Reveal some kind of alternate ending where he was good all along.

Watching his secret hopes shatter right in front of me is heartbreaking.

"I was tired of her nagging. Told her to go to the deli for lunch, called the hit."

His father called the hit on the mother of his children.

Oh my fucking god.

"We'll have to set up something similar for her." He tips his head my way. "Already talked to Paulie about it; he agrees. I was hoping we could wait until the wedding, wait for the Russos to become family, but I can't see it. She's playing games, Dante."

He's speaking like what he admitted didn't just destroy his son.

He's speaking like I'm not in the room.

He's speaking like he's some higher power who doesn't have to abide by human fucking decency.

"She's a cunt just like her mother, just like your mother. They all think they can get power. Look what happened to fuckin' Tony: let Teresa feel that power for too long and now we're stuck with her and he's a guest of the state."

When my eyes move from Carmine to Dante again, the anger and aggression have left his face.

It's blank.

He flipped the switch.

He's stone-cold mafioso.

He's the man I watched break another man's wrist for touching me.

He's the man who ordered his second to *take care* of another for calling me a name.

He's the man who threatened to ruin a woman's family for being mean to me.

And he's staring at a man who wants to have me *killed*.

I don't fear for my life in this room.

I fear for how Dante will feel when this is all done and over with.

"We'll be doing no such thing," Dante says, his voice cool and smooth. His father pauses before speaking.

"We absolutely will," Carmine says.

"That's my wife you're threatening." The room goes cold. "You threaten my wife's life, and I'll have no choice but to end yours."

"Your—" Carmine starts, confused, but I know before Dante moves.

I know that Dante revealing our secret does not bode well for Carmine Anthony Carluccio, Senior.

And that's confirmed when Dante takes a step forward, wrapping his hand around his father's throat, tightening, cutting off his air supply.

Carmine's eyes bug then shift to mine.

And there I see it.

He's begging for me to help him.

Ironic, really.

He now sees the feral anger and aggression that's confined to Dante's eyes.

Funny how in his time of need, he turns to the woman he tried to destroy minutes before.

"Delilah, go to your room," Dante says, his voice low and even. His hand is wrapped around his father's throat, but not enough to do harm, just enough to contain.

Carmine's hands scratch at his son's grip, but there's no use.

I know that.

I'm sure Carmine knows that.

"Dante—" I start, trying to argue.

"Delilah. Go to your room."

His words are curt, his eyes never leaving his father's, and I know this, in a way, is the ultimate test.

I've fought Dante on nearly every step of this since we started.

I've insisted I have my hand in everything, needing to do this *together*. Needing not just to be some pretty trophy.

But this is the test.

When it comes down to it, when push comes to shove, will I listen to my husband? Will we work like a team with trust and understanding, letting the other take on a task when necessary.

"I love you," I say, leaving it at that before I turn to leave.

I don't tell him not to do anything too brash.

I don't tell him not to hurt his father.

I don't even tell him I'll see him tonight.

I just remind him that I love him, hoping he knows that I mean that no matter what happens in this room, before I walk out, heading to my room and getting ready for bed.

And Dante doesn't come to me that night.

The next morning, when I wake up, the house is in shambles.

Carmine Carluccio has died in his sleep.

THIRTY-EIGHT

-Lilah-

I wear red to the funeral.

Dante told me I couldn't wear sparkles, that we shouldn't celebrate Carmine's death in the public eye.

It still felt like a celebration to me.

I figured a dark, bloodred was as close as I'd get to giving one last fuck you to this horrible, horrible man.

I hope he's looking up at us from Hell.

I hope he's screaming into the void, trying to curse us.

I hope every last person he fucked over is torturing him slowly.

The funeral is four days after Carmine is found unresponsive in his bed the morning after he cornered me.

For four days, Dante and I didn't speak about what happened, other than for him to talk through the emotions behind finding out about the truth of his mother's death.

For four days, I never asked him what happened after I left that room. And I never will.

I've seen the shadows, the moments where he remembers, the flashes that will forever haunt him.

If he needs me, he knows I'll be there, but I will never push him. Ever.

It's as I'm thinking this, the clouds blocking the sun as we stand in the graveyard, Carmine having been lowered into the ground less than an hour before, when I feel a presence behind me.

"What on earth are you wearing, Delilah?" The words are spoken in angry, hushed breaths.

I don't have to turn to know who it is.

I don't answer.

Instead, my eyes scan the graveyard of black outfits until I find Dante shaking hands with some man in a dark suit, not a hint of grief on either of their faces.

He, too, is fighting the celebration, despite him having to wrestle with the fact that it's his father who passed—and how it happened.

This morning, as I got dressed alone, I wondered if anyone would grieve Carmine Carluccio.

But that's not where my mind is right now.

It's on the hand that just grabbed my elbow.

On the cold, familiar fingers.

"Delilah, I'm speaking to you," the voice says, and he tugs until I face him.

Shane Turner.

The man who raised me.

The man who wanted me tied to the Carluccio family for his own benefit.

The man who conspired with the man who is six feet under to kill my rightful father.

"What are you doing here, Shane?" I ask, keeping my face relaxed. I try and tug my arm from his grip, but he tightens it. My eyes scan the crowd again, not a single set of eyes on us, Dante still too far away.

Where the hell is Marco?

Where is Roddy?

I don't even see my *fiancé*, not that I think he would be much help right now.

"A colleague passed. I'm here to pay my respects."

"God, what would the press think of that? Wholesome, honorable Shane Turner considers himself *colleagues* with a mafia Don. Strange bedfellows," I say with a sarcastic tone.

"What the fuck are you wearing, Delilah?" he repeats. "If someone gets a photo of you in that, it will be all over the headlines that *my daughter* wore *red* to a *goddamn funeral*. Fuck. Get in the car. We're leaving."

His fingers tug again, but I ignore the sharp pain, smiling with all the venom that's been stewing under my skin for months.

Years, if I let myself be honest.

It's so interesting how he worries about my image still.

"I'm not going anywhere with you, Shane."

"Stop this fuckin' game, Delilah," he says through gritted teeth, tugging again.

I'm sure I'll have a bruise there tomorrow.

Is it fucked that I hope I do so the family has to retaliate against this piece of shit once and for all?

"Not a game. You are fucking dead to me, Shane. And if you make the decision to come back into the land of the living, I promise you, you will regret it."

"*Get in the fucking car.*" His eyes are dark, angry, his jaw tight as he tries to argue with me while keeping his face press ready.

"Absolutely not. Now let go of me. You're hurting me."

"You leave a single mark on that woman, you'll regret the day you were born," a raspy older voice says from behind me. "You gotta lotta *cazzos* showing up here like this, putting your hands on her, even *thinking* you have any sway. You're lucky you're still fuckin' breathing."

Turner's fingers loosen from my arm as he turns his head, staring at the man who spoke.

I actually smile when I see his face melt just a hair. When I see the panic and disbelief fill his eyes.

I don't know which smile this is—it's not the siren, planning his demise.

He's not worth that.

Maybe instead, it's the jilted princess, smiling as she watches her captor face her dragons.

Because standing there in all black is Alfredo Russo, my grandfather, his face a mask of fury.

He's flanked by Marco, his dark glasses on despite the gloomy weather, and Jason, both men with firm jaws.

I smile at Shane, who drops his hand instantly. I move my arm, shaking it and swiping where his hand was, like he left a layer of dust I want off my skin.

"You okay, princess?" Marco asks.

"All good, big guy," I say, and even with the glasses, I can see the eye roll. Jason's lips twitch and I raise an eyebrow at him as if to say, *Get used to it. You're next.* "Nice to see you, Jason. Didn't expect you . . . on this side." The words mean more than just this side of the graveyard.

"Talked to my old friend. Got some information. Made some decisions." I smile for real now.

"Good to know."

"Now, Turner, you owe our Delilah here an apology," Alfredo says, tipping his chin.

"I'll do no such thing," Shane says, and I could have told you he'd have that reaction—the man never admits a fault.

I give him an exaggerated cringe.

"If I were you, I'd just do what the man asked."

"I won't be apologizing to some whore who came to a funeral in a slutty red dress like some kind of call girl."

My eyes go wide, comically so.

Seems we've dropped the father act.

Good.

"Funny, because I became a stripper to pay off your remaining debts and get you blacklisted from any game in the tristate." His eyes go wide—just a hair. "No one there has ever treated me like a call girl. In fact, the only person who actually sold my time and my body, in any way, was you, right?"

All three men to my left go tight at my words.

Guess my husband didn't share my history.

"All those dates with senators' sons? The galas . . . the luncheons . . . all with different men on my arm who needed an image boost."

"That wasn't—" Shane starts, trying to save his ass.

I warned him, to be fair. Told him to walk away.

"It was. But that's behind us now." I step forward, tipping my chin up. "I don't want to see you again. Not in my presence. Not at events. In fact, I don't even want to see you in the fucking *news.*"

"You're being ridiculous—"

"She's not. She told you her expectations. You either adhere to them or there are consequences," Marco says, his voice firm.

Have I mentioned lately how much I *love* Marco?

"I'm a mayor. I can't just stay off the news," Shane argues.

"Perfect. Quit," Alfredo says.

Shane actually has the balls to laugh.

"You're insane, old man," he says, but the laugh stifles quickly when both Jason and Marco step forward, arms crossed on their chests.

I cringe at Shane. "Eeek. Bad move."

"I can't just quit being mayor. I have . . . I have work. I have bills to pay. I have—"

"Never stopped you before when you were making Lola pay your debts." The area around us goes quiet, and the air goes cold. "All those debts you racked up, never worried about the bills you had to pay. Always had her, right?"

"That's not—"

"Quit," I say, the words firm, the idea growing in my mind. "Quit or you'll have a challenger next term. Quit or I'll make your life a living fucking hell."

"Delilah—"

"We have a guy already, a friend of the family. Would do well in your place. With the backing of your daughter and Lilah, I can guarantee he'll win."

"The town loves me," Shane says. "No one could beat me."

"You know Samuel Citrino?" Arturo asks, naming a family friend who, for years, I was sure would marry my sister. "A friend of mine. Would love to see him take over. Make it easy for him to do so or we'll make it hard on you."

Shane's skin goes white.

He knows what they're saying is true—how, I don't know. But somehow, Sam is endorsed by the Russos, and that means bad news for Shane.

"You don't have to decide here, yeah?" Arturo says, slapping Shane on the back way too hard. He flinches. "We'll set up a meeting. Make sure your assistant knows to accept it, Turner."

The meaning is not lost.

Accept the meeting or we're *making* you.

Shane doesn't even look my way as he nods and walks off.

A fucking coward.

And then I feel it.

Eyes.

Burning on my skin.

And when I look to the right, I see him—Dante, shaking hands with a mourner, his head facing me, his jaw tight.

God, if I don't appease him, he'll come racing over here.

I give my husband a small smile, but a genuine one, and even from here, I can see his jaw relax. His eyes flick to Marco, and mine do as well, catching him nodding at Dante.

The silent, *She's good. I got her* is transmitted across the graveyard.

"You say the word, that man is as good as gone, Delilah," Alfredo says under his breath, and I go back to looking at him. "I have more than enough reason to do the job myself. But he's your blood, in a way. You make that call."

All the more reason I regret not knowing this family sooner.

The respect.

The kindness.

Giving me the ability to make decisions that impact me and for my family to trust that I'll make the right decision.

"That's . . . I appreciate it. But he's Lola's father. I don't . . ." I sigh, looking at the light-grey sky. "I have no parents. It doesn't feel great. Lola doesn't have a good father, but I don't want her to have that. She'd still mourn him." I don't look at Alfredo when I answer, instead looking around, avoiding eyes.

I'm embarrassed.

Does it make me weak? Not wanting to punish a man who harmed my family and me so terribly?

Will he think less of me?

But then a warm finger is under my chin, tipping and moving my head until I'm staring up at my grandfather.

"That's brave. That's kind. You're a good woman, Delilah. Better than me." I make a pained smile, his words proving my fears right. It's weak. It's— "But your father. He would have made that decision. He was a better man than I could ever hope to be, and I know he's proud right now. I know I am."

I don't know what to say.

I don't know how to respond.

The words are stuck in my throat with no way out.

Alfredo fills the silence.

"Have your husband reach out, yes? We have family matters to discuss and a proper wedding to plan." My eyes widen, but when I look around and see no one in ear shot, I speak.

"How did you . . ." I catch my second smiling behind him. "Fucking Marco," I murmur.

"Fuckin' Marco," Alfredo says in agreement, and all I can do is smile.

THIRTY-NINE

-Lilah-

"He's not going to be Don, is he, Delilah?"

The voice comes from behind me as I'm setting up the main room for Carmine Carluccio's celebration of life later that afternoon.

As if there is anything to celebrate about that horrible human's life.

In my opinion, we should be celebrating his fucking *death*.

But I can't quite say *that* without raising a few eyebrows.

So instead, I'm preparing the room where my engagement party was held just a few months ago for the group of people who wish to honor Carmine.

God, that feel like a lifetime ago.

But right now, I'm turning to face Teresa Carluccio, Paulie's mother, dressed in a pretty black dress, her dark hair pinned on top of her head that's tipped to the side, staring at me.

"I . . . I don't know what you're talking about," I say.

I don't fully think it's a lie because I'm not completely sure what she's saying, what she's asking.

Everyone in this family asks questions in layers, saying one set of words but expecting another set of answers.

"Paulie. You have a plan, don't you?" she asks.

"Teresa, I—"

"Delilah, if he becomes Don, that's my death warrant." I don't say anything.

She told me Paulie attempted to put a hit out on her, told me she had information on Tony to keep him quiet, to keep herself safe.

But if Paulie, unhinged, chaotic, uncaring Paulie, got the title . . .

"You're married," she says, not an accusation but a fact.

Silence.

How the *fuck* do I respond to this?

I want to trust her. My mother trusted her so I want to, and she opened up to me, shared information that was vital to me moving forward with my plan.

But what happens if she's playing her own game, same as I? What if she's working for Paulie or even someone else and is trying to get information from me?

Trying to put me in danger?

This entire family feels like such a minefield these days, one wrong step away from blowing everything apart.

"You married Dante, didn't you? That's not Paulie's ring." Her head tips to the engagement ring Dante gave me in Lake George, then to the thin gold band on my right ring finger. "Not sure what his plan was, offering you to Paulie, but you were never going to be his. You two are going to be at the top, aren't you?"

I force myself to loosen, dropping my shoulders, regulating my breathing.

"Teresa, I don't know what—"

"Of course. You won't admit that; you're too smart. Who knows what my motivation is? You keep that instinct, Lilah. You keep it to protect yourself at all times. Before you reveal anything, ever, you make sure you have something worse. Something that could destroy them. You need . . . Okay. Look. I was the one who put Tony away."

The world stops spinning.

"I'm sorry, what?"

"We're on the same side, Lilah. I'm the one who put Tony away."

"Teresa, I—" My eyes are wide as she cuts me off.

"Did you know that he offered to take in your mother?" She's staring at her nails like she's bored, but I know she's not. She's at full attention as she confesses what I think might be her deepest secrets.

"He had Paulie and he was married to me, but he wanted to toss all of that, marry your mother. It would be a win for him—he'd get the girl who turned him down once upon a time, ease that giant fuckin' ego of his, and have a connection to you, the Russo heir. Carmine might have planted that seed, manipulative shit that he was, but Tony let it grow. He let it fester."

"I . . . I'm sorry. I—"

Teresa continues, not even paying attention to me.

I think she's in another world, a history she'd rather forget.

"Your mother turned him down, smart woman she was." Finally, she stops looking at her nails and moves her eyes to me. "I wouldn't have known any of this if it wasn't for her." She sits in a decorative armchair next to the table I'm setting up with photos from Carmine's life, putting her arms on the armrests and leaning forward. "Your mother told me about the plan to replace me with her. Called me up and we had coffee and cannoli and started planning."

Silence lingers and I feel the need to fill it.

My curiosity can't resist.

"Planning?"

"You're a lot like your mother, Delilah. She'd be proud." Her smile is motherly and it warms me in a strange way, despite the panic and confusion coursing through me. "Together we planned to take down Tony. Send him away where he wouldn't do any more damage. Keep him away from you." I feel my mouth open, but she keeps speaking. "Your mother had the ears of politicians from Turner and her father. I had the proof. Just had to whisper to the right people, get the right information into the right hands. The feds were dying for what I had—evidence that Tony and Carmine were doing the pump and dump scheme on stocks. They would do anything to get it." She shrugs then smiles. "I just wanted to stay anonymous and free so I could watch the empire fall apart."

"My mother . . ."

"Your mother was a good friend of mine. Knew her since I was little. God, you look so much like her, Lilah, it's insane. And you, now? What you're doing? Dismantling this toxic, poisonous family, working to build it back up from the bottom? Fuck. She'd be so damn proud." A part of me lights up with the words.

Another part is so incredibly confused.

She's made mention, of course—of knowing my mom, knowing the plan, knowing more than anyone would think. But this? I could have never imagined.

"But . . . Paulie is Tony's son. Didn't you . . . ?"

Teresa's smile turns sharp.

"Paulie is Tony's, but he's not mine. A product of a million and seven affairs, but this one he didn't catch quick enough to offer his normal . . . settlement. So instead, he paid off his *goumad* and took the kid in because he needed an heir anyway. Made me pretend it was mine. Perfect little family. He never even fucked me, Deilah. It was an arranged marriage to benefit the families, but wasn't it just *hilarious* when I refused to let him sleep with me even after we were wed?"

Her smile is near devious and I see the pride there.

The marriage was forced, but she maintained that control.

"But he got an heir either way, made me pretend I was hiding a pregnancy with baggy clothes, the whole nine. And then one morning, I woke up and I was a mother. Something I never fucking wanted. I spent years treating Paulie like he was mine, doing everything I could to counter the fuckin' poison that is the Carluccio blood. But he's a selfish, greedy little shit just like his father. And where he wants to take this family? He's dangerous, Delilah."

As she drops her bomb, I stare blankly at her.

"Teresa, I—"

"I owe a debt to your mother." I don't speak, unsure of what to say but also afraid to interrupt and have her stop. "She wanted revenge for herself, but she's the one who dug through years and years of information and found the scheme, the proof. She knew I wanted to stay comfortable but get out from under Tony's thumb. He went away, and I got the house. I'm still a made man's wife, still get his cut of things. And he gets to rot in prison."

She looks off to some point behind me and I know instinctively she's in another world. "I got freedom, and she got Turner, cancer, and her daughters being tortured by this family."

"I haven't been tortured, Teresa," I say, my voice going soft and consoling, as if I need to reassure her and assuage her guilt.

"Because you're too fuckin' strong to let any man tear you down, *bella*." Her hand goes to my cheek and it feels . . . good. It's nice to have a woman in this house on my side, someone who sees and understands me. "But that doesn't mean that I don't owe your mother. That I didn't want to help you in your own goals."

"You've been . . ."

"I sent that picture of Paulie fucking Dario's wife to the Russos. Knew they'd give it to the right person. Dante got it, correct?"

My gut churns at the thought of this woman in front of me hiring a private investigator and then getting images of who the world thinks of as her blood fucking the wife of one of his Capos.

"I didn't look, don't worry," she says with a smile. "The PI gave me the images. I just wrote on the envelope." For some reason, I smile as well.

Despite this unbelievable, chaotic mess, I smile.

"Does . . . Does Dante know all of this?"

"No."

"Dante doesn't know that you're not Paulie's mother?"

"The only people who know that are Paulie, Tony, and Carmine."

"And his mother?"

Teresa shrugs.

"Never heard from her again. Risky business, fucking a married made man and then getting pregnant on purpose. Can't say what happened, but I know she was convinced one way or another to keep her mouth shut." My heart broke for the woman who lost her child to this family, whether she wanted to keep him or not.

"They're poison, Lilah. Tony. Carmine. Paulie. Something's just not right with them. They can't live without the power. Fuck, look at Carmine—he could have gone down instead of Tony but refused. Let his son take the fall for him." I bite my lip.

"He's good though, Lilah," she whispers. Her fingers go out, touching the St. Christopher medal that burns on my skin. "He got all of her. She was good. Would have loved you. He's good." She says the words looking at me, eyes wide like she's trying to tell me to trust her, and I can't decide if I should. If I should believe her, confess to her, give more to her the way she's given to me.

"And your mother would be proud," she says, pulling me into a hug and pressing her lips to my hair, her eyes watering. When she pulls back, those eyes are near overflowing, and she puts both hands on my cheeks before she presses another kiss to my forehead. "Hey, Marco. Just us girls being girls," she says, louder now, to someone behind me.

"You good, Lilah?" I hear from behind me, the familiar sound nearly turning my own tears on.

"I'm good, Marco," I say, my voice cracking as I turn away from Teresa to see my friend.

And when I turn to look back, she's already gone.

"People are starting to arrive. We have to go," he says, and I nod, completely unsure how Teresa made it all these years in this home knowing all of these secrets.

FORTY

-Lilah-

I'm in the kitchen, putting appetizers and dips into bowls to bring into the main room where everyone is gathered for Carmine's celebration of life, when it happens.

He walks in on a mission, eyes locked to where I stand, and I put down he bag I was holding, turning to face him fully and crossing my arms on my chest.

"What do you want, Paulie?"

"I know everything." It's not his words that send the tiniest shiver down my spine.

It's the smell of liquor on his breath and the utterly insane look in his eyes.

"You'll have to use your big boy words for me to understand what you're saying," I say, poking the bear I should very much leave alone.

"You think you're so fucking smart, so fucking important, don't you?" I continue to stare at the man in front of me but don't answer. A sickening smile crosses his lips and I just know a bomb is behind it.

"I know Dante killed Carmine."

And *this* is why my husband and I never spoke of what happened once I left that room.

Because when I reply, it's the truth.

"I don't know anything about that, Paulie. From what I was told, Carmine had sleep apnea for years. Forgot to put on his machine and died peacefully, God rest his soul."

He punches a cabinet when he doesn't get the reaction he wants, leaving a fist-sized dent in the wood before growling, the sound angry and aggressive.

"Stop with the *fucking games.*" Paulie moves, pacing like a caged animal. "It was supposed to be you, you know. You were supposed to be the one whose *life we're celebrating* tonight."

"What are you talking about?" I ask, but, of course, I know the answer—Carmine said he and Paulie already spoke about it, about how I had to go.

I was to be taken out as soon as they realized I had flipped all of Paulie's men, pulling them to my side.

Instead, Carmine was the man who fell.

"Why would I have been killed, Paulie? Your family wants the connection to mine. It would stir up unresolved issues; it could start a war."

"A war the Russos couldn't fight."

It's then that I make a mistake.

I forget to play dumb.

I forget to be the dumb blonde with good bloodlines who is just here to join the families.

Partially because I am *so damn tired* of idiotic men who can barely remember to wash their asses assuming I don't know anything.

I raise an eyebrow, leaning a hip into the counter as I cross my arms on my chest.

"How would you win any war, Paulie, if all of your men were mourning my death?" I tip my head to the side and give him a taunting half smile. "That black eye is healing up pretty slow. Looks like you could use some more sleep. Are you eating okay? Or is the guilt from putting a hit out on your own fucking mother eating at you?"

Red creeps up his neck, anger encompassing his face.

"You're a fucking cunt. *That's* why you need to be gone. I know what you've been doing, turning my fucking men against me. Just like my whore of a mom did to my father, turned all of his men so they were loyal to her. Made it so if anything happened to her, they'd all have questions, so she had a safety net to destroy all of us."

You know, I thought I liked Teresa before, and now I *fucking love her*. Seeing how much her even breathing clean air riles up this asshole brings me so much joy.

"And you know—Carmine was willing to let it happen. Was willing to wait, let you keep pulling your strings until we were fucking married so he could have that tie to the Russos. But he didn't know what I do."

He takes a step forward and I know before he speaks what he's about to say.

Somehow, Paulie found out about us.

"But you're already married, aren't you, Delilah? And even better, you're married to a Carluccio."

In this moment, I know I have to make a decision.

Do I deny it and try and talk my way out?

Or do I admit it and start the end now?

I choose the latter, tipping my chin up as I start to talk.

"Oops. You got me, Paulie." I smile, moving my eyes over him like I'm trying to decode him. "You know, your uncle really threw me for a loop, announcing my engagement to you." I turn again, giving him my back as if I'm not scared of what he might do while I'm not watching him, resuming my job of filling bowls with chips.

I refuse to let him see the shaking of my hands.

The way this confrontation is impacting me.

"But by then we were already married, already committed to the same vision." I face him, taking my place with my hips against the counter, my arms crossed, shaking hands hidden. "Your family needs to be stopped, Paulie. And I'm going to be the one to do it."

"Who the fuck do you think you are?"

I ignore him and keep speaking.

"You're a poison to this family, just like your grandfather was. We're going back to the way it used to be—helping the community, making money, living life, but not fucking over the innocent."

"You don't know anything. That's not how it fucking *works*." He steps forward, pinning me to the counter the way he did months ago in the back room of Jerzy Girls, but this time, I don't panic.

I'm no longer a scared princess without the whole picture. I've come into my own, have become the all-knowing queen who is tired of the petulant prince's tantrums.

I stare in his psychotic eyes and lay it out for him.

"You'll be given a choice, Paulie: fall in fucking line or go down," I say, my chin held high. I'm almost relieved this is happening. I'm tired of hiding. I'm tired of not being a queen.

I'm tired of not being Dante's.

"What does that mean?" he asks, his face barely an inch from mine.

If someone walked in, it would look like a lover's spat or like he was about to kiss me.

"It means whatever you want it to mean. It means don't be fucking stupid. It means you play by our rules—*my rules*—or you're done."

"Who the fuck do you think you are?" he asks, spit flying from his angry mouth onto my face.

But then a new voice joins the fold.

"She's your new Donna, Paulie. Don't be a fucking idiot and get yourself killed just because you can't stand the idea of not being a piece of trash."

It's not Dante.

It's not Marco.

It's *Teresa*.

She walks into the room in a tight black dress, heels clicking on marble tile as she does, her arms crossed on her chest and shaking her head like she's never been so disappointed.

"Get the fuck out of here, Mother."

"No," she says, clearly shocking her son. Paulie moves away from me, taking a step toward his mother.

"No?"

"Paulie, I think you forget, I don't have to play by your rules."

"Just because you have shit on—" She smiles before interrupting him.

"Do you really think it's just him, Paulie? That my long list of lies and wrongdoings is limited to *Tony fucking Carluccio*?" She rolls her eyes like he's an absolute idiot. "Do you think that's what was keeping you or your grandfather or any of the men who you thought bowed to you from taking me out? No, Paulie. I have something on *everyone*. You don't get as far as I have, live as long and as well as I have without ammunition."

"What could you possibly have on me, Teresa?"

Gone is *Mother*.

Gone is respect.

Her smile is feline and if I were Paulie, I would be scared.

But instead, I smile as well, knowing Teresa is on *my* side.

"The cop you were working with? Setting up that prostitution ring, trying to sell the girls out of the club? Yeah, he seemed real willing to spill about all of your secrets as soon as I got some bourbon in him and showed him some leg. Your whole plan, names, dates, process—all on a recording."

The room is silent as I take that in, as Paulie tries to understand what she just said.

"How—"

"Because you're messy. Your ego gets in the way; you pick shitty partners. Honestly, Paulie, you can't even clock a shitty fucking PI. The PI I hired to track you, to catch you getting fucking messy? He said he barely had to hide himself when he was on your tail. You're so wrapped up in your fucking god complex that you don't see reality. That's where your uncle wins, you know. He understands his weaknesses. It's what got your grandfather killed, what got your father in prison for life."

"Are you saying you did those, too?"

"Not all of them," she says with a smile.

"I should—"

"You should what, Paulie?" a new voice asks, and that one I know better than the back of my hand.

Dante.

My love.

All heads turn to look at him, but he only has eyes for me.

How much he heard, I don't know, but he doesn't hide us.

Not anymore.

Instead, he walks right to me, putting an arm around my waist, tugging me in front of him as he presses a kiss to my hair.

"The game is over. You're never going to rule this family, Paulie."

"We'll see what the men sa—"

"I already spoke with all of them. There was a meeting," Dante says, and I see it then.

The flicker.

Whether it's panic or shock or indignance or something else all together, I'm not sure, but it's there and he wanted to hide it but failed.

"A meeting?"

"There was a meeting the night after Carmine died."

"And where was I?"

"Not invited?" I ask, a small smile in my voice. The room goes cold before Dante finishes.

"You weren't there, but we were, and Lilah and I were sworn in with the men. Unanimous decision. Ask any of them."

Silence takes over the kitchen again as Paulie stares at his uncle, trying to decode his words, not understanding their meaning, but pride stopping him from asking.

I, of course, can't resist a quick little push.

"Go ahead, Paulie. Ask," I say with a little chuckle.

"What the fuck are you talking about?"

"I'm talking about how Lilah and myself are Don and Donna of the Carluccio family together. It was decided and sealed into the books three nights ago.

I remember it then, the meeting coming to mind.

FORTY-ONE

-Lilah-

I've been in the room once before—for that first family meeting I was a part of—but this time, I'm not dressed to kill.

I'm dressed to rule.

A tight, long-sleeve red shirt tucked into tight dark jeans, a pair of simple heels, and my gun is in the waistband at my back. Instead of my hair being down and pretty, trying to win over the men, it's pulled up into a high pony, my face free from any strands. Simple makeup, red lips.

The St. Christopher out, the metal warm on my skin.

And most importantly, my wedding band on the correct finger, the ostentatious engagement ring on top of it.

And Dante at my side.

The family is here—Dante's men, Paulie's men, the men who were once Carmine's and Tony's.

And now, *my* men.

Marco stands next to Sal Conte and Alfredo Russo, who are in attendance at my insistence.

It's happening now.

"What's going on?" Jason asks, and I turn my head to him, staring at a man I could see as a friend. A brother.

I don't hesitate, don't mince words.

"Dante and I are married." A whisper of shock runs through the room, through the men, and it's interesting to watch the reactions.

Marco is stone-faced.

Alfredo smiles.

Tino's eyes go wide, the look almost humorous, like we completely blindsided him.

A few men share the look, though most are a bit more subtle, but some . . . Some look like they had a suspicion confirmed. Or like things just make a little bit more sense.

Dario is one of them.

Jason is another.

"I came to Jerzy Girls about six months ago with the intent of taking down the Carluccio family and proving myself worthy of heading the Russo family." My eyes meet Sal's as I say that, and he gives me a small smile, tipping his head in my direction. A tiny acknowledgement, an apology of sorts. "Eventually, Dante and I formed a connection and realized we had a similar goal."

"So Dante wants to take down the Carluccio family?" Vinnie says, outrage tinging his voice.

"I want to bring this family back to the glory it once held," Dante says, staring him down. "Hudson City once held this family in high regard, not because they feared us, but because for as much shit we did, we gave back. We helped the community, made it a good place to be. We were a *part* of it, not a negative aspect of it." There's an expectant silence the carries through the room as Dante makes eye contact with the men one by one. He's about to speak again, but Silvero does.

"I remember those days. Back when Anthony was in charge. It was good. We all made money, were comfortable, but there weren't RICO charges breathing down our necks. We didn't have people whispering every time we walked into a restaurant."

"It was easier. Had time for family, and the family was more . . . familial," Martino, one of the older made men, says, agreeing.

"Okay, but what the fuck does this all even mean?" Tino asks, and I smile at him.

"It means that back then, it was all for one and one for all. The power was more equal. It was less of a dictatorship. Men weren't disappearing just for disagreeing with the Don."

Glances are made and met among the men.

"Dante and I plan to bring that back. Carmine is gone. We plan to work together with the Russos, ease tensions, and return to the good days. Push the club more, expand there. The games will still happen in the back rooms with vetted clients, but we'll be pickier. No more paid protection around the city, no more transport, and sure as fuck no drugs."

"What about the girls?" Tino asks, and my eyes meet his.

I know he's asking with the knowledge of what Paulie's plans are and how that applies to his girlfriend.

"The only connection the family will have with the girls is if they're dancing or serving. It ends there. And just like now, we'll make sure they're well taken care of, that they are safe. As we expand, we can add things like helping them get into school if they want, childcare—whatever. We can make this community—and the women who live here—thrive."

There's less silence as the men murmur amongst themselves, and when I look at Dante, he's looking down at me, too.

I read it there.

This just might work. We just might have them, he's saying.

And then the question comes.

"What about Paulie? I thought he was taking over," someone asks —I'm not even sure who. It doesn't really matter. They're all wondering. I sigh and feel Dante do the same, but Marco speaks before either of us can.

"Paulie is poison to this family, same as Carmine was." Noise increases, an argument on the tips of tongues. "How many of you know Carmine had the option to go down when Tony did?"

This brings silence.

"Feds had both of their names on the papers. Carmine could have taken the fall, let Tony lead the family. Instead, he wanted the power and to stay free. He pushed Tony to take the fall, and, well . . ."

Silence again.

"He sold out Tony?"

"He didn't bring the information to the feds, but he didn't stop it from happening when he could. And he was training Paulie to be just like him. To take the family too deep, to get darker. You get caught running a ring like Paulie wants, you go to federal prison for life."

Silence.

"Jason, who would raise Bethanny?" I ask quietly. His face goes white, but I don't take the time to stop and wait for an answer. "Silvero, how many years you got left, you think? Jamie's pregnant, right? You wanna meet that grandbaby?" His face is a near mirror of Jason's.

All those months of learning these men, gaining their trust, letting them tell me about their lives and all the things that Paulie never saw value in—it pays off now.

"Tino, money is good doing what Paulie wants you to do. I get that. But do you think he'll care that Sammi is yours if she can make him more money by selling her?"

"Jesus Christ," he murmurs under his breath.

Silence fills the room.

"So, what're the options?"

Dante sighs and I speak, trying to appease everyone.

"We're here to talk to you all. Dante is the right person to take over this family. I think that's incredibly clear to all of you at this point."

"And you?"

"When the time comes," I say, looking over at Alfredo, "I'm taking over the Russos. Until then, I'm going to assist Dante."

"She'll be ruling alongside me," Dante corrects.

"So, what, the Russo whore gets—"

Santo, one of the lower-level made men I haven't gotten too close with starts, but he doesn't get the chance to finish. Dante moves before I can even take a break and his hand is on his collar, holding the man above the ground. His feet kick, but Dante doesn't flinch.

"Lilah's being nice, being easy. Trying to tell you all everything so you can make a fuckin' educated decision. But she won't tell you that the decision is be respectful and choose the right head or get the fuck out. And when I say *get the fuck out,* I mean get fuckin' taken out."

It's so totally fucked, but I get a little hot watching him.

My heart races and my pussy flutters at this man protecting my honor.

"You gonna fuckin' play nice? You gonna respect your Donna?" The man's eyes go wide and I smile.

Might as well lean into the position, after all.

And then he nods.

Dante puts him down.

"I will not tolerate a single one of you talking down to my wife. I draw the line there. I vow to be a fair and just Don, to value the family above all else. To bring us into the future, to build better. But I will do that with Lilah at my side. She will not just be my wife—we are a team."

"You're merging the families," Jason says, his voice low and not quite shocked, but still nearly.

"We'll be running the families together. If it works to merge, if it benefits all of us equally, yes. But until then, Dante and I will be running the Carluccio family while Alfredo teaches me more about the family I was born into."

I get stares but also, a few nods.

Finally, Jason stands.

"I vote for Dante and Delilah. Both of them. I think they can take the family in the direction it needs to go," he says, shocking me to my core.

"I second that," Marco says, standing, his voice booming.

"Third," Tino says with a smile.

And then slowly, I watch every man in the room vote in favor of Dante.

And me.

And hours later, after a very old-school ceremony and a few drinks, I walk out the Donna of the Carluccio crime family.

"I'm gonna fuckin—" Paulie starts, but before he can say more, four men walk in, Marco at the front.

"It's time for the service," he says, and Dante nods, leading me and Teresa out of the room, Paulie left to try and put together his new reality.

"Should we be worried?" I ask under my breath as we walk toward the room where the ceremony will be.

"I have Jason and Tino on him, keeping an eye."

"You don't think he'll do anything crazy, right?" It's probably bad luck even putting that out into the universe.

"He's drunk and he's Paulie and you're in the same building as him. I won't take a single chance."

My hand holding his squeezes and he looks down and smiles at me as we enter the living room.

And we enter as the heads of this family.

FORTY-TWO

-Lilah-

"We're here today to honor Carmine Carluccio, a man of honor and integrity," Dante says not long after, his words ringing in the large room that once held my engagement party.

I force myself not to scoff before feeling an elbow in my side—Teresa. Her own lips are pursed, as she's trying to fight a smile.

This whole thing is a sham.

But a sham we must go along with in order to maintain the proper image.

"He served for a long time, reminding us of the code of this family: honor, trust, and community." I widen my eyes in humor and look at Teresa again.

Her face mirrors my own.

I understand what he's doing—reminding the room of mourners of who Carmine should have been and what the family once was, so when change happens, it's fresh on their minds.

So that when the changes happen, people are happy to see them, happy to see that *Dante* is the one who brought them upon us.

My husband is nothing if not wise.

"My father—"

Before he can finish his sentence, there's a noise.

The door slams open, banging against the wall as it does, and in the doorway stands Paulie.

A Paulie who clearly is completely unhinged, dots of blood on his white dress shirt, his eyes showing . . . nothing.

Not anger.

Not rage.

Not even sadness.

They're blank as if he's gone from the world.

A hint of true fear shakes through me when I see him.

"This is all a fucking scam," Paulie shouts.

Confusion and shock roll through the room, and I hear Teresa mutter a curse under her breath. But I don't look to her. Instead, I look to Dante, his jaw tight, his eyes narrowed on his nephew.

"Paulie, man, let's—"

"I'm tired of talking. Tired of this bullshit. They've been planning this for months. Years, for all we know."

"Paulie—"

"He's fucking her, you know," he shouts, pointing at me, and I look to Paulie and decide I truly fucking hate this man.

"Paulie, you're making a scene," I say, the words tired even to my own ears.

"Good! They should know you're a whore and that he's a backstabber."

"The family was meant to be his all along, Paulie," I say, trying to both reassure the room of onlookers and calm Paulie in any way I can. "Carmine just saw you as a new opportunity to play games and an easier puppet to control than Dante."

"Where're Jason and Tino, Paulie?" Dante asks, and then I remember that they were watching him. I look at the specks of blood on his shirt.

Oh fuck.

"Tino is out of commission right now, the fuckin' traitor. And Jason—"

A breath of relief leaves my chest as the man in question runs into the room, his chest heaving, his own shirt a bit more blood covered than Paulie's.

"Paulie, you gotta stop this shit," Jason says, looking to the man he once thought he'd be working right under with an expression of panic.

It's a terrifying picture on this normally calm, assured man.

"Jason, where's Tino?" I ask, not letting the quaver reach my voice.

"Tino's knocked out, got him settled and came right here."

Another breath of relief.

Knocked out isn't great, but it's better than dead, I suppose.

"What is going on here?" a man asks, and I recognize him as a town council member—an old friend of Carmine's and a man who, according to Dante, receives regular kickbacks from the family.

"Sir, I think it would be a good time to step out. It seems there's a bit of a family issue," Dante says. "Emotions are high with my father's passing, and Paulie is clearly struggling." The man looks to Dante, about to nod and agree, but then Paulie speaks.

"Oh, what? You don't want the world to know what a fucking traitor you are?"

"I don't want everyone to know how fucking far gone you are and to start questioning the surety of the fuckin' family, Paulie," Dante says through gritted teeth, but I'm slightly relieved to watch a few people start to move, to walk toward the exit of the room.

"Family," Paulie says with a brisk laugh. "What the fuck do you care about the family?"

"Paulie—" I try, the eyes in the room growing more intense.

This is family business.

Not for the world to watch.

"Shut the fuck up, you whore," he says, and Dante's body goes stiff. His eyes shift from wanting to get Paulie out of this room to wanting to beat his ass.

Jason sees it too.

"Man, don't—" he starts, moving toward his friend, but Paulie turns to him

"Stand the fuck back. I'll deal with you next."

Gasps fill the room, several people pulling in air, and I look around at the memorial still filled with mourners.

But it's also filled with the Carluccio family. Men. Made men.

My made men, in a way.

I needed that. That reminder that Dante and I are in control now. This needs to end.

I stand straighter, rolling my shoulders back.

"Paulie, he has nothing to do with this," Dante says, his voice calm and low, his hands at his sides moving gently, trying to appease his nephew as he takes a step closer.

Slowly.

It's like he's approaching a rabid, wounded animal.

I wonder for a moment if, like a rabid animal, we'll be forced to put him down.

I wonder what that would do to Dante, taking out his nephew after what happened with Carmine. How much more would that hurt his soul?

Blood is thicker than water, but does it weigh even more when that blood is on your hands?

"You're right. It's all about you and that fucking whore," Paulie says, turning from Jason to Dante, and I can't help but think if I would be willing to sacrifice Jason, to make Bethanny fatherless, in order to save Dante.

And if I tell the truth of my answer, that I would sacrifice everyone and anyone to keep Dante safe, does that damn me to Hell?

Or am I already headed there anyway?

Paulie moves, stepping into the room, everyone giving him a wide berth. Even without a weapon in his hands, he gives off an unhinged, psychotic-break type of energy that has everyone backing away. I look around, making note of who is still in the room—elderly men and women, old friends of Carmine's, women and children who don't need to be here for this . . .

Fuck.

What a goddamn mess.

My eyes move to Jason and then to Roddy.

"Get them out of here," I say, issuing orders to the men and tipping my head in the direction of a group huddled together. "Then someone go check on Tino, make sure he's good. If needed, call an ambulance." The men nod and I watch Jason quickly move to a woman with a small girl, both shaking with fear, and leading them toward the exit.

"What, you take fuckin' orders from this cunt now?" he yells at who was once his second. "A fucking piece of pussy walks in, turns you all against me, and what? You just follow her?"

"Paulie, it's not like that. These people don't need to be here for—"

"Shut the *fuck up,* you stupid bitch," Paulie screams, taking a step toward me and barely, just *barely,* touching my arm.

Before I can respond, Dante fucking loses it, taking three steps in my direction before bellowing at his nephew. "Don't you even fuckin' think of putting your hands on my wife!"

The room, most of whom probably still assumed I was dutifully engaged to Paulie Carluccio, goes crazy at Dante's words. With them, I pull a page out of his and Marco's book, shaking my head at the ceiling because this is *so not the right fucking time.*

"Head in the fuckin' game, Delilah," Marco says behind me, his voice low and on guard. I don't know when he got there, but I'm glad to have him near, to have him on my side.

"Oh, what, you all didn't know?" Paulie says, a sick, chaotic laugh coming from his chest. He's completely gone, any speck of a respectable, put-together man evaporating now that the truth has come out. "Yeah, Dante's apparently been *fucking my fiancée* and even went so far as to fucking marry her."

"That's not—" I start because that's not what happened. That's not how this worked, not how any of it worked, and I refuse to let him twist that aspect of my life.

"No one *fucking asked you!*" he shouts, pointing a finger at me unsteadily.

I watch as it shakes, his hand unsteady.

From drink?

From nerves?

Does it even mater anymore?

"*Paulie!*" Dante shouts at his nephew, but I keep staring at him, crossing my arms on my chest.

"Paulie, this is fucking ridiculous. Be a fuckin' man and have a real conversation with us about this. You want a position of power? Fuckin' prove you can handle it. All I've seen is you fuckin' around, messing with your men's wives, getting drunk, hitting women—"

"That was your fault!" he says, turning to me, and I try not to smile despite the serious moment because he's right.

And it's a fault I'm still proud of.

"You did this, you fucking whore. Just like your mother, use—"

"Do not," I say, all humor evaporating, and move a step forward. Marco tries to grab my arm but I shake it off, and I also ignore the way Dante says my name low and furious, a warning. "Do not speak about my mother."

"A fuckin' whore. Fuckin' a Russo then gets pregnant by that mayor. Then fucks the Russo again. He's dead because of her, you know. Your father's death was your mother's fault."

I shake my head at him.

"And your father got his *goumad* pregnant and forced Teresa to claim you as her own. The two of you and your scum of a grandfather treated her so terribly, she made sure Tony got his. So I guess we've got that in common, Paulie, fucking over our fathers and all."

"*Delilah—*" Dante starts, but I shake my head.

"If we're doing this, let's do it," I say, holding my hands out at my sides as if to say, *Game on.*

"This was all a setup to get Dante in charge," Paulie says, stepping back from me, his voice petulant and frustrated.

"See, that's your issue, Paulie. It was your father's problem, and your grandfather's: assuming that women have no power, no ambition. But really, at the end of the day, women are your downfall. Underestimating the women around you? *That* will get you killed. Women know all in this family—the men are just too fucking stupid to see it." I see Teresa out of the corner of my eye, and though I wondered for a moment if she'd be mad I spilled her secrets, I see she has a smile on her lips.

She approves.

I can almost hear the words now.

Your mother would be proud.

A small, near imperceptible warmth starts to grow in me.

"You treat your men like shit, Paulie."

"The fuck—"

"You treat you man like shit, boss them around like they're your indebted minions instead of your family. As if they work *for* you and not *with* you. Your arrogance made it so fucking easy to play. So yeah, I pulled them to my side, encouraged them to be loyal to me instead of you, but it wasn't hard. I didn't have to tell lies or spin fantasies to make it happen. They were willing. You treat people like shit, and they won't be yours for long."

"Dante told you—"

"I walked in that office months ago and offered you a deal. You only saw a pretty, young thing you could manipulate, use, and sell. I saw an idiotic man who was so wrapped up in himself, he wouldn't see what I really wanted. I came in that office to take you down, Paulie. Take down your family."

For a moment, I forget there is a room full of people around us.

Family.

Friends.

Associates.

People who, over time, will probably hear this story manipulated seven ways from Sunday, so they might as well hear my side of it before it gets too far from the truth.

"I had a plan: learn what I need to, find the weak spots, take down the Carluccios. Funny, it seems my mother and Teresa once did something similar. A would-be Russo and a Carluccio working together to make men pay." I smile like it's funny. "You know, it was my mother who found the paperwork outlining the pump and dump scheme. Handed it over to Teresa, made sure it got to the right people." I smile as I watch the gears move slowly behind drunken eyes. "There it is. You're getting it now."

"My father . . ."

"It could have been Carmine, but of course, he's so fuckin' selfish he wouldn't save his own son if it meant losing power. So down went Tony. But that's history. We're talking about the present."

I'm honestly surprised at this point Dante hasn't interrupted, and when I quickly glance over at him, he's staring straight at his nephew, waiting for the slightest movement in case he needs to step in.

But still, he lets me have my moment.

Letting me shine.

Letting me be queen.

"The present? You're forcing a fuckin' takeover."

"I didn't force a goddamn thing," I say simply.

"That's bullshi—"

"I'm bringing the Carluccios back to their grandest moment: before your grandfather took control, dragged this family down. Before my father was killed because my mother turned down yours. Back to before your family put a mark on a literal newborn baby, planning to somehow marry her off into your family to gain control. But again, men forget that women can want revenge, too. So when I found out, I came here looking to make your family pay for what it did to mine. Instead, I decided I wanted it for myself."

"So what, you stole Don from me because you're a vengeful cunt?" I feel the air change.

Uh oh. He called me a bad name and now Dante is rising from his corner, ready to defend my honor.

"Paulie, you were never going to be Don," Dante says, his hands in his pockets, posture easy, as if he doesn't care.

But that muscle in his jaw is tight, the one I like to lick when we're alone, and I can tell he's about to lose it.

"The fuck I wasn't—"

"You couldn't handle this. Do you really think I was just going to *give you this family?* Let you tear it down? I would give you two years before you had the entire organization incarcerated."

"Carmine—"

"Carmine wanted you in charge because he didn't want me in charge."

"Even more reason—"

"You think that if you went against him, he wouldn't have had you taken out, Paulie? You weren't smart enough to gain loyalty, not the kind that would keep you safe."

"He wouldn't—"

"He had my mother killed."

Silence fills the space.

We haven't talked about this either. About the revelations that were brought to light that night in Carmine's office, about the news that undoubtedly haunts Dante.

"I don't—"

"Men liked her too much; she had too many opinions. Had his own wife murdered and then played the mourning widower like a pro. Do you think there's a universe where he wouldn't do the same to you?"

Paulie's face changes just a bit. He's not sure how to process this information.

"He was loyal to no one. Not his men. Not his wife. Not his children. It wouldn't have changed just because you were in the picture."

"That's not—"

"It is," Dante says, and for a moment, I think he'll get through to him. That we can move past this as a family, that this will blow over.

And then something snaps.

"Fuck this." Paulie reaches behind him and I know.

I know what he's doing.

Others do as well, the few people who aren't family and are still in the room to watch the drama unfold shifting toward the door, fleeing for safety.

The next thing I know, Paulie has a gun in his hand and it's pointed toward Dante.

"Lilah, out," Dante barks, and I feel Marco place his hand on my arm, eager to obey Dante's command, but I can't move.

I can't breathe.

I can't take my eyes off Paulie, who has his gun pointed directly at my husband.

"Paulie—" Jason starts, at some point returning to the room after helping people out. He starts walking toward him slowly, but Paulie points the gun in his direction, causing him to freeze.

My mind thinks of Bethanny, his sweet daughter who bragged for an hour straight about her *amazing* father the time I went to the hospital to visit her when she had pneumonia.

I think about Marco, who told me Jason is his oldest friend, how he brought him into the family, how he's good, he just bet on the wrong Carluccio.

I think about how he defended me when Paulie hit me.

"Paulie, I'm the one you have an issue with," I say, my words low and easy, like I don't actually care. "Talk with me, not my men."

Because, really, that's what they are now. I'm in charge of this family, of these men. It's my job to keep them safe, to keep this family safe.

"Delilah . . . ," Dante starts, but then the gun is pointed to me and his words trail off, panic and fear seeping from him and into the room.

"I'm the one who took your spot, after all, right? I'm the one who showed your men your true colors, made them understand you're not the right person to be Don." I feel rather than see Dante take a small step closer to me.

"You fuckin whore—"

"That's what happens, though, Paulie, when you fuck your men's wives. When you deny them a life outside of just serving you. When you punish them for disagreeing with you. When you hit a woman who wanted to go over *wedding plans* with you. You showed who you were all on your own, Paulie. I didn't do anything except help to pull it out of you."

"This was all a fucking setup, you sick fuck! This was always your plan! Steal it all from me, fuck everyone over!"

"She didn't steal anything. It was never *yours*," Dante says, and I want to curse at him, watching Paulie move his focus from me to my husband, the barrel of the gun pointed at Dante's chest now.

My blood runs cold.

"Don't be fuckin' stupid, Paulie."

"What does it even matter anymore?" He waves the gun about, pointing at different people in the room. "She's a fuckin' traitor, gathering shit to keep herself in Chanel and anyone who crosses her in fuckin' prison," he says when he looks at Teresa. "My men." His eyes move toward Gian standing near the exit, to Dario who also came back at some point. Even Silvero, who was once most loyal to Carmine.

All of them, my mind now registers, are holding weapons, all pointed at Paulie.

I'm not sure when that happened, but it further proves my point. He laughs when he speaks, like it's a joke. "*My men* all voted against me, following some *puttana* who gave them a little bit of attention. And now my fuckin' men are *threatening* me, willing to take me down for trying to make this shit right." He points the gun to where Jason stands, now also pointing a weapon at Paulie.

"And Carmine's fuckin' dead, killed by *him.*" He points the gun at Dante again and I feel sick.

But then it happens.

It moves back to me.

"But it all started with you. Maybe if you're gone . . . " His words trail off and the rest happens in excruciatingly slow detail.

You know how they say when a tragedy happens before your eyes, your mind slows it down?

Slows it down and remembers ever millisecond?

Yeah.

That's what happens as I watch Paulie move, his eyes feral and crazy. His hands are shaking, the weapon moving with them, but that doesn't really matter when there's a gun pointed at you.

There is noise all around—Teresa yells something, my grandfather shouts, Marco's deep voice bellows, but I can only hear one single thing.

Only one noise registers in my mind.

The sound of Dante breathing.

Or, I guess it's something I *don't* hear, because he stops.

Before he even moves, I know what his plan is.

"No!" I shout like some kind of movie cliché, and I don't even know who I'm saying it to—Dante or Paulie or the universe at large.

Because right as Paulie's finger presses the trigger, Dante moves, pushing me until he's in the line of the bullet.

He falls to the floor.

FORTY-THREE

-Lilah-

God, god, god, FUCK.

The world speeds up again.

Men—four of them—move to Paulie, if not a few moments too late, and restrain him.

I'm shocked no one shot him, but in a way, I'm relieved.

If someone gets to have his blood on their hands, I want it to be me,

"You fucking idiot!" I shout.

I'm not talking to Paulie, though.

I'm yelling at my idiotic husband who just took a fucking *bullet* for me.

"You *fucking idiot!* I can't believe you just fucking did that, Carmine Dante Romano Carluccio!"

"Delilah, get the fuck out of here," he says as I move to him on the floor, trying to find exactly where he was hit.

"Til death do us part my ass, Dante. You die, I'm finding a way to hold you in fucking *purgatory* until *I die* so I can torture your ass." He smiles and relief pours through me before I see a dark stain starting to bloom on the dark gray of his suit jacket. "Fuck, fuck, fuck. Where were you hit, you dumbass!? Can you stop being Mister Tough Guy for fucking once and tell me where you're hurt?"

"Lilah, wrong time," he says, tipping his chin. "Please, for the love of god, go to Marco. Get out of here." When I look to where he tipped his chin, I see that the men who have been holding back Paulie are struggling.

Somehow, in that moment, it becomes clear.

I can't leave.

I can't let Marco take me out, keep me safe.

This is the moment I become the Donna.

I was sworn in, but this is the true test.

If this doesn't end now, it never will. I'll be living in fear of this man for the rest of my life. One way or another, Paulie has to be done tonight.

And after everything he's put me through, everything his father and his grandfather put my family through, I want to be the one to do it.

More importantly, I don't want his blood on Dante's hands. Dante, who is moving to sitting despite the blood stain growing, fumbling for his weapon to point it at his nephew.

It's my turn to get some blood on my soul.

If Dante is already damned to Hell, I better make sure I meet him there.

Quickly, I stand, reaching down to the slit of my long dress I changed into for the party, grabbing the small weapon I placed into my garter at the top of the thigh-high stockings I wore today.

"Jesus fuckin' Christ," I hear Marco say in dismay, but it doesn't matter.

"Lilah!" I hear Dante shout through gritted teeth, but that doesn't matter either.

I have one shot.

One shot before I lose my chance.

The men can't hold him much longer.

So just like how Dante taught me, I turn off the distractions.

You want to rule beside me? Then I need to know you know how to protect yourself.

I aim, remembering my practice, the memory of Dante in my ear clear as day.

Gut shot. You hit a man there, not a great shot of him making it without a hospital trip.

Definitely a mob princess, going for the kneecaps. You hit there, they can't come after you, but they can still shoot. Gotta decide if you want to run or finish the job.

And then, I shoot.

And Paulie Carluccio falls to the ground.

FORTY-FOUR

-Lilah-

"He's asking for you," the doctor says, walking into the waiting room.

He doesn't have to call my name, knowing my face and knowing that when he walks into this room, I will inevitably attack him, asking for updates and if I can go back and see my husband.

He's asking for you.

The most beautiful words I've ever heard in my life.

Except, maybe, when Dante says *covered in you.*

Those words are the ones seared in my brain forever.

The hallway has the absolute worst lighting, the fluorescents pinging off shiny white tile in a way that is supposed to look clean and sanitized but instead always makes me anxious and over-whelmed. I'm walked down the hall, stopping at a different door than the last time they brought me back right after the surgery when he was still sedated, but alive.

Blissfully *alive.*

"He's still under heavy medication for the pain and from the surgery," the doctor says. "He's mostly saying gibberish. His left side is bandaged and there are plenty of monitors and IVs so it might look scary, but you can rest knowing the worst is over." I nod, preparing myself as he opens the door and ushers me in.

"I'll give you two privacy," he says. "Just hit the nurses' button if you need anything."

"Thank you. Another man is down at the cafeteria getting coffee. Can you send him down when he's back? Big Black man, name is Marco. He'll want to see Dante as well," I say, and the nurse who came with the doctor gives me a weird look, like she thinks we're a throuple or something, but I don't care.

I give her my mob boss glare, which probably needs some work, raising an eyebrow as if waiting for her response before she turns slightly red and nods.

"Of course, will do," she says then scurries off.

I smile. Maybe my glare doesn't need as much work as I thought.

But all of that is gone the moment I walk in and see my husband in the hospital bed, monitors beeping, IV stands all around administering fluids.

His dark hair is a mess, his skin paler then normal, and he looks absolutely ridiculous in the light-blue hospital gown, but he's there.

He's alive.

And his eyes are open and pointed at me.

A cry bubbles in my throat, coming out in a croak as I speed his way, the too big sweatshirt and sweatpants Marco bought in the gift shop to get me out of bloody clothes slowing me down, but I don't care.

Because Dante is lying there and he's alive and he's looking at me with love and relief and a part of me knows the worst is behind us.

Not just the surgery, but all of it: the family mess, Carmine, Paulie, the men.

It's all done.

And we're free.

I move to his side, unsure of how to move, how to touch him, how to make sure I don't hurt him when all I want to do is crawl in that little bed and snuggle in and reassure myself that he's here. He's alive. He's safe.

My hand moves to his jaw, a five o'clock shadow rough on my palm and a tear falling without my permission onto his nose. I bend forward as his free hand moves up into my hair, pulling me closer, and I watch his eyes that are still a bit glazed and unfocused go soft.

"Missed you," he says, his voice croaky and hoarse after surgery, and I realize I was wrong.

Those are the most beautiful words I've heard in my life.

FORTY-FIVE

-Dante-

"Please, for the love of god, stop fussing," I say, batting at my wife's hands.

"Dante, I'm going to be fussing over you until you fucking die, so get used to it." I glare at her, giving her a look that should say I'm over her dramatics, but I'm secretly fighting a smile.

She's been like this since the paramedics came, originally to help out Tino. He ended up just with a concussion from hitting his head when Paulie knocked him back as they tried to restrain him.

Instead, I was the one who left on a stretcher. Somehow, my wife batted her eyes or showed her tits or maybe just demanded in that no-nonsense way that she be allowed into the ambulance with me, where she continued to berate me for moving in front of a bullet for her.

"I swear to god, Dante, you ever think of doing that kind of shit again, I'll be the one to put a bullet in you," she'd said through gritted teeth, mad despite the fact that there were paramedics working to keep the blood in my body.

It was a joke, something to keep her mind occupied, but I could see what was beneath it.

The terror.

The horror.

The panic.

The woman loves me almost as much as I love her, and knowing I put myself in danger to save her was killing her.

So to get that look off her face, I agreed, telling her I wouldn't be using my body as a human shield from here on out. The look melted, just a hair.

I lied, of course.

I'd put my body in front of a goddamned firing squad, jump on an atom bomb, run into a burning building if it meant her survival.

If I die before I'm old and gray, it will be with the knowledge that my wife is safe, in one piece, and breathing fresh air.

The problem is, I think she feels the same way.

A lifetime of strife.

Upon being rushed to the ER, the doctors quickly informed my wife (who was attempting to scrub up and sit in the operating room with me) that I would be fine, that I needed a few stitches and to be put under to remove some kind of fragment, and that she'd be called to my bedside upon my being rolled out of the operating room.

She argued, of course.

There were tears that broke something so fucking deep in me.

I saw it on her face, the way she was gearing up to be the queen at battle, to argue with the doctors until she got her way. I saw Marco standing behind her, an arm wrapped around her middle to keep her back.

"*Fiorella*," I said, my voice weak and tired, part from the exhaustion and part from the medication. "*Fiorella*, please. Let them fix me. You sit in the waiting room with Marco and when I'm all good, you come back and check on me."

She stared at me for long moments, and it was all there—the fear and panic and hurt in her eyes.

"I promise, baby. I'll be fine."

Another long minute and from my periphery, I could see the nurse getting irritated by our long goodbye, annoyed that my wife was stopping her from doing her job. She was just about to interrupt, to tell us to say goodbye, but I lifted my hand in her direction, urging her to shut up until my wife was ready.

That, of course, was a shit idea when I realized it was the arm Paulie shot, a searing pain running through me with the small gesture.

It turned out that worked in my favor, though, when Lilah's eyes went wide, the fear and nerves leaving and the need to take care of me pushing in instead.

"Go. Take him," she said to the doctor in the room. He nodded and the nurse began moving things to prepare to roll me down the hall. Lilah came over to me, placing a gentle hand on my face, a hand that I tried to ignore was shaking. "Please, for the love of god, Dante, come back to me." Her eyes watered and every muscle in my body ached to take care of her.

To get rid of her nerves, of her sadness, and replace it with confidence and happiness.

"Love you, *fiorella*. See you soon," I said, and she let go of me, walking off to where I knew Marco would take care of her.

And now she's here in the room with me, fluffing fuckin' pillows and giving me shit every time I ask the nurses when I'll be out of this hellhole.

"Good to see everyone is back to normal," I hear from the doorway and look over to where Marco is filling the frame, leaning on it with a small smile on his lips.

"Can you take off those stupid fuckin' sunglasses?" I say, tipping my chin toward my second.

Lilah's second.

Our second?

I guess there's still a lot to figure out in this new life.

"Stop it, Dante. They're his signature look." I glance at my wife with exasperation, attempting to hide the humor I find in her words. Marco doesn't bother, the smile growing wider on his face.

"His signature look?" I ask, giving my wife a raised eyebrow. Her smile widens.

"Yes, Dante. His signature look. Like my nails," she says, wiggling her fingers with pointy red tips. "And your . . . scowl." Marco lets out a guffaw of a laugh, walking in and sitting in a guest chair in the corner, sprawling like he was invited to be there.

"My scowl?"

"It's the only consistency I can think of."

"You're a little brat, you know that?"

"I'm your brat," she says with a smile, and despite the numbed pain in my arm and the fact that I'm laid up in a hospital bed after *being shot*, my cock twitches at her words.

"Once we get home, you can be my little brat all you want—"

"Jesus fucking Christ, I'm right here," Marco groans. Lilah's laugh tinkles through the room, and I glare at my oldest friend.

"No one asked you to be here, Marco."

"Dante! Rude!"

This is my life now.

My wife and my former second teaming up on me.

Marco just smiles, white teeth blinding against dark skin.

"What are you doing here?" I ask, knowing that the chances of Marco just popping in to check on my well-being a second time are slim to none.

He sighs, confirming my thoughts.

"Got some updates."

"Updates?"

"Gotta lot of updates, but a few I wanted to share before you get released. Ease any . . . anxieties." I stare, waiting for him to keep speaking. "Spoke with the department before I came here. No further investigation into Lilah for Paulie's death. Self-defense. He shot at her husband, hit her a few days prior. Enough witnesses to confirm there was no malice, no planning on her end. They want her to come down next week, give her formal statement, but she's clear."

"But . . ." Lilah looks around like she isn't sure if she should be speaking.

"All good. No bugs, no ears," Marco says. She nods, looking at me.

"I'm not licensed. That gun wasn't registered to me."

"Yes, it was," Marco says. "And yes, you are." There's that smile on his lips, and Lilah looks confused.

"I never—"

"We did though," I say, squeezing her hand. "We know . . . We know the right people to make it happen. Everything was aboveboard."

"Or at the very least, looked that way," Marco says. The look on her face is almost cute as the wheels turn, as she starts to understand what we're saying.

"Other updates?" I ask, moving the conversation along.

"Met with the men. They have everything under control. They're still on board with the changes in the family. If anything, the chaos cemented the need for you two to be in charge," Marco says.

I can almost feel the relief pouring off Lilah.

She's been worried about that, about how what went down would be seen by the family. If her taking down Paulie would give them a sour taste, if it would make them question her.

I knew all along it would be the opposite, if anything.

Watching Lilah stand up for the family, stand up and be brave as fuck would only make the men more loyal to her.

"So they . . . ," she starts, looking around. "They aren't mad?"
Marco laughs.

"Jason's mad you stood in front of a gun a mad man was pointing, but other than that, no. They love you, Lilah."

"Interesting," she says, deep in thought. It makes me laugh, the movement jerking at sore muscles and stitched flesh and making me cringe.

"Oh god! Should we get the nurse? Are you okay?" Lilah asks, jumping up. I swat at her hands.

"Jesus Christ, Lilah, no. Stop it. I'm gonna lose my shit if you don't stop hovering."

"I'm gonna be hovering until you fucking die, Dante Carluccio. Better get used to it," she says, and I roll my eyes, feigning annoyance while Marco laughs.

But what I don't tell her is I will endure her fussing and hovering every day of my goddamn life if it means I get to spend every moment with this woman.

FORTY-SIX

-Lilah-

A few hours later, as I sit in Dante's hospital room, we have another visitor. One I've been dreading seeing, all thing considered. I squeeze my husband's hand and he does the same, reassuring me as I smile at her.

"Knock, knock," Teresa says, standing in the doorway. "Mind some company?"

"Of course not, come in," Dante says, tipping his head into the room. She walks in, standing in front of a chair but not sitting.

Moments pass before I finally speak.

"I'm sorry for your loss, Teresa," I say, staring at the woman. She's dressed in a black dress similar to the one she wore at the celebration of life just yesterday, her hair a bit tousled but otherwise the perfect, put-together mob wife.

I should take notes.

Paulie Carluccio was announced dead on arrival when the medics entered at the home. With so many witnesses, keeping the death in the family was too risky, and the proper channels needed to be taken.

The cops came, letting me go in the ambulance to the hospital with my husband before questioning me in the hall while Dante was in surgery. The bullet thankfully missed anything important, the wound mostly superficial. I was told a centimeter or two to the left and it would have been a much grimmer tale.

In the hospital waiting room, I explained how my husband and I were honoring the life of his deceased father, how his nephew was going through some things with his father in prison and now his grandfather's death. I showed the bruise on my cheek, having intentionally washed my face in the bathroom to remove the pile of concealer, and explained that Paulie was so off kilter, he hit me just a few days prior.

Jason was my witness to the assault, confirming that Paulie had hoped to marry me and he lost his mind when he found out about my secret wedding to his uncle.

Once they were done interviewing me, the police walked off and I watched the detectives speak with first Teresa, who sat with a handkerchief to her face, then with Alfredo Russo, who showed up about two hours after we arrived at the hospital. According to Marco, he stayed behind handling cleanup and getting the guests home safely.

After a suspicious handshake between the officers and my grandfather, they left, leaving me a voicemail stating that I may need me to come down at some point to give a formal statement, but all seemed clear on their end and I was free to go without having the awful circumstance on my record.

Horrible circumstance out of your control, they said.

Teresa looks around the room, at the television that is broadcasting the local news. They're currently showing a group of reporters right outside this very hospital with a bright-yellow headline at the bottom that reads *Carluccio heir shot by nephew at private celebration of life, one death reported at the Carluccio home.*

"It would have happened eventually. It's not like . . ." She looks around, avoiding my eyes. "He wasn't really mine."

"That doesn't matter," I say, moving from Dante and walking to hold her hand. "You said it yourself, you spent years treating him like your own. Like he was your son. That can't be easy, seeing what you saw. Losing him. If . . ." I look over at Dante, knowing that while I don't like admitting this out loud, he probably understands better than most, with his own complex relationship with his father. "If something were to happen to Shane, it might be a relief at the end of the day, but I'd still mourn him. Especially if I saw what you did."

Teresa sighs, gripping my hand a bit harder before letting go and walking toward large window.

"They're all here to catch a sound bite, aren't they?" she says, looking down at the reporters below.

"Marco will escort you out the back, get you home without seeing any of them," Dante says. "He'll be waiting for you outside."

"Do we have someone making a statement at all?"

"Lawyers will be speaking on our behalf."

"Carmine used to do it," she says. "All the press. Loved that, being in front of everyone, giving them a glimpse into it, knowing he was telling lies out in front of the world."

"Yeah, he was quite a piece of work," I say with a sigh. "We should have someone on the payroll. A spokesperson. A representative for the family," I say, looking to Dante. "A friendly face people can trust, especially as we start to work with the community again." He nods and I put it on my mental list.

It feels a mile long right now.

"I could, you know," Teresa says.

"Could what?"

"Be the spokesperson. I . . . I want to have a bigger hand in the family. I know I basically am just here because of Tony, but . . . this is my life. I have nothing else but this family."

I look at her with understanding because I get it.

If something happened where there was no Russo family for me to head and Dante passed, I would be lost. I'd need some kind of tie to the family, something that kept me in the life.

I don't know if you can just go back, live a normal, carefree life after you know the secrets we do.

I look to my husband, asking him but already knowing what I'll do next.

Thankfully, he nods, understanding.

"We'd pay you, of course," I say, looking at Teresa.

In a way, the woman has become a confidant to me. A kindred spirit.

A second mother.

She knew her and how she fit into this life best, after all.

Maybe that's what Teresa is to me—a lifeline to the part of my mother I never knew.

"That's not—"

"Aboveboard, Teresa. We need to start working on getting some things legitimized. And I don't want to be working with the press nonstop."

"Neither do I," Dante says. "And I know Marco would rather get shot than do it."

She stares at me, and it's then I see it.

Hesitance.

"If you don't want to, that's—"

"It's not that," she says.

"What is it then, Teresa? Is it Tony? Is it what happened with him and what part you had in it? You handed over the intel, but he did that to himself," Dante says.

"It's not that. It's . . ." She looks around with a sigh. "I've spent the last twenty years collecting information on everyone. All of you. The men, Marco—I knew about Marco's tie to the Russos years ago." My eyes go wide and a tiny, almost imperceptible smile plays on her lips. "Knowledge is power and in a family where the men thought women had none, I knew I was safe with knowledge," she says with a shrug. "But if I work for you . . ." There's a long pause.

"It's fine, Teresa. I get it," Dante says, his voice low.

"Do you want what I have?" she asks, and it's strange hearing this strong, confident woman nervous, her voice shaking just a bit. "There's some on you, Dante. And . . . god I'm a bitch, but you too, Lilah."

"Rumors or proof?" I ask, looking at her, knowing there's a huge different between the two.

"Receipts, statements, recordings. Proof, Lilah. The kind of things that would hold up in court. I have everything I would need for everyone to fall." I can almost hear the sound of Dante's jaw grinding with the need to defend me, but I speak before he can.

Change needs to happen in this family.

A lifetime of lies and deceit and unrestrained power and greed nearly killed all of us. Nearly ruined this town and hurt so many fucking people along the way.

With a new chapter starting, I want to change that.

"Keep it," I say softly. Dante reaches out, grabbing my hand near painfully, but I brush him off. "Is it safe? Somewhere no one will find it?" She nods.

I trust her. I know that if I went looking for whatever she has, I'd never find it. "Keep it. If the darkness ever wins, if Dante or I ever go too far, use it."

Dante's body loosens as he understands what I'm saying, what I'm implying.

"I'm still not comfortable, L—" he starts, but I cut him off, shaking my head but keeping my eyes on Teresa.

"I don't care. Keep it safe, Teresa, yeah?" The room is painfully silent. "The old rule is out. We're playing new games; there are new rules. Less darkness, less greed. A balance of power. I don't want things to go the way they were when Carmine was in charge ever again. I don't . . . I want my kids to grow up knowing that. The men to know that we're holding ourselves responsible, that we can't just do whatever the fuck we want without worrying about consequences."

She stares at me for a full minute where I can hear my pulse pounding in my ears, where I panic, wondering if I made the wrong decision. I made it so this woman could destroy all of us in an instant, if she so desired.

But then she nods, standing and moving toward the door.

In the last moment, she turns to me with a smile.

"She be real proud, Lilah."

"What?" I ask, confused.

"Your mom. She'd be really proud of you." And then she's gone.

"Lilah . . . ," Dante says, his voice low and exasperated.

"I don't want to hear it. We're starting this with integrity. We keep it, there's no need to worry."

"And if Teresa decides she's mad at one of us?"

"That won't happen," I say, sitting on the side of the bed and brushing Dante's hair back gently, red nails getting lost in the dark hue. His eyes drift shut, whether from the feeling of my hands on him or from the meds working their way through his system, I have no idea.

"And if it does?" he asks, eyes still closed.

I stay silent, watching him, continuing to run my fingers through his hair and marveling at how lucky we are.

At how it's all over.

It's all behind us now.

And how a beautiful future full of so much hope and potential and happiness lies before us.

He opens his eyes then narrows them, looking at me.

"*Delilah.*"

"If it happens for some strange reason . . . I may have taken a few pages out of her and my mom's books." His lips tip up just a hair.

"You have something on her, don't you? Even the scales?" I smile and shrug my shoulders.

"Who knows. Hopefully, it will never come to that." His smile widens and the hand of his good arm moves up, grazing the skin of my arm then landing at the base my neck and tangling in the hair there.

"So fuckin' smart, my wife."

"Keep that in mind if you ever try to fuck me over."

"I would never," he says then pulls me down, pressing his lips to mine.

I know now that we're going to have that beautiful life he promised me.

I know now my words all those years ago were true, that somehow, even then, I knew.

Life is beautiful if you let it be.

He scoots over, making room on the tiny hospital room bed, tugging me until I lie next to him even though I know the nurse is going to give him shit for it when she sees me here.

Whatever.

"So, what's next?" I ask what feels like hours later, using my hand to brush his hair to the side. He's still pale but gaining color, and I'm pretty sure we'll get the okay to go home tomorrow.

If not, I think Dante might force me to break him out of here.

"Next?"

"Well. You're Don. That's . . . done."

"And you're Donna." I smile at him.

"I am, aren't I?"

He smiles and I can't resist pressing my lips to his again.

"My queen," he whispers against them.

"I just want to be yours."

"That was always a given, *fiorella*. You had no choice in the world but to be mine." I sigh, love and happiness and comfort filling my veins in a way I haven't let happen since those days in the cabin.

"So, what do we do next? Family meeting? Meeting with the Russos? Dismantle the patriarchy?" He laughs, the sound jerking his body and causing a hiss of pain.

"Shit, I should—" I say, trying to move out of the bed.

"Do not even think about leaving this bed, Delilah Antonia Carluccio-Russo." I smile at the use of my full name and the way he smiles saying it. "I think I owe you a wedding," he says, and my smile widens to the point where it almost hurts my face.

"Yeah. You do."

"A big one."

"Huge," I say in a whisper.

"But first, Lake George. We need a vacation."

EPILOGUE

-Six months later-
-Lilah-

"Baby, you already had a bachelorette party," Dante says, watching me pull thigh-high tights on, my thumbs running the line of the lace until they lie flat. "Why do you need another?" I stop and stare at the man who, technically speaking, is already my husband, and tip my head to the side.

"Dante, are you telling me that if I wanted seventeen bachelorette parties, you wouldn't be making me complex Pinterest boards to decide all seventeen destinations and their themes?"

"I don't even know what Pinterest is." I raise an eyebrow because we both know that's not the point. He takes two steps closer to me as I slip on a pair of sky-high heels and then takes both of my hands, pulling me up until I'm right against him. One arm wraps my waist, and the other goes to my chin, tipping it up until I'm looking at him, his eyes dark and serious. "But yeah. I would." I smile.

I knew that answer, of course.

"But if you don't go, I could bury my face in your pussy all night and make you scream my name until your voice is hoarse." His head dips, licking the spot under my ear and then blowing on it.

God, this man.

"But you'll do that anyway when I get home," I say, my voice shaky. His arm around my waist tugs me in closer until I can feel how he's hard in his slacks, not having changed after a day at the club.

"But I could do it *now*." The way his voice goes low sends vibrations from his chest to mine, our bodies lined up perfectly, and it takes everything in me to push him away until he steps back.

"Give me this, honey. I want the whole nine."

"You're having a wedding with four hundred people attending and three outfit changes." I raise an eyebrow. "And a month-long honeymoon." I tip my head and he shakes his, staring at the ceiling in a very familiar move.

I smile, my red lips pulling as I do.

"Exactly," I say, confirming that I know without a shadow of a doubt that I will always get whatever I want with this man. He's still shaking his head as he smiles, pulling me in and speaking with his lips against mine, brushing there.

"This is going to be my life, isn't it?" he asks.

"What?" I say in a whisper.

"You giving me puppy-dog eyes, gettin' whatever you want."

"Would you want it any other way?" I ask.

"Not even for a moment." He presses his lips to mine before stepping away and turning me so my back is to him and I'm facing the door, slapping my ass. "Now go before I lose all will to let you and fuck you all night long, keeping you away from your party."

"I love you, Dante," I say over my shoulder, blowing a kiss to him.

"And I you, *fiorella*. Now go. Keep me updated, please," he says.

"Always," I reply, thinking of just *how* I would like to keep him updated.

Two hours later

I'm drunk.

Come home.

It's my party. I can't just leave.

Sure you can. I'll call Marco now, tell him to bring you home.

I'm having fun.

You'd have more fun on my cock.

Yeah?

Yeah.

Why?

Because I'd be fucking you.

What else?

You tell me.

I'd be in your lap, face-to-face.

Yeah?

And I'd move so my clit rubs on you, and I'd squeeze hard on your cock inside me.

Fuck, baby. Come home.

My nails would be in your hair and I'd moan your name, baby.

Lilah.

L: Would you suck on my nipples, baby?

I'd do whatever the fuck you want me to do.
Now come home and I'll make it happen.

You come here.

He doesn't reply.

My clit throbs just from those texts and the liquor in my system, but I don't have time to question anything because Sammi grabs my arm, shaking me and pointing at the stage where Fancy is coming out, ready to give us a show.

I fucking love it here.

About ten minutes later, I feel it.

It's loud and it's hot and my body is sticky with sweat from dancing and shouting and hooting as I throw singles at the girls giving us a show, but still—I feel it.

The prickle of electricity from behind me has my hair standing on end.

"What?" Candy says from beside me, and when I look at her, her face is confused.

"He's here," I say, and she looks even more confused, but when I turn my head, my words are confirmed.

Dante is striding through the club, phone in hand, walking our way.

"Sweet baby Jesus," Sammi says under her breath as we all watch him coming, his eyes locked to mine.

"Ope, there goes Lilah's night," Candy says with a laugh. I can't respond, though, because my husband is closing in on us, a plain, white, fitted undershirt tucked into a pair of slacks like he couldn't even bother to put his shirt back on before leaving the house and coming to get me.

But why?

And then my drunk ass remembers the texts I was sending not long ago, before I got distracted, and the smile grows on my lips.

He sees it and despite the fact that he doesn't slow, doesn't smile at me, I see it in his eyes. The warmth that grows there. The humor.

Finally, he's to where I'm sitting, his hand reaching down to grab the back of my neck and pull, lifting me up onto shaky knees and pulling me into him, kissing me like I didn't just leave the house a few hours ago.

Cheers and groans and a, *Get a room!* come, but I ignore them, making out with my husband slash fiancé in a crowded strip club while some of my favorite friends flounce around topless nearby.

My life is utterly insane, and I *utterly adore it.*

When he finally breaks the kiss, his hand leaves my neck, trailing my arm until it's at my wrist then tugging.

"See you later, ladies," he says and, as we retreat. Sammi and Candy scream and laugh before going back to the task of throwing singles at strippers and enjoying the night.

"What are we doing, Dante?" I ask with a giggle, stumbling in my too-high heels. He pauses, catching me as always and dipping to pick me up bridal style. Then he takes long strides to a door that I still can't walk past without thinking of him.

"Something I've been thinking about for a fucking lifetime, Delilah." He walks through the door, locking it behind him and setting me down before moving to a corner where the music settings are and messing with it before soft, sultry music flows into the room.

"*Oh my god,*" I whisper, looking around and understanding what he's saying. "Are we really doing this?" I ask, scanning the familiar room, old memories coming back like warm caresses.

This is where it all started, Dante and I.

The questions and answers.

Dante sitting in the shadows, fighting the urge to steal me and hide me away.

Paying to spend time with me.

Becoming mine.

"Fuck yeah, we are," he says, moving to take an all too familiar seat. He sits there and leans back, kicking his legs out and crossing them, his head falling to the shadows.

"God, this brings back memories," I say with a smile, the low music playing the same way it did back then.

"It's bringing back how I always wanted to fuck you every time we were in this room like that." With three drinks in my system, the music enters my veins, forcing my body to move to the beat. A low, quiet groan falls from Dante's lips, and it sends a bold of heat through my body.

"You never even touched me when we were in here like this."

"I knew if I ever did, I'd never stop," he says as I move to the panel that controls the music, turning it up just a bit.

"You also never let me undress when I was in here with you," I say, my voice husky with the promise of what's to come.

"Jesus, Lilah. Knew if I saw you like that, your perfect body on display for me and me alone, I'd lose any desire to play it safe. I'd steal you away, lock you in the compound until you agreed to be mine." My breathing goes wonky as I move a hand to the back of my dress where a zipper sits low, tugging it down and loosening the material.

"I would have, you know," I say, swaying my hips. "Agreed to be yours." My hand moves to the thin strap of the red dress, pushing it down my shoulder and repeating it on the other side until the top of the dress falls down to my waist, leaving me in just a thin bra with low cups on top. My thumbs move into the dress, pushing it over my hips until it falls to the ground.

"That's a lie." His words are low, his eyes locked on where my thumbs are pushing down fabric.

"We've always had a pull, Dante. You know that. I would have fallen for you the way I did one way or another." I step out of the dress, kicking it to the side until I'm standing before him in thigh-high tights with lacy tops, a thin red bra, and a high-cut red satin thong.

He doesn't say anything for a long moment as he takes me in. I continue swaying, moving my hands above my head as I do.

"No, my Lilah wouldn't. You're too stubborn, too brave. You would have fought me at every turn." I smile, doing a turn to show him the back of me, where my panties disappear, where a tiny red bow sits on top of my ass. He inhales. "Not that you didn't do that anyway."

"True," I say, turning back around to face him, moving my thumb to the strap of my bra, sliding it down.

I can feel Dante's eyes burning on me.

"You like me stubborn though."

"I like you any way I can get you," he says, and again, I smile. His smile is sweeter though, filled with the knowledge of how true and honest his words are.

He does.

He'll take me however he can.

"Stubborn," he says, and I move my fingers to the other strap. "Patient." I push it down. "Loving. Teasing. Siren. Queen." Each word repairs a part inside of me, the ones he's constantly reinforcing that get damaged in the day-to-day when my mind starts to win. When I hear Turner's voice telling me I'm not good enough, when the voices who doubt me start to speak.

And each day, Dante repairs It.

He's never bored of the job, never exhausted by the responsibility.

Instead, he treats it like an honor.

My fingers move to the back clasp of the bra, letting it fall to the ground.

There's a sharp intake of breath as it does. I shimmy my shoulders, my tits gently moving as I do, and Dante curses under his breath.

"Yeah, it's good I didn't let you do this all those months ago."

"Why's that?" I ask, flipping my hair before moving my thumbs to the waistband of my underwear, pushing them down until I'm just in my heels and thigh-highs.

"Because I would have done this," he says, and then he leans toward me, wrapping an arm around my waist and tugging me forward. I stumble a bit, but he catches me, and finally, I settle on his lap, straddling him, his hard cock right where I need it most despite the layer of fabric between us. His arm on my waist moves me, rocking me against him and making a deep moan fall from me.

His free hand moves into my hair, tugging the way he loves to, the pull searing in a way *I* love, the move synched perfectly with my clit.

"Oh, god, fuck," I murmur as his mouth meets my neck, biting the spot beneath my ear, his teeth just a bit too hard to be called a love bite.

"At home, waiting for you to come home to me, all fucking tipsy and ready to fuck. Wanted you to have this, have this night with your girls, but then you go and fucking start texting me. Telling me what you need, telling me to come to you." Another moan as he grinds me on his bulge, my clit scraping on the fabric and sending a bolt of heat through me.

"I didn't think—oh, fuck, Dante,"

"That I'd come? Don't you know by now, Delilah?" He uses my hair to tug me back, to make it so I can stare in his eyes as he speaks. "You tell me what you need, I make it fucking happen. You wanted to rule; I made you a queen. You wanted to be mine and mine alone and for the word to know it; I'm marrying you twice. You needed me to barge in, fuck you good to ease the ache? I'm right here, baby."

A heavy breath comes from my chest as I start to move on my own, his hand helping but also slowly moving, over my hip, down the leg straddling him, then back up and in, tickling the sensitive skin of my inner thigh, his rough thumb hitting the crease where my leg meets, where I need him most.

"Dante," I whimper.

"What is it, baby?"

"You know."

"Tell me anyway."

"I need you." His face is in my neck, his breathing hard there as he pants against my skin.

He might be playing the game of riling me up, but he needs me just as bad.

"I need you to fuck me, Dante. I'm so fucking empty without you," I moan, and he groans against my neck, pushing me down again to grind, but this time, I'm riding his hand.

One finger slips in.

"Fuck, you're so wet for me."

"Always," I whisper, and I know he hears it even over the music.

Another finger slides in as the first comes out, two now filling and stretching me.

"Ride these, baby," he says, his thumb moving to rest on my clit. I move my hips forward and back, reeling at the way it makes his thumb rub me how I need. Slowly, I start to rock back and forth and he stills his fingers, letting me use him for my own pleasure.

I'm in control.

"It's so good, Dante," I moan, swirling my hips this time until his finger grazes my G-spot.

"That's it, baby. Is this what you needed? Me, finger fucking this sweet pussy?" He's still fully clothed while I'm naked other than my heels and stockings and as always, I love it.

And he knows it.

"Such a dirty fucking girl, sending me filthy texts, trying to get me hard, making me come all the way here, getting naked and then sitting in my lap. You're going to leave your mark on my pants, aren't you? I'm gonna have to drive home with your pussy on me."

The thought of that fuels me, my body igniting.

"Should I take your ass tonight, Delilah? Fill you good? Or will your pussy miss my cock too much?" His breathing is heavy in my ear, riling me up, my pussy clamping down on his fingers as his words drive me higher and higher.

"Fuck, my girl likes that, doesn't she?" His teeth nip my ear. "Maybe we'll do both. Let you come on my cock here in this room, the way I always wanted, then when you come home to me, I'll press you down into the bed and fuck your ass until you scream my name."

I moan deep, my head tipping back, and I beg, "God, yes, please." My hips continue to move, continue to take me higher with each tiny rock.

"Tell me what you want." His head dips down, the hand in my hair pulling me back so his mouth can reach my peaked nipple. His mouth closes over it, sucking it in, making me moan again.

"I want to ride your cock, Dante. Please, fuck," I beg, needing more. Anything.

Him.

His teeth dig into my nipple, the pain playing off the pleasure until I'm clamping down on his fingers, so fucking close.

"Dante," I yell, unable to form words anymore, but of course, he knows.

"I know, *fiorella*. Give me a second and I'll make it better," he says, his hand working between us, undoing his zipper and pulling himself out with a low groan. My hand moves there, swiping his out of the way so I can grip him, working him once, twice. "Jesus," he groans then moves both hands to my hips, lifting me while I position him where I need him most, a well-oiled machine working together.

Once he's notched, the tip wet with me, he moves, slamming me down onto him. I moan, my head tipping back, eyes closed as he fills me, bringing me the kind of peace I only get when he's inside me, when we're together like this.

"So fucking perfect," he says, his face going into my neck, one hand pressing on my hip to hold me down, to keep himself deep in me, the other moving to my hair to tug hard, bringing me back to the land of the living.

Using that hand in my hair, he moves my face until my lips are right in front of his and I'm breathing his air, his eyes on me.

"You are fucking mine, Delilah. Don't you ever forget that," he says against my lips.

As if I ever could.

But I know he wants more of an answer than that.

"Yours," I say and watch his eyes dilate further with the word, even in the shadows.

"Ride me," he orders, and I have no option other than to abide, letting the toes of my stilettos hit the floor on either side of the low chair then moving, grinding my clit on his pelvis, lifting and falling on his cock. He tugs my hair until I'm looking at the ceiling, my back arched, riding him, on display for my husband.

"Jesus fucking Christ," he says through gritted teeth. "Fuck. How'd I get so fucking lucky?" The hand not keeping me from falling moves, trailing my side, up, up, until there's a thumb moving over my nipple then back down, skimming over my hip and in. [NG1]

"That's it, baby. Keep riding me; keep taking my cock deep." His thumb moves to cover my clit. "Take me as you come on my cock and don't you fuckin' stop," he demands, and the pressure inside me builds, my entire body on overdrive. I want to fill myself, to grind on him until I explode, but still, I obey. I'm moving up and down, fucking myself on his cock when it happens, when I explode, my head tipping back farther, a low, guttural moan coming from my chest as I explode.

But I keep moving.

Keep fucking him as I come, overwhelmed by how quickly it builds again, his thumb still going at my clit, the hand on my hip digging in more as he gets close.

"Fuck, yes, yes," he groans, watching me come undone, watching it build for a second time. "Take me with you, baby. Fuck, just look at you. A goddamned dream, that's what you are."

"Dante—" I start.

"I know, Lilah. Fill yourself and take me with you," he says, and I do as he asks, slamming down, filling myself deep to the point where there's a twinge of pain before I scream his name and come.

And as I do, my name comes through his gritted teeth, the sound a mix of pleasure and all-consuming pain as I feel him pulse inside of me.

I leave the private room that smells of sweat and sex, notably lacking the thigh-highs I went in with and having gained crazy sex hair. As I walk toward the bar where Joey is serving, I get a round of applause.

Dante is barely a foot behind me as I walk, winking at Candy and Sammi who give hilarious screams.

"Bitch just got the GOOD dick!" Fancy yells from the stage.

"How do you know it was the good dick, Fancy?" Roddy says, and I try to ignore the fact that my friends, employees, and men are all gossiping about my sex life.

I'll probably feel more shame in the morning, but right now, I'm feeling too good to care.

"Are you kidding me? Look at her. She can barely walk straight," Candy says, and I smile in their direction, throwing a wink before Joey slides a shot of tequila and a lime in front of me. Dante comes up behind me, placing a kiss in my hair and putting an arm around my waist. When I turn to him, I offer him the shot, but he shakes his head.

"Gonna head home."

"Home?" I ask, shocked.

"Yeah. You get nice and drunk. When you're done, Marco and the boys will make sure you get to me in one piece, make sure your girls get home okay. I'll be waiting for round two." There's a devilish smile on his lips and I return it.

"Oh, Jesus, I don't know if I can handle a round two," I murmur, and Joey laughs, having overheard. Dante's face moves to my neck, licking the skin there before he bites my earlobe.

"You've got a while to prepare. When you're ready, come home to me."

And then he kisses me one last time before turning away and leaving me to enjoy my bachelorette party at the strip club he owns.

We own.

"You're one lucky bitch," Candy says, watching Dante talk with Marco in the corner before leaving.

"Yeah. I know," I say before I go back to tipping the hard-working girls shaking their asses for my entertainment.

Hey reader!!

In this last section of the epilogue and Dante and Lilah's story, there is a mention of pregnancy. If you are struggling with infertility, miscarriage, or if for *any* reason you don't enjoy reading about that topic, you can skip the last few passages and know that Dante and Lilah have their own happily ever after.

You are loved, you are important, and you are seen.

Love,
 Morgan

Five years later

"Am I under arrest?" I ask, my brow raised at the arrogant officer.

His jaw tightens.

He knows what comes next.

I smile my siren's smile.

"No, Mrs. Carluccio. You are not under arrest."

My smile widens as I stand, my red bottoms clicking on cheap linoleum as I do.

"Well. Then you won't mind if I head out, will you?"

He sighs but closes his manila folder as I walk out of the interrogation room.

And then I move out of the building, ducking into the blacked-out car and ordering Marco to take me to my husband so I can ream his ass out.

Just another day in the life.

"Carmine Dante Romano Carluccio, where the hell are you?" I call as soon as I walk in the door of our home.

It's not the compound, not anymore. For our one-year anniversary, my husband bought me my dream home.

Not too big, but big enough to house the kids I told him I wanted, big enough to host family parties, and most importantly, big enough so our room is far enough from any future gremlins.

I don't plan to stop letting my husband rail me just because there are kids under our roof.

And with the lack of cars out front, I know only my husband is home.

"Dante!" I yell again, walking through the foyer toward the kitchen, not because that's where he normally is, but because that electricity is pulling me there.

And when I walk into the kitchen, I stand in the entryway, putting my hands on my hips, staring at my handsome husband.

The hair at his temples has gone just a bit more salt and pepper, the lines on his face a bit deeper, but he's still as handsome as that first time I saw him all those years ago as a drunk girl in Jersey City playing dress up as Rapunzel.

His *fiorella*.

Though these days, the laugh lines are a bit more prominent than his frown lines, and I like to think that's all my doing.

He sits back, leaning into the chair before looking at me.

"Why do I feel like I'm about to get yelled at?" he says, a smile on his lips.

I glare.

"Ah, because I am." The smile grows. "Where were you when you got angry?" he asks as if that will help him remember which of the things he's done recently got me mad.

"The police station," I say, deadpan, and he sits up straighter, the furrow in his brow forming.

"The police station?"

"*Yes*, Dante. Apparently, Shane Turner has gotten himself in deep once again and told the police that his daughter would come help out. Sat in a fuckin' interrogation room for twenty minutes, them telling me about all the trouble Shane's been getting into and how he's claiming that it's all *my* fault."

Thunder crosses my husband's face, and I fight the way it makes my belly flutter in a good way.

"*Your fault?*" Dante says angrily. "Where the fuck was Marco?"

"Marco drove me there and then dropped me off here." I smile, watching Dante's frown deepen.

Good.

"And why didn't he tell *me?*" That thick brow is raised like he thinks *I'm* the one about to get in trouble when it's very much him in the doghouse.

"I told him not to."

"Why?"

"Because I wanted to see the look on your face when I walk in and tell you I spent twenty minutes in a *police station*." He looks to the sky and mumbles to himself.

"Delilah—"

"How long?" I ask, staring at him, my hands on my hips.

He stops.

He stops and that's when I know he's been hiding this from me.

"Dante."

He sighs and stands from his chair, moving around the kitchen island, a hand out to me.

"Delilah—"

I step back, pointing a single red-tipped finger at him.

"You tell me everything, we can talk. Until then, you stay there."

He gives me an annoyed look and rolls his eyes but doesn't argue.

"He's been on my radar for a year."

"*A year?*"

"Not even near us, over in New Hampshire, but I know people and they keep me updated on things."

"New Hampshire?!"

"He lost that election to Sam and left the state, you know that." I do. Alfredo kept his word, working closely with a family friend to make sure Shane Turner was not elected the next time he was up, and when Shane lost, he fled the state in shame.

"Why did he go to New Hampshire?"

"Why does the man do *anything* he does, Lilah?"

Valid.

"So, why are the Hudson City detectives talking to me about him?"

"You tell me," he says, and I just raise an eyebrow at him.

He sighs when he realizes I'm not telling him anything without learning whatever he knows.

"I don't know the full details," he says. "I'll get them, but I didn't even know he was in the state."

"He's detained downtown right now." Dante runs a hand through his hair and sighs.

"He's been racking up debts up north. On my radar only in the sense that I needed to know if he started to come back. A year ago, I had to send Tino up there, have a few words."

"A year ago," I say, annoyed. "Tino never mentioned it to me."

"He wasn't supposed to, so glad to know he did his fuckin' job." I cross my arms on my chest.

"We said no more secrets, Dante."

"No more secrets about the family. But this? This would do you no good. Nothing you could do about it, and all it would be was a stressor, something for you to worry about, and Lilah, you've worried enough about this goddamn man for a fuckin' lifetime." He reduces the gap between us, putting a hand on each side of my face.

"Made it my mission for you to live easy, Delilah. That includes keeping shit from you sometimes." I make a face, but he keeps talking. "If there is something that you cannot act upon, something that will cause you stress, I will not be telling you. I will not apologize for that. You are my wife, and I live to keep you happy and safe. If it's not about the family, not about business, I'm not telling you." I grind my teeth before speaking again.

"What about Lola—"

"Talked to Ben, and he agreed." My mouth drops open.

"*What?*"

"Called Ben up nine months ago when Turner started to get in deep. Wanted his opinion. His wife's father was in some shit, and I know he feels the same I do about that man. He agreed that until it impacted you two, we wouldn't burden you with it."

"You called up my brother-in-law?" I scrunch my nose, feeling tears there.

Betrayal, maybe.

"He's my brother-in-law too, technically." I roll my eyes. "But yes. I needed to pull him in, get his opinion." Dante moves then, dipping and lifting me, walking me to the couch in the living room and sitting, making me straddle his lap. "Now, tell me what the cops said."

"Nothing much. Apparently, he left New Hampshire and had a warrant there. He got stopped in Hudson City with an expired registration, and they arrested him."

"Why was he in Hudson City?" Dante asks, and I sigh.

This he will not like.

"Apparently, he was on his way to Jerzy Girls," I say, my voice low. "He wanted to talk with you."

"With me?" Dante says, his voice shocked. "Why the fuck would he want to talk with me?" I give him a look that tells him *exactly* why he would want to talk to the Don of the Carluccio-Russo family.

"Fine, why the fuck would he think *I* wanted to talk with *him*."

"No idea. They couldn't give me an answer. Eventually, I got tired of being there, asked if they had a warrant for me, and left when they said no."

"Good fucking girl," he says, a smirk on his face.

"Dante—"

"I'll figure out whatever else I need to know tonight when I have Marco look into it. Gut tells me that Turner is officially not our problem and that he'll be a guest of the state sometime soon."

He presses his lips to mine.

"Now that that's handled," Dante says, moving so I'm lying on my back and he's hovering over me.

"It's not handled, Dante!"

"It is, baby. He's in custody; he's done. I'll have Teresa do her magic later, send over whatever she has in her fucking psychotic file."

"You're gonna—"

"I'm not gonna do shit, Lilah. He did it. But I *will* be making sure we can be done with him once and for all." My stomach drops despite the fact that I haven't seen or heard from the man in over five years. That time had the lowest stress of my whole life, despite literally revamping an entire crime family.

"Prison."

"Unless you have other ideas..."

"He's Lola's father, Dante," I say, my voice quiet. His hand moves, brushing my hair back.

"Ben and I agreed it would be best for your sister to do this if he ever came back to town, tried to contact you girls again."

"You talked to Ben about that too?"

"He brought it up." My heart flutters a bit, knowing Lola has that. A man so worried about her mental well-being that he told my *mafia husband* that he wanted her father locked up if he tried to contact her again. "You disagree?" he asks, and I know what he means.

Do I disagree that Turner should be put away?

Nope.

He can see that on my face, of course.

"That's what I thought. So, we'll make it so he can't bother you two anymore, and that's it." I sigh. "Now, let's talk about something else," he says.

I look to the ceiling and shake my head.

"We have dinner plans tonight. We don't have time—"

"Wanna tell me what I found in the bathroom garbage?" he asks, his lips to my neck, and my body freezes.

I don't respond.

His lips move to my ear.

"Was it yours, *fiorella?*"

I don't respond.

I'm panicked.

I'm panicked because I don't know how *he'll* respond. Will he be happy? Will he be angry? Will he—

But as always, he knows.

Dante always knows.

"Because if it was, I need you to cancel those reservations at Trattoria, Lilah. I need to celebrate with my wife. Alone."

My heart fills with his words, and my head turns gently in his direction.

"Would you be happy?" He tries to lift his head, but I can't handle that, can't see his face right now.

I'm so irrationally afraid of what I'll see there.

As always, he knows.

He knows my fears and my joys.

"I would do absolutely anything on this earth to give you everything you want, Delilah. I'd kill men. I'd steal the world. I'd buy you every pair of red-bottom shoes on the planet. You being in this universe, sleeping in my bed every damn night makes me the happiest man on this planet." My heart pumps, tears pricking at the backs of my eyes.

"But nothing—and I mean nothing, Delilah—would make me happier than you making me a father."

I start to cry silent tears with that.

"It was mine, Dante," I whisper.

He breathes something that sounds like tears of his own, and that's confirmed when wet warmth hits my collarbone.

"I'll allow these tears. Happy tears."

And then I lose it, remembering his promise all those years ago.

You don't cry because you're sad anymore. You cry when you marry me again in front of five hundred fucking people. You cry when you tell me you're carrying my kid. You cry when we name a little boy after your dad or a little girl after my mother. You don't cry because of what they took from you. You cry because of what I give you.

And he has stuck to that ever since.

15 years later

"Eliza Carluccio, I swear to *fucking god,* if you do not stop whining, I'm making your father turn this car around and we're going home," I say, turning around in my seat and staring at my 14-year-old daughter. She's sitting in the back seat next to her younger brother, arms crossed on her chest and glaring at me.

"Good. I don't want to go to *stupid* Lake George anyway." I suck my teeth and look at the ceiling, praying for some higher power to come save me.

Please.

Anyone.

"You know, if I turn around, we're stuck in the car with her bitching for another three hours, yeah?" That's my wise, handsome, *pushover* of a husband who loves his little girl more than life itself. I give him the side eye, and he smiles. "Liza, baby, you gotta cut the shit."

"Daddy—"

"Your mother and I have been coming here—"

"Since the day you got married, yeah, yeah, yeah, I know. I just . . ." She huffs and looks out the window, her jaw tight in a familiar way.

Familiar because it's the way my jaw looks when I'm frustrated and trying to figure it out, trying to decide how much I want to reveal.

I'd put money on the fact that she's gnawing on her lip.

"Juliana is having a pool party tomorrow."

"Great, when we get home, we'll have a bigger party and invite her."

In Dante's world, that's how you solve a problem with the women in your life.

Give them whatever they want.

"She *wasn't invited*," Turo, our son younger than Liza by just a year, says with a mean smile.

It's not actually mean, but mean in the way that younger siblings get when they're about to cause their sister mental suffering.

I know it well.

But on the bright side, I now know why my daughter is being so cranky.

"Because of *Mom*," says Turo. My boy is named after the father I never knew, while my daughter is named after Dante's mother and Teresa. Her middle name honors my mother's best friend, just like my mom once promised would happen.

Or *Gonna Teresa*, as my kids call her.

"Because of your mother?" Dante asks, clearly confused.

I'm not.

"All of those fuckin' mothers at that uptight goddamn school you insisted on hate me," I grumble under my breath.

I see Dante's smile.

"Is it because you give them the fuckin' death stare when they look at me?"

Yes.

"No."

"It's because Mom never wears fucking normal mom clothes, and Mrs. Giordano doesn't like how Mr. Giordano looks at her."

"*Eliza!*" I say, holding onto the dash as Dante swerves. "Language!"

"Mr. Giordano *what?*" Dante asks, moving over the fact that our 14-year-old just dropped an f-bomb without hesitation and moving to the fact that someone's husband looks at me too often.

Still as protective as ever.

"Mr. Giordano has a wandering eye, apparently," Liza says with an eye roll.

"Okay, look, you're not allowed to play with Juliana anymore," I say. "I am so not comfortable with you being there."

"Why do you know her father has a wandering eye?" Dante asks, voice firm.

"Her mother told her," Turo explains.

"Steven Giordano?" he asks, looking at me. I give him wide eyes, knowing what he's going to say.

"Dante—" His name comes through gritted teeth, but it's no use.

"Comes into the club a lot. Lot of private dances."

"Jesus fuckin—"

"Juliana's dad gets *private dances?!*" Liza says with a teenage girl screech. "Oh my god, this is *gold!*"

"Eliza Teresa, you do not fucking bring that up *ever*," I say, turning in my seat to speak to her directly, mom glare firmly in place.

"But, Mom—"

"Family rule, Eliza. Family information stays family information," my husband says, and I know he's looking in the rearview at his daughter when she meets his glare, puppy dog eyes on.

"Daddy—" she starts, trying to win over her father, but I know she won't.

Not this time.

"Listen to your mother, Eliza. You don't bring that shit up, not ever, you hear?"

You hear is Daddy Dante for *nothing you say will sway me, now agree.*

"But I—"

"Eliza, you confirm you hear me right fuckin' now." Turning again to look at our daughter, I see her jaw tight and her eyes watering in anger.

"God, you both are the *worst*," she shouts, frustrated tears falling.

"I know," I say, turning back around because there will be no reasoning with her as she stares out the window and pouts angrily.

"I wish I were in a different freakin' family," she murmurs under her breath, and even though I know it's said in anger, my heart pulls a bit. Dante's hand moves across the console, squeezing my thigh as he keeps his eyes on the road.

I can only sigh, hoping once we get to the cabin, she'll turn her attitude around.

***

"You know, your dad took me here right after we got married," I say, my hand moving across the glass display cases. We've been in Lake George for a full day, and Liza still has a shit attitude. Dante told me it was time for her and me to have some time together, to mend fences. I turn to face her.

"The first time or the second time?" she asks, lifting an eyebrow.

God.

She's such a little shit sometimes.

But she's also *so fucking me*, I can't be mad for long.

Dante calls her his best payback for making him put up with my *drama* all the time.

As if he didn't come into this relationship with his own boatload.

"The first time." Her nose scrunches, and I hear an old voice, a familiar voice, before she can speak.

"Lilah! What a surprise!" I turn and smile.

"Julius. It's lovely to see you."

"You as well, it's been a while."

"Family, ya know?" He just smiles, turning to look at my daughter.

Dante says she looks nothing like him, that we're two peas in a pod. He likes to say when we walk into a room together, everyone quiets a bit, shocked to see the two most beautiful girls in one place.

He's full of shit, of course, but it makes Liza smile.

But when she's like this—pouty and broody and irritated—I see her father.

The way her brow never crinkles, the way her jaw sets tightly, the way her eyes, the same dark caramel as her father's, go just a bit darker . . .

All Dante.

"This her?" he asks, and it's like a flashback to another time.

"Yes. This is our Liza," I say, moving an arm to Liza's hip, pulling her closer.

"She looks just like Dante," Julius says, and whether he knows it or not, he just dished out her favorite compliment.

Her back straightens, her jaw loosens just a hair, and the tiniest smile comes to her lips.

Liza loves to be told she's like her dad.

"Do you have it?" I ask my old friend, letting go of my daughter and stepping up to the glass. Julius doesn't even say anything, just nods and turns, grabbing a small bag.

"Thank you, Julius. Dante covered it, yes?" I ask, and he nods before I say our goodbyes (Liza being too much of a bratty shit to do more than wave) before leaving.

An hour later, we're parked in a secluded area facing the lake, Liza silent.

"You know, I didn't always live like this," I say, my voice quiet. I don't say more, waiting for my daughter to say something. Anything.

"What?" she says, turning to face me.

"I wasn't always . . . I wasn't always in the family, you know."

Liza goes silent, her eyes getting wide.

We don't talk about *the family* with the kids.

They have a bare understanding of who we are, of what we do. As they get older, we've had to answer questions, had to explain whispers, but we never give more info than necessary.

Finally, though, it's time.

"Auntie Lola and I were raised by a mayor where Lola and Ben live still. I thought he was my dad for a while and, well, you know. He wasn't."

"Because you're a Russo," she says, quiet, and I nod.

She knows that part, knows that Lola is my half-sister, that Turo is named after her grandfather none of us ever met.

She's seen the framed photo of my father holding newborn me.

"Yes. And . . . it took a while for me to know that. I spent so long not understanding things about me, about myself. About my family. Got weird looks and never . . . I never fit in. And then I met your dad." Silence.

We've never spoken of this either.

No sweet stories of how mom and dad met, no photos from first dates.

"I came to the family to take them down."

"*What?!*" my daughter shouts, and I don't bother to fight the smile.

"I found out who I really was, that I was a Russo. There's a history between the Carluccios and the Russos. Not all of it is great. I . . . I wanted revenge." When she stares at me, it's like a small, integral part of how she sees me has shifted.

"And I wanted to be in charge."

Again, her face changes just a bit.

"Liza, you're the oldest." Her little brow furrows, and I see Dante there again, in her eyes. "You're the oldest, which means one day, you'll get a choice." Her tongue comes out to lick her lips. "I want you to have everything in your life, Liza. I want you happy first and foremost. If that means you run off to fuckin' Alabama and never come to Jersey except for on the holidays as soon as you turn 18, then I'll be happy for you. If that means you go to school and you become some kind of tech wiz and live in California and run some crazy company, I'll be the first to invest. But if that means you stay here and you take an interest in what's going on in the family, you have first dibs, Liza."

She's silent, and I let us sit in that silence.

I'm not sure if she's even in the mood to talk, if she's still mad or hurt that she wasn't invited to some party or that she has to spend a week away from her friends.

I don't look at her.

I don't push her.

I just stare at the water.

And finally, she speaks.

"What you guys do . . . it's . . . it's not normal, is it?" I smile but still don't look at her.

"No, baby. It's not normal."

"But it's . . . it's good, right?" Her words tremble, and I reach out to grab her hand, the one that once grabbed onto a single finger. That finger is now nearly the size of my own.

I let her feel how my hands tremble just as well.

Let her feel my nerves.

"It's . . . gray."

"Gray?"

"Sometimes things aren't good or bad. They're right in the middle."

"And you and Daddy are . . . gray."

"I guess. But we try to balance it, Liz." I sigh. "I worked really freaking hard, and so did your father, to make it so the family benefits not just us, but Hudson City. We work every day to make sure we leave a legacy that means something. And sometimes that gets . . . gray."

"Gray," my daughter says, the word hanging in the air between us.

"You don't have to decide now. But I figured . . . I figured it was time. To talk to you about it. I didn't have a mom when I was your age, and I wish I had someone to help me understand what I could be, if I wanted it."

Another few minutes pass, and I watch a flock of geese fly over the lake, squawking as they go.

"If I . . . If I wanted to do what you're talking about, what you do. It would be me? Not Turo? He's . . . He's the boy."

I smile at her.

I smile wide because she might look like Dante, but god, is she all me.

"Baby, you'll learn eventually that men only *think* they rule the world. Women? Women are the ones who really make it turn."

She smiles at me, and I swear, it's the first genuine thing I've seen from her other than annoyance in months.

The teenage years have been painful.

"I got you this. It's become . . . kind of a tradition," I say, handing her the thin velvet box. "You don't have to wear it, not now. And I don't want you to think that if you do wear it, you're committing to something. I just . . . I wanted you to have it."

I watch her hands—not tiny, but not fully grown—with the chipped purple polish move to open the box. When she does, she keeps staring at it.

"Is this Daddy's?"

In the box is a St. Christopher on a delicate gold chain.

"It's yours."

"Is it yours?" she asks, looking at my neck where the old gold medal still sits warm against my skin.

"It's yours, Liza. St. Christopher. It's for protection. Your grandmother gave one to Daddy when he was young, then he gave his to me. We bought a new one for you father when we came here right after we got married at the same jewelry store we just got yours."

She keeps staring.

"Protection because . . ."

"Because if you do one day end up choosing the family, it's good to have. And if you don't, well, a little more protection doesn't hurt." I watch her fingers graze the chain gently, like she's afraid to touch it.

Like if she does, she's accepting some kind of fate she isn't sure she wants.

"It doesn't mean anything if you don't want it to, L—" I start, but then I stop again.

Her hands move to the box, taking the chain out. I watch those little hands move, holding the thin chain to me then turning away when I accept it. Her back to me, Liza lifts her long blonde hair out of the way before looking over her shoulder at me.

"Can you put it on me?" she asks, her own voice low and soft.

Nervous.

"Of course," I say through the lump in my throat, and then I put the St Christopher medal on my daughter's neck.

When we get home, Liza skips ahead of me, turning at the front door.

"I'm gonna go call Jeremy, okay?" she asks. Jeremy is the real reason she is annoyed to be here for a full week, a week away from her first real boyfriend. Her father absolutely despises the boy because he knows as well as I do that he's going to break her heart into a million little pieces one day. It took weeks of promises and sweet words and quiet discussions just to get him to approve her first date.

It kills him, watching her grow up.

His little *principessa*.

"I won't tell him about . . ." She touches the necklace with a smile. "You know." I shake my head in a, *God help me* kind of way.

"Twenty minutes, Eliza," I say, and then she nods, skipping into the little cabin before moving right to her room on the first floor and slamming the door behind her.

I drop the bags from our shopping excursion in the middle of the living room, looking to the ceiling and shaking my head.

Dante's laugh fills the room, and I don't watch, but I know he's getting closer. Electricity snaps, even now.

And then he wraps an arm around my waist, pulling me in close, my hand moving to rake through his hair that is more silver than dark now. His head goes to my neck and it's then he says the words that always flow through me.

The words he always says if we spend any longer than two hours apart.

"Missed you."

ACKNOWLEDGMENTS

I want to say writing these acknowledgements gets easier, but truth be told I can barely spell the word, much less remember everyone who helps me and keeps me sane.

But still, I've built a community of the most *amazing* human beings on this planet. People who hype me up like no other, people who talk me off the ledge, people who brainstorm with me. And I want them to know how much they mean to me.

First and foremost, thank you Alex. You think I'm lying when I tell you I brag about you all the time, which I find hilarious. Every day you take over the chaos so I can sit in my little office and live in a fantasy world. I'm grateful every day I went to that house party and met a real life book boyfriend.

Next: Ryan, Owen, and Ella. Please never read this or any of my books, but if you do, let's never ever speak of it. But thanks for letting me be your mom and for being awesome.

Thank you Lindsey. Thank you for keeping my head on straight, handling the little things that stress me out, and for always telling me your proud of me because you know that's what I need. I'm so damn proud of you and watching you find your passion has been amazing.

Thank you Norma Gambini for taking the chaos and typos and turning it into an actual book people can read. Thank you for always hyping me up in the comments and telling me what exactly the girlies are going to love.

Thank you Madi from Madicantstopreading. Thank you for the amazing cover. Thank you for being the voice of reason and the Type

A we need to stay on track. Thank you for group chats with my heroes as the title and bending over backwards to help with literally anything. I love you to death. Capitalist Barbie until we die.

Thank you Steph from stephlivesinpages. Thank you for being the ultimate hype girl. Thank you for keeping me from drowning in imposter syndrome and reminding me that I'm kind of okay at this. Thank you for sprinting with me and helping me brainstorm. You are going to so such amazing things this year and I'm so glad I get to be a part of that. I love you a million times over.

Thank you to my ARC team, the true stars of any hint of success this book will receive. You take my crazy stories and help me share them with the world. I can't thank you enough.

Thank you to Booktok—yes, the whole damn thing—because without you, this would all be something I dream about but never do. Thank you for enduring my cringeworthy videos, finding gems, liking and sharing and reading my books. It makes me cry if I think too long about how much you have changed my life.

But most of all: thank YOU, sweet, beautiful reader. I've loved books for as long as I can remember and when I wrote my first book, I published it thinking there was no way people would enjoy it. You all laughed in my face and demanded I give you more. Being able to share these people and stories with you all has been life changing.

So, thank you from the absolute bottom of my heart.

I love you all.

WHAT'S NEXT?

If you haven't read it yet, Bittersweet is Lilah's sister Lola's story, and a prequel of sorts. It's on Kindle Unlimited here!

Most life changes start with a wake up call.

Lola Turner's wake up call came in the form of saving her politician father one too many times.

Now she's determined to be 'New Lola' - the version of herself that has always been hiding beneath duty, guilt, promises, and secrets since her mother passed away when she was 15.

But the problem with a wake up call is you're the only one to get it. So even though she's moving on, starting her own bakery on the Ocean View boardwalk, the mess that her father always seems to get himself into still is finding its way to her.

Ben Coleman left his hometown and the family business that should have been his to pursue his true passion: art and tattooing. Coleman Ink has become his world, and he's tailored the business to fit his life the way he wants it, rather than the life that was originally laid out for him.

Until early one morning he's woken up by what he thinks is an intruder only to find it's just his new neighbor. His new neighbor, who has no regard for her own safety, wakes up way too early, and seems to have made it her job to tempt him.

But what happens when the grumpy neighbor decides that it's his job to keep her safe, even if she drives him insane? Will Lola open up and share her burden with someone else? Will she be able to keep her family's secrets without getting hurt?

Bittersweet is a contemporary grumpy sunshine, enemies to lovers romance. It is book three in the Ocean View series, but can be read as a standalone.

It is a full-length romance with a Happily Ever After that features sexually explicit material and profanity. This book is intended for 18+

WANT THE CHANCE TO WIN KINDLE STICKERS AND SIGNED COPIES?

Leave an honest review on Amazon or Goodreads and send the link to reviewteam@authormorganelizabeth.com and you'll be entered to win a signed copy of one of Morgan Elizabeth's books and a pack of bookish stickers!

Each email is an entry (you can send one email with your Goodreads review and another with your Kindle review for two entries per book) and two winners will be chosen at the beginning of each month!

ALSO BY MORGAN ELIZABETH

The Springbrook Hills Series

The Distraction

The Protector

The Substitution

The Connection

Holiday Standalone, interconnected with SBH:

Tis the Season for Revenge

The Ocean View Series

The Ex Files

Walking Red Flag

Bittersweet

The Mastermind Duet

Ivory Tower

Diamond Fortress

ABOUT THE AUTHOR

Morgan is a born and raised Jersey girl, living there with her two boys, toddler daughter, and mechanic husband. She's addicted to iced espresso, barbecue chips, and Starburst jellybeans. She usually has headphones on, listening to some spicy audiobook or Taylor Swift. There is rarely an in between.

Writing has been her calling for as long as she can remember. There's a framed 'page one' of a book she wrote at seven hanging in her childhood home to prove the point. Her entire life she's crafted stories in her mind, begging to be released but it wasn't until recently she finally gave them the reigns.

I'm so grateful you've agreed to take this journey with me.

Stay up to date via TikTok and Instagram

Stay up to date with future stories, get sneak peeks and bonus chapters by joining the Reader Group on Facebook!